THE DAYS NEVER KNOW

THE DAYS NEVER KNOW

MARY MACDONALD BELL

ANDRE DEUTSCH

First published in Great Britain in 1992 by
André Deutsch Limited
105-6 Great Russell Street London WC1B 3LJ

British Library Cataloguing in Publication Data
Bell, Mary Macdonald
    The days never know.
    I. Title
    823.914 [F]
    ISBN 0–233–98742–8

Typeset by Falcon Graphic Art Ltd
Wallington, Surrey
Printed in Finland by
WSOY

To Mum and Dad

'What is life? It is as the little shadow that runs across the grass and loses itself in the sunset.'

Last words of Crowfoot, Chief of the Blackfoot Tribe
1830-1890

Acknowledgements

Special thanks go to Roger Turner for his generous support in the writing of this book. Likewise to Donna Denyer for all her help with the research and her hospitality. Thanks also to Janet Williamson of the Edmonton Provincial Archives, to Esther Whitby at Deutsch, and to Angie Bell for her attendance at the birth.

The title is a quotation from
Ralph Waldo Emerson (1803-1882)

'The years teach much which the days
never know.'

PART
1

1

Scotland, Tuesday 4th March, 1890

The change from night to day was barely perceptible in the grey light that struggled to filter through storm clouds above the Firth of Forth. Sea and sky merged in a monotonous slate sheet, a steady drizzle obscuring the Edinburgh shoreline across the water. Usually the dock-sides of Burntisland harbour would just have been coming to life at this early hour – but it was no ordinary day. Most of Fife had declared a public holiday to mark the opening of the new Forth Bridge by the Prince of Wales, and the people had come out in their thousands. The tiny port was crammed to overflowing, and a hubbub of excited voices sent the sea-gulls screaming aloft to soar on the stiffening breeze. There was a huge demand for places on the ferries crossing the river estuary to South Queensferry. Already long queues had formed outside the ticket offices and would-be passengers found themselves faced with a tedious wait. Periodically, someone would start up a song. Then others would join in, clapping their hands and stamping their feet in an effort to restore warmth to their numbed limbs. Meanwhile the hot-pie vendors were enjoying a brisk trade with those who were able to afford their exorbitant prices, leaving the less well-off to sniff in resigned envy at the enticing aroma of rich onion gravy.

Frances Rintoul and Jeannie Adamson had started their journey from West Wemyss in the dark, hours before and they now presented a sorry sight. Standing cold and bedraggled in a stationary line for tickets, their high spirits had been dampened by the interminable waiting. Frances kept her feet moving but the worn boots did little to warm her frozen toes. Warily she scanned the multitude for any unwelcome glimpse of a familiar face, avoiding attention by drawing the coarse woollen scarf about her head and shoulders. Though framed by escaping strands of rain-darkened hair and half-hidden in shadow, there was a compelling directness in her clear, hazel eyes. In spite of the cold there was a bloom in her features, something which held the onlooker for a second longer than most. And yet if the memory lasted it was impossible to say why. At eighteen,

Frances was mostly unaware of these arresting traits and never used them as instruments to her advantage. Similarly she was gifted with a thick sable richness of brown hair which she regarded more as a cumbrous affliction than something to be cherished as the envy of her peers.

'Do ye see anyone?' Jeannie stood on tiptoe but her view was still marred by the shoulders of the crowd.

'No, I told ye we'd be all right,' Frances retorted abruptly. Her plump friend shivered beside her, knuckles showing blue where she clutched the thin shawl. Still the queue did not move and Frances felt her patience giving way. Suddenly she could stand it no longer. 'I didna come all the way from the Wemyss to freeze to my death! Come on,' she declared and began to shove her way through the masses.

Jeannie followed, looking back regretfully as the people shuffled forward and swallowed up the space where they had been. 'We've lost our place,' she said plaintively, 'we'll never get on a boat now.'

Frances pushed the scarf back off her head, glad to be moving and free of the jostling throng. She led the way along the quayside, enquiring at each boat they passed. Most were deserted, and the crews of the others showed no interest in going out into the rough waters of the Forth that morning.

'Try Archie on the railway company steamer,' said one boatman, pointing to the end of the docks. 'I think they'll be taking folk.'

The goods steamer was tied up at the furthest jetty. With an air of resignation, the first mate sat on a capstan in the rain and smoked a cigarette. He made no acknowledgement of the two girls as they approached. 'Are ye taking passengers today?' Frances asked, undeterred by his manner.

Archie Rannoch looked up slowly, almost contemptuously. 'Aye, lassie, we are that. But there's no many willing to spoil their Sunday best on this auld bucket of rust.'

'Well, as ye can see, this isn't my Sunday best,' she laughed. Archie shrugged, gave a little jerk of the head to indicate his assent and, before he knew it, she had gathered up her skirts and clambered aboard.

Jeannie was still standing on the dock. She looked doubtfully at the battered hull and grimy smoke-stack but, seeing her dithering, Archie put out his hand and roughly hauled her on to the boat. He waved to the open deck. 'There's no passenger lounge on this ship, ladies. So you'd better find something to hold onto, it'll be a rough crossing.' He took the coppers offered as payment and pocketed them. 'And I suppose you two will be wanting a sight of the Prince like the rest?'

'It's the bridge I want to see,' said Frances, picking her way between packing cases.

Archie spat into the water. 'Dinna talk to me about that bridge! I've watched it grow out the water for eight years, and every foot higher it grew, the closer I came to being out a job. I've no work after today because of their fine, new bridge – and me with five bairns to feed!' He hawked over the side again. 'Well, ye better make the most of your trip, lassies – it's the last this ship'll make.'

They watched him go about his work, grim-faced. 'Oh, the poor man,' Jeannie whispered.

'Blethers,' said Frances, settling herself between two large sacks. 'There's no shortage of work for seamen around here. He's just scunnered at losing an easy job.'

'Shh, or he'll hear ye.' Jeannie wedged herself in beside her friend. Then she asked, 'Do ye think it'll be awful rough?'

'Probably,' said Frances, vaguely. They had been the last to come aboard and she was having a good look round at the other passengers huddled between crates and bundles. Only a handful were eager enough to brave the crossing in the open.

'Oh, I hope I dinna spew,' Jeannie said dolefully. The smell of wet clothing and canvas mingled with the pervasive malodorous stench of rotting seaweed and fish.

'Well, if ye do, do it over that way.' Frances tried to make light of her misery and poked her in the ribs. 'Ye canna be sick – a good Wemyss lassie like you! What'll folk say?'

The reference to home touched a gloomy chord with Jeannie. 'We'd best no let on where we've been,' she warned.

'Well, I'll no say anything. Ye ken my father would kill me for taking the day off work.'

Jeannie paused. 'I bet you'll tell Gavin, though?'

'I might,' Frances said contrarily, though the flicker of a smile crossed her face at the mention of his name. 'I dinna tell him everything.'

'Och, ye do.' Jeannie fidgeted, trying to get comfortable. 'So, he's no asked ye yet, then?'

Frances ignored the well-worn provocation. There was more than a hint of impatience in her voice as she elbowed her friend again. 'Move over a bit, you're squashing me.'

'No, you move, I've no room here.' Jeannie nudged her in

5

return with equal vehemence. 'I sometimes wonder why Gavin puts up with ye, you're that ill-natured.'

'I am no!'

'Ye are so. And forbye, you would try anybody's patience.' Jeannie shivered and was reminded of her hunger as she looked back down the quay. 'Oh I wish we'd enough to buy one of those pies.' Then she laughed. 'But I'll no need to worry about being sick – I've nothing to bring up!'

Soon, the steamship pulled away from the harbour and out into the rolling swell of the Forth. Once beyond the shelter of the sea wall, the full force of the storm hit them and the icy wind whipped around and sprayed needles of rain into their faces. They clung on desperately as the boat pitched and tossed on the waves, struggling to make headway up-river against the tide. The howling gale and beat of the engines made conversation impossible and Jeannie pulled her coat and shawl tight around her, burying herself as far down as she could.

Meanwhile Frances stared ahead, eager for her first glimpse of the bridge. The weather made the skipper cautious and instead of taking the more direct route, the steamer hugged the coastline. So it seemed like an eternity before they at last rounded the headland at Aberdour and the great iron structure loomed into view. At first it was frightening in its immensity, dwarfing everything around. The building of such a colossus was inconceivable to a girl who had rarely left West Wemyss. There, everything was on a smaller scale, and life and work revolved around the mines and the men who worked underground. Never in her life had she seen anything as imposing as the giant now before her, and even the very storm seemed to quieten, as though tamed by its monumental presence. She arose, drawn to the prow with eyes wide in wonder. Straining against the roaring wind like a figurehead carved on the bows, she willed the boat closer to the three massive steel diamonds that vaulted the chasm. As the ship drew under the bridge, she turned her head up to the soaring network of girders that slashed the sullen sky and was momentarily oblivious to everything else, lost in the grandeur.

It was Archie's sour voice that brought her attention back from the bridge. 'Look at them,' he was saying, pointing to the dozens of little craft swarming at the bases of the immense support piers, 'running to see the mighty Prince of Wales.'

'It's no the Prince they've come for,' Frances replied simply as she resumed her scan of the framework above.

Archie followed her eyes. 'It'll be like the Tay Bridge, mark my words,' he grumbled, 'it's no a dozen years since that was blewn down. This one'll go just the same.' Then, muttering to himself, he turned and lurched back to the shelter of the wheelhouse.

Because of the large number of boats on the river, it was almost another hour before their steamer could get into the landing stage at South Queensferry. Once they joined the crowds lining the shore, the two girls were swept up in the infectious excitement as they promenaded back and forth with everyone else viewing the bridge. All over it the diminutive figures of workmen scurried about making last-minute preparations for the royal opening. The high approach viaducts were festooned with bunting, and a Guard of Honour lined the walkways on either side of the tracks. Down below, military bands were playing to entertain the spectators, and the Hawes Inn was doing a roaring trade in glasses of hot, sweet rum punch.

'I've seen enough from down here,' Frances said, noticing the signs that pointed uphill. 'Let's go to the new station. We'll get a better view.' The steep climb to Dalmeny soon brought warmth back to the two girls after their freezing boat journey. As they approached the crest of the hill they could see the new Forth Bridge station standing decked in readiness for the ceremony and the royal train that would be the first to cross the river. Everywhere there was a carnival atmosphere but, at the top of the rise, they found their way barred by a force from the local constabulary.

An officious looking sergeant in a large waterproof cape stepped forward. 'And where do ye think you two are going?' he said with raised hands, obviously relishing the role he had been assigned for the day.

'We want a good sight of the train going over the bridge – we'll no be any trouble.'

Frances attempted to pass him but the sergeant stopped her, his bulky arm pushing her back roughly. 'I'll make sure of that. Can ye no read?' he said waving to a sign. ' "NO PUBLIC ACCESS" '.

'Well, who are all those folk up there?' She pointed towards the group on the platform.

'Use your eyes, lassie. Now, do they look like public to you?' Scanning the figures, she could make out the fancy hats and furs under the umbrellas. The message was clear and the two girls slowly turned to walk away, leaving the sergeant shaking his head and smiling.

Once he had disappeared back onto the platform, Frances stopped in her tracks. 'We've taken a day off our work, been on the road since the first grey light, got frozen and soaked through, then thrown about on that rickety boat.' Her tone was emphatic. 'I dinna ken about you, but I'm no giving up now we've come this far.'

Jeannie knew better than to try and persuade her differently and she shrugged in resignation. 'All right, but what can we do? Ye heard the policeman, the station's only for toffs.'

Frances glanced around her. At the side of the fencing was a clump of dense bushes. 'Maybe we can see something from in there,' she said as she pulled Jeannie into them. It quickly became apparent, however, that they would see nothing, but before they could leave, the police sergeant resumed his post on the pathway and they were forced to remain where they were.

From their hiding place they craned their necks in vain to catch a glimpse of what was going on. Time passed and there was a lot of noise and commotion. Then a band struck up. They heard the cheers of the crowd as the Prince arrived and boarded the train; they heard the clanking engine spit steam as it set off along the track; they heard the train's whistle scream as it moved onto the bridge; and way down below a warship in the Forth boomed out a salute. But they saw nothing.

The train receded in the distance and the two looked at each other miserably. The place had grown silent and, peering out gingerly, Frances saw the crowds withdraw from the rain-washed platforms into the warmth of the station waiting-rooms. Suddenly she was forced to duck into the bushes again as two soldiers from the Guard of Honour strolled by, pausing at the fence.

'Christ, I thought I'd frozen stiff out there!' exclaimed one, lighting his cigarette. 'At least we've a while before the auld bugger's due back.'

'Aye,' answered his crony, 'ye may depend his Highness'll no be freezing his royal arse in this wind!' They moved on, leaving the platform deserted.

Jeannie gasped, stunned by their irreverent comments and slapped her hand to her mouth to stifle a snigger. Frances was also thinking about what had been said but it was the significance of the words that interested her. The platform was empty and they could take advantage of the interval before the train returned. If they were careful, they could get up onto the bridge without being seen. 'Come on, this is our chance,' she whispered. She stood up and, making sure that the soldiers had vanished, began clambering over the fence. Desperate not to be left behind a second time, Jeannie struggled to hoist herself across the wooden slats.

8

'Och, ye great lump of suet. Here, grab my hand!' Frances urged as she roughly pulled her over and they tumbled together onto the deserted platform. Giggling, they helped each other up and ran unobserved down onto the track, away from the station and towards the bridge. Soon, they were too breathless to laugh. The view had been deceptive and the size of the bridge had made it seem much closer than it was. The great granite archway that stood at the end of the viaduct was almost half a mile away and, as they ran headlong towards it, the fierce wind snatched at their clothing and threatened to blow them from the high track. Reaching the arch, they huddled in its lee, sheltering from the blast. A temporary wooden platform had been specially built for the occasion at the side of the rails where they stood and there was plenty of room. They looked back towards the station buildings which now seemed small and insignificant as the stone gateway to the bridge towered high above them.

'Well, was this no worth it?' said Frances, putting her arm around her friend.

Panting with the exertion, Jeannie still looked doubtful. 'Frances, we could get in awful trouble for being up here. Think of what would happen if Doig found out – he'd give us the sack for sure!'

'I told ye, dinna worry. He'll no find out, you'll see. And this'll be a day to remember for us. From here, we'll have a great sight of the train on its way back . . .' She continued to try and placate Jeannie, to reassure her that the adventure well outweighed the risk. But gradually her words tapered off, cut short as another threat loomed, challenging the very point she made. Frances glanced over her shoulder. To her dismay, the official party had already poured out of the waiting-rooms and were again on the platform. Time had passed quicker than she thought. Now, all the high-ranking officials, warmed by their hot toddies, were advancing down the track to witness the last part of the ceremony and greet the royal train on its return. Even at that distance, the sight of so many dignitaries heading in their direction was a terrifying prospect. Flanked by the soldiers, the throng of notables gradually came more sharply into focus, tottering towards them. The ladies in their fur coats hung onto their escorts and clutched at their elaborate feather hats. Nearer and nearer they drew, their curious, unfamiliar voices babbling above the sound of the wind.

'Oh my God,' Jeannie whined, 'what'll we do?' Panicking, Frances looked around for a means of escape. In the great arm of the cantilever that soared from the viaduct, she spotted an open access hatch.

'Quick! In there,' she ordered and, with little time to spare, they managed to climb inside, closing the metal cover over their heads. After a few minutes, muffled snatches of conversation could be heard from outside as the privileged guests gathered on the wooden platform.

The two girls cowered together in the darkness. Jeannie wanted to cry but stifled the noise so only a vague echo of her whimpering resounded in the chamber. It was freezing, encapsulated in cold ringing steel, like a tomb, she thought. By this point her disenchantment with Frances was total, yet it was not an unfamiliar feeling. Once again she had been drawn into an escapade which had developed into something more than she had bargained for.

Looking around, Frances could see a glimmer of daylight coming from another opening high above them and feeling they were safe enough now curiosity began to take over from fear. Tucking her skirt into her drawers she put her first foot on the metal ladder.

'What the hell are ye doing!' Jeannie hissed, grabbing at her ankle.

'Och, you'll be all right here for a bit,' Frances whispered in reply. 'I'm just going up there for a look. If you're no coming with me then let go my foot.'

Jeannie had absolutely no intention of following this time and remained in huddled silence as her friend ascended the iron rungs.

Reaching the upper hatch, Frances had to use all her strength to lift it open. As she did so, the freezing air was sucked in. Nervously, she poked her head up through the hole and the wind screamed and whipped at her hair. Almost knocked off balance by its force, she had to grab a girder to steady herself. She clung on until sure of a safe stronghold and her fear slowly subsided. Only then did she look around and gasped as she took in the view.

For a few moments, the storm clouds and rain had been swept away by the wind, and the panorama of the Forth Valley and estuary lay before her. To the south sprawled Leith and Edinburgh with Arthur's Seat and the Pentlands rising in the distance. Below her, strung along the river, lay Inchkeith, Inchcolm, Inchmikery and Cramond Island; beyond were the May Island and the Bass Rock. Looking over the north shore to Fife, she could see Aberdour, Burntisland and Kinghorn before the coast curved away, hiding the coal-mining communities and her own village of West Wemyss.

Gradually, her attention drifted from the view and she became aware of the many workmen perched, like her, on the girders above the track. These were the bridge builders. Familiar with the altitude, they hung like spiders against the web of steel, at ease in the dangerous environment. Their strength and endurance had turned the dream

10

of a link across the Forth into a reality and now they watched as the official ceremonies marked their achievement.

Even higher than Frances, two of them sat astride the iron rafters on the other side. They were dressed in heavy work-clothes, jackets buttoned against the cold and their caps jammed down to prevent them flying away in the wind. The dark-haired one saw her first and nudged his companion who looked across with concern. Then, realising that she was neither in danger nor afraid, he grinned. Pulling off his cap and ramming it in his pocket, he stood up on the beam and waved to her. Uncertainly, she released an arm from the stanchion she was clinging to and gave a hesitant little wave in return. He reacted effusively to this gesture and proceeded to make even greater efforts to retain her attention. But the battering wind drowned his voice and she could only watch as his thick hair ruffled wildly while she wondered at the ease with which he leaned casually, almost carelessly, against the bar. Then, quite suddenly, his foot slipped and he fell backwards.

Frances gave a cry and shut her eyes to the horror of his fall. Her heart thudded in the few seconds that passed but when she opened them, she saw that the man had caught the spar below and now swung easily with both hands. He winked across at her – even at that distance it was undeniable. She felt confused and not a little angry at being teased in such a way. Irritated that she had allowed herself to be taken in by it all, she decided to ignore him and looked away.

His fellow workers had enjoyed the prank and now, to their further delight, the man began to give a unique performance in order to recapture her attention. Far down below moved the swollen waters of the Forth that had claimed so many lives during the building of the bridge but the man showed no fear. He was at one with the giant framework he had helped to create. Despite her annoyance, Frances found herself mesmerised by the display. As he swung around the criss-crossed ironwork he seemed, like the gulls that wheeled above him, an untamed spirit of the air caught in the sudden shafts of light that burst through the re-gathering clouds. There was an aura about him that held the attention of all the onlookers and gradually, with the rest, she was drawn into the spell. It was hard to tell where strong, muscled arm met relentless steel as he spun and tumbled through the air. Every time she thought he had outreached himself, he effortlessly found a handhold and swung away on another trajectory. Between each skilful feat, he was cheered on by his fellow workers. Pausing momentarily, he would acknowledge the applause, but it was in her

11

direction that the man bowed dramatically low and Frances was made uncomfortably aware that the show was just for her.

At last he stopped, his broad chest rising and falling as he gasped for breath after his exertions. He looked across, unsmiling now, with a questioning expression on his brown, weathered face. Even at that distance, she could feel the directness of his eyes as they burned into hers. It was an unsettling sensation that sent a rush of blood to her face despite the fierce cold.

The spell was abruptly broken by a distant blast on the returning train's whistle. At the far end of the bridge, Frances saw tiny billowing plumes of smoke as the engine advanced. In the next few minutes the sound gradually grew into a roaring rumble. She felt transfixed. There was no time to escape and she held on desperately, praying she would not be seen. Nearer it drew, whistle screaming against the thunderous clanking of its power, eventually creaking to a halt mere feet below where she sat. Her eyes were blurred by the smoke but as it cleared, though she scanned the bars above, the men had disappeared. Looking down again, she held her breath and her heart raced. Not thirty feet below, the royal party had emerged.

No one saw her crouched figure, half-hidden on the girder above. The Prince stepped heavily from the train, clutching his top hat with both hands to stop it blowing away in the gale. Shouting at the top of his voice, he announced, 'Ladies and gentlemen, I now declare the Forth Bridge open.' Frances momentarily forgot her fear as she caught his inadequate words through the hiss of the wind. It seemed a paltry, bland statement for such a magnificent engineering conquest and she wondered what the men who built it would have thought. But strangely, they had vanished and the reality of her predicament forced her to weigh up the options. Whether to sit tight and wait until the train had gone – or to get back into the hatch as quickly as possible. She decided on the latter and drew herself up unsteadily. As she edged her way along the girder, a ripple of polite applause rose from the sea of heads below. The ladies curtsied and the men doffed their toppers, everyone trying to court the attention of the Prince. But, no sooner had he uttered his meagre little dedication, than he had turned away and was climbing back aboard into the warmth of the sumptuous carriage.

The heads continued their bobbing and bowing beneath the canopy of umbrellas as the train drew off. Then Frances became aware that one face among them, contorted with rage, was turned towards hers and she found herself staring into the menacing eyes of Euphemia Doig.

2

It was late when Frances and Jeannie returned home, trudging up the pebbled beach in exhausted silence. Lying on the very edge of the Fife coast, West Wemyss seemed nevertheless to have turned its back on the sea. None of the houses along the shore faced seawards and the black winding-towers of the collieries showed that here life concentrated on the bounty under the water rather than in it. From the harbour crammed with coal-carrying barges, the road rose to meet the main street where the houses curved away inland before sweeping down to the seashore again at the other side of town. The roads were a patchwork of cobbles and churned dirt with noisome open sewers running in channels down the middle. With no street lighting, all that could be seen in the darkness was the whitewashed clock-tower. The Rintoul home was next to it, part of a monotonous row of terraced cottages, each indistinguishable from the other under the red-tiled roofs.

The two girls parted at the foot of one of the steep wynds. 'Mind and no say anything,' hissed Frances, glancing around nervously. 'Ye ken what you're like with your big mouth.'

'Me? – It's no me ye have to worry about. It was you that Effie Doig saw up the bridge.'

'There was a lot of folk there and with all that smoke and steam, she canna prove it. I've told ye, when we get to work the morn just act like nothing happened. We'll be all right.'

'Aye, and how many times have I heard that?' Jeannie grumbled as she turned and walked away in a huff.

Frances hurried on down the High Street, aware that the lateness of the hour would likely provoke an inquisition at home. But she reassured herself with the thought that at least her father would not be back from work. The front door burst open before she could push it and she almost collided with her mother who was coming out carrying two battered and rusting buckets.

'Where have ye been?' shouted Jessie Rintoul. 'Ye should've been back from your work hours ago.' Frances was too tired to answer. Wearied from her exhilarating day at the bridge and the arduous journey home, she merely shrugged in an attempt to make light of it. The pails were shoved into her hands. 'Away and get the water for your father's bath. And shut that door before ye let all the heat out!'

13

Frances went to the pump and started to crank the handle. The icy water was slow to rise to the well-head and then only came in a weak trickle. Her arms ached, and she was chilled through but there would be no respite until the household had been prepared for the return of the working men. The whole focus of the family was her father and brother and their shifts at the mine. They were on the back shift that week and would not be home until around half-past ten. Though it was already late, Frances would not be allowed to go to bed until the water had been heated and a meal cooked. And in the morning she would have to rise at her usual hour for the long walk to the linoleum factory at Kirkcaldy where she and Jeannie worked.

Returning to the kitchen, she put the water on to boil, pulled off her wet coat and hung it on the pulley above the fire. The room was filling up with steam and condensation trickled down the walls. Yet her grandfather sat to one side of the hearth, seemingly oblivious. 'Hello Grandad, how are ye?' she said, smiling at the old man.

He did not look up but squeezed her hand, his gaze far away, fixed on the heart of the glowing coals.

'He's been right bad today,' Jessie replied for him. 'Can hardly draw breath.' She laid a bowl on the table with some large slices of bread. 'Here, come and have this before your father gets in.'

Gratefully, Frances ate the warming broth. When she had finished, she was still hungry but knew better than ask for more. Until the men were fed and satisfied, there would be nothing else to eat.

'So where have ye been then?'

Frances had known it was coming. 'Och, we just fell to blethering and forgot the time.' Nervously keeping her eyes lowered, she mopped up the last dregs of soup with her bread.

'But it's near nine o'clock, lassie! I'm telling ye, next time your father can deal with ye.' Jessie's admonishments were as usual deflected by preoccupation with the task in hand. 'And another thing,' she added, starting to scrub the potatoes, 'Gavin was round for ye past tea-time.'

Frances paused, the last morsel of bread half-way to her mouth. Jessie noticed the look of disappointment on her daughter's face. 'Aye, well, it's your own fault – there's no point in scowling at me. If you'd be here when you were supposed to be —'

'What time did he leave?' Frances butted in.

'It must've been over an hour he waited! It was past eight when he left. Why he bothers with ye I dinna ken!' Frances tried to interrupt but Jessie continued without pausing for breath. 'What could ye have to talk to Jeannie about all that time? He was right

14

let down that ye didna come. Still, he bided a while and had a crack with Grandad.'

'What was he saying then?' Frances was relieved to turn the talk away from her late arrival home.

The old man roused himself. 'He was telling me about his work with the union during the pit strike.' He wheezed, growing hoarser as he spoke. 'A grand laddie is Gavin, aye thinking of other folk . . .' His voice tailed off, crumbling into a breaking coughing fit.

Jessie went over to him and pulled the blanket closer round the gaunt body now wracked with choking. She held him till relief came and he spat the viscid black mucus into the fire. Then, gently patting his shoulder, she turned back to her chores. She wrapped a cloth around the scalding pot handle and shifted it to the side of the fire. Another pan was filled and her swollen red knuckles whitened as she lifted the weight. 'Well, dinna just sit there, come and give me a hand. I've had to do all this myself.' She got out the tin bath and started to fill it.

Frances looked on. At forty-three, Jessie Rintoul had brought up three children after losing her first two in infancy and now there was her own ailing father to care for. Laid off without any means of support, he was totally dependent on the family. Frances could not remember a time when her mother had seemed young or happy. Dark circles underlined the tired eyes that stared from her taut, anxious face – how different from the elegant ladies seen at the bridge that morning. The thought provoked a shudder of anger and Frances felt her hands tremble as she swept her plate and things from the table and dumped them in the enamel bowl. The water was covered in a greasy scum, but to get more meant another trip to the pump and she was too tired. As she washed, she was gripped by the fear of her own inexorable future. Watching her hands redden in the cold water, she knew that in twenty years there would be nothing to distinguish her from her mother now. She wished she could share the excitement of the day with her but knew that to do so would only invite misunderstanding and criticism, followed by the inevitable row.

'Hurry up with that. Lay the table and help Grandad ben the hoose before your father gets in.' Jessie's voice now held a tinge of anxiety as well as impatience.

Frances finished rinsing the dishes and put out the plates and cutlery on the threadbare table-cloth. In a daze, she rubbed ineffectually at the stains as the memories of the day kept crowding back.

'What in God's name is the matter with ye?' In exasperation Jessie grabbed the spoons from her hand and shoved her towards the bedroom. 'Put Grandad to bed, and then get away to your own, for you're just a hindrance to me here.'

Frances went through into the cramped back room. The tiny space was filled by her own bed and a second larger one which was shared by her brother and grandfather. An old sheet hung from a piece of string between the two beds as a token gesture to privacy. Shivering in the cold after the heat of the kitchen, she turned down the covers for her grandfather. Then, going back through, she helped the old man from his chair and supported him as he walked unsteadily to the bed.

'This is no job for a young lassie.' He sighed as she eased off his slippers.

'Ye ken I dinna mind, Grandad.'

He fumbled with the buttons of his gallowses. 'Aye, but ye should be looking after your own man in your own hoose – no having to pander to an auld scunner like me.' He slipped down the tops of his trousers and as Frances pulled them off, he leaned forward conspiratorially and whispered, 'I'll bet Gavin wouldn't take so long to get his breeks off if it was you and him in here!'

Frances felt her cheeks redden as she piled his clothes at the foot of the bed and pulled the covers up over him. 'Just you be quiet, ye dirty auld thing, and get to sleep.' She leaned over and kissed him and he held her hand a moment, his eyes a little misty. 'I'd like to see ye wed afore I go, hen.'

'Time enough for that, Grandad.' She kissed him again. 'You'll be dancing at our wedding, never fear.' She moved to the other side of the partitioning sheet and undressed, watching through a crack in the door as her mother continued the preparations for the men's return. Snuffing out the candle, she lay back on the cold sheets and tried to block out the rasping sound of her grandfather's breathing. She hoped that sleep would come quickly. So often she was kept awake by relentless coughing from the old man. If not that, then there was her brother's snoring or, worst of all, her father's voice raised in anger from the other room. Closing her eyes, Frances let her mind wander back over the day, and the glimpse she had been offered of a wider world. The view from the heights of the great iron bridge had made her own life seem so confined, and the unknown man, flying in the face of danger, had evoked an elusive spirit of freedom. Feelings of restlessness kept sleep at bay and it was long after the moon rose in the clearing sky that she finally succumbed to exhaustion in a troubled slumber.

3

Elspeth Douglas looked up at the clock as her grandson entered. 'My, but you're late tonight,' she murmured, rising stiffly from the old armchair by the side of the hearth.

He bent to kiss her. 'It's all right, dinna stir yourself, I'll make the tea.' Gavin pulled off his cap and slung his jacket on the back of the door but she was already on her feet. He gave a resigned sigh and slumped into the chair, watching her move about the kitchen at the tranquil, measured pace she had always used throughout her seventy-four years.

Though she rarely left the house any more, there was little happening in West Wemyss that slipped her notice. Unlike the village gossips, who picked over the failings of their neighbours with glee, Elspeth was known for her genuine concern and sound advice whenever anyone came to her with their troubles. In her own way, she studied the human personality: a worried look, a sigh spoke volumes to her as she watched the generations around her move into each new phase. Her own grandson was not disposed to confiding his innermost thoughts but she read them just the same, the silences often betraying more than the spoken word.

'You've been a long while at the Rintouls,' she said, pouring water into the teapot. 'How was Frances?'

Gavin settled himself into a chair. 'She wasn't back from her work so I didn't get to see her.' He loosened the laces of his tackety boots and heaved them off one by one. His toes began to thaw as he stretched his long legs to warm them by the blazing fire. Then, shuffling through a pile of papers by his side, he selected one and began to read.

Elspeth handed him a cup of tea. 'Maybe if ye gave her as much attention as your books, she'd be there when ye went round.'

He took the cup but did not answer; it was a familiar provocation lately. The old woman seated herself again and gathered up her knitting. 'So what's kept ye all this time?' she asked.

Gavin looked up. 'I stayed a while with Mrs Rintoul and auld Wullie.'

'And how's the poor man keeping?'

17

'I told him ye were asking after him, Grandma, but ye ken he's no doing so well these days. The Black Spit has got him so he canna speak without coughing. God, it pains ye to hear it.' He tapped the paper he held and his voice became animated. 'I'm working on this now to present to the Company. We've got to get compensation organised for the likes of Wullie, laid off with their health. Obviously it's the mines that's killing them, and that's the coal company's responsibility. We're suffering and they're the ones who should pay for it!'

Elspeth nodded and began to count her stitches. 'Aye, but it's no me ye need to convince,' she said calmly.

He paused, then smiled, realising he had got carried away and returned to his reading.

'Ye were there a fair while, then?' she continued with gentle persistence. The mantel clock ticked relentlessly. He made a note with his pencil and tried to concentrate. She looked over her glasses. 'Well?'

'When Frances didn't come back, I went up to the Institute. I had a bit of union business to sort out.'

Elspeth gave a little sigh of exasperation just loud enough to be noticed. She put down her knitting and stirred her tea noisily. 'Och, if it's no your work, it's your books. If it's no your books, it's the union. Since they started that Federation last year, it's all you've thought about.'

Gavin threw down the pencil. 'Look, I thought you approved of my work with the union – mind what the pit did to Grandpa and my dad!'

The old woman waited until the heat had gone out of the moment. 'Son, let's give the union a rest for a minute, can we?' she said quietly. 'Where's the fun in your life? When was the last time ye took Frances out to the dancing?' He tried to interrupt, but she continued undeterred. 'Once the pair of ye are married, there'll be time enough for the serious side of life. You'll no court her with a load of union speeches.'

'Grandma, Frances understands what I'm trying to do. She's no like the other lassies . . .'

'Oh, aye? And you're an expert, are ye?' He opened his mouth to protest but she continued regardless. 'I've kent Frances since she was a bairn. She has a good heart, but she's like any other young lass – I'm no so old that I canna mind myself when I was eighteen. All I'm saying is ye should take more heed of her.'

18

'That's no fair.' He was suddenly self-conscious, and he mumbled the rest. 'Ye ken how I feel about Frances.'

'Aye but does she?'

The few seconds of silence that followed confirmed her point. Elspeth leaned forward and patted his hand persuasively. 'She'll no wait forever, son, d'ye hear me?'

Gavin's expression was still one of embarrassment. 'You'll no believe this, but I was going to talk to her the night. I dinna ken why but every time I decide to make a move where Frances is concerned, I seem to make a mess of it.' He sighed and rubbed his eyes. 'I'd worked it all out, what I was going to say to her – and then she's no even hame when I go round.'

'Just as well, by the sound of it.' Elspeth got up and refilled their cups. 'Ye worked it all out in your head and went to negotiate – like she was a pit manager instead of your lassie.'

'Och, Grandma!'

'Just for once, Gavin, will you let your heart speak for ye? If you do, then Frances will listen.'

He nodded and met her eyes at last. 'I'll speak to her on Sunday, after the kirk. And I'll say it right this time.'

Elspeth wanted to say more but let the moment go and they returned to silence. She had not meant to hurt him but was relieved that she had spoken her mind. Later, when she looked up from her knitting, she saw the papers slide from his fingers as his dark head drooped forward in sleep. Exhaustion had overwhelmed him. This earnest dedication to right the world's wrongs was all very well, she thought, but a full day's shift, followed by pressing demands from the union was no life for a young man. She went over and stroked his hair, looking down into the face, so peaceful when the care had left it. Sighing, she started to tidy the clutter away from around his feet. As she moved his jacket to hang it up, a slim book fell from the pocket. Retrieving it, she saw that it was not some dry political discourse as she had expected. 'The Love Ballads and Songs of Robert Burns' was embossed on the spine in gold. Her stiff fingers smoothed across the fine leather binding, and she flipped open the front cover. She recognised her grandson's bold writing in the inscription on the first page and smiled as she read the words he had obviously penned for Frances. 'Och, why did I worry?' she whispered inwardly, moved by what she had just read. She slipped the book back into his jacket pocket and gently shook him awake. 'Wheesht now, away to bed – and dinna let me see a light under your door.'

4

The linoleum factories standing at the top of Pathhead dominated the high shoreline looking down onto the Forth. The ruins of Ravenscraig Castle were lost in the shadow of the great red-brick buildings that reared up twelve and fifteen stories above the sands like a latter-day fortress. Walkways arched like buttresses across Factory Road, connecting the Nether Street works to the newer buildings behind and making the roadway between them a dark and brooding canyon. Lying low in the sky, a weak March sun caught the glass-canopied roofs of the blocking and pattern-cutting rooms. In these warm, light-filled eyries of privilege, the designers and cutters created the printing blocks used to make the brightly-coloured floor covering that was in such demand throughout the Empire. And on each of the many levels below, enormous cavernous rooms were filled with the machinery that spewed out mile after mile of linoleum. After baking in the towering ovens, the rolls of finished floor cloth finally came to rest in the bleak, draught-swept realms of despatch where gangs of women worked. During their midday break, the women sat astride these rolls hunched in groups, while the department foreman moved among them.

'Keep your head down, here comes Jimmy Reid,' Frances warned Jeannie.

He paused and eyed them censoriously. 'And where were you two yesterday?'

'I'm awful sorry, Mr Reid, my grandad was poorly and I had to bide home and watch him,' Frances mumbled with a mouth full of bread.

'Aye, well you'll likely be docked a day's pay,' he grunted. 'And what about you, Adamson – I suppose you've got an ailing relative too?'

'What? – oh no, sir, I wasn't well,' Jeannie faltered, her voice trembling. Despite being coached for an hour on the walk from West Wemyss to Pathhead, she was not a convincing liar. But fortunately for them, the foreman let it go at that and walked off without pursuing the matter.

The two looked at each other.

'See! I told ye we'd be all right.'

'But Mrs Doig saw ye. Ye said so yourself.'

'Well, maybe she didn't see me after all. I got out of the way as quick as I could. And she's as blind as a bat anyway, with those muckle glasses she wears. What I'd like to know is how she got up there with all the toffs.'

'Who cares about that? At least ye both saw it. I spent the whole time down a hole in the dark for my trouble.'

A loud bell signalled the end of their break and the faces of the women grew weary as they dragged themselves up from the floor. Reluctantly, they returned to work and the task of cutting the linoleum and rolling it up in sheets of coarse jute began all over again.

Frances hauled a heavy roll onto the bogey and wheeled it over the stone floor to the loading bay. The doors leading to the yard were wide open, letting in the cold breeze from the sea and clouds of dusty fibres swirled around the work area. The stench of linseed oil pervaded the atmosphere and everything was caked in a waxy grime. Suddenly a warning shout from behind made her jump.

'Falling roll!' the voice cried, followed by a thunderous crash. All activity ceased and a stunned silence descended on the women. Jimmy strode into the middle of the bay to where a large cylinder had toppled on its side. Peeling back the wrapping, he shook his head in a hopeless gesture. The linoleum, brittle in the cold, had shattered like so much glass, rendering the entire roll worthless. 'Who was moving this?' he demanded, looking round.

One of the men came forward nervously. 'It was me, Mr Reid. I dinna ken how it happened.'

The foreman thought for a minute then spoke.

'Right, come with me. We'd better see Mr Doig about this.' The two walked away, watched in frozen apprehension by the rest of the work-force. 'Well, get on with it!' he turned and shouted back, the sudden force of his voice jolting them into activity.

A few minutes later, brisk footsteps could be heard as the two men returned, coming down the wooden stairway that led from the manager's office in the corner of the despatch area. Preceding them, exuding an unmistakable aura of authority, was the short stocky figure of Archibald Doig. As Despatch Manager he often liked to talk of his workers as a cheery, satisfied lot but in truth it was his tyrannical régime which ensured that no one stepped out of line. Far from being satisfied, their faces betrayed only fear as he approached. Very little escaped his notice and, when it did, his wife Euphemia, as his chief clerk, was well placed to be his eyes and ears. Hated by the workers and vaguely mistrusted by the other managers, Doig's determination to rise higher in the company had left him few allies. His wife who shared his ruthless ambition was detested even more than he by the women who worked for them.

When he marched onto the floor of the warehouse, all conversation abruptly ceased. No one dared look up as he moved among them, his thumbs tucked into a waistcoat which stretched tightly over his barrel-chest and stomach. He came to a halt in front of the shattered roll and poked it with his toe. As he stared down, his little bird-like eyes narrowed in anger. 'How many times have you been warned about carelessness, MacPherson?'

'I'm sorry, sir, it was an accident . . .'

'Oh, aye, you will be sorry.' He spun round to face the man. 'Have you any idea how much that roll was worth before you dropped it?' He jabbed a finger into the other's chest, pushing him backwards.

'Er, no sir.'

'Well, you'll find out soon enough, for it'll be coming out of your wages for a few years.'

'Oh Mr Doig, please sir, ye can't!'

A smug expression flooded Doig's features. 'Oh no? Well, you have the choice. You pay for the damage you've done, or you're dismissed. Think on it, MacPherson, and let me know what you decide.' With that, he turned and made his way towards the stairs.

High up, from the office window his wife watched the scene on the floor below. A thin smile spread over Euphemia Doig's lips as she tapped on the glass to attract his notice. When he glanced up, she pointed behind him, mouthing words he could not make out. Looking around, he caught sight of the object of her attention and nodded in acknowledgement. Frances kept her head down but could tell he was making straight for where she stood. Not until his rasping voice barked at her did she look up.

He stood staring at her for a few moments, deliberately savouring her nervous discomfort, then said, in a clipped and contemptuous tone: 'I want you and Adamson in my office after you've clocked out tonight. Do I make myself clear?'

'Yes sir,' she faltered, almost bobbing a curtsey and hating herself for her diffidence.

Doig then turned to the foreman. 'And I want to see you now, Reid!' With that, he smartly marched away, his lackey nervously tripping after him.

Frances and Jeannie watched out for Jimmy's return but when he came back from the office he looked grim and would not catch their eye. There was no opportunity to talk and both knew his manner did not bode well for them. Soon after punching their time cards, it was with heavy hearts that they presented themselves at the door of Doig's office. He sat in readiness, dwarfed by his enormous desk and tapping the blotter with podgy fingers. From the corner, his wife watched with gloating triumph as the two girls entered, her eyes gleaming malevolently behind her thick, pebble glasses.

'Where were you yesterday?' he snapped at Frances. She swallowed hard and repeated what she had told Jimmy.

'And you?' he asked. Jeannie's reply was barely audible.

Suddenly he was on his feet. 'You're a pair of lying wee toerags!' His fat neck and red face bulged with anger. 'Ye were seen cavorting about the new bridge,' he hissed.

Frances decided to brazen it out. 'You're mistaken, Mr Doig. I was in the Wemyss all day. So was Jeannie.' She spoke quietly, trying to keep a cool head.

This infuriated Euphemia Doig. 'I saw you Rintoul,' she burst out, her yellowing teeth bared in anger. 'You were standing above his Royal Highness, laughing in a most disrespectful way.'

Both girls tried to speak but Doig held up his hand for silence. 'You cannot deny it,' he said. 'You were seen. That's all there is to it.'

Frances hesitated, but knew it was useless to continue. 'All right,' she said, 'I was there. But no Jeannie. Ye didn't see her, I was there myself.'

Again Doig interjected. 'Blethers!' he roared. 'Wherever you are, she's no far away. Like a collie dog.' There was silence. He pulled out a handkerchief and wiped his neck and forehead. Then, regaining his composure, he sat back down. 'I'm not an unjust man, and though I suspect that Adamson was with you, I have no proof.' He looked contemptuously at Jeannie. 'You'll be docked a day's wages.'

'Thank you, Mr Doig.' She glanced at Frances who winked back reassuringly.

'Right then, away with ye.' Nervously, she fled the room and he waited till the door closed. 'But you, Rintoul.' His voice was low and quiet, menacing in its composure. 'You are dismissed with immediate effect.'

Frances couldn't believe it. She had expected to lose a couple of days' pay, but not given the sack. 'That's no fair, Mr Doig.'

'Enough of your lip,' he shouted. 'I've had my fill of ye. If ye were a good worker, I'd keep ye on. But you're a trouble-maker, Rintoul. You've no respect.' Now on her feet behind him, Mrs Doig egged her

23

husband on, her head bobbing up and down in agreement. He took out his pocket watch. 'Right, get out,' he said impatiently. 'You can collect what money you're due at the gate-house on Friday.'

For a few moments she stood still, disbelieving, but it soon became clear that the interview was over. Frances felt curiously detached about losing her job, but the obvious pleasure the Doigs had taken from the distasteful interview left her angry. As she walked towards the door, she turned to face the complacent pair and said, with candour, 'I wouldn't wear that hat again ye had on yesterday, Mrs Doig. Ye looked like a burst haggis. God alone knows what the Prince of Wales must've thought!'

'Oh, no, he didn't give ye the sack!' Jeannie was in tears as they started the long walk home along the beach towards West Wemyss. She had waited at the foot of the Ravenscraig steps for Frances to catch her up.

'It's all right. I'll get another job no bother.' Anger still drove her and she was walking quickly, making Jeannie half-run to keep up.

'But what will your father say?'

'He'll no say anything. He'll let his belt do the talking for him.' Her pace slackened and she shrugged. They walked in silence round the crags on which stood the old castle. The tide was going out, leaving the sand wet and strewn with debris after the storm of the day before.

'I knew there'd be trouble if we went to that bridge.'

'Oh, for Christ's sake, Jeannie, stop going on about it – I canna live like a nun in the Wemyss all my life! Is it no worth losing a lousy job to have had a bit of fun and excitement for a change?'

'That's you all over! Dinna mind the consequences, just do as ye please!' Jeannie moaned. 'You've always been that way, thinking of yourself and no worrying about anybody else.' She started whimpering again. 'I've got to tell my mother my wages'll be short this week. You're no the only one that'll get a hammering.'

They passed Dysart where the lights in the cottages around St Serf's tower made a welcome break in the darkness. There was nothing to say and each was lost in her own private thoughts. Jeannie would not be comforted. Her feet were tired of treading the stones and it was not long before she made off in the direction of the road. Alone, Frances dawdled, flinging skimmers into the sea and wishing she could be somewhere else. The prospect of going home with the news was daunting and yet it was not so much her father's reaction that she feared. Something wider and less obvious now troubled her. The humdrum reality of work and home life had become unendurable, and she felt a growing sense of emptiness and isolation that seemed to drain the energy from her.

The heat of the house blasted her raw cheeks as she opened the door. Her mother did not look up. 'You're late again,' she said as she fussed around the fire, preparing the meal. Frances stood unmoving, trying to find the right words to break the news. Jessie Rintoul stirred the stew and tasted it with a spoon. As she added the salt, she became conscious of the silence and turned towards her daughter. 'Well? Are ye no taking off your coat?' she asked.

'Ma, sit down a minute will ye?'

'What are ye talking about lassie, I've no time for —'

Frances interrupted. 'I lost my job today,' she blurted out.

'What?' Jessie paled and slumped into a chair. It was as if a cold wind had blown through the kitchen. The old man was roused from his fireside slumber aware of a sudden change in the atmosphere. 'Is that Frances home?' he asked.

'Aye, I'm home, Grandad.' She went over and kissed him.

'What's wrong?' Starting to cough, he choked on the words and she helped him to clear the phlegm from his chest.

'She's lost her job, Grandad.' Jessie stared in shock. 'Taking days off again, no doubt? Or was it something else this time?'

'I dinna want to discuss it, Mother.'

'Well, lassie, your father'll want to discuss it!'

Frances pulled off her damp mittens and laid them on the hearth. 'Och, I'll get another job in no time, you'll see,' she said casually.

'He'll no see it like that, Frances!' Her mother shook her head ruefully. 'That'll no be good enough for your father! Ye better have a right good explanation ready for when he gets home!' There was an edge of fear in her voice as she began to weigh up the likely consequences. 'What is wrong with ye? We never had this carry on with Chrissie or Rob.'

'I've told ye, it'll be all right.'

'No, it'll no be all right! We've had nothing but bother with ye. First it was the school, always cheeking up to the masters, and now this – it's the second time you've lost your job since ye started working . . .' She began to weep into her apron, her thin shoulders convulsing as the sobs shook her.

'Oh, Ma, dinna greet,' Frances knelt down beside her, 'ye ken I'm sorry.'

Jessie was not to be consoled. 'Just when things were coming right,' she said, wiping her eyes and nose. 'It's a long while since we've had a harsh word in this house and this'll make him dancing mad – ye shouldn't do that to your father, ye ken how worked up he gets – it'll make him ill.'

Frances bit her tongue, knowing there was no point in arguing. She pulled off her coat with an air of defeat.

Suddenly aware of the time, Jessie jumped up again, her mind already focussed on the remaining chores. 'He'll be home soon,' she warned. 'Look, away ben the hoose and keep out of his road. I'll speak to him first.'

Frances turned in the doorway. 'No, Mother, there's no need, I'll speak to him myself,' she declared and went through into the bedroom. Behind her, the old man struggled to clear his throat in an effort to fend off another bout of coughing.

After ten, when the back shift ended, Mr Rintoul came home with Rob. Very little was said as they washed and then sat down to their meal. Henry was a large, heavily built man whose swarthy features were emphasised by the patina of fine coal dust that could never be entirely dislodged. Sitting opposite each other, the two men devoured their food hungrily. In the dim light, it was only the grey flecks in Henry's hair that distinguished him from his son. Both had a permanent frown, a look of distrust in the deep-set eyes that dissuaded any casual approach. Mrs Rintoul sat by the fire mending, her eyes alert in case they should call for more.

In the other room, Frances bided her time. When she thought the moment was right, she came through and her mother looked up anxiously. 'Frances has to speak to ye, Dad,' she faltered.

'She can hold her tongue till I'm finished,' he said brusquely and ignored them as the normal meal-time silence resumed. Frances stood at the end of the table and waited. From time to time, her father eyed her coldly while the only sounds in the room came from the clink of cutlery against plates and her grandfather's troubled breathing.

'I'll take another couple of tatties, Jessie,' Henry said, holding his plate out to his wife.

She jumped up and spooned the vegetables from the pot. 'What about you, son?' she asked but Rob shook his head and continued to bolt his food.

Eventually, Henry pushed his plate away and leaned back in his chair while his wife fussed around clearing up. All the time, her watchful eyes darted nervously between husband and daughter. At last he spoke, his gaze as contemptuous as his words. 'Well, what is it that's so important ye have to interrupt my dinner?' A movement distracted him as Rob made to get up. 'Did I say you could leave the table, Rob?' The boy sat back down and Henry returned his attention to Frances. 'Right, lassie, we're all waiting to hear ye.'

There was no easy way to tell him. She took a deep breath. 'I've had to leave my job.'

She saw the change in his expression as his face darkened in a scowl. 'What for?' he demanded.

Frances looked down but spoke clearly. 'I missed work on Tuesday to see the new bridge being opened and Doig sacked me.'

'Ye did what! What did I tell ye the last time?' She did not answer and looked up again, bracing herself for the onslaught. For a few seconds he paused, then he shouted, 'Ye daft, lazy slattern!' as his chair jolted forward.

'Dad, it's all right. I'll get another job.' She tried to placate him and backed away slightly.

'Bloody right, you'll get another job! Do ye think I'll keep ye when you're no bringing in a wage?' He gripped the table with both hands. 'The sooner that Douglas laddie marries ye and takes ye off my hands, the better. Let him put up with your carrying-on. I'm sick of the shame and disgrace you bring on me and this family.' Rising to his feet he started to pull off his thick belt. 'You're no too big for a leathering, and by Christ you'll no forget this one!'

Rob looked away, then took his chance to get up and slip unseen into the other room.

'Henry, leave the lassie.' The old man wheezed, trying to push himself from the chair.

'Be quiet, Wullie, this is none of your business.' Grandad turned his attention back to the fire, his eyes bright with tears. Frances watched as her mother lifted the dirty dishes into the sink and began to scrub them vigorously. Like so often before, she faced her father alone.

As he advanced towards her he finally tugged the belt free and raised it above his head. Shaking, Frances backed towards the fireplace. 'Come away from the fire,' he barked at her, knowing if he swung the belt now it would cause havoc and probably injure the old man. She did not move. 'Come away from the fire!' He made a grab for her and she edged further back.

Suddenly, the fear was gone. Reaching behind, her hand fell on the pot handle and she swung the pan of boiling liquid between them. 'I'm no taking another hiding from ye, Father,' she said, dangerously quiet. 'Touch me and I'll blind ye with this.'

No one spoke. For what seemed an age, the two faced each other. Then, Grandad began to cough convulsively. Frances still stared at her father, her arms trembling under the weight of the steaming pan. At last, with an angry roar, he threw down the belt in frustration. 'You're no daughter of mine! God alone knows what devil o' hell spawned ye, but you've a black and wicked nature.' He glared at his shaking wife. 'See she's out of my sight by the time I get back.' He stormed out, slamming the door.

The silence that followed was almost palpable, as if the room was reeling from the shock. Frances replaced the pot on the stove and went across to her mother. 'Come on Ma, it's over now,' she said in an effort to stop her tremulous weeping.

But Jessie would not be comforted and pushed Frances's arm away. 'Oh, ye think so?' Her voice shook weakly but the look in her eyes was hard and cold. 'Well, it's no over by a long chalk.'

Later that night, Frances lay restless in the narrow bed but it was not the hoarse breathing that kept her awake. Gazing through the small window frame, she watched clouds scud across a stormy sky till finally sleep came. She did not hear her father return. What roused her was the sound of sudden blows and her mother's stifled cries as his drunken rage finally found a target. Jumping up, she ran to the door, but her arm was gripped tightly by her brother.

'Dinna be daft!' he hissed. 'Ye were lucky before that he was sober.' He pushed her roughly back to her bed. 'If ye go ben there now, he'll maim ye for life.'

She pleaded with him. 'Do something!'

'What can I do?' he whispered. And in the dim moonlight she saw her own shame mirrored in his face as he turned away. Crawling back under the covers, she lay in cold despair until the dawn.

5

It did not take long before events in the Rintoul household provoked gossip which filtered through the village. Henry Rintoul enjoyed an otherwise considerable status in the community but for the singular impediment of his younger daughter. In such a small place, opinions needed scant foundation and, once formed, quickly became entrenched. As it was, Frances did little to dispel the myth that she was defiant and insubordinate, having long since given up the fight to redeem herself in their eyes. Three days after the row with her father, it was obvious that she was the focus of attention for the Sunday congregation. She shifted uncomfortably in the pew, wedged between her mother and Rob as her ears caught snatches of whispers. In an attempt to ignore them, she thumbed the worn hymn book on her lap and kept her head down. At length, the welcome sound of her sister's voice assailed her from behind. Chrissie was there as usual with her six children, one of whom had smuggled a catapult into the church. Discreetly, and with a careful aim, the boy directed a missile at the minister's wife. It found a target on the unsuspecting woman's hat where the feather twitched and came loose drifting limply down her back. The children snorted with giggles and Chrissie arraigned them with threats to keep quiet. Frustrated in her efforts, she leaned forward and turned her attention to Frances. 'I heard there's been right ructions at home. Folk are having a rare claiver with ye.' She, too, had heard the tittle-tattle.

'Just look at them.' Frances frowned. 'All done up in their Sunday best, sitting in the house of God with nothing better to do than blether about me.'

Chrissie grinned. 'Well, you've got to admit ye give them enough to talk about, don't ye?' She looked around, then asked, 'Is Gavin here?'

'Aye, he's sitting over there.' Frances pointed a few rows ahead.

'Does he ken about all this?'

'I suppose he must've heard – I've no seen him since I lost my job.'

'I wonder what he'll have to say about that?'

'It's got nothing to do with him.' Her response was swift but there was an edge of uncertainty in the defiance.

'You're daft to talk like that when ye ken you'll be wed before the summer's out.'

Frances coloured slightly. 'Well, he's no asked me yet.'

'Aye, and whose fault is that?' There was no reply and Chrissie continued. 'Och Frances, ye should've nabbed him long ago,' she whispered wistfully. 'Look at him. God, if I could turn the clock back, I'd be chasing ye to the altar!'

Suppressed laughter bubbled to the surface and the two women giggled like young girls. Frances looked at the tired face of her sister and wished she could roll the years back. In a very short time, Chrissie had changed from carefree bride to world-weary mother. Tiny red veins gave a deceptive rosiness to her cheeks and her eyes darted anxiously within pain-dimmed shadows. She thought little of herself, and her appearance betrayed a life surrendered to the service of her family and her man.

When she had recovered her composure Frances asked, 'Where's Jack, is he no with ye today?'

'No, he bided at home, his chest's bad again.' There was a sigh. 'I only hope it's no the stourie lungs he's got.' The prospect of Chrissie losing her husband was too awful to contemplate. A brooding silence descended and neither spoke of it again. All the men in the town were miners. All faced the same risks to their lives and the attendant consequences to their families.

Disturbed by the thought, Frances looked across at Gavin and suddenly felt the same twinge of fear for him. These were the beginnings of something she knew she would learn to cope with if they were to share a life. At work he suffered his own particular burden, handicapped by his tall frame as he crouched at the coal face in the confined channels and drifts underground. Even here in the church, he looked somewhat restricted, hunched and uncomfortable in his Sunday suit. Yet there was a strength and permanence about him which made it seem unfair to fear the future when now he sat mere yards from her, his presence sure and indestructible. Frances watched him without his knowledge, his dark brows drawn in concentration on problems at the pit or worried by some union question. Or was he thinking of her she wondered? The notion moved her. True, Gavin had a pensive side to his nature, never more earnest than when he spoke about his work. But when he was with her he displayed a tenderness she had not known possible in a man. Though life was serious and those times were all too few, she could almost bear the waiting in between. And Chrissie was right, he was attractive. He personified the fortune-teller's stock image of tall, dark and handsome and was popular amongst the Wemyss women who teased him remorselessly for it. Frances knew many of them thought her an unworthy match but, since the age of sixteen when first she had walked out with him, he had not shown even a passing interest in anyone else.

They had not seen each other for a week and in that time so much had happened. She hoped that after the service they could steal some time alone together. But the hope was underlaid with a vague anxiety which she did not understand. This restiveness was new to her and she sensed with a growing apprehension that it was just marginally out of control. At that moment Gavin turned round and gazed across the heads until he caught her eye. He smiled at her and she felt the uneasiness vanish and smiled back.

The service was about to begin and again Chrissie's voice sounded from behind. 'Will you bairns sit still, or I'll skelp ye!' she said, confiscating the catapult.

The minister led them through the first hymns and prayers before launching with zealous determination into his sermon. For such a small, thin man the Reverend Hezekiah Black had a surprisingly rich and sonorous voice that could be heard above the singing of the congregation. Frances hoped he would not get carried into the realms of hell-fire, brimstone and damnation that morning. The lurid accounts of life-after-death in the nether regions always left her feeling slightly soiled and with a headache from his shouting.

'Friends and parishioners of St Adrian's: the theme of this morning's sermon is the virtue of family life.' The sanctimonious tone was accompanied by an emotionless smile and Frances fancied that he was looking directly at her. 'The Apostle, Saint Paul, gave us guidance almost two thousand years ago on the sanctity of the family.' He opened the great, thick Bible that stood on the lectern. 'Paul's epistle to the Ephesians, chapter six. "Children, obey your parents in the Lord: for this is right. Honour thy father and mother (which is the first commandment) that it may be well with thee and thou mayest live long on the earth. And ye fathers, provoke not your children to wrath; but bring them up in the nurture and admonition of the Lord." ' Frances sighed heavily, louder than she had intended, and her father scowled at her from the end of the row.

The minister closed the book and looked round at the assembled faces before him. 'The community is itself like a great family to which we all belong and to which we owe a service – just as within the body of our own families, we have unquestionable obligations.' There were a few concurring murmurs in the congregation and Frances wondered idly if the day would ever come when the sermon would not be about obligations. 'There is nothing more wholesome than the enrichment we receive from family life,' he continued. 'To be a participant in that, no matter how mean or seemingly insignificant a role we play, is to be in harmony with the natural order of things. Only in that way can we learn to serve God. Of course, not everyone has the good fortune to play that part. But those of us who are denied the bosom of the family through death or misfortune may take comfort from the fact that they can be of service to their fellow man, that wider family that I spoke of before.'

Frances looked across at Gavin's bowed head. Was he contemplating his own loss, what little there was left of the Douglases in West Wemyss? Was he the living proof of the preacher's words

31

the way he threw himself into his union work? But strangely it was not pity she felt. Instead she was overwhelmed by the sense that she was slipping away from him and needed to reach out and take hold of him to reassure herself. Then, as soon as they had come, these unsettling thoughts passed and the penetrating voice resumed.

The minister held up his hand and gave an ingratiating smile. 'Now, I know some of you are thinking of the converse side of what I am saying. I speak of the force of darkness that sometimes rears its head within the household – the occasional cross word that leads to another, and before they know it, mother is pitted against daughter, father against son.' At this point Frances knew they were in for another tour of the Devil's domain. She stopped listening altogether and continued to pick away at the hymn book which was now disintegrating in her lap.

Relief came at last when the congregation poured out into the little churchyard and stood around chatting in groups. The Rintouls remained together, Chrissie's children chasing each other rowdily between the adults. Periodically, they were joined by others but Frances hung back embarrassed by some of the looks she was getting and unwilling to talk. Finally, Gavin came up and was welcomed by them all. He acknowledged Frances somewhat self-consciously in the presence of her parents and was careful to bestow equal attention on the rest of the family. The children clamoured to be noticed and he swung one of them onto his shoulders while the others tugged at his legs, demanding the same treatment.

'How's Elspeth keeping?' Jessie Rintoul was asking.

'Och, she's fine,' he said. 'But her rheumatism was playing her up this morning, and sitting in the cold kirk didna seem a good idea, so she stayed at home.' The child pulled the cap from his head and ruffled his hair. He laughed and swung the boy down to ground level where Chrissie was chastising them for being a nuisance. Gavin talked for a while to her about Jack, enquiring if they were coping while he was off work. But though his concern was genuine, all the time he was mindful of Frances in the background and his eyes kept wandering in her direction.

Once all the news had been exchanged, he squared himself and asked politely if it was all right to walk out with Frances. Her father paused and his brows drew together in a frown. Seeing this, Gavin gently persisted. 'Please, Mr Rintoul, no for long – just to take a turn along the beach with me?'

Frances watched in anticipation. Then her father let out a sigh and reluctantly gave his permission. 'Aye, away and talk some sense into her,' he said with a dismissive wave of the hand, 'and mind ye have her back afore dinner.'

As if a huge weight had been lifted from them, the two headed through the side gate and onto the beach. It was blustery but mild, the first spring-like day they had had that year and once they were on the sand, Frances undid the laces on her tight boots, pulled them off and stuffed her stockings inside. Gavin picked them up for her as she ran ahead towards the outcrop of rock on which stood Wemyss Castle. He got the impression she was slightly uneasy, not surprising he supposed in the light of recent events. 'Can we no find somewhere else that's quiet?' he called. Other couples and families were already starting to appear strolling near by.

At the back of the beach was a dense wood bounded by a wall. 'Come on. Let's go through here for a change,' she suggested, equally keen to be free of the crowds.

The woods were part of the Estate of the family which owned the mines, and Gavin was reluctant to trespass. 'We're no bairns, Frances. We canna just go running through the Estate – are you no in enough bother already?'

Unaffected by the rebuke she eased open the weed-clogged old door. Though she expected an initial resistance from Gavin, she knew him well enough to be sure he would follow her. Once they were both inside the wall, he tied her boots together and hung them around his neck. Then she took his hand and drew him forward into the wood. Immediately, the wind abated under the dark canopy of trees and they were enclosed by an unfamiliar privacy. Gradually Gavin began to relax and slipped his arm around her waist.

'Ma said ye were round on Tuesday, I'm sorry I missed ye,' Frances said, squeezing his hand in added apology.

'Och, it doesn't matter.'

'But it does – it's been ages since I've seen ye,' she said, leaning her head against his shoulder as they walked.

'Aye, but you've been busy though – cheeking up to Doig and losing your job I hear.'

'It wasn't like that.' She jumped ahead and faced him. 'I had one day off to see the new bridge – oh, Gavin, it was braw – ye should've been there!'

He shook his head and sighed with mock severity. 'Aye, and I'd have lost my job as well – then where would we be, eh?'

She was undeterred by his reproach, still carried away by the memory of the experience. 'You've no idea how grand it was – it was so big. And there were bands, and lots of folk. Me and Jeannie sneaked up to the station and from there we managed to climb up onto the bridge itself —'

He stopped in his tracks. 'Ye what? How could ye be that stupid — ye could've killed yourself!'

Frances frowned and looked away dispirited but he quickly caught her hand and drew her back. He was anxious not to spoil their time together and checked his disapproval with a smile. 'You're impossible!' he said, trying to lighten the mood.

'So are you! If it had been one of your pals at the pit that was sacked, you'd've had plenty to say. When it's me and Doig, ye take his side.'

'Are ye telling me ye were no in the wrong?'

'Well, it was worth it,' she said with a little contrite shrug. Then she broke free and ran ahead, laughing as she disappeared through the trees.

Gavin tried to concentrate on what he wanted to say, though things were not going exactly as he had planned. Loosening his collar he followed, calling out cautiously, so as not to draw attention. Hearing no footfall on the soft ground, he looked around. But she was nowhere to be seen and he called again, louder this time, his eyes scanning the woods for a movement. 'Frances, stop this, where are ye?'

Suddenly, a rustling sound came from above and he glanced up to find her seated on an overhead branch swinging her legs. Her cheeks glowed with exhilaration and dark coils of tousled hair sprang loose as she unpinned her hat, sending it spinning to the ground. Her clothes had become somewhat dishevelled in the effort and Gavin was baffled as to how she had achieved the climb. He eyed her quizzically. 'Aye, very clever. But just how are ye to get down from there?'

She stuck her nose in the air. 'Maybe I'll no come down.'

'Ye will if I pull ye!' he grinned, grabbing her feet and making her wobble unsteadily. Then she squealed as she lost her balance completely and tipped backwards with a loud yell that sent the wood pigeons flapping skywards. He managed to catch her awkwardly but stumbled and together they fell to the ground with an ungainly thud. Both were laughing breathlessly, uncontrollably, all fear of discovery momentarily lost in the chaos. They looked at each other in the pause that followed then he put his hand gently around her face and drew her mouth towards his. The embrace had a tender familiarity and she responded with ease, moving nearer as her cold hands found their way into the warm recesses of his jacket.

'That's more like it,' he said, stroking her hair. 'It's good to see ye smile. Ye looked so glum in the kirk this morning.'

Frances sighed. 'Did I? Aye well, my father's making my life a misery right now — he took it bad about the job.'

'He didn't hit ye?'

'No.' She shuddered at the memory. 'But the place is like a dead-hoose — he'll no speak to me.'

Gavin shook his head ruefully. 'Ye're a right one for getting yerself into a scrape.' But he didn't care about that, and never had. Each time she alienated herself further from work or family, he saw her drawing closer to him. So close in fact that he was almost sure the time was now right to settle it once and for all. He kissed her again, hoping gently to turn the conversation round to thoughts of the future. 'And what are ye going to do now?' he asked.

But the reply was not quite what he bargained for. 'Do ye think my father would let me sit around the hoose with no money coming in?' She shrugged. 'I've been picking coal at the bings these past three days.'

Suddenly his face darkened. 'I'll no have a wife of mine picking coal.'

She drew back from him with an arch look. 'Gavin, in case it's slipped your notice, I'm no your wife yet.'

He paused, embarrassed. 'Well, I think now's as good a time as any.'

'Oh ye do, do ye?' She frowned. 'And I suppose that was a proposal?'

He reddened, fingering the little book in his pocket, wondering if this was the right moment to give it to her. 'I ken I'm no very good with words,' he began, slowly drawing it out.

'Oh, but ye are — when it matters to ye!' Resentment surfaced from somewhere deep inside and she pulled away, rounding on him angrily. 'I've heard ye speaking at the union meetings — ye've got them eating out of your hand. Ye stir their blood till they're cheering and clapping. And I've seen grown men greeting when you're reciting Burns.' Frustrated, she pushed her hands into the tussocks of grass in front of her, tearing them up by the roots. 'But with me, you're a lump o' stone!'

Gavin was taken aback by the outburst and quickly returned the book to his pocket before she saw it. He tried to make amends and fought to retain a grip on the situation but she stubbornly got up and moved away a few paces. 'All right, all right, I'm sorry,' he said in a chastened voice, unsure now of how to proceed. He came up beside her and put his arm over her shoulder. 'What's got into ye, Frances? You're that restless you'll no give me a chance.' He eased her round to face him. 'I said I'm sorry. Speaking to you is twice as hard as facing a union meeting. I got the words all mixed up.'

'It's no that,' she protested. 'It's just that, well, ye seem to think I should be that glad . . .' He looked hurt and she quickly amended her remark. 'Och, I dinna mean it like that. It's no you, it's just that when I look around I dinna see the same rosy picture of the future that you do.'

'Why do I spend so much time up at the union, eh? Do ye think I want us to live like this for ever? I'm working for change. I want to see improvements for our bairns, better conditions at the mine.' But in the midst of this he noticed her expression had changed and it suddenly looked as if she might cry. 'What, what is it?' he said, immediately concerned.

'I was thinking about us, just you and me.' Frances swallowed hard, trying to stave off the tears. 'But the way you talk makes that seem selfish.'

His voice softened. 'There'll be time for us, lass, I promise ye. You're all cooped up in that wee space, ye canna breathe there, that's what's wrong. Ye ken there's only me and Grandma at home. When we're married we can have our own room.'

'Aye, but for how long, Gavin? Once we've two bairns running round the place, we'll be bulging out the door like everybody else in the Wemyss.'

He sat down dolefully again at the base of the tree and put his hands in his pockets. 'Would that be so awful? Christ, Frances, we love each other – I canna think of anything better than to share my life with you and to bring up our own bairns. If you dinna see it that way, what is it ye want then?'

Frances looked down at him. His face bore a sad, blank expression and she slumped to her knees beside him. 'When I was a wee lassie, I always thought there had to be more to life than this. But now I'm grown up I see that everything just carries on the same as before. You're born here, ye marry here, ye die. Nobody leaves.'

'That's the way it is, Frances. I wish right now I could offer ye more . . .' He shrugged. 'But ye have to change things from inside if ye want them to be any different.'

'I ken you're right,' she said weakly.

'For what it's worth, I dinna intend to stay a miner all my life.'

Unwittingly she had wounded him and blanched to think how little effort it took. She touched his face. 'It's worth a lot.'

Seizing on this, he gripped her shoulders. 'Enough for ye to be my wife?' A flicker of anticipation pulsed in his eyes. 'Say yes, Frances. I'm no like your father – I swear I'll never give ye cause to regret it.'

She laughed self-consciously at the sudden ardent outburst but Gavin did not flinch. He continued to stare into her face, trying to maintain a calm exterior but hardly concealing the urgency she knew to be there. 'Yes,' she said quietly.

His grip relaxed and he let out a deep sigh as he wrapped his arms around her body. 'I love you.' The voice was muffled, whispered from somewhere in the tangled mass of her hair, but she heard it just the same.

'I know,' she said, hoping desperately that it would be enough.

6

Easter came around and the annual Links Market was again in full swing. Every night Kirkcaldy was mobbed with folk from far and wide, eager to see what the fair had to offer. Down the length of the sea front, glinting paraffin lamps illuminated the stalls and side shows. There were carousels, helter-skelters and tents with fluttering pennants. Posters and placards announced the arrival of amazing new acts attempting greater feats of daring, while strange animals from foreign lands added to an exotic mix of the curious and the bizarre. All around, shrieking, happy voices rose above the relentless barrel organ as people came in their droves, encouraged out of doors by the milder weather and the optimism of spring. It was as if the gloom of winter had been lifted by the arrival of the fair and a new spirit pervaded.

With their contracts ended, several of the builders from the Forth Bridge were drawn to the Links Market to take a holiday and blow some of their pay. Many who had worked together over the years now faced parting with their old comrades. This was particularly true of two riveters, William Munroe and Carlo Bagiotti who had developed the kind of mutual trust born out of dependence on a fellow worker, a special relationship only those who had braved the elements at that fearful altitude could know. The conditions on the bridge were often treacherous and in their time they had seen thirty men plunge to their deaths in the water below.

William was glad it was over. In September 1886, he had presented himself for work at the Forth Bridge site and had stayed on to see it completed. It was out of character for him to remain so long in one place for in his twenty-five years, he had turned his hand to almost as many different jobs. Without family or ties, his credo had always been to take work where he could get it, save what he could and then move on without a backward glance. People liked him and he knew it. His manner was perceived as carefree rather than insubordinate and where the same behaviour in others might be seen as flouting convention, he somehow got away with it. It was this gallus confidence that prevented him from viewing the world too seriously and secured his popularity among men and women alike. Though familiar with hardship, he retained a characteristic insouciance that shone through even the most dire circumstances. Sometimes in the chaos of their over-crowded lodgings, where the briggers lived crushed together with only cheap ale to blur the harsh reality, William would be persuaded to take up the fiddle and, as the sweet sound drifted through the house, many would grow quiet and think of home.

Carlo thought of home. Unlike William, the bond of family to him was very strong but, along with so many other migrant workers, he had crossed a continent for the guarantee of employment and a regular wage. In a sense, they were both displaced persons, which perhaps explained the understanding there was between them. Carlo would go back to Italy fluent in a new language but spoken with a distinctive hint of his friend's Scots brogue. William had his own plans too. But for now all the two men wanted was an entertaining diversion so they came to the Links Market to unwind for a while before a different world claimed each of them.

From the top of the Ferris wheel they enjoyed a unique view of the activities below. The wheel was making its debut at the fair and only the most intrepid would give it a try. Despite this, a long queue snaked round the enclosure, though many had second thoughts when their own turn came. William and Carlo, who had been first to get on, now waited impatiently for the seats to fill up. Eventually the great wheel creaked into motion and the gondola in which they were sitting began to turn. The crowd marvelled and squeals of delight went up as they watched it spin slowly on its axis.

William felt disappointed and he quickly grew restless. Even at the height of its momentum, it never really gathered much speed and the experience was tame in comparison with his own of the last few years. He looked down through the metal spokes and spars and watched in vague amusement as the other passengers clung on fearfully. Far below on the opposite side of the wheel, a young woman sat alone. Though she held the safety bar firmly, it was clear she was unafraid and enjoying the ride. His eyes followed fascinated as she rhythmically came into view and was lost again. He concentrated hard on the cyclical image, sensing something familiar about her. Then suddenly he remembered and nudged his friend. 'Carlo, look down there – is that no the lassie from the bridge?'

He jumped to his feet and called out to her, waving his arms, but Carlo roughly hauled him back into the seat. 'What's the matter – you want to kill yourself?' William reluctantly complied and sat down again but throughout the remainder of the ride, he did not avert his eyes from the figure below.

With another revolution, the wheel slowly came to a halt and started to discharge its human cargo. Being at the bottom, the girl alighted first and William grew agitated as he and Carlo waited their turn to get off. He had failed to catch her eye and watched with desperation as she disappeared into the fair. 'Can ye no make this thing shift a bit faster?' he shouted to the attendant below but received only a scowl in return. The intermittent jerking movement continued until William's exasperation grew unbearable. With a curse, he clambered on to the hand-rail and swung himself down through the mechanism before jumping the last few feet to ground level.

'E matto, e amore.' Carlo shrugged as he watched his friend making off into the crowd.

As the tent flap dropped behind the two girls, the bustling sounds of the fair became muffled and distant. They waited nervously, cocooned in the dim light with the smell of damp grass and canvas filling their nostrils.

'I'm no sure this is such a good idea.'

'Och, Frances, aren't ye just a bit curious about the future?' Jeannie whispered enthusiastically, looking around at the astrological charts hung from the tent poles.

'Christ, I dinna need a fortune-teller to ken what lies ahead for me!'

'Ye dinna sound too pleased for a lass that's to be married in a week and I ken dozens who'd change places with ye. What would Gavin think if he could hear ye talk like that?'

Frances sighed but was spared the need to answer when they were interrupted by a hoarse voice. 'Well, come away in lassies.' The 'Mystic Madame Zelda' emerged from the shadows holding a spirit lamp, her brass jewellery catching the light as she moved with a swish of her flowing robes. The gloom was barely illuminated by the smoking lamp and this gave an added Bohemian mystery to the atmosphere. A scrawny dog had followed at the gypsy's heels and it came over to sniff around their feet. Frances ignored the dog but Jeannie bent down to pat its mangy head. With no warning growl, the animal snapped at her hand and she recoiled with a squeak of fright.

'Get out o' here!' Zelda spat, kicking the hapless beast in the ribs. It yelped and slunk off into a dark corner, licking its side. The gypsy hung the lamp on a tent pole and turned to weigh up the two young women before her. Then, satisfied she had got the measure of them, she gave a toothless grin and pulled forward a small table and two chairs. 'Now, there's nothing to fear, my dears,' she said, noticing a slight reticence on their part. 'Just sit ye down, cross my palm with a coin – a silver one gets better results – and all will be revealed.' She tightened her lips and held out her hand expectantly.

'You first,' Jeannie whispered, and stepped backwards, leaving her friend no option. Reluctantly, Frances sat on the edge of the chair, pulled off her mittens and offered a coin. In a flash it was snatched and secreted in some dark recess of Zelda's gown.

'So, ye want to know the future?' Zelda fixed Frances with an unblinking stare and received a hesitant nod in response. 'Well, then, we'll ask the crystal to tell us what lies ahead for ye.' From beneath the table a glass sphere was produced and placed between them. Crooning in a low chant, the old woman began passing her hands over the ball. As she sang her dirge, she swayed back and forth, her eyes opening and closing in intermittent spasms. The jerking movements of her head seemed to loosen her wild hair, and a corona of dark, crackling strands rose to frame her ecstatic features.

Frances shivered and watched the gnarled fingers fluttering in time to the droning, incoherent words. The smoke from the lamp clung in an oily mist around the table and the tent seemed to grow even darker and colder. Long minutes passed until gradually she became intrigued as she imagined a faint glow emanating from within the crystal. Although she strained to see more clearly, it became difficult to focus on the movements of the swooping hands as the light began to pulse in time with her own heartbeat. Suddenly, the harsh voice stopped. Frances waited what seemed ages in the unsettling silence with only Jeannie's nervous breathing in the background. Zelda peered into the globe with a deep concentration in her marble-like eyes.

'What do ye see?' Frances whispered.

'Have patience and dinna interrupt!' Zelda's reprimand came like a whiplash through the brooding quiet and both girls jumped. 'The crystal tells me everything in its own good time.' She resumed her tuneless keening over the ball.

Frances hung on a little longer but she had become bored. 'Are ye seeing something now?' she prompted again.

'There's a wilful streak in ye, that's for sure.' Zelda frowned and turned her attention back to the crystal. 'Ah, but now, what's this?'

'What? What can ye see?' Frances leaned forward eagerly, and Jeannie moved up to her side, almost pushing her off her seat.

Zelda spoke the words in a monotone. 'I can see trouble at home.'

Frances sat back in her chair. 'Oh aye? And who doesn't have trouble at home?'

'True enough,' the gypsy conceded, not looking up. A few moments passed before she spoke again. 'But you'll be out of it soon. I see you're to be wed.'

'That's right, next week,' the voice came from behind. 'How did ye ken?'

'Shut up Jeannie,' Frances barked, 'dinna tell her everything!'

'Ye think I didn't know that? Lassie, this is a gift I have, special powers.' Zelda pursed her lips in annoyance. 'I dinna need hints to see into the future.'

'Well, prove it. Tell me who I'm to marry.'

The old woman snorted in derision. 'I canna do that.'

'Why no?'

'Ye obviously dinna ken how this works, lassie.' The voice was smooth, like honey. 'I see things in the ball – omens and warnings, signals for those that heed them.' Then her eyes flashed white against her dark skin. 'It doesn't give out names and addresses! Now hold your tongue, you're breaking the spell.'

'All right then, what is he like?' Undeterred, Frances leaned forward again and looked for herself into the glass.

Zelda pulled it back out of reach. 'It's hard to tell. I can see a dark figure, a tall man – a miner perhaps?' She stole a quick glance at Frances's impassive face. 'And there's a bairn.' A long, loud sigh came from across the table and she threw her hands up

41

in anger. 'Look lassie, you're no to be the next queen of England, if that's what ye think! I only read the future, I dinna make it – what do ye expect for a penny?'

Frances shrugged in frustration. 'I expect ye to tell me something I didn't ken myself.' She held forward her coal-blackened hands in a challenging gesture. 'Anyone could work out from these where I come from – there's a fair chance I'd marry a miner! And a bairn will be no surprise once we're wed —'

'Ye didn't listen, did ye? I didn't say it was *his* bairn.' Zelda leaned back smugly in her chair, a sly look on her face.

'What?' There was a moment of silence while the words sunk in. 'Whose bairn, then? Well, dinna just sit there if there's more to tell!'

'There's more all right – but you've had your money's worth.' Her tone annoyed Zelda who was used to being treated with a degree of reverence. 'You'll have to pay up for a further reading. Is it no worth it for a wee bit o' silver?'

Jeannie was nodding in agreement as she fumbled in her purse. 'Aye, come on, let's find out.'

'But I've had no time at all,' Frances said, stunned by the unfairness of it all. 'And you've told me nothing.' Her voice rose angrily. 'You're just an auld fraud!'

'Oh aye?' The old crone stabbed the air indignantly with her bony finger. 'Well, I'll give ye this for free,' she hissed. Pulling her hand from her pocket she leaned back, dramatically sweeping it across the lamp and a flaring light sprang up with a choking cloud of smoke. Momentarily, the two girls were blinded. The dog in the corner growled, baring its teeth, and the air seemed to chill around them. The acrid, metallic fumes cleared slowly and when their eyes adjusted to the darkness again, Zelda stood holding the glass ball high above her head. A dark, whirling redness played across the crystal's surface, the scarlet ripples reflected in the old woman's arms and face. 'There's blood for you.' Her voice was deep and sinister. 'Blood and death.'

'Oh Frances, dinna get her roosed or she'll put a curse on us,' Jeannie gasped from behind.

Frances buttoned her coat and drew on her mittens. 'It's all blethers, Jeannie, and a bit of trickery to impress us.' She stood and looked Zelda coldly in the eye.

The gypsy lowered her arms and sneered. 'You're cursed already, my lass. I've no need to waste my power.'

'Well, I wasted my money.' She turned to Jeannie. 'You can bide if ye want.'

William was waiting outside the tent. He was caught off guard as she barged past and almost knocked him over in her rage. 'Here, hang on a minute!' he called, stumbling after her but Frances was oblivious. Desperate, he jumped in front, barred the way and stopped her in her tracks. 'Do ye no remember me?' he asked breathlessly. The original words he had planned were lost and he was annoyed with himself for the clumsy introduction. Frances was still preoccupied and looked up blankly. Nevertheless, he persevered. 'I'll kill myself if ye dinna remember me!'

She was confused but his smile brought a flood of recognition and suddenly the frown left her face. 'I remember ye nearly killed yourself up on that bridge,' she said.

William sighed with relief. 'Well, it was worth it.'

They stood awkwardly facing each other. Frances's eyes were almost level with his, which in close proximity were a potent blue even more interesting in their concentration than before. When he pulled off his cap, a thatch of tawny hair flopped forward and he pushed it back off his face with a natural gesture before offering his hand. 'I'm William Munroe. What about you?' As she told him her name he took her hand and held it just a little longer than she thought proper. 'So, er, what did the auld spaewife foretell?' he laughed. 'Did she see me in her crystal ball?' Frances frowned again, not wishing to be reminded, and pulled her hand away. 'Oh, I didna mean any offence,' he said swiftly making amends. She smiled at him nervously and he noticed her glance back at the tent for sign of Jeannie. 'Your friend will be out in a minute, dinna worry. I'm no going to steal ye away!'

'I'm no worried about you,' she said hotly. 'I just dinna ken what's going on in there – Jeannie will believe anything.'

'Come on, dinna fash yourself – look, here's Carlo.' William indicated a dark-haired wiry figure coming in their direction.

Carlo shouted across cheerfully as he approached. He extracted a toffee-apple from the sticky clutch he carried in his fist and handed it to Frances. 'This for you.' They were clearly a novelty he had not come across before and she accepted his gesture without a second thought. He inclined his head towards her and spoke in a mock conspiratorial tone. 'One month my friend is looking for you but where you go? He say, Carlo my heart is broke.'

Frances shot a disquieting glance at William who looked equally embarrassed by the revelation. He snatched one of the apples and shoved it into Carlo's mouth to silence him. 'Dinna listen to him – ye ken what the Italians are like, all hopeless romantics!' This

43

lessened the discomfort of the moment and she found it hard to stifle a smile.

Just then Jeannie emerged from the tent wearing a dour expression. She stared over at them, paused for a second and approached the group warily. Frances drew her towards them. 'Are ye all right?' she asked, squeezing her shoulder. There was an uneasy silence punctuated by a further round of awkward introductions.

William proffered his arm to Frances. 'If it's no too forward of me, would ye care to take a turn with us round the fair?'

Jeannie's mouth dropped open in surprise and she looked uncertainly at the two men. 'Come over there,' she whispered to Frances. 'I want to speak to ye.'

They moved away a few paces. 'All right what's the matter, what did she say that's upset ye?' Frances asked, assuming Madame Zelda to be the cause of her anxiety.

'Never mind that,' Jeannie interjected angrily. 'Who are they?' She pointed across at William and Carlo who nodded and smiled in her direction. Frances explained but it was not well received. 'Are ye mad? You're getting married in a few days' time – what if somebody sees ye?'

'Sees what? For heaven's sake, we're only talking; there's no harm in that.'

'But ye ken what briggers are like. And one of them's Italian – he's probably even a Catholic!'

'Ach, so what? We'll no burn in hell.'

Jeannie folded her arms stubbornly. 'Aye well, it doesn't seem right,' she sniffed.

'You please yourself then. I dinna care what folk think. I'm nobody's wife yet and I've a right to a bit of fun before I'm wed.' Jeannie watched as her friend turned and walked away. With a martyred look she decided she must reluctantly follow suit in the now necessary role of chaperon. In response, the first thing Carlo did was to divest himself of the fourth toffee-apple which occupied much of her attention while the other two moved off ahead.

Frances was impressed by William. It was patently clear that this was his intention but still she allowed herself to be fascinated as he talked with an amusing lightness and engaging enthusiasm. He was uninterested in the humdrum aspects of her life and thankfully did not probe for information about her family or her work. Even so, his manner displayed a familiarity she thought inappropriate. There was a physical ease in his behaviour. He touched her a lot, only peripheral gestures but there was an implied intimacy that she found

44

at times disconcerting. She quickly decided she had the measure of him. Despite this, he made it easy for her to laugh and she soon forgot not only the unpleasantness with Madame Zelda but much else besides.

The four made their way through the milling crowds between the stalls. 'Have ye been in to the circus yet?' William asked as they came to Pinder's Great Marquee. This was deemed to be one of the highlights of the market and the billboards outside announced: 'Sophia, Queen of the Lofty Wire!' and 'The Human Cannonball!'. Seeing their wide-eyed expressions, he did not wait for an answer. He paid the entrance fee and they found seats near the ringside.

Rousing trumpets brought plumed horses into the ring. They were followed by performing dogs that jumped through hoops of fire, then the colourful spectacle of the acrobats and jugglers. At last a hush went through the crowd and the drums rolled. Jeannie forgot her vigilance and gave a little gasp as Sophia came out onto the wire high above them. The tiny figure with her unwieldy balancing pole moved gingerly, one step at a time. As she reached the middle, she did a little turn and carefully picked her way back. The audience roared its approval when she finally made it to the landing stage again and waved to them.

Typically however, William was not too impressed. He lowered his head towards Frances. 'We were higher than that and we didna have a safety net,' he whispered. She could feel his breath on her neck as he continued talking, seemingly no longer interested in the show. 'So tell me, what happened to ye that day – I searched the crowds but ye just disappeared?'

'I wasn't supposed to be there.' She shrugged, deciding there was no point in concealing that aspect of the truth. 'Somebody saw me and I had to leave quick.'

'Oh dear, I hope it didna get ye into trouble?' He smiled expectantly but Frances did not answer him and kept her gaze straight ahead. William decided not to press the matter. 'Well, maybe I can make up for it now,' he said, casually slipping his arm around her shoulder.

'Maybe,' she said, slowly removing it.

In between acts, the band played and clowns performed around the edge of the ring. The finale of the show was the 'Human Cannonball' but the ringmaster's stirring introduction did not prepare them for the portly figure that appeared.

'My God,' William exclaimed to general amusement, 'if they can stuff him into the cannon, they'll never blow him back out!'

They were still laughing when they came out and this cheerful mood prevailed throughout the rest of the evening. At the back of the beach was a grassy strip illuminated by the lights of the stalls and they flopped down for a welcome rest. This time Carlo was handing out ice-creams but his face quickly screwed up in an expression of distaste. 'This you call *gelato*?' he complained. Then, seeing the other two were absorbed in conversation, he diplomatically engaged Jeannie in a convoluted exposition of how real Italian ice-cream should be made.

William turned to Frances and took her hand. The fingers protruding from her mittens were raw and, though she had scrubbed them before coming out, the coal grime was deeply ingrained. Anticipating his thoughts, she pulled her hand away but not before she was noticed by two Wemyss women passing close by. Frances winced as she heard their accusing voices. 'There's that Rintoul lassie with another man – the roarie bizzum!'

She imagined William must have heard it too but if he did, he chose not to comment. Instead he lay back with his hand behind his head. 'Go on then, tell me about yourself,' he said.

'There's no much to say,' Frances replied abruptly. She did not want to lose her grip on the situation but knew she could not persist in deflecting the subject away from herself without raising suspicion. Instead, she talked of her impressions of the new Forth Bridge, the risk she took in going there and the repercussions. It was reassuring to relate this to someone who passed no judgement and she gave a little embarrassed laugh. 'Now ye ken why my fingers are black.' In the pause that followed, she wondered if perhaps she had said too much.

But William was wide-eyed. 'And all that to get a better view from the bridge . . .' he said, smiling.

Frances changed the subject. 'So, what about you, William Munroe? I can see you're no the type to be staying round here for long.'

He grinned at her. 'Aye, well it has its attractions.'

'But seriously,' she pressed him, 'what will you do now?'

He stared at the sky. 'Oh, my plans are already made,' he said wistfully. 'I'm off to Canada.'

'Canada!' she breathed in wonder. It was so totally alien to her experience that for a moment she could not find anything else to say and was annoyed at her own ignorance. 'I think I had a cousin in the East Neuk went out there . . . or was it America?'

He grinned. 'There's a difference, ye ken. Aye, but Canada's the place. Great open spaces, rolling plains, wild mountains. A man could have a chance out there – a different kind of life.' Frances could hear the hope in his voice as he went on to tell her of the work to be had on the railroad. 'They're building a new branch of the Canadian Pacific, a line from Calgary to Edmonton.' As he spoke, his face became animated. 'I'll get fixed up on one of the crews. It'll be hard work to start with but give it a year and I should have enough to work a wee homestead.'

'What's a homestead?'

'It's a hundred and sixty acres of virgin land for farming. The Canadian government give them away free in return for a guarantee to work it for three years.' Frances listened enviously as he talked of his dream. He turned towards her. 'All my life I've worked,' he said, 'since I was seven years old and lugging a cart round the streets. I've gutted fish, I've humped coal, I've built bridges – I was the best damn riveter they had on the Forth.'

Carlo overheard. 'This is true,' he chimed in.

William smiled and acknowledged the compliment but finished in earnest. 'So now I'm going to get a bit of what's owing to me.'

'What do ye mean, owing?'

'I dinna have a house or a family, nor a thing to my name. I sold my tools, even gave away my fiddle to Sandy Dees. So ye see I've nothing to lose here. But out there in the new world, well, I'm going to build myself the first real home I've ever had – I'm thinking it's long overdue.'

Frances twisted the grass in front of her. 'How soon before ye go?' she asked impassively.

'Oh, no for another week yet,' he replied brightly. 'Time enough to see ye again if you'd like. That is, if you're no courting.'

She stood up without looking at him and brushed the dirt from her skirt. 'I've got to be getting home now.'

He reached up and grabbed her hand. 'What's your rush? We've no been all through the fair yet.'

'I'm sorry, I have to go.'

There was an awkward silence. Carlo helped Jeannie to her feet and walked with her to the road. 'Are ye coming? We'll be late again.' Jeannie called back to where Frances still stood uncertainly.

William got up. 'Well, when can we meet again? Come on, it's only a bit of fun.' He noticed her glance across anxiously at Jeannie and Carlo and lowered his voice. 'Dinna mind them – come yourself. How about Tuesday?'

'No,' she whispered.

'Wednesday then, same time,' he insisted. 'I'll be here waiting for ye.'

7

Frances had no intention of returning to the Links Market and so there seemed little point in confiding the invitation to Jeannie or speaking further about their encounter. Her work at the pit-head ceased and she was expected to spend the rest of the week in preparation for the impending marriage. She visited Elspeth several times, delivering bed linen and helping her to organise the house but found it hard to muster enthusiasm. 'You're awful quiet like,' the old woman had observed.

'Och, I'm all right. I just wish I could see a bit more of Gavin.'

'Dinna worry, there'll be time enough once you're married.'

'Aye, so everybody keeps telling me.'

Elspeth could see the girl was unsettled. 'Listen, hen, you look tired.' She took the bundle of clothes from Frances's arms. 'Away and have a walk on the beach – the fresh air'll bring some colour to your cheeks. I'll finish this.'

Frances did not argue. The prospect of a few moments' solitude and reflection on her own was too appealing. She made her way to the shore, relishing the fresh breeze that swept up from the incoming tide. Despite her desire to be alone, she wished that Gavin was there. What few opportunities she had had to be with him were all too brief and Frances felt she needed him now more than ever before. She had the uneasy sense that when they were not together, it was as if he did not exist and the feeling that everything was getting out of control returned now, only more strongly. In what should have been a time of busy anticipation, she had begun to feel quite desolate.

A severe change in the weather also had not helped. Over the past three days, squally winds and fierce rains had confined her at home indoors and, though there was much to do, the bickering atmosphere was becoming intolerable. Henry Rintoul had lost no opportunity to remind his daughter of the burden of expense which her wedding presented. 'I thought he would be glad to be rid of me,' she had complained to her mother, but both knew inwardly that with one less woman to do his bidding, his comforts would be significantly reduced. As for the cost, since she was allowed to retain only a measly

48

portion of her earnings, she knew she had virtually paid for it herself. Besides, it was hardly to be a grand affair. Wemyss weddings were short, lack-lustre and often expedient. People did their best with what little they had and, as Frances had stitched along a line of pins in an effort to alter Chrissie's old dress, she saw no reason to assume hers would be any different.

When she and Gavin had visited the manse, the Reverend Black's discourse on matrimony was little short of his usual Sunday sermon. He concentrated heavily on the role which duty had to play, giving no preview of anything which might provoke optimism, and the interview had left her strangely empty. Gavin however was unabashed. As they left by the garden gate he had put his arm round her, assuring her there was a whole other side to marriage that the crag-faced cleric could only dream of.

Now, walking along the stony sea-shore, Frances found her mind drawn back to the fair. Remembering the colour and music and sense of excitement seemed to emphasise her current bleak mood. It was therefore almost inevitable that what she had thrust to the back of her mind now beamed in the fore-front as the bright focus of an otherwise strained week.

The secret meeting on Wednesday fulfilled all that Frances had hoped. She and William went through the market exhausting every stall and side show, pitched balls at every coconut-shy and rode all the carousels. He was not short of money, having put aside his savings and earmarked the rest for the pursuit of a good time. Frances imagined she was just one component of that good time but enjoying his company, a feeling that seemed to be genuinely reciprocated, she was willing to play her part. It was an unusual experience devoted entirely to indulgence of the moment, where neither the past nor the future intruded. As such, it took on a heady intoxicating quality. They both laughed a lot, unmindful of others' eyes and only when the afternoon drew to a close did Frances realise how disinclined she was to end it there.

'I canna take all these home with me!' she exclaimed, loaded down with knick-knacks and novelties, the trophies of their gamesmanship.

'Why not? Ye won them fair and square.'

'Och, ye won most of them yourself,' she protested.

'Well, there must be bairns in the family who could have them.'
She looked uncomfortable with the idea and William was curious.
'Do your folk ken where ye are today, did ye tell them about me?'

She shook her head. 'Is that no asking for trouble, Frances? I mean, ye make it look sneaky doing this behind their backs.'

'It's my own business,' she said flatly.

'Ye're full o' secrets,' he grinned, 'have ye maybe a husband at home you're no telling me about?'

Frances felt anxious as she was reminded of Gavin and guiltily laughed off the suggestion. She was thankful that he did not pursue the subject but the mood had been broken and she remained confused by her thoughts for the rest of the evening. While she was with him, William invaded her life totally. He brought an instant thrill to what was otherwise mundane and made anything seem possible. He teased out that part of her character which others sought to subdue, making her feel brave, reckless and above all, dissatisfied. It was grim to think that in a couple of days the fair would be over for another year. Packed up, the great horse-drawn caravans would move off, leaving only rutted wheel marks in the mud and brown patches on the grass where once they stood. And in the same way William would be gone too. She knew that these last few hours would fade, dream-like, almost as if they had never occurred and she stared ahead dismally, uncertain whether to be reassured by the thought.

'What are ye thinking?' His voice penetrated her contemplation.

They were in the 'Freak Show' in front of a platform where a man in a bowler hat was extolling the qualities of his latest exhibit: 'Juliet the Giantess. See, ladies and gentlemen, eight feet two and still growing!'

'She looks so sad,' said Frances as the gargantuan girl was made to do a turn.

'Aye, and she's no the only one. What's got into ye, eh?' William pulled a face at her and tried to make her smile. 'We came to have a good time, remember?' Frances made an effort to shrug off the mood and look cheerful for him but he wasn't fooled. 'Come on then,' he said drawing her away, 'let's get out of here.'

She left the pile of souvenirs behind and followed him out of the tent. They emerged into the deepening twilight, the stalls now lit in a festive atmosphere and Frances grew worried about the time. 'It must be late.'

'Dinna go yet.' There was an impatience in his voice and he caught her hand to try and persuade her to stay.

The thought of going home held no attraction for Frances but to delay would mean certain confrontation with her father. 'I must,' she said bluntly.

'Well at least let me see ye home?'

That too was impossible. It was bad enough to risk being seen in Kirkcaldy but she could not take the chance on the road to West Wemyss. 'No, I'll wait at the works for Jeannie and go back with her.'

They left the sea-front and made their way slowly into the town. William looked disappointed. 'Ye act like you're ashamed to be seen with me.'

'And you act like we're courting,' she retorted. 'It was just a bit of fun – ye said so yourself. Dinna try to make more of it than that.'

They walked on towards the dark buttresses of the linoleum works. 'When can I see ye again?' he asked.

She was surprised by the question. 'I thought ye were away in a couple of days?'

'Aye, but there's a dance at the Corn Exchange tomorrow night, I'd like it fine if you'd come – just one last time?'

She shook her head and had to smile at his temerity. 'You'll no give up, will ye?'

'What's the matter, ye do ken how to dance?'

'Me? That's a daft question,' she said. 'I'm famed for it round here.' She gave a twirl in front of him to demonstrate.

He tried to appear suitably impressed. 'No bad, but I'm telling ye Frances, you've met your match with me.'

'Oh, we'll see about that!' she challenged. Amused by how skilfully he had manoeuvred her into accepting, she was nonetheless too excited by the prospect of such a rare treat to refuse.

They came to a halt at the gates. 'Come on, let me see ye home,' he tried once more to coax her.

But again she heeded the warning voice inside. 'No. I've said I'll come to the dance so please go now, I'll be fine.'

Reluctantly he conceded to her wish and as he walked away, called after her, 'Tomorrow night then – and dinna be late!'

After he had gone she remained, a lone figure at the factory entrance. It was almost dark and she stamped her feet and blew on her hands against the crisp, chill air. From within the walls came the muffled, cheery voices of the workers as they finished for the day. Yet she no longer belonged here and, far from being a comfort, the sounds made her feel alienated and remote. In a sudden change of heart, she turned, drew her shawl about her and decided not to wait.

8

Frances stood before the mirror and stared at her reflection. What looked back at her was a stranger with actions and intentions beyond the scope of her control. As if through a window, she watched herself bend over the bowl to wash, performing the task with involuntary gestures for which she bore no responsibility. The neglected bridal dress hung limply against the bedroom wall but she ignored it, searching through the wooden chest for the appropriate garment. A skirt with movement in it, one in which she could go dancing.

Jessie Rintoul entered holding a pile of folded sheets over her arm. 'Have ye tried on that dress yet?' she asked without looking at her daughter. Getting no reply, she turned round and her eyes opened wide in prelude to yet another heated exchange. 'What's going on here?'

'I'm just away out for a wee while,' Frances responded, trying to make light of the fact.

'Well, I never heard the like! You're getting married on Saturday, do ye no ken there's work to be done?'

'What? I've finished all the sewing.'

'There's piles of ironing for a start, and dozens of cakes and scones to be mixed and taken to the bakehouse —'

'Nothing that canna wait till tomorrow.'

Mrs Rintoul put her hands on her hips in an ineffectual gesture of exasperation. 'And just where is it ye think you're going?'

'Into Kirkcaldy if ye must ken – just a night out with the lassies.'

'Away to see your fancy man, more like!' There was an uneasy pause. 'Ye canna fool me, Frances, I've heard talk —'

'Och Mother, ye dinna have to believe everything ye hear – let me be.' Frances pulled on a blouse and freed her hair from its collar, shaking her head as she did so. A vibrant mass of thick hair fell over her shoulders and hid her face as she did up the buttons. She swept it back and straightened the collar, smoothing her hands slowly down over her breasts onto her waist. In the light of the conversation, those gestures, natural enough in a woman dressing, were perceived as brazenly provocative by Mrs Rintoul. She looked her daughter up and down and Frances caught her disapproving gaze in the mirror.

'Don't look at me like that,' she challenged. 'It's nigh on a year since I was last at the dancing – ye dinna begrudge me one wee fling before I'm wed?'

'It's nothing to me, but what about Gavin? What kind of a wife do ye think you'll make for him, behaving like this?'

Frances rounded on her. 'Look Ma, we're no married yet and I don't intend to aye be at his beck and call once we are. I'm no going to spend my life cowering in fear of my man – I've seen enough of that.'

'Watch your mouth girl!'

'Och, dinna pretend it's Gavin you're worried about, when I ken fine you've more concern for what my father'll say when he gets home.'

'And so should you for he'll no stand for this, Frances – you're driving him to an early grave with all your carrying on!'

'Me? Ye canna blame me for the way he is. Stop begowking yourself, you're always taking his part. Just for once can ye no let it be? He'll be drinking down at the Institute till late and be home with a belly full of beer none the wiser – he doesn't need to know, unless you tell him.'

Mrs Rintoul shook her head despairingly. 'I never thought I'd live to see the day you'd speak to me like this, Frances,' she said wearily and turned to leave the room. 'You're more like your father than ye know. And I tell ye, lassie, you're heading for a fall. Mind what I'm saying.'

Frances tried to ignore the pain she had seen in her mother's eyes. She stood there a while trembling from the intensity of the confrontation, aware that she had spoken her mind as never before. Yet still a residue of anger remained because in her heart she knew it would change nothing. She sighed heavily and returned to the mirror. Deftly she pinned up her hair and stood back to examine her appearance. Despite the fraught atmosphere, she was mildly surprised with what she saw. Her mother may have been right about her behaviour, yet strangely the impending marriage, far from dissuading Frances from going out, did more to encourage her – and the pleasure of anticipation radiated her features. Turning this way and that, she raised her skirts and took a few practice steps. Her father would be mad with rage if he found out but the knowledge that she would very soon be married and safe beyond his reach somehow justified the risk. She loved Gavin, she had always loved Gavin, so what was the harm? For now, she was going dancing.

The music from the Corn Exchange could be heard well down the street and the doorway bulged with folk trying to see in. Some, the worse for drink, were slumped outside and Frances stepped around them as she attempted to look over the heads. Exhilarating sounds drifted through and the infectious spirit of the dancing made her nervous with excitement. She pushed her way in, all the time watching out for sign of William.

The box and fiddle band were just ending a Strathspey and a raucous cheer went up from the crowd as they retired breathless to the benches and trestles that bordered the great room. The space cleared revealed a scattering of sawdust, cigarette ends and an occasional button which had sprung free in the exertion. Frances scanned the hall for a familiar face. Miners, linoleum workers, jute weavers were there; coopers, fishwives and farm-hands. Smoke tumbled in the shafts of yellow light that illuminated the dance floor and their drab clothes were softened in the glow.

Again, the players struck up and the cheering hordes surged forward for Circassian circle. Frances found herself drawn into the well of the dance when suddenly a firm hand gripped hers. She turned and William was there beside her. He smiled and tried to say something but there was no time for conversation as they were pulled inexorably into the throng. The people abandoned themselves to the momentum of the circle. Boots thudded on the dusty boards and they whirled round whooping and clapping in time to the beat. After the cold night air, Frances felt the colour restored to her cheeks as she was warmed by the atmosphere. Though it was somewhat lacking in discipline, she enjoyed the spirited, untamed style of William's dancing. An Eightsome reel followed and she joined in enthusiastically. They could not talk for the noise and the movement. One moment they were together and touching, the next on opposite sides of the set. Others lost their balance and were hurled into the massed onlookers at the sidelines. And so it went on. One wild reel led to another, followed by a jig or a march and a reel again. By the end of the set, the dancers were out of breath, their faces red and shining. Bubbling laughter gave way to puffing sighs and smiles as everyone drew back, some limping, some flapping their outer garments to cool them down.

The band took a break, sitting back to fill their tankards and light their pipes. William put his arm around Frances's waist and guided her off the dance floor to sit down against the wall. As the people began to relax and take refreshment he noticed the lull and turned to her. 'I'll be back in a minute.'

'Where are ye going?'

'You'll see,' he said, touching her cheek for a moment.

She watched him stroll across the floor to the bandstand and sensed a new and unexpected dimension of intimacy had crept into their brief relationship. She did not know when it had happened but she was both disturbed and seduced by the change.

William crouched beside the players, talking with them but she could not hear what was said. Then he took up one of the fiddles and plucked it twice to check the tuning. Slowly the room grew quiet as he raised the fiddle to his chin. The gallery became hushed and people began to turn their heads towards him while he drew out the first chord, waiting for the silence to be complete. A few knowing sighs went up from those who recognised the lament but as he started playing, the painful sweetness of it was felt by all. Frances listened inspired. All the power and noise and mayhem of the dancing was now quelled by the tenderness of the sound. Lovers drew closer to each other and there were a few moist eyes amongst the older faces. As he played, William stepped down from the dais. He inclined his head, acknowledging the smiles from the people lining the floor and slowly moved towards Frances. Her heart beat quickened as he approached drawing nearer and coming face to face for the final refrain. She had no doubt that the performance had been just for her. No one in the place doubted it either and, for a few seconds, the room remained still.

Then suddenly a cheer went up that filled the rafters. William nodded to the appreciative crowd as they roared their approval shouting 'More! More!' He turned to Frances but she was clapping and cheering too. There was nothing else to do but give them what they wanted. So, with a lively note, William's fiddle burst into the 'Hangman's Reel'. He tapped his feet to accompany the music and quickly the people joined in. Soon the intermittent clapping became thunderous pounding in time to the beat. Frances stepped forward boldly into the space and, facing William, she gathered up her skirts and danced with hands on hips. The crowd erupted, cheering and whooping, shouting their encouragement to her, 'Go on lass, lift your feet up!' William quickened the tempo and her feet responded, as if to challenge him. Delight shone in his eyes as he dipped and turned, following the unrestrained movements of her body. One by one the other players took up their instruments and joined in as the music turned into an unbridled reel. William thrust the fiddle aside and grabbed Frances's hand to swing her over the floor. Several times her feet left the ground as they wheeled round, her eyes bright with daring, her hair now loose and flying. Urged by the frenzied crowd, they whirled wildly on, faster and faster.

The room was spinning and the atmosphere now so highly charged that the band decided they must end it before someone got hurt. The box-player tipped the wink to the others and adroitly they led into the gentle lilt of a Hebridean boat song. As they did so, Frances and William, breathless and panting, flopped into each other's arms. Flushed with excitement they moved together and the physical potency of the reel was diffused into a warm drifting waltz. Gradually, people merged onto the floor to join them and they became just another couple in their midst.

At length she came to her senses. 'William, it must be getting late, I should go.'

'Can I walk ye home?'

She hesitated and felt danger in the pause. But by now the house would be ringing with the inebriated snores of her father. There would be no need for explanations until the morning, though she knew in the cold light of day the guilt would weigh heavily. Yet it seemed a cruel severance to part in the busy street, to end such a night with a blunt goodbye among a faceless crowd. She looked at William's hopeful expression and smiled back. 'All right, ye may.'

The tide was out and they took the low road back to West Wemyss along the beach. It was a cold, blowy night but strangely quiet in the shadow of the rocks. The moon's reflection dappled in fragments on the water and only their footfall on the displaced pebbles broke the sound of the raking waves, withdrawing in a sensual underflow sucking little slurries from the pools. Carefully they picked their way over the stones, both feeling a current through the touch of their hands but reluctant to speak.

As they trudged on, Frances became preoccupied with the thought of William's impending departure. 'So you'll be leaving soon then?' she asked, keeping a lightness in her voice.

'Aye, I should be up to Burt's tomorrow to book my ticket.' His own voice was flat.

Frances had often passed Burt's window in Kirkcaldy and had seen their display in the *Fifeshire Advertiser*:

'Ye must be awful excited,' she said. He let go of her hand and hung back a bit, spinning a stone at the water and watching it skim the surface like a flying fish. She continued walking and eventually he caught her up, but his mood had altered and he seemed uncharacteristically quiet.

Past Dysart, they came round the headland and stopped to gaze up at the figure carved in relief on the red rocks above the shore path. Surmounted by protective railings, the manacled prisoner stood chained to a huge ring and staple. Locked irrevocably in the sandstone, his expression was one of desperation and despair.

'The "Man i' the Rock". It was a weaver from Dysart who made it years ago,' Frances explained. 'I used to be right scared of it when I was a wee lassie and run past quick so it wouldn't get me.'

'And what about now?'

She smiled wanly. 'Now I ken just how he feels.' She leaned against a rock and watched the water come in and slap at the encrusted barnacles, smoothing down the green hair of the seaweed as it withdrew. He moved towards her and she could feel his hands slip beneath her shawl and press her body to his. Breath mingled and disappeared on the frosty air as his mouth brushed hers then held it in a kiss. For a moment she did not notice the cold or the damp or the rough stone grazing her back.

Then suddenly, with her heart thumping tremulously she fought free of the embrace and pushed him away. 'What the hell do ye think you're doing!'

He jumped backwards, surprised by the rebuff and spread his hands in a gesture of surrender. 'I'm sorry . . .'

'So ye should be! Ye think ye can come here and have your bit of fun with me and next thing you're away the other side of the world. I ken what you're like – I've met your kind before!' Frances was angry with herself for allowing her emotions to burst to the surface and she stumbled off, determined that William should not see the tears that now coursed down her face.

He caught up with her at Blair Point and seized her arm. 'Listen, how was I to ken how ye felt – you've been that canny . . .'

'Leave me alone, what do ye want from me?' The moon was brilliant against a coal-black sky and the spectre of the Victoria Pit with its huge winding wheels hung over West Wemyss. Intermittent clanking could be heard from the rigging as boats gently rolled in the harbour.

'I want ye to come with me.'

For a moment Frances continued to wrest herself from his grasp. Then suddenly she stopped and looked at him as the impact of his words sank home. 'Ye mean to Canada?' He nodded. She stepped back a few paces and gave a faint hysterical laugh. 'And when did ye make your mind up about this?'

'From the first minute I clapped eyes on ye.'

'Oh aye, very likely.'

'It's true,' he insisted. 'I ken it's short notice, Frances – I would've asked ye before but I didna think you'd come.'

'And ye think I'll come now?' she challenged sarcastically.

The words came out in a rush. 'We could get married at the docks before we go —'

'But ye don't even know me!'

'I ken enough to see you'd make a good wife out there. I didna consider marrying before because first I have to save enough to get the homestead started. That'll take nigh on a year working on the railroad and I never thought you'd wait. But if ye come now, even if it's a bit rough to begin with, you're strong and I ken ye could cope.'

'God, you've got it all worked out. And I'm supposed to drop everything, just like that?'

'Well, sometimes that's the best way. I take it ye dinna think much of this place,' he observed. 'You've said so yourself enough times – what have ye got to look forward to here?'

Frances grimly considered his words. She thought of Gavin but the time to tell that bit of truth had long since passed. She looked across the narrow span of the village as it crouched against the shoreline. A few lights were glinting but hardly a soul was about. Here she had a place, a fixed role in the scheme of things like generations of others before her. For a moment she was safe with the thought but the stimulation, the visceral edge in William's proposition kept clawing her back. Her glance drifted over the Estate wall and into the trees that hid the castle beyond. She belonged to the immutable order that permeated every part of life here and she doubted that even Gavin, with his vision of a better future, could change that. Somewhere over the woods an owl hooted and again she felt the

strong arms tighten around her. 'Come with me then, why don't
ye?'

Those words remained suffused in her head like a drug she had
inhaled and could not shake. Within the Glass Cave the two sat
side by side and stared out towards the grey dawnlight. Of all the
Wemyss caves this one alone held special memories for Frances.
Listening to the muted roar of the sea she remembered how it had
been her secret hiding place as a child when life at home became
unbearable. Now here she was, in a sense hiding again. She and
William had talked long into the night. Much of the time was taken
up in persuading him of the need for anonymity. His offer to meet
with her family and talk to her father was quashed by the strength
of her determination to avoid it. She insisted she could deal with that
herself, he was to be in no way involved with her imminent departure
and was to stay out of West Wemyss for the next two days until
she joined him. Those were her terms and once he had reluctantly
agreed to them, plans for the journey were laid and arrangements
were made. It was only then Frances inwardly surrendered to what
she had always believed unthinkable, yet perhaps had known was
inevitable – she would not marry Gavin. Instead she would board
a ship bound for the other side of the world with this stranger who
now sat next to her.

Shivering suddenly, she moved closer to him seeking comfort
and reassurance. He stirred from his own thoughts, slipped his
arm around her waist and asked, 'Are ye cold?'

She shook her head and burrowed further into his strong embrace.
The decision to leave had filled her with alarm. Now, a rage of swift
and intense emotions battled within her and she could not conceal
the trembling they induced. William responded by enfolding her in
his arms. He kissed her face, at first gently soothing and whispering
her name. Then slowly his mouth became keener, pressing more
urgently to hers. She was bewildered by the sensation. His ardent
and unfamiliar hands began to move over her body and she could
feel the arousal in his breathing as he held her tighter. Suddenly a
different and more immediate panic pumped in her chest.

'No!' Her voice echoed small and tremulous and she hated
the sound of it. Pulling back from him, she extricated herself
from his grip. For a brief moment, she was faintly disturbed
by the prospect that he might force himself upon her. Either
that, or scorn the lack of experience she had so far only hinted
at.

He let her draw away and looked steadily at her. 'It's all right Frances, I thought ye . . .'

'I ken what ye thought,' she said in a little choking voice.

As she turned her head away, he could see her eyes were wet with tears and her shoulders heaved convulsively with threatened sobbing. 'I'm sorry,' he said, trying to offer words of reassurance. He was hesitant to touch her again, aware of how vulnerable she felt. 'Ye're right enough, there's a time for that when we're married, lass.' All the weight of her decision showed in her face and he opened his arms. 'Come here,' he said tenderly. 'Dinna worry, just hold on to me.'

Frances slumped against him and allowed herself to be soothed like a child while he murmured words that meant nothing and signified everything. She was exhausted but could only achieve a half-sleep as her emotions continued to torment her. The chance she had longed for was now within reach – she ought to be glad. But instead she remained locked in combat with the spectre that rose again and again to confound her hopes. The intruder was Gavin and she wondered how long it would be before she could live with the leaving.

9

The impending storm hit with full force the following night. Turbulent and menacing, the seas could be heard crashing against the rocks as Frances, rain-soaked but unseen, rushed into the shelter of the close. Taut with anticipation she forced herself to obey one painful duty before she left and, hurrying up the stairs she rapped hard twice on the door. From within came the sound of the old woman slowly rousing herself and her swollen hands fidgeting with the latch to open it.

Elspeth Douglas smiled when she saw who it was. 'Oh lassie, you're droukit. Come away in out the cold,' she said, welcoming her into the warm room. 'We didna expect ye.'

Frances entered and looked around uneasily. 'Gavin's no here, is he?'

'Dinna worry, you'll no be seeing him tonight. The lads are getting in a drink for him at the Institute when he comes off his shift,' Elspeth explained, laughing. 'He'll be fu' by now.'

Frances sat down. 'Are ye all right then, Grandma?' she began casually, but when she held out her hands to the fire she noticed they were trembling.

Elspeth noticed too but bided her time. 'Same as before, I canna complain. But just listen to that wind out there!' She set the kettle on the fire. 'Oh what a busy week we've had. No doubt you'll be glad when it's over?' There was no reply. She put out her gnarled hand and touched Frances, pushing back wet strands of hair and feeling a hard tension in the young shoulders. Elspeth took her face and turned it towards her own. 'You're that pale, have ye eaten today?' she enquired softly.

Frances shrugged off the question. She felt impatient and distracted, unable to form the words but equally terrified of letting her guard down. She pulled her knees up under her chin to stave off the tremors.

The tea was forgotten. 'Has there been trouble at home?' Elspeth ventured gravely, now recognising the signs that something serious had happened. She patted the hunched figure before her. 'Come on, lassie, better out than in. Tell me what's wrong.'

Frances made a little gasping sound and her body heaved with a sudden convulsive shudder. 'Oh Grandma, I'm sorry,' she groaned as tears spilled from her red-rimmed eyes.

'My God, I've never seen ye like this – what is it that's brought this on?' Elspeth waited, endeavouring to assess the situation for herself. 'Child, if you'll no tell me, what can I do? I ken you've had a trying time at home but ye can soon put all that behind ye. Once you're here ye can make a new start and be happy. And I ken Gavin's no been that attentive to ye as he should these past few days but —'

'Shut up!' Frances put her hands over her ears and shouted again, 'Shut up, will ye?'

Elspeth was stunned by the force of the response and, though her face did not betray it, a gnawing dread now filled her senses.

Frances quickly got to her feet, pulled a small folded piece of paper from her pocket and laid it on the table. 'Don't ask me to explain, but I canna stay,' she said brusquely. 'Just see he gets this.'

The old woman looked from it to the girl before her. 'What's this then? Are ye no speaking to each other? If it's a wee tiff ye can surely sort it out.'

'Och, ye don't understand, I'm no talking about a wee tiff. Me and Gavin are finished – the note explains everything.'

'What the . . . I must be hearing things. And what's brought this on all of a sudden?' Elspeth waited but no reply was forthcoming. 'Is there some other laddie that's turned your head? I ken there's been a bit talk but I didn't take any notice.'

Frances blanched visibly. 'Aye,' she faltered, 'but it's no like ye think.'

'No? Then can Gavin expect ye to turn up at the kirk tomorrow?'

Frances looked away. 'He's better off without me, Grandma.'

'Och, ye ken fine that's blethers. He's been a different man since ye said ye'd have him, I ken that better than anyone. Now he's got the chance of a good future with you, something to look forward to. You're surely no going to throw it all away on some stupid whimsy.'

'My mind's made up.' Frances struggled to remain in control but could hear the timidity in her own voice.

The old woman paused and steadied herself. She put her hand under Frances's chin and held her face towards her. 'Dinna do this to him, lassie,' she said quietly, 'no on the eve of your wedding.'

'Better now than too late.'

Elspeth pushed the face away from hers, it was clear she was losing the fight. 'I just canna believe ye would do such a thing,' she said shaking her head. 'He doesn't deserve this.'

'I ken Grandma, the last thing I want is to hurt Gavin.'

'Then forget this foolishness, child, it's no too late.' There was no response and no hope lingered in the silence. Elspeth wiped her eyes with the corner of her apron. 'Does your family ken about this – what does your father have to say?'

Frances winced, recalling the awful confrontation at home shortly before. She would have preferred it if he had beaten her but with a sombre finality he had pointed to the door. No words had accompanied the awesome gesture, he merely waited until she obeyed. All the while Jessie had whimpered pitiably in the background as the other two looked on impotently.

'I had to leave there and then,' Frances explained, 'he wouldn't even let me get my clothes. All I've got is what I'm standing in.'

Elspeth gazed with moist eyes into the fire. 'Well, I can't say I'm surprised. If I didna have a wee bit care left for ye I'd have done the same myself.' She shook her head defeatedly again. 'He must have something right special this lad, that's all I can say.'

'He's taking me to Canada, Grandma.'

'Canada!' she breathed, amazed.

Frances felt her resolve weaken. She desperately wanted to redeem herself in the old woman's eyes. 'I ken I've hurt ye,' she said, 'but do ye no see, it's my one chance to get away from the Wemyss. Ye always said yourself there wasn't much here . . .' But at that point she was overwhelmed by emotion and broke down into uncontrollable tears. 'Oh God, I'm so sorry.'

'Well, all I can say is I hope ye ken what you're doing.'

Frances rubbed her nose on her sleeve. 'I do,' she sniffed, then moved to the door and lifted the latch. 'I have to go now. I'll miss ye.'

'Wait.' Elspeth got to her feet unsteadily and shuffled through to the other room. There she rummaged in a trunk and brought out a plaid shawl. 'Here, take this,' she said, wrapping it around Frances's shoulders, 'it was my wedding gift to ye, it's a Douglas. You'll be needing it where you're going.'

Tears welled again as the ample arms held her close. 'Dinna be roosed with me, Grandma. I do love him . . .'

'Shh, I ken that.'

Frances blew her nose on the hankie that was offered. 'Do ye think he'll take it bad?' she ventured.

'Aye, he'll take it bad — but ye ken that right enough yourself.' Then, drawing her to her bosom, Elspeth held her strongly. 'Just see that man takes care o' ye,' she said and her voice cracked with sadness. Frances could not speak. She clung tight for a moment then rushed from the house.

Outside, she leaned against the cold wet wall of the house and took in deep breaths. A wailing shrieking wind buffeted her clothes and the air was salty with the spray of the sea's fury. The dark streets were dead but for the sound of a distant footfall, a heavy crunch of hob-nailed boots on the puddled cobbles. Frances crouched furtively in the shadows waiting for whoever it was to pass. She felt like a fugitive in her own town and wished only to be rid of the place without meeting another soul. But there was an urgency in the steps that were now approaching faster, a thinly veiled desperation and she somehow knew it was Gavin. In a panic, she drew the shawl around her head and shoulders and rushed down the stone steps, colliding headlong with him as he turned into the dark close. Save for the gleam of his eyes and the miner's graith, he was black as the night that engulfed them. The familiar coal-dust smell rose from his body and she stepped back uneasily, hoping he had not recognised her.

'Frances?' He gently pushed the shawl back off her face. She could not make out his expression but felt the anxiety in the seconds that followed. He had heard something, of that there was no doubt, yet he hesitated, unwilling to substantiate the awful rumour. He tried a smile and she saw the slash of white teeth across the pitch-dark features. 'They say it's bad luck to see your intended the night before you're wed.'

She mumbled an inaudible reply and backed away from him.

'What do ye think?' he said, more earnestly now. 'Is it bad for us?' He took her arm and restrained her. 'Well?' He waited. 'Answer me, Frances!'

'Yes,' she said weakly.

'How bad?'

'Dinna ask me to explain, I've left ye a note at the house,' she choked through her tears.

'And our wedding the morn, is it to be?' She shook her head slowly and he stared as if unable to comprehend the gesture. 'So it's true then.'

Frances could hear the contempt in his tone. 'I didna mean to hurt ye, Gavin,' she stammered, trying to get away but his grip tightened on her arm.

'Dinna talk to me about hurt!' he shouted, his voice booming through the passageways and sending the rats scurrying. 'Ye carry on behind my back and I'm the last to hear of it. You've got the whole town laughing at me and ye wait till the night before to tell me we're no to be married! Christ woman, ye think that doesn't hurt!'

The whites of his eyes flashed angrily and she recoiled from his accusing stare. For the first time, she feared him and the power of his scorn as he towered over her. 'Please, try to understand,' she begged.

'I understand fine! The woman I wanted for my wife turned out to be nothing but a whoor!'

'No, it wasn't like that!'

He raised the back of his hand to strike her and she flinched, anticipating the blow. Instead it remained suspended. Then with an anguished gasp he thrust her aside and she fell against the wall. He looked down at her, a threatening coldness in his voice. 'I've been a bloody fool. You've led me a fine dance these years, Frances Rintoul,' he said and slowly began to mount the stairs. 'I wish I'd never known ye, and I hope to God I never see ye again!' Frances slumped to the floor and weakly called after him but with a resounding crash, the door slammed and he was gone.

*

Later that night, when the coals were reduced to embers, Gavin read again the little note. He had a tightness in his chest from holding back the despair that was waiting to overwhelm him and now, whilst Elspeth dozed, he let the tears come freely. She opened one eye and saw him bent forward with his head in his hands but she did not stir. In a hopeless gesture he crumpled the fragment into his fist and held it a few seconds before flinging it to the back of the fire. At the same time, the little book dropped from his lap onto the floor. He reached down to pick it up and read, with a mixture of humiliation and sorrow the message he had inscribed at a time of such hope.

Frances, if I could find the words to tell you how much I love you, they would fill ten thousand books like this. But I know when the moment comes they will fail me. So let the Bard speak for me – pick any page at random and know in your heart that the sentiment is mine.

Yours ay, Gavin

The book slid from between his fingers and fluttered noiselessly to the floor. Vacantly he stared at the open page and for a moment did not discern the couplet it revealed. Then all too soon the bitter irony in the words came sadly home to him:

'And my fause luver staw the rose,
But left the thorn wi' me.'

PART
2

1

As they stood side by side in front of the ship's captain, William glanced uncertainly at Frances. In the three days since their departure from Kirkcaldy she seemed to have withdrawn behind an impenetrable wall he was powerless to break down. When they set sail, she had stared out beyond the complex rigging that obscured the horizon, ignoring the choking funnels that droned against the backdrop of vivacious activity. Hundreds of people thronged the dock-side and she had remained impassive, watching them receding until Greenock itself had become a dull smear in the distance, merging into oblivion.

With no time to go through the formalities on shore in Glasgow, William had somehow persuaded the captain to marry them on board, though he assented with little enthusiasm. Now, on the cramped and noisy deck of the *Devonia*, the couple were to be joined in matrimony by a joyless, perfunctory ceremony that smacked of convenience, and their uneasiness was apparent to everyone. For the first time, William began to experience doubts about the precipitous course he had launched them on. Unable to cajole Frances out of her silent depression, his own normally boisterous nature had also given way to a subdued self-consciousness.

The captain viewed them with suspicion and before going ahead with the formalities he took Frances aside. 'Are you sure this is what you want, my girl? You don't seem too keen.' He followed her quick glance at William. 'Don't worry about him. Come on, speak up, I don't have all day.'

She forced a smile. 'Yes, it's what I want. It's just the leaving that's no easy.'

He saw the tears come to her eyes and thought he understood. 'Aye, it's hard right enough, my dear.' Convinced that nothing serious was amiss, his brusque manner then returned. 'Well, let's get on with it. I've a ship to run.'

The ceremony began but Frances found it impossible to concentrate. Bleak and cheerless ostracism from the place she knew so well had weakened her resolve and though she had refused to let the diminishing shores provoke regret, the memory of her mother's haunting eyes brought thoughts of home.

'Frances Ellen Rintoul, wilt thou have this man to thy wedded husband . . .' The words rang in her head like an accusation. 'This man.' Not the one she had promised herself to, but this stranger. Her fingers picked at the frayed edges of the shawl and she noticed the black smudge was still visible where Gavin had grasped it. She shuddered to think of their parting and imagined him now, alone and tormented once the heat of his anger had died. The captain's gravelly voice continued. 'Wilt thou obey him, and serve him, love, honour, and keep him in sickness and in health . . .' She looked down at William's feet in line next to hers. They were unfamiliar and she considered how little she really knew of him. Yet here she was committing herself to a lifetime ahead – 'so long as ye both shall live' – when in truth the future was a blank and unknown quantity lying somewhere beyond the distant line where sea meets sky. She swallowed hard as the utter vulnerability of her situation pulled at her heart like a great, heavy weight and her grip on William's hand tightened.

A short cough in the pause that followed made her glance up. 'I will,' she said quickly, responding to the anticipation on their faces and forcing herself to cancel out any chafing doubts she might have harboured. William's expression relaxed into a smile for the first time that day.

The captain led them through the responses then asked, 'Have ye a ring, son?'

'Oh, aye.' William produced the ring from his waistcoat pocket and carefully pushed it onto her finger. Frances was briefly distracted and mildly surprised by this, wondering when and where he had acquired it. His hand still held hers as he softly pledged his vow. 'With this ring I thee wed, with my body I thee worship, and with all my worldly goods I thee endow.'

The captain shut his book and barely paused to announce, 'You're man and wife,' before turning away. They kissed and it was over.

The whole experience had been uncanny in its simplicity and Frances half-imagined she would wake up out of the dream at any moment. But the ring was there on her finger, the heaving ship swung about on the waves and she was unmistakably Mrs Munroe, bound for Canada. They were well out to sea by now and she gripped the deck-rail to steady herself as the last of the gulls deserted the vessel. William came up behind her and put his arms round her waist, his chin resting on her shoulder. His eyes followed the direction of her gaze, not back towards

70

Scotland but ahead into the westering sun. 'Scared?' he asked softly.

'Aye, just a bit,' she said, holding her stomach taut and hoping he would not feel her tremble.

'You're no changing your mind?'

'Too late for that now.'

'What do ye mean?'

She turned round and smiled to reassure him, hoping she too might be convinced by the utterance of the words. 'It's all right, I'm no changing my mind.'

He drew her to him, his jacket shielding them both from the raw wind. 'I'm scared too, Frances,' he confessed. Strangely, it helped her a little to know that he had his doubts too. 'It's a big thing we're doing, lass,' he went on, 'more so for you, since you've no had time to think on it – and you'll no tell me what ye left behind ye. I ken it must be hard to sever from your family and the folk ye love —'

'Do ye?' she interrupted cynically, re-visited by guilt for what she had done.

William looked chastened. 'All right, I've no kin to speak of myself. But I can try to understand if you'll talk to me about it – was there another lad maybe?'

A look of alarm came briefly into her eyes before her expression changed and softened persuasively. 'It's true I'm worried about the future, who wouldn't be. But I've made my decision and I've no regrets.' She gave a little laugh. 'Heavens, we just married, William. What more proof do ye want!'

'Mrs Munroe.' He touched the ring on her finger. 'Strange, isn't it?' Encouraged by her words, his enthusiasm returned. 'Aye, you're right. We don't need what's behind us now. We'll make our own family and a life for ourselves the way we want it. I tell ye, all we have to do is look after each other and stick together. What can go wrong?'

She smiled at his infectious optimism and kissed his forehead. 'Aye, what can go wrong?'

William responded by pulling her closer, the heat from his body seeming to drive through into her very bones. 'Let's go down,' he murmured. 'We can find a corner, away from everybody else.'

In the chilling breeze that swept the open deck, they both shivered again. But now it was from an anticipation that replaced their earlier fears. Because they had boarded as single ticket-holders they were forced to remain in segregated quarters, a prerequisite the captain had insisted upon despite their marriage. Hence there seemed little chance of a honeymoon or any intimate solitude until land-fall, four thousand miles away. Below decks, the ocean's freshness gave way to a foul-smelling closeness of unaired bedding, stale food and primitive toilets. Emigrant quarters provided the absolute bare essentials and no more, since the shipping companies reasoned that those escaping the slums of the cities could neither expect nor demand any better. Somehow, in all the chaos that precipitated their departure, Frances had given this little consideration until now. Accepting they would have to remain apart during the voyage, she was not prepared for the idea that they should snatch some time alone together. She could hardly imagine circumstances less conducive to intimacy.

They wandered through the labyrinth of steerage class and it felt as though they were down a mine. There were no port-holes and the dim lighting made little impression on the darkness. Cargo that would not fit in the holds was dumped in the passageways and everywhere shadowy figures sprawled on coils of rope or boxes. Though the rolling of the ship was still minimal, through the thin partition walls came the sound of people being sick. Mingled with the constant throb of the engines was the inconsolable crying of children, terrified by their strange and inhospitable new surroundings.

After the chill of the open deck, the heat made Frances light-headed. In her heavy clothes, the claustrophobic warmth sent perspiration trickling down her back. They came at last to a deserted spot where the passage ended in an immense watertight bulkhead. Finding a dark corner away from the scrutiny they embraced again. William held Frances close then shifted the shawl from her shoulders as his mouth moved over her neck. She tried to respond with affection, to muster some passion for the moment but was too acutely aware of a sense of degradation. Then all at once the heat and the smells and the noise overwhelmed her. Unable to stand his proximity, she gasped incoherently and pushed him away knowing she must surrender to nausea. Embarrassment and shame released the other emotions she had held at bay for so long and she collapsed sobbing and still retching into her own mess. The physical indignity seemed an added punishment to the guilt and remorse and she cried aloud with the injustice of it all. She felt herself being pulled gently to her feet and heard William's voice break through the barrier of pain in her head. 'Come on, it's all right, I'll take ye back to lie down.' He practically had to carry her, fighting against the increasingly violent swaying of the liner. In the dingy quarters Frances shared, he laid her carefully on her bunk. 'Will I get ye something to drink? Some tea maybe?' he asked.

The very thought of the strong, stewed swill they served made her gag again. 'Just leave me,' she gasped, turning her face to the wall.

'And I thought ye were a good sailor!' He tried to joke but she was deathly white and looked almost unconscious.

An older woman entered. 'It's all right, son,' she said patting William's arm. 'I'll keep an eye on her. Away ye go.' She started to undress Frances, peeling off the soiled clothes and dropping them in a heap on the floor.

William watched uncertainly. 'Is there nothing I can do?' he said.

'She'll be fine here. It'll pass in time – nobody ever died o' seasickness. Now, out ye go or you'll just get in bother for being in the women's section.'

Reluctantly, he left and made his way out on deck. The sun had almost sunk beyond the horizon and a giant red streak lay beckoning like a road across the sea. He stayed watching it fragment and dissolve until darkness filled the sky and only the ghostly phosphorescent lights rippled on the waters.

As the old steamship rolled west on its Atlantic crossing, Frances remained overwhelmed by the strong sensation of nausea. Unable to endure the relentless pitching of the ship, she stayed in her bunk. The weather continued to worsen and more and more of the passengers took to their cabins where the stench of vomit permeated everything. William, in contrast, was unaffected. He came when he could to check on her, sitting on the edge of the bunk and holding her hand. They talked little but Frances was grateful for the unspoken support, the strength he tried to will into her. She found that if she remained lying down, the feeling of sickness could be kept back but the least movement brought searing waves of dizzy retching and trips to the inadequate filthy latrines became a nightmare.

This resulting enforced idleness provided a curious pressure release for all her emotions. Though she suffered, everything else was temporarily blotted out, her bodily misery leaving no room to analyse her feelings or make sense of what she had done. Much of the time she dozed fitfully until her exhausted mind twisted recent events and disturbingly changed them into vivid dreams that jerked her awake again. As each agonising hour slowly passed, she wanted nothing more than to be off the swaying old craft and onto firm ground.

Stormy weather followed them all the way over to the North American coast but, unfortunately for Frances, the misery did not end there. Once on the long-awaited firm ground, they faced a train journey that would take them right across Canada. At first, relief at being ashore more than made up for the discomforts of the crowded immigrant car they were to travel in, but she soon came to detest the train as much as the ship. One incessant motion was exchanged for another. There was still no privacy and they found themselves crammed in among the same faces with whom they had shared the awful sea crossing. The carriage was packed with railroad workers and settlers, their wives striving to placate the squalling children who fretted in the restricted space. Food was prepared with difficulty on a wood-burning stove in the middle of the car. There was no sanitary provision so despite frequent stops, dysentery was prevalent and the flies tormented everyone. Again, William seemed undaunted by the wretchedness. When he roused her from a slumped, bleary stupor to point out some new sight, Frances could see his eyes bright and marvelling at the strangeness of it all and she tried hard to enthuse in return. As the great iron engine continued chuntering west, they passed through a rocky water-land, rich in tamarac and jack-pine. The terrain was fragmented by lakes, some as big as seas, dotted with tiny islands and tree-fringed shores. William held the children up to the narrow window to see the beaver dams and the tell-tale whorl of their snouts under the shimmering surface. In places, the track would wind through narrow man-made canyons in the rock, torn apart by dynamite and brute force in the building of the railroad.

After a few days, the ground began to level out. The endless, rolling grasslands of the plains stretched all around them, occasionally pock-marked by a solitary homestead, a smoking dot on the horizon huddled timorously, it seemed, against the enormity of the sky. The quality of the soil for farming was discussed at great length between the men, and arguments about which were the best crops raged on into the night. William listened with interest but Frances could only smile wanly, relieved that their journey was almost over.

The rigours of three weeks' travelling had left her weak and emaciated, but gradually her eyes were opened to the new country and as she slowly recovered her strength an irrepressible enthusiasm bubbled to the surface. William's joy at his bride's renewed optimism left him heady with excitement. He chattered endlessly about his plans for their future and she let herself fall under the spell of his vision while the horrors of the journey slowly faded into memory.

74

In the wide flatness of the open plains, Calgary could be seen long before it was reached and eager faces were squashed together straining to get a view from the carriage. On the horizon to the west was the long, ragged line of the Rocky Mountains from whose snow-capped peaks the Bow River rushed in an icy blue torrent, snaking through the town and into the hazy distance.

When at last they alighted, it was disconcerting to walk in the wide, bustling streets after their incarceration in the train. The coming of the Canadian Pacific railroad had transformed Calgary from a trading post to a burgeoning frontier town of four thousand people. Its dirt roads were thronging with carts and horses, crowds of construction workers, wagons piled to overflowing with farm produce, and herds of cattle being driven to the pens. The surrounding rich farmland was bringing in a steady trickle of homesteaders but, with the prospect of a new branch line running north, this would soon rise to a flood. Well before its launch with the official sod-turning ceremony, work on the railroad to Edmonton had already commenced. In the dry heat of mid-July, a large grading outfit was camped out in the Nose Creek Valley some miles to the north and, in the absence of one central recruiting agency, William realised he would have to go there to secure work. But his immediate plan was to spend at least a few days in town, in a comfortable room that did not roll like a ship or rattle like a train.

Though it was only a cheap boarding-house on the outskirts of town, Frances was enthralled when the landlady showed them the bedroom and bathroom. 'God, William, this is bigger than our whole house in the Wemyss,' she exclaimed, running over to admire the voluminous tub and gleaming brass fitments.

'There's plenty of hot water,' said the woman tactfully, eyeing their dishevelled state. 'Have a good soak and get rid of the dust from the train.'

Though Frances felt sinful at having a bath in the middle of the day, she luxuriated for over an hour before William hammered at the door and implored her to let him have his turn. Then while he bathed, she lay in bed enjoying the scent of clean linen that mingled with the fresh smells of the prairie drifting in through the open window. The shimmering afternoon heat seemed to dull the noises outside into a drowsy lullaby and her warm contentment sent her almost to sleep when she heard him come quietly into the room. As he slid under the covers beside her, she felt a momentary panic and her body stiffened. Then his hand slowly stroked her hair, turning her face towards him. There was none of the urgency in his touch this time, his manner gentle but sure. He sighed into her ear as his lips brushed against her. 'Frances.'

The sound of her name blurred the concentration of her thoughts. Though barely touching her skin, his fingers seemed to burn her as they explored her trembling body. Unnerved by the excited new sensations which mixed with her fear, she tried to contain the moment but her innocence denied her control. The strength of his caress grew less tentative. She heard her name murmured again, urgently now as the rhythm of his breathing quickened. His hands became more determined and he eased himself across her, guiding her body to meet his. The feeling was uncanny. She wanted to summon her instincts to respond to his passion but a sudden physical pain burst through her. She gave out a smothered little gasp but he held on to her and told her not to be afraid. He waited and gradually her heartbeat slowed. Then, as the fear subsided and she grew calmer, his own arousal was again intensified to a pitch of desire. She felt somewhat detached from the act when, all too quickly, it appeared to be over. He lay heavily on top of her and she experienced a vague disappointment. The anticipation that had stimulated her amorous sensibility in the past was now defused by the reality.

William drew back from her and searched her face. 'I wasn't too rough?'

She smiled faintly but could not think of anything to say. She had expected to feel different but apart from the pain, which had been very real, the rest was almost as if it had not happened. Yet William now dozed in a glow of contentment and it was clear he had experienced pleasure in their encounter. Frances was kept awake by a sense of confusion and denial. She now wondered tentatively if what had just passed was the sum total she could expect from the conjugal bed.

As if in response to her thoughts William stirred. 'It will be all right next time,' he assured her drowsily and she lifted her head to admit his arm.

Time passed and the room grew stifling, the heat and dampness of the bed making them languorous. Frances put out her hand and stroked the contours of his face. It was a good face she thought. He opened one eye and looked at her, the blue intensity catching her unawares. She wanted to answer his expression but words seemed inadequate. Instead she kissed him awake and let the touch of her mouth speak for itself. He turned towards her, sharing her desire and carefully urged her responses, gently arousing. At last she held him willingly and gave in to the pleasure that flooded her body. But before it subsided she found herself weeping without understanding or even caring why.

Two days of relative comfort left them drugged with the luxury of time alone together. No one knew them there or made judgement. Without the inhibitory effect of prying eyes, wagging tongues or other people's expectations, they had the rare freedom to indulge unhurriedly in the discovery of one another. On the ship, William had half feared that she might weaken to a point beyond recovery. But Frances was gradually reviving and already he could see signs of the grit and tenacity only hinted at in the short days of their acquaintance back in Scotland. A return to health and an awareness of her entirely dependent state had strengthened her resolve and forged a deepening commitment to him. There were times when the significance of that weighed like a burden, reminding her of the utter vulnerability of her situation. But for the most part she was able to see the destructiveness in such thoughts, and held them at bay. However, there were compensations. She grew closer in her affection for him and soon learned that there were times when he needed her as much as she did him. He had high hopes, enthusiasm and was not afraid of hard work. Yet his plans, when pared down to the detail, were muddled and unfocussed. Frances was surprised, indeed amused to find herself in the unfamiliar role of occasionally exerting a restraining influence. It gave a kind of equilibrium to the partnership.

The day after their arrival, they went out to explore the exciting new land they had come to. After enquiries at local offices, they made arrangements to ride out to the railroad at the end of that week with one of the convoys of supply-wagons which left town daily. The time before their departure then had to be spent in a hasty shopping spree, purchasing a tent and the provisions they would need to take with them.

'I like the idea of living in a tent – it's romantic.' It was their last night in Calgary and Frances flopped back on to the bed where William lay sprawled against the pillows. She nestled her head into his shoulder and ran her hand over his damp chest, tugging at the fine blond hair that had darkened with sweat. The heat was penetrating, even at that late hour, and the thin curtains hung limp on the breathless air of the open windows.

He slid his arm under her, pulling her closer. 'I wouldn't call a construction camp full of railroad builders romantic – it'll no be like this ye ken.' His voice was still slow and slurred from their love-making, his eyes half-shut in prelude to sleep.

Frances however, was wide awake. 'Are ye sure you'll be able to find a job?' Getting no response, she nudged him till he opened his eyes. 'I mean, if there's that many men out there already?'

'Och, it'll be all right,' he said absently, caressing her bare shoulder. 'There'll be plenty of work for skilled men like me. And the money should be good too – hopefully it should only take a few months to save enough for the —'

'Homestead.' Frances sighed as she finished the sentence for him. She pushed his hand away, wanting his full concentration. 'Honestly, William, have ye thought about this – what do you or me know about farming?'

He pulled a face and sat up. 'Probably as much as half the other folk that've come out here. But we'll learn, you'll see, and we'll have land of our own Frances, something we'd never have back home.' As usual his casual optimism was unshakeable.

'Do ye think I could get work at the camp too, if I try?'

'Oh, ye fancy yourself as a spiker or a navvy, do ye?' he grinned.

She prodded him hard in the ribs. 'No. Ye ken what I mean, anything – cook, cleaner, laundry-woman. Just so I can help us save a bit more. If you're determined to have this homestead, we'll need all the money we can get.'

'I'd no thought about it,' he shrugged, 'but right enough, it would be good if you could earn something – I ken you wouldn't want to be a kept woman.'

'Huh,' she laughed, 'fine chance of that!'

'Oh, I canna imagine anyone keeping you in your place, least of all me – I wouldn't dare to try!'

'Why, ye cheeky bugger, Munroe.'

He feigned shock at her language. 'Well, you've a navvy's mouth on ye if nothing else.'

She grabbed the pillow and walloped it hard against him, sending little tufts into the air. In retaliation, he hurled it back at her but she ducked and it skidded over the floor, feathers flying like a snowfall in the heavy air. Someone was knocking on the ceiling and he fell back on to the bed, trying to stifle his laughter. Frances pulled herself on top of him and forced his hands above his head. 'Now, apologise for that or . . .'

'You'll what?' he challenged. Then gradually his eyes softened as her hair fell over his face and her mouth covered his. When she released him, he was watching her with a different expression. 'I do love you, Frances,' he said suddenly, almost as if surprised by the sound of his own voice.

For a solitary second, an echo of these words seemed to shoot through her. But almost as quickly, the moment passed and she was back in the room with the hushed warmth of the night and the blue eyes looking into hers. 'Then show me,' she whispered, now strangely needful of assurance.

2

Out at the Nose Creek camp, they pitched their tent beside what seemed like a hundred others. The weather was hot and the nights stayed warm and light till late. There were a few other women in the camp, some of whom Frances thought to be of dubious reputation and she kept her distance from them. The rest spent their days doing laundry and cooking for their men but she was determined not to do likewise. Within hours of arriving, she had found work helping to serve from the food tent. There was no pay as such but in return their meals were free and this would enable them to save with little expenditure of their own. Toh Seng, the cook, said she could start straight away and she returned, bursting with excitement, to tell William the news.

He however, had not been so fortunate, discovering that there would be a long wait before track-laying commenced. Dispirited, he sat in the tent with Frances.

She put her arms round him and shook him. 'Dinna be so down about it, there must be something ye can do. Ye did say ye would take anything.'

He mentioned he was considering joining a lower-paid grading team while there was still a need for men. 'But at what they're paying, we could be here forever before we save enough to get out.'

'Look, take it for the time being. If something better turns up, ye can change.' She felt glad that for once she was able to encourage him instead of the other way round.

'I suppose you're right.' He looked unenthusiastic and climbed to his feet. 'I'll away and sign up now.'

She took his hand and squeezed it. 'We'll cope – just remember, ye need a job if all our plans are to come to anything.'

He smiled and leaned down to kiss her. 'Aye, you're right. I suppose there's no harm in making do for the time being.'

He sauntered idly through the camp, aware that he was still reluctant to commit himself to the work on the grading. Then, as he passed one of the engineers' tents, he heard a strong Scots voice shouting from inside. Drawn to the timbre of the accent, William peered round the opening to the tent. Inside, a man sat at a makeshift desk opposite a younger, obviously subordinate clerk who shifted uneasily as a tirade of abuse was flung at him.

'Ye couldna build a doll's house, never mind a bloody railroad.' The elder man continued and waved a sheaf of drawings in the air. 'Where's my survey? We can't trust to luck and just hope we've built the damn line on solid ground.'

'But Mr Dewar, there's been problems . . .'

'To hell with you and your problems.' The papers were tossed at the hapless youth. 'I've a schedule to stick to and I need somebody as can deal with problems. You're fired. Away and work for Thomson or somebody else before you have me bankrupt.'

William was almost knocked to the ground as the young man barged out, blushing furiously. Behind him the engineer returned to his work, absorbed by the charts laid out before him and contemplatively stroking his distinctive white beard.

'Mr Dewar?' William pulled off his cap and entered cautiously.

The man looked up. 'Aye, what is it, son?' His tone was still angry. 'I'm busy here.'

'I'm sorry to bother ye, sir, my name's William Munroe,' he coughed, nervously, 'I'm after a job and no having much success. I wondered if . . .'

Dewar relaxed and offered his hand. 'Always glad to meet a fellow Scot,' he smiled. 'Take a seat, Munroe, and tell me what's brought ye to this side of the world?'

William explained he had come to Calgary anticipating that they might be recruiting for the track-laying teams. 'I thought maybe I could get myself a foreman position – but I don't quite understand the system here.'

Dewar sighed. 'It's confusing I know. The road-bed work has been split up and let in short-order contracts to the construction companies – they're all working on different sections at a time. I'm overseeing a couple of the surveys and we'll be hard pressed to keep ahead of them, I can tell you.' He paused, fingering his beard again. 'What kind of work did ye do back home?'

'I was a riveter on the Forth Bridge these past four years. Maybe you've no heard of it.'

'Oh, but indeed I have. A feat of modern engineering, that bridge.' Dewar was impressed. 'Ye should be proud to have been involved.'

William looked at the floor. 'I am, sir, but it's no helping me here.'

Dewar was pensive for a moment. 'I don't know of any work round here that would suit ye, son – at least not like you've been used to.'

'I'm desperate, sir, I'll take anything.'

'Mm, you mean that? Well, would you consider coming along with us, joining the survey team?'

'Oh yes, sir! But I have to be honest with ye, I dinna ken much about surveying.'

Dewar eyed him eagerly. 'If you saw the imbecile that just left, you'll know what I'm up against. We've too much work and no enough experienced men. Now, I've got two surveyors who handle the actual survey and we've a good Indian scout to guide us. My assistant, Matthew Daniels, effectively leads the team but he could sorely do with some help. I'm only out there overseeing it from time to time. As you can tell,' he waved at the disorder around him, 'most of my work is here, and I've got another team to supervise as well.'

'What exactly would I be doing then?'

'We need someone to keep an accurate account of the loads they'll have to haul. You'll get instructions at each stage – numbers of men, horses, and so on. Then there's gravel and track to be considered. It's only record-keeping essentially and I know you're no office clerk, Munroe, but if you worked on the Forth, you'll know what it takes to get something built – same principle.' He paused and waited for a response.

'Aye, you're right there,' said William, confidently.

Dewar pressed on, sensing a growing enthusiasm. 'And it's a rough life out there – I need someone strong and reliable who can take it. I've already sacked one and I've no stomach for interviewing a load of others. In my opinion, you'd do excellently. What do you say?' William was flattered by the engineer's praise but still he paused. Dewar saw him waver. 'It's just a wee outfit, only six men and not answerable to anyone but me. They're camped a good bit north of here by now and just keep moving on as the ground is covered – I think the independent life would suit ye. Come on, man. There's no problem is there?'

He held out his hand, and William made his decision. 'It's a deal, Mr Dewar,' he said, shaking on it. It seemed an inauspicious moment to bring up his marriage.

'Don't ye see?' he tried to reason with her later. 'On the money Dewar's willing to pay me, we can be out of here sooner than we thought.'

'Oh aye? And how often will I see ye?' she snapped back.

'The team's up around Red Deer just now — there's a stage comes by on the trail — I can get word to ye.'

Frances whipped round to him, her face angrily flushed. 'Think what you're saying!'

He kept his voice calm although his face had reddened also. 'It's a straight choice. We could have a year or more together moving with the railroad or six to seven months apart until I'm finished. Then we'd be able to get on to the farm right away.'

'I prefer the first choice,' she said stubbornly.

'That's ridiculous.'

'Ye asked my opinion.'

'But it doesn't make sense, Frances.'

'It makes sense for me to be with ye,' she shouted.

William put his finger to his mouth. 'Shh,' he interrupted. 'Do ye want to wake up half the camp?'

'I dinna care! I'm your wife, no somebody to be left at the end of the line and picked up when you're finished with your work.'

'That's no fair.' He gripped her shoulders. 'Ye think I wanted this? It was me that asked ye to come in the first place, or had ye forgotten that?'

'I've no forgotten! I remember ye wanted me to come with ye right away instead of leaving me waiting in the Wemyss — what's the difference if ye disappear off for months on end?'

He paused and an uncharacteristic firmness came into his voice. 'The difference is I want this homestead even more now, Frances. I want it for you and me and our bairns to grow up in — and as far as I'm concerned, I'll do anything to make that possible — the sooner the better.'

She looked down at the floor but he put his hand under her chin and raised her face towards his, speaking more softly now. 'That's all that's keeping me going — or I couldn't bear the thought of being away from ye — ye ken that, don't ye?' Frances felt defeated. Yes, she knew he loved her but that was not the argument. 'Trust me, it'll be all right,' he whispered soothingly.

She pulled away, a hard knot still inside her. 'You promised we would stay together,' she said. When he did not answer, she turned and left the tent, feeling the need to walk off the unbearable tension before she lost her temper completely.

Later that night, when there was still the vaguest trace of violet in the sky, Frances opened her eyes to see William's seated form at the end of the bed-roll. He was pensively smoking a cigarette, his outline shadowed against the canvas. As she watched him, the sense of desolation gave way to an irrepressible need to make amends. It was true she felt disregarded, indeed wronged by his decision, but she tried to convince herself it would ultimately benefit them both. A fear of her own vulnerability made it essential to come to terms with him now and though she doubted she could tolerate his absence for even a day, she wanted to let him know she would try.

Leaning forward she touched him and felt his hand fold firmly over hers. For a few moments they stayed like that without speaking. 'Och, come here to me,' she sighed at last and drew him down into her arms. As they kissed she could taste the salt tears on his eyelids. It was strangely affecting to know such pain so soon when only the day before they had been filled with unbounded optimism.

'I'm sorry, Frances,' he sighed deeply and pressed against her. There was no further need for words. They held each other and expressed with their bodies the ache which his impending departure now quickened to a keener sting.

3

Three weeks had passed since that day and Frances had heard nothing, seen nothing of William. Laying an arm over her damp forehead to shield her face, she squinted at the early morning sun as it slanted through the slit in the tent. Only half awake, her mind and body were still numb with the dregs of sleep. But it was only seconds before the pain of emptiness flooded her consciousness again, as it did relentlessly with every day that passed. Nothing in her experience had prepared her for this loneliness and she feared she could not make it through another night.

Outside the noisy mayhem of the camp assaulted her ears. Teamsters bawled at their horses and there was a great clanking and thudding of hooves as they set off to plough the road and haul the immense scrapers over it to make a flat bed in readiness for the track. And above all rose the voices of the men as they shouted instructions and milled about the site. Frances stretched under the covers and sighed. Every day was a monotonous chore of slopping beans and salt-pork onto plates and ladling tea into tin mugs as the leering queue of navvies shuffled past her. She was brow-beaten by Toh Seng, who swatted her with his cloth at every opportunity and even now she could hear his voice calling for her above the hubbub.

'You come here to work, not sleep,' he shrieked, poking his head through the flap and jostling her with his foot. 'Move! Now!'

'All right, all right,' she yelled, pushing the foot away. 'I'm coming.'

Frances rolled off the mattress and fumbled for her clothes. Her head was aching from lack of sleep and the flies were already buzzing around inside the tent. Roughly she fastened her blouse and broke a button in the process. She looked for her boots and could only find one. Throwing things aside she cursed, fuelling the anger simmering within. Toh Seng was shrieking at her again and she grabbed her apron and raised it to pull over her head. Then quite suddenly, almost calmly, she knew she had reached the limit of her endurance and the moment of decision had arrived.

The stage dropped her off at Old Ross's stopping house. It was the nearest to the survey camp, the driver explained. Frances waited as her trunk was lowered to the ground and said goodbye to the other passengers, two brothers who were homesteading at Red Deer. She was not sure if they were German or Austrian but, since they could not converse with her, nor she with them, there was little room for inquisition on the journey, and for that she was thankful.

Ross's was a large, log-built house with a grass roof. There were several out-buildings and a couple of horses were fenced off in an enclosure. Inside, it was spacious and comfortable and for a moment, Frances was tempted to stay a while.

'I believe the team's camped about a mile and a half east of here,' the keeper told her. 'I can send someone out to tell them you're here if you like?'

'No.' She almost shouted at him. 'No, that's all right, I'll walk out there myself, it's light till late.' She smiled to reassure the man, who looked at her questioningly. 'I want it to be a surprise, you see.' Then, arranging to collect the trunk later and, despite his protestations, she set off across the hill alone.

In places the ground was boggy and several times Frances felt her boots sink in the mire. She quickly grew disorientated when thick clumps of trees had to be negotiated and struggled to keep her sense of direction. There were flashing glimpses of deer, occasional darting rabbits and strange little furry creatures that scurried into holes whistling furiously at her approach. She half-wondered about wolves, but decided quickly to dispel any negative thoughts and put them from her mind.

At last a shallow valley opened ahead and a thin pall of smoke rose from a fire. Relieved to have arrived, Frances stumbled towards the camp site. She could see the debris of felled trees they had used for firewood and to make cross-poles for two tents which were pitched on one side of the clearing. Further back on the other side stood a tipi, smoke puffing from its apex.

The men sat eating on a stony bit of ground around the fire. As she approached, the conversation died and they stood up in surprise. William gaped in amazement, his spoon poised half way to his mouth. She dropped her bundle and ran forward to him. 'Oh, William, I'm that glad I've found ye!'

The men started laughing under their breath and he pulled away, embarrassed. 'What the hell are ye doing here?'

'I've come to be with you,' she said plaintively. 'I couldn't stand it another day.'

He drew her to one side. 'So you thought you could just turn up here?' Then, as he realised the predicament she had put him in, his anger grew. 'You knew what I was coming to. Look around – do ye think ye can stay here?' He swore in exasperation. 'We agreed —'

'No. *You* decided – I didna get a choice.' Her own temper was beginning to flare. 'Well, I've made my decision now and I'm here. We stay together, William, or we're finished.' Frances glared around her as the other men shuffled their feet uneasily and tried to ignore the row taking place only yards away from them. The two surveyors continued the business of stowing away their instruments in a box and a little way off, a rather more dishevelled individual proceeded to feed the horses.

Suddenly, Frances was aware of a fourth man who emerged from one of the tents. 'Good grief,' he exclaimed, seeing her. 'Where did you appear from?' William gave an uneasy explanation and the man turned abruptly to face her. 'You realise you can't stay here, Mrs Munroe,' he said blandly.

She ignored him. 'Who's he? I thought Mr Dewar was in charge.' William winced visibly and opened his mouth to speak but the other man interrupted.

'Mrs Munroe, I'm Matthew Daniels, assistant engineer. And

85

when Mr Dewar is not in camp, I'll thank you to know I'm in charge.'

'I've come all the way from Calgary —' she began but he ignored her attempts to explain.

'There's no place for a woman here. You'll simply have to go back.'

William decided to intervene. 'Look, Mr Daniels, I see your point, and it was wrong of her to come out here – but it's getting dark now. Can we no leave it till morning – it's no a good walk to Ross's, even in the light.'

'Where's she going to sleep, man?' Daniels said in an exasperated voice. 'We've no provision for married quarters.'

The men shifted about uncomfortably and Frances began to realise just how disruptive her presence was. She sniffed loudly, picked up her bundle and walked away.

'Frances ...' William ran after her. 'Ye canna go back. It's getting dark.'

She shook off his hand. 'It's what you want, is it no? And him!' She glared back at Daniels and continued walking. 'Well, to hell with the pair of you!'

William caught up with her again. 'You'll get yourself lost. Now stop this.' He held her arm firmly, refusing to let go until he felt her relax. 'Come back and we'll sort something out.'

'What about him?'

'I'll square it with him – for tonight anyway.' He put his arm round her shoulder and drew her back towards the tents. 'But you'll have to go in the morning.'

Daniels was unhappy about the situation but grudgingly accepted that she must stay the night. 'I'll see if we can put her in with Pi'taki,' he said, and walked off towards the tipi.

William saw the curiosity on Frances's face. 'That's Broken Claw's tent. He's the scout with this outfit – Blackfoot Indian.'

'I'm no sleeping with him!'

'Dinna be daft, of course you're no sleeping with him. He's away with Dewar until tomorrow. His wife's here, though. She works as the camp packer, moving the tents and that.'

'Wife? I thought all this carry on was because you couldn't have women out here. And there's been one here all the time ...'

Before he could answer, Daniels emerged from the tipi. 'Old Pi'taki's none too happy about it,' he shrugged, 'but she's agreed – providing it's only the one night.'

Frances did not welcome the idea either but the engineer made it clear there was no other option. She was told to help herself from the stew-pot hanging over the fire but one whiff told her she would rather go hungry. William introduced her to the other men who were still considerably embarrassed at what had happened. The two surveyors, Randall and Marsh, doffed their hats politely as she was introduced to them and then scuttled into their tent, quickly followed by Ben, who seemed more at home with the horses than in the presence of a woman.

Daniels made no move, obviously determined to give them no time to themselves and, after a brief good night, Frances walked across the clearing and nervously entered the tipi. She carried her shawl and an oil lamp which, when raised, cast an eerie shadow over the pyramidal slope of the wall. The sleeping form on the floor was indistinguishable as a human body, only a hunched mound under a cover that rose and fell with her breathing. The fire had been dowsed and an acrid smell permeated the space. Letting the flap drop behind her, Frances carefully stepped over the buckskin packages and hides that lined the interior. She felt miserable about the reception she had got on her arrival and did not look forward to the morning, knowing that she must give up and return to Calgary.

With the plaid shawl over her shoulders she sat glumly and pulled her knees up under her chin. As she did so, the mound beside her shifted and turned round. Two narrow eyes glittered from within deeply furrowed brows as the lamp-light played across the face that emerged. Frances felt suddenly quite frightened. She had seen little respect conveyed to the natives in Calgary and had assumed a like-minded attitude towards them herself. They had seemed a rather dejected lot, with an aura of defeat about them and there was little sign of the 'noble warriors' she recalled from her brother's storybooks. But she had to admit the stare of this woman was uncanny. She could feel the hostility directed at her through those eyes. Their intense, alert animosity was in stark contrast to the face, dark and unmoving like old, carved wood.

Pi'taki sat up, still fixing her with a penetrating look. The light picked out an ochre stain in the parting of her hair which lay in black oily braids about her shoulders. She put out a brown, leathery hand and tried to touch Frances, who recoiled with a mixture of fear and revulsion. Again the hand came forward, gingerly reaching out. It was the shawl she seemed fascinated by and her fingers smoothed down the fold of it. Frances tugged it from her reach. 'Keep your thieving hands off,' she hissed, trying to put a warning authority in her voice. The hand immediately withdrew and Pi'taki made a sonorous, grunting sound. Then, hauling the

87

covers back over her shoulders, she lay down and turned to face the wall.

Confused, afraid, and most of all cold, Frances sat with her arms wrapped around her knees to keep warm. The plaid shawl offered little protection against the vast, cold night that descended over the plains. For hours she retained her vigilance and increased her fear by imagining brutal acts which might be visited on her during the night. Shivering, she listened to the hoarse breathing that accompanied Pi'taki's sleep as the light from the oil lamp waned and picked out the strange markings that covered the walls. Little brown and red figures oscillated in the flickering glow like tadpoles in a pool. The arched, minimal shapes of horses, clustered conical tipis and darting arrows came to life in the dying shadows. These ancient and sacred symbols depicting the legends of the Blackfoot mesmerised her as they moved before her eyes, rhythmically emerging and fading, dulling her senses and drawing her into sleep.

4

The men were already up as the morning's first light licked the surrounding hills. Randall revived the fire while Marsh peered dimly into a propped mirror and tried to shave, his braces flopping loosely at his side. William was busy rolling up charts and maps, keeping one eye on the tipi and wondering when Frances would emerge. He could see Daniels was growing impatient and he decided to go and call her out himself. As he drew near, he could hear a growing commotion within its skin walls, and he smiled in surprise as Frances came stumbling out of the opening, her boots tossed after her.

'Thrown ye out then, has she?' he laughed. The others joined in the mirth and she stood regarding them angrily with hands on hips. Then, remembering the shawl, she dived back inside to retrieve it. Pi'taki was holding it against her face when it was snatched vigorously from her grasp.

'And you're no having that!' Frances yelled and stormed back out. The general amusement had reached a pitch now. 'What are ye all laughing at?' she shouted, confronting them and giving William a particularly scolding stare. 'She's a mad-woman – I could've been murdered!'

'Och Frances, she's harmless.' William took her hand and pulled her towards the camp-fire. As he did so, he caught Daniels frowning at them. 'We'll have to hurry. I'll take ye back to Ross's, but I canna hold things up here.' He lifted the kettle from the fire and pushed the stew-pot onto the flames. 'Have something to eat quick and then we'll go.'

She peered into the blackened pot. 'I'm no eating that!'

'There's nothing wrong with it.'

As he spoke, two figures rode into the camp and the men seemed to jump to attention. The portly man who exuded an air of authority she assumed to be Angus Dewar, and the man riding beside could be none other than Broken Claw. He had the same carved and burnished skin of his wife with deeply grooved lines around the nostrils and eyes, eyes that seemed focussed on the distant horizon even when his curious gaze rested on Frances. His long hair hung limply under a dusty old black hat, but he too had a dignified bearing, which was emphasised by Pi'taki's dutiful ministrations. She led his horse away and returned to prepare food in the tipi, her husband following her in.

Dewar could see he was in the midst of some drama but was not in a hurry to unravel it. He strolled over to the fire and casually accepted the tea that was offered. 'What's going on here then?' he asked, bushy eyebrows raised.

Daniels spoke up. 'This woman's presence was entirely unexpected, sir. I've told Munroe she'll have to go.'

'All right, Matt, I'll handle this.' He looked at William. 'Enlighten me, son.' William offered the facts a little uneasily and was relieved to see a smile break across Dewar's face. 'Why did you no tell me you had your wife along?' he said, regarding Frances. She was now determined to have her say.

'Mr Dewar, I canna wait on my own for months at the end of the track – let me bide here. There must be something I can do to earn my keep?'

'Well now, lassie, we have rules about women tagging along with the crews, and for good reason – it tends to cause trouble.'

'But I wouldn't be any trouble —'

He held up his hand and continued. 'Now, just a minute. Far be it for me to break up a young marriage before it's hardly begun,' he said. 'But tell me, what kind of a life do you think you'd have here?'

'I wouldn't care,' she replied. 'Please, dinna make me go back.'

There was an uneasy pause and he spoke again. 'Well, I don't rightly know what you could do . . .'

'I can cook.' Frances looked hopefully at the faces of the other men but they seemed uninterested.

Dewar was unsure of how to resolve the situation and anxious to get on with the day's work. 'Let me have a word with my assistant here,' he said, motioning to Daniels to follow him into the tent. 'If you want to make yourself useful, you could fix me something to eat.' Frances thought at first she had imagined it, but she was sure he winked at her, unseen by the others.

She rolled up her sleeves and grabbed the bubbling pot from the fire. 'Right,' she said, 'show me the stores and where you get the water.'

Unclear about what was happening, William pointed in the direction of a nearby stream and watched bewildered as she dashed off eagerly. He started to help the others and they all became so immersed in preparation for the day's work that they did not notice her return. Randall was the first to detect the smell wafting over from the fire and he sniffed the air luxuriously. Soon the others were distracted from their chores too and gathered around Frances to make a closer inspection of the anticipated breakfast. Before long they were all eagerly placing their orders. Even Daniels could not resist the seductive aroma of fried bacon and pancakes and followed his nose for a second helping.

'I take it then, gentlemen, that you all agree to Mrs Munroe accompanying us as camp cook?' Angus Dewar glanced around at them as they tucked in hungrily. 'Voice your objections now, if you have any.' As he had expected, no one uttered a word and before he departed once more, a schedule of work for Frances had been drawn up. Apart from the cooking, it was agreed that all other camp duties would be shared with Pi'taki. Frances was none too pleased about this but relieved that she was allowed to stay.

The question of sleeping quarters was settled by moving all the equipment into one tent, leaving barely enough room for Frances and William to squeeze in at night. The rest of the men all had to cram into the second tent together. William was ill at ease with the arrangement. He disliked being singled out and so spent much of his time working and talking with the others till late. Frances began to wonder if it had all been worth it for the precious little time they spent together, speaking in hushed tones, cramped among the undignified jumble of boxes and gear in that confined space. She was aware that she was on a tight rein and did not want to upset the rhythm of life in the camp. The men treated her amiably enough, though she suspected this tolerance was more out of deference to William than any genuine acceptance on their part. Often she would sneak a glance over to the pointed smoking tipi which seemed to stand aloof from all their chaos.

She and Pi'taki were now thrown together and frequently spent more time in each other's company than with their husbands. Before he left for an extended trip to South Edmonton, Angus Dewar had made it clear he wanted them through to Wolf Creek by the end of August. This meant the men were usually gone on ahead by sunrise and if it was a day to strike camp, the two women would be left to clean and clear away the cooking utensils and store the food. They then set about rolling up the bedding and dismantling the tents, rarely speaking to each other, though Frances knew that Pi'taki understood her language. They worked side by side in relative silence, each regarding the other with concealed curiosity. Frances was still wary of Pi'taki but the initial fear had gone. Observing her from the corner of her eye, she wondered how old Pi'taki might be. Older than her mother? Old enough to be her grandmother? It was hard to tell from such a face and her clothes made it impossible to judge from her body. She wore a long shift-like garment made of two deer skins sewn together, with some bead-work for decoration. Short leggings were gartered below her knees and extended to her flopping moccasins. When it was cold, she wore an old Hudson's Bay Company blanket over her shoulders, though Frances knew she would dearly love to exchange it for the plaid shawl. Sheathed in a pouch at her side hung a large, horn-handled knife. At first, Frances had been nervous of it but soon came to realise its many and varied uses.

Whatever her age however, there was no doubting the strength of the woman. Once they had struck camp and loaded the packs on to the horses, Pi'taki would dismantle the tipi, bundle all her belongings on to a travois sled and haul it to the next site. The travois was designed to be pulled by a horse, but she donned the yoke herself and moved off without complaint. Frances thought it a primitive way to behave and said so to William one evening as they sat in the opening of their tent.

'The woman's no better than a pack-horse.' She gestured to where Pi'taki was busily erecting the tipi while Broken Claw sat smoking his pipe.

'Don't interfere, it's their way,' he responded.

'And he's no much friendlier than her. Why do ye need them here? They dinna seem to like it much.'

'He's a good guide, and we need him to negotiate with some of the Indians around here. He likes it better than being stuck on a reserve. As for Pi'taki . . .' He shrugged. 'Mr Dewar says she lost all her children years ago in a measles epidemic, it's the only reason she's here with us, otherwise she'd be back on the reserve. Now she just lives to serve her man.' He thought for a moment. 'Suppose old Broken Claw's got the right idea – only wish I could keep you in line like that!'

Frances did not laugh. 'It's no so different for me,' she said flatly.

'What do ye mean by that?'

'Well, I'm still fetching and carrying for a load of men.'

'You're no going to start complaining again, are ye?'

'No,' she sighed, 'it's just that when ye think about it, I dinna get treated any better than the squaw.'

William grew impatient. 'Well, maybe you should do as she does, and ignore it,' he replied tersely. Frances was annoyed by this and made to speak but he grabbed her arm and silenced her. 'Look, there's nothing I can do about it. I canna change the way things are. You either stay here and make the best of it or pack up and go back to Calgary – make your choice.' With that, he rose and left her sitting stunned by the outburst. As Frances watched him join the other men, she felt herself seethe with rage. Angrily, she got up and kicked a pail across the ground before walking off towards the nearby stream.

Meanwhile, at the other side of the clearing, Pi'taki watched from the shadows of the tipi. Strange behaviour between man and wife, she thought.

5

By the end of the month the little survey team was about twelve miles from Wolf Creek. All the talk was of the progress in construction on the railroad and each night Frances sat apart from the men eating her supper in silence.

Dewar had visited them again and given the news. 'Have to press on, lads,' he had said. 'The graders'll be on your tail in no time. We expect them to have a hundred and sixty miles ready for track by the autumn – they'll be north of Red Deer in a couple of weeks.'

She could not see what all the fuss was about but it seemed to put a new urgency into the work. The next morning, Dewar departed and the men went ahead early for Wolf Creek, leaving the women alone in the silent camp. Only snatches of bird song could be heard in the trees and the smoke from the doused fire hung strangely on the heavy atmosphere. The heat was already intense and the sun glistened through a soupy sky. In the distance a long train of wagons was silhouetted against the hazy blur. Following the trail, they slowly moved along the skyline like a retreating army, eight oxen per wagon straining in the harness. These were the freighters bringing huge loads of hay for the teams of horses that would be used in the grading. Frances had often seen the enormous ten-ton lots they were laying down every five miles along the proposed route of the railroad.

She tied a cotton square round her head to keep the sweat from her eyes as she and Pi'taki worked to break up the camp. They had a pattern, a kind of unsaid order in which things were done that had developed out of the wish to remain separated in their duties. As such, they spoke little, and rarely with a civil tongue.

'Give me the rope.'

'Och, get it yourself.' This was the usual nature of communication.

After a similar exchange that particular morning, Pi'taki scooped all the dishes up into a bucket and sulkily went down to the creek to wash them. Frances was glad to be rid of her for a while and continued to work, humming to herself as she shook out the bedding from the tents. The pack-horses snorted as the dust irritated their nostrils. But for their heavy breathing, and the flap of the blankets as she aired them, she might have heard the sudden footfall on the stones. As it was, they appeared as if from nowhere and she was surprised when she looked round to see five men standing in the entrance to the camp. The cover went limp in her hand and she shielded her eyes from the sun's glare with the other.

'Morning. I didn't hear ye coming,' she called to them. A couple of the men removed their hats and there were uneasy smiles all round. They were unshaven and dishevelled, as if they had slept in their clothes. She thought they could be settlers or freighters who had been on the trail for days and asked, 'Are ye from round here?'

A large man came forward, wiping his hands on his grimy shirt-front. 'Just passin' through, ma'am.' He seemed agitated. 'Just looking for a little hospitality.' The others grinned animatedly from behind him.

There was something wrong Frances thought, as she tried to get the measure of them. 'Some coffee, maybe?' she offered, going to the fire. There was still heat in it and she squatted down to set the kettle on. She heard heavy footsteps as the man's boots came to rest close by her and her eyes followed the line of his body as she rose to face him. He gripped her arm firmly and kicked the ashes over the flames to deaden them.

'Not the kind of hospitality we had in mind,' he said in a cold, steely voice.

It took a few seconds before Frances realised the danger she was in. Blinded by the light of the sun, she scanned the face that now bore down on her. She could see the sweat come in runnels and cling in shining beads to his moustache. There was a residue of liquor on his breath and in the oppressive heat the animal smell from his body was sour and acrid. Snatching off his hat, he threw it to the ground, revealing an almost bald head with a few greasy tails of hair plastered against it. She was about to yell out but a large hand clamped across her mouth while with the other he pushed her arms in a tight grip behind her body. With legs flaying, she kicked out while the man thrust her backwards through the tent flap and onto the ground. Wild terror flickered across her features as she struggled under the leaden weight that pinned her down and she tried to sink her teeth into the palm that smothered her face and muffled her screams.

The air in the confinement of the tent was thick and close. The man was breathing heavily now, his rheumy eyes glittering. He let go his grip to wipe off the sweat and in an instant, Frances managed to pull one arm free. With desperate fingers she scrabbled and scraped the floor for a chain or a pole, anything to beat off her attacker. But the survey equipment had all gone on ahead and for once there was nothing within reach. The man laughed as she pounded his chest with her fist before he again constrained her. He tugged the cloth from her hair and pushed it deeply into her mouth, gagging her.

'Get in here and hold her down,' he bawled to the others.

They squeezed into the cramped space and her arms were pulled out and held against the floor. Astride her on his knees the man roughly unbuckled his belt and slowly she stopped struggling as the inevitable horror began to take hold. For a second, the only sound or movement seemed to be the frantic thudding of her heart amplified in her ears. Brilliant, hazy daylight coursed in through the triangular opening of the tent and the air became stifling. Choked by the scarf in her mouth, she felt she would suffocate and the faces that looked down on her seemed like a pack of wolves circling two adversaries, hungry for the remains. Roughened hands urgently thrust back the folds of unfamiliar petticoats, fumbling with the string of her drawers and the man spat impatiently, tearing at the cotton material. The others gripped her ankles and her legs were pushed apart. She thought she might faint and closed her eyes half in hope, half in resignation.

Suddenly, all the commotion stopped, frozen. No one moved. It was as if a spell had been cast over them and all the antagonists were turned to stone. Frances felt the hands on her body slowly relax their grip and slide off. Her chest heaved as she struggled to breathe through the gag but nothing else moved except the buzzing flies. Confused, she looked at the others and their tense faces conveyed fear. The man was still crouched over her. Then she saw the sunlight flash across the long, cold blade that was held against his throat. The very presence of its scathing edge was violence itself, without imagining what havoc it might wreak on human flesh. And to look into the eyes of the one who wielded it was to know that horror was possible.

A thin line of blood seeped into the folds of the man's sweaty neck. He was panting like a dog in terror, fearing that at any moment he would hear the sound of his own breath escaping as his throat was cut. Frances gave a little gasp as she saw the brown knuckles tense over the horned handle.

'She ain't bluffin', Jake, she ain't bluffin' I tell ya,' one of the men gulped.

Pi'taki motioned to Frances to get out and she scrambled to her feet. Stumbling into the open, she ripped the scarf from her mouth and drew in great draughts of air. The men sprinted out after her, making a frenzied escape through the trees to the clearing where they had left their steeds. Clouds of dust were thrown up as they galloped off, leaving their leader behind.

In a daze, Frances made her way down to the creek where she hitched up her skirt and waded in knee-deep. As if to cleanse herself of what might have been, she carelessly sloshed the water between her legs. At the same time she was vaguely aware of Jake's muffled scream and urgent running footsteps as he bolted for his horse. But when she returned to the camp, only the knife cleaned of the gore was driven in the dirt to remind her. Vacantly she slumped beside the dying embers, pulling her knees up to her chin and shivering slightly as if she was cold. She was only dimly conscious of the other woman who was hastily rekindling the fire and blowing on the sticks to raise a flame.

Pi'taki squatted beside her and wrapped a blanket round her trembling shoulders. Then she heated an aromatic tea in a small tin and thrust it forward. Dutifully Frances sipped the strange bitter liquid and very gradually she felt a little warmth coming back to her body. She watched Pi'taki tying up the bed-rolls and loading them onto the mules, packing the saddle-bags and filling the water bottles. Feeling guilty, Frances tried to get up but her legs weakened beneath her and she was made to stay by the fire.

She was unaware of the extent of time passing but the sun was high overhead when the sound of hooves drew near again. Pi'taki went forward as the familiar figure of Daniels rode into view.

'What in hell have you two been doing?' he shouted, swinging down from the saddle. 'We get back hungry an' thirsty and there ain't no food waitin' – ain't even a camp. You should've been well on our trail by now.' Getting no reply, he strode around in frustrated anger, pausing to take in the hunched, motionless figure seated by the fire. 'And what's got into you?' he said gesturing to Frances but she remained detached and still.

'She is sick,' Pi'taki offered in blunt explanation.

'So sick she can't speak up for herself?' Daniels pushed back his hat brim and groaned in exasperation. 'Damn, this is all we need. Knew it would hold us up bringin' darned women on the trail . . . Well, you better tell her, if she's gonna carry on like this she better get off back to Calgary. We ain't got the time for lookin' after sickly folk on this trip.' He turned and walked briskly back to his steed. 'Pi'taki, we have to make Wolf Creek by sundown or there'll be trouble. Move this lot – with or without her.' Then as he remounted, the horse wheeled round, reared once and galloped away.

How they achieved the trail to Wolf Creek Frances never knew. The first time she was fully aware of what was going on around her was when later she opened her eyes and found that she was lying in her own tent. Unsteadily she got to her feet and went outside. The men had not yet returned and the camp was peaceful. Dusk was just drawing in and she saw that all the gear had been unloaded, the other tents were pitched and already a good fire was roaring. She went across to where Pi'taki was distributing hay to the horses and stood, consumed with the inadequacy of how she might express her gratitude.

'Pi'taki, I . . .'

The other woman looked up. 'Now you are well?' she half-asked, half-stated.

Frances smiled. 'Yes, yes I'm fine now, I had a good sleep.' She paused, searching with difficulty for the right words but was interrupted before she spoke.

'Good.' Pi'taki gestured towards the fire. 'Start cooking. Soon the men will be back.'

Later that evening, when everyone was fed and retiring for the night, William joined Frances in their tent. It was the first opportunity they had had to talk all day. He smiled, leaned across and kissed her. 'I hear you were having a job keeping up with us,' he joked. 'When Daniels came back and said ye were dawdling way behind —'

'Is that what he said?' she asked still confused.

'Aye, ye should've seen the faces – we had to go without our dinner!'

Frances's mind raced to interpret the events of the day. Obviously Daniels had not thought it important enough to tell William of her 'illness'. And, since Pi'taki had managed to make camp by the appointed deadline, it was clear nothing more had been said. Dimly she remembered the care she had received from the older woman, the gentle solicitude that had lulled her back into a sense of security. She could breathe freely now – it was almost as if the horror of a few hours ago had never happened. She peered out into the night. Across the clearing, Broken Claw sat before the fire smoking a long pipe. In time, Pi'taki emerged and sat beside him, her legs folded under her and the plaid shawl held fondly about her shoulders. As Frances watched, in her mind she was momentarily transported thousands of miles back to West Wemyss. She remembered the love with which the shawl had been given to her and sensed, despite everything, that Elspeth Douglas would not have disapproved.

William's voice came from behind. 'I see Pi'taki got her hands on that shawl after all. What happened, don't tell me you gave it to her?'

'What if I did?'

'Nothing, but I thought you were always at each other's throats?'

Frances shrugged off the remark. 'Och, I wasn't feeling well this morning, and she was good to me. It's just a way of saying thank you.'

'What was wrong, ye didn't say ye were poorly?' He sounded concerned but when he looked at her face there was colour in her cheeks. 'Ye seem all right to me.'

'I am,' she replied, 'dinna worry, it's over now.'

6

The long, hot summer seemed endless, with no sign of autumn breaking the glorious weather. The relationship continued to improve between the two women and a new sense of harmony settled over the camp. Frances and Pi'taki spent longer together, becoming better acquainted and more tolerant of each other's ways. A trust had developed and, in time, something approaching friendship began to emerge. By the end of September there was a grading party north of Red Deer, advancing on the survey team with all speed. They were now up among the Bear Hills where the native people on the reserve were showing some resistance to the survey crossing their land. Day after day, Broken Claw spent hours in negotiation between them and the chief engineer and it was not until mid-October that a satisfactory agreement was reached and surveying could recommence.

During the wait, reports had reached their camp of an epidemic afflicting the horses used by the grading teams. William went to see Dewar on his return. 'This business with the horses is a worry,' he said. 'It looks as though a couple of ours have taken bad. We've isolated them, but losing two now will hold up the work.'

'Aye, you could be right.' The engineer looked thoughtful. 'I tell you what, I've to go up to Edmonton the day after tomorrow. If you come with me, you could bring back replacements.'

William was delighted to be asked to go. In the copies of the *Edmonton Bulletin* that Dewar brought back to camp, he had seen notices advertising a forthcoming agricultural show. 'Could I ask you a favour, Mr Dewar?'

'What is it?'

'This trip to Edmonton would be a chance for me and Frances to check out the farming prospects in the area. And I wondered . . .'

'You wondered if she could come along with us.' Dewar pondered the idea and smiled. 'I don't see why not, son. You've had little enough time to yourselves – I suppose a few days away from camp will do you both good, eh?'

'Oh, it's braw to be out together like this!' Frances clung to William's arm as they walked up the main street of Edmonton.

He smiled and put his hand over hers. 'I'm supposed to be here working.'

She pulled a face. 'You arranged about the horses, and so you've done all you can today. And Mr Dewar said we don't need to go back till tomorrow.'

The prospect of a whole extra day on their own had put them both in a holiday mood. They walked up and down surveying the shops, peering at the rows of bottles and jars in Daly's drug store, sampling the fresh-baked bread in the bakery, and tasting the preserves and pickles that were on display to be judged for prizes in the show. The Edmonton Agricultural Society was holding its annual exhibition and farmers had come from all around to show their livestock and crops. The Hudson's Bay Company would be presenting a silver cup to the winner and competition was fierce. All the farmers were settlers who had originated in other places, some from other countries, and many had never worked the land before. William was intrigued by this since he would soon find himself in the same situation. With growing enthusiasm, they wandered between the stalls, William asking questions. They found that everyone was eager to talk about homesteading and he became engrossed in conversations about the quality of the grain, the best time to sow, the problem of threshing operations, even the varieties of hens that had been introduced.

Late in the afternoon, William and Frances took a break and sat down on the grass at the back of McCauley's Livery Stables. 'Listen to this,' he said to her, avidly reading from a pamphlet he had picked up. 'Last year there was a late frost in all the eastern states, Manitoba and the southern part of the Northwest – but absolutely none at Edmonton!' He flipped the pages. 'And here it says that during the years of drought, Edmonton still had a higher yield of grain than anywhere else.'

'Well, they would say that, wouldn't they?' she laughed. 'It's written by the Edmonton Board of Trade. They'd hardly say it was the same as everyplace else.'

But William was transfixed. As he read further, he became convinced of the perfect suitability of that part of the land for farming. 'No danger of drought, blizzards, grasshoppers – plenty of water and timber – this is ideal for us,' he declared, slapping the paper with the back of his hand. 'Dinna laugh, I'm serious. This is going to be our future home.'

'I know,' she said tenderly, 'but ye canna believe all ye read in that.'

He was not listening. 'Let's go into the Dominion Lands Agency,' he said suddenly.

'What for?'

'I just want to see how much settlement there is around here.'

'But, William, it's too soon for that – you'll just go getting yourself all worked up when ye canna do anything about it yet.'

'There's no harm in looking – come on,' he begged and so, resignedly, she got to her feet.

In the land registry office, the clerk patiently explained all the rules and procedures. 'You get six months,' he said, 'but as it's late in the year now, we extend it till the first of June, next year. Remember though, you've got to take possession and be living on the homestead site by first of June.' Once William heard that there was no stopping him. The ten dollars was on the table before they had even selected the spot.

'You're mad,' Frances whispered as the clerk went to get the township register. 'We canna move in till next year. What's the point of paying for it now?'

'You heard the man, there's settlers arriving every week. If we dinna get our money down now, we'll get left with the dregs.'

'Well, I hope we can save enough in the time.'

'We've got till next year. Besides, the railroad'll be here by then and that'll bring settlers flooding in. We've got to take this chance now, while we can.'

She had not the heart to deter him further. He was so absorbed in the moment and after all the weeks of hard work it was wonderful to have such hope, to share such excitement in the future. When they came out, he wheeled her round and round. 'The south-east quarter of section two, township fifty-two, range twenty-seven, west of the fourth meridian!' He repeated the co-ordinates of the land they had selected over and over again. 'We're landed gentry now!'

'Hardly gentry,' she laughed.

'Just you wait and see. Give it time and we'll be making a success of it – I guarantee ye. Now, let's celebrate, Mrs Munroe!'

The next morning, they set off early after packing food for the journey in the cart and hitching the extra horses to the back. Frances, enjoying the luxury of a real bed for a change, grumbled at having to leave so early, but William insisted. 'It's a long way to Wolf Creek and I have a wee detour in mind.' She was intrigued but he refused to say any more.

They set off up the bumpy trail and headed into the beautiful rich rolling countryside beyond South Edmonton. The sky was the fiercest blue and yawned above and ahead of them with an expansiveness only possible in such terrain. Around midday, William pulled up at a spot along the Battle River valley.

Frances stood up in the cart and looked about her. 'Oh, what a lovely place,' she breathed.

'Aye, I thought you might like it. Worth getting up for, eh?' He led the horses to the trees and tethered them.

'How did ye know about it?' she asked, as he came back and lifted her down.

'The surveyors were all over this land before they agreed on the route of the railroad. I remember Randall mentioning it – I think this must be the spot he meant.'

She looked around and took in the sight. 'It's strange. I feel like we're the first folk ever to have come here.'

A babble of bird song and the distant rushing of water on the huge river-bed were the only sounds that disturbed the calm. They took off their boots and with bare feet on the cool grass walked to where the eddying waters merged in a slow-moving pool. Standing together, they watched the amber-jewelled sunlight dazzle the surface of the water. The lonely call of the loon echoed upstream from the dark green recesses and a heron darted, emerging with a flash of silver in its beak. It was impossible to say a word that could make greater sense of the place and they stood, unspeaking, penetrated by its beauty.

The heat and the stillness bore down on them. With a sudden movement William tore the shirt from his sweat-soaked back and, taking a long run up to the river's edge, he jumped high and noisily, hitting the water like an explosion. The eruption as he submerged drove the birds from the trees in a profusion of colour and alarmed calls that quickly faded into silence. Frances remained entranced by the serenity of the place, watching him as he ducked and dived under the surface, emerging in the leaf-thrown shadows at the far side and calling her to join him.

Slowly she unbuttoned her blouse and peeled off the constricting garment. It dropped to the ground still retaining the shape of her body. Unlaced, the cotton bodice followed. The heavy skirt and petticoats slumped after it in a heap at her feet. Stepping out of the flowering pile of discarded clothes, she tugged at the combs and released the weight of her hair. Then, unencumbered, she slipped into the water.

William was transfixed by the sight of her nakedness. He watched her strong beautiful body descend with ease into the pool, her hair spreading out on the surface. He gazed as though it was an illusion,

101

something ephemeral that might disperse at any moment if he took his eyes away. With hardly a ripple she dipped under the surface. Coming up again she shook her head and swinging droplets curved in a wide arc falling like rain about her. William felt the breath catch in his throat as she swam rhythmically towards him. She reached out her hand and drew him to her. Still mesmerised he felt her legs entwine around him. She pressed her mouth sensuously to his and as she did so, the silk of her water-borne hair fell slithering over his shoulders.

'This is unexpected,' he breathed.

Frances looked into the sharp blue of his eyes, made all the more stunning by the intermittent flickers of sunlight. 'Ah well, it was you that taught me to make the most of the unexpected.'

'And was I right Frances, are ye happy that ye came away with me?'

As if in answer, she embraced him again. Then taking him by the hands, she drew him out of the water and together they lay down in the lengthening shadows between the trees. Warmed by the golden afternoon, the canopy of branches overhead became an echo chamber for the mellifluous sounds of their love-making.

William pulled the blanket around to cover her shoulders, pushing back wet tendrils of hair from her forehead as he gazed at her. 'Ye never spoke of it but I ken a woman like you must have left a sweetheart behind.'

The reminder of the past jarred, strangely at odds with this all too rare and tender moment. Where once such a mention would have brought a stab of desperation to torment her, now there was only a residue of sadness. Briefly it stirred within her, then settled again.

'A woman like me?' She smiled reassuringly into his face. 'I was just a lassie, and it all seems so long ago.'

'Aye it does,' he agreed. 'Think how far we've come in such a short time. You've no regrets, Frances?'

She kissed him again. What regrets there were had no place here and she could not change what had gone before. She had made her choice and now felt she could live with the decision. A sureness of the future was growing within her and a deepening love for this man was an added bonus to the chance she had taken in following him.

William thought of the last few months and was humbled by an awareness of the times he might have lost her. His desire at that moment was so strong that he was seized with a sudden irrational fear that she might somehow leave him now. Though she was about to speak he put his fingers to her mouth, driven by a sudden need to make amends.

'I ken it's no been easy, Frances, putting up with living in that wee camp but I swear I'll make it up to ye. I promise this time next year it will all be different. We'll have our first harvest in and you'll be rocking on your own front porch, watching the sun go down.'

She wanted to reassure him of her faith in him but before she could, she saw the familiar urgency come into his eyes. He pulled her close again and, with a desperation that had been absent in their earlier, more languorous love-making, kissed her hungrily now as if life itself depended on it.

Later, as the cart dawdled homewards, they sat wrapped in each other's arms, instilled with the intoxication of the day. A flamy sunset filled the sky and the great bronze bowl of the sun cast a massive shadow behind them as it slowly slid towards the earth.

7

By the late autumn, the survey camp was preparing to move back and spend the winter at Red Deer. Frances greatly looked forward to this. The weather had suddenly turned much colder and living in tents was no longer the novelty it had been. She was growing tired of the early rising, the constant packing and unpacking and the relentless, routine chores. Some days, her muscles ached and she felt light-headed with the strain of lifting, and even the simple act of bending down became arduous. Though Frances tried to hide her fatigue, Pi'taki seemed to sense it and more often than not she took on the heaviest duties. It was hard to imagine getting through the day without her help but soon she and Broken Claw were due to return to their own people and Frances knew she would miss her.

When news reached the camp that several of the men in the Red Deer grading team had gone down with typhoid, Frances became worried. She grew fearful that her lassitude, feelings of weakness and sick frailty were early symptoms of the disease and wondered how she would find the words to tell William. When he was asleep, she wept silently and, in the day time, hid her distress from Pi'taki and tried to push the dread from her mind.

At twilight one evening, they sat together waiting for the men to return to camp. A great fire crackled before them, taking the chill off the air but Frances was gloomy and stared into the flames. She felt vaguely nauseous. Her back ached no matter which position she tried and it was no longer possible to conceal her discomfort.

'I don't know what's the matter with me,' she yawned. 'I'm that tired.'

Pi'taki prodded the glowing embers with a stick and took a light for her slender pipe. Wisps of pungent smoke curled into the atmosphere as she puffed, savouring the tranquillity of the moment. Then quite suddenly and with calm assurance in her voice, she spoke.

'It is the baby.'

Frances's mouth dropped open, all signs of her discomfort momentarily forgotten. 'What did ye say?' Pi'taki did not reply. She had made herself plain and there was no need to repeat it. Frances stood up and felt her stomach. She looked again at the old woman. 'Ye mean I'm pregnant – this is no the fever?'

Pi'taki sucked her teeth. 'Tsst, fever!' She spat the word disdainfully as if the very thought was ridiculous.

'I'm pregnant?' Frances whispered, disbelieving. Then she said it again, out loud to convince herself and immediately her discomfort disappeared. Without thinking she flung her arms around Pi'taki's neck in gratitude, as if somehow she had been responsible for the miracle. As she did so, she fancied she saw the ghost of a smile drift across her weather-beaten features.

The men returned, the news was announced and there were many good-natured, if somewhat self-conscious congratulations for the mother and father-to-be. In the middle of the night, William shook Frances awake. 'What if it comes before we're on the homestead?' he whispered anxiously. In all the excitement, he had forgotten to ask when the baby was due.

'Och, dinna worry about that,' she smiled. 'He'll no be born till July.'

'It's to be a lad then, is it? And how did ye work that out?'

'Pi'taki said so. She told me he'll be born in July, when the okonoki berries start to swell. A boy, that's what she said.'

'God almighty, Frances, and you believed her?'

'Of course I believed her.'

'I suppose she knows everything, does she?' William was sarcastic.

The conviction in her voice silenced him. 'Aye, I think maybe she does.'

Shortly after that, Pi'taki and Broken Claw left the camp. Frances awoke one morning to find the tipi gone. There were no fond farewells, no promises to meet again and, though she had expected it soon, she felt strangely rebuffed by their sudden disappearance. She had come to look on Pi'taki as a friend and would miss her sure presence, her dependable strength. The blunt departure left an unexplained emptiness in her life but, as the days passed, her thoughts became ever more concentrated on the future.

William had decided to finish work in the spring of the following year. This would give him a month to prepare things on the homestead and be resident by the required date of occupancy. Frances agreed she would remain with the big grading camp until he returned for her. With luck and hard work, they would be well settled on their land before the birth of their child.

8

With only a month's respite, when the snows were at their worst, the work on the Calgary to Edmonton railroad continued unabated. A large outfit of men wintered at Red Deer and William got work supervising a grading team. Life in the new camp was very different. The mobile box-cars moved along the track and so kept up with the body of workers as the rails were laid. It was a big change in routine for Frances with no more dismantling tents and equipment every few days. There were however, a great many more people around and, since the graders were always miles ahead, she saw less of William now. She resumed service with Toh Seng in the bustling activity of the food wagon, and it was far more suited to her advanced state of pregnancy than the heavy work of the survey camp.

As planned, William quit work on the first day of May, by which time rails were laid to the Blind Man river crossing. There were a lot of men who were sorry to see him go and, before the stage arrived to take him to Edmonton, he moved among them, saying his goodbyes. Frances waited with the baggage and watched as they slapped him on the back, wishing him well and shaking his hand. She knew he would miss their companionship and wondered how he would fare out on the desolate plains by himself. The night before, he had talked at length into the small hours and mused about how much he could achieve on their land in a month before he returned for her.

'The first thing is to get the well dug,' he explained, 'there's no shortage of water if ye go down twenty or thirty feet. I'll get that out the way before I start on the house. Plenty of timber round there, and if I can hire a bit of local help, we'll build ye the finest house you've ever lived in!'

'Dinna push yourself, there's a limit to what ye can do. And stop worrying about the house – I'll be glad just to be out of a tent.'

But William was unstoppable. Once again he had that voracious hope in his bright eyes and would not entertain a negative thought. 'A fine house, my lass, just like I said, is that no right, Rory?' He patted her swollen bulge under the covers and she smiled resignedly. There had been more talk – about what could still be planted out at that late date, the farming implements he would get in Edmonton, what size of cart he would need to buy to make the journey from there, and much else. But Frances had lost the thread of it. Exhaustion overcame her and she was in deep sleep before he realised she was no longer listening.

Their homestead plot lay far to the north west of the rail camp and the country between was rough and dangerous. 'Dinna try and come back over the hills,' Frances warned as she kissed him goodbye the next morning. He seemed impatient but she persisted. 'Leave the cart in Edmonton and come back for me on the stage, now promise.'

'Och woman, it's you who should be taking care,' he said, without answering the point. Before she could insist, he held her close, feeling the warm mound of her belly against him. 'I reckon you'll be moved up around the Bear Hills by the first of June so I'll come for ye there.' She nodded and the coachman blew a whistle to summon William aboard. 'I love ye,' he whispered, taking both her hands in his and kissing the knuckles. With that he swung his baggage up on top and climbed inside.

'The first of June,' she murmured as she watched him leaning dangerously out of the window, waving his cap in the air and shouting to the well-wishers. Then all at once, the stage disappeared up the trail, leaving only a cloud of dust.

That evening, Frances walked around the camp, unable to sleep. William would just be arriving in Edmonton, she thought. She imagined him rising early the next day, full of enthusiasm and off to McCauley's to choose a good horse. They had agreed that a second-hand cart would save them a bit and the same for a plough if he could get it. Then it would be into the hardware store for the tools, nails, rope and wire – the endless items of self-sufficiency. So preoccupied was she with these thoughts, that she almost walked by the tipi without noticing it. Frances stood and stared at the markings that had become so familiar to her the year before and realised with delight that Pi'taki and Broken Claw had returned.

The foreman, who had replaced William, explained to her later. 'We're pushin' up through Indian country now and don't want no trouble. Broken Claw knows how to keep the peace – he's a good negotiator just like his chief Crowfoot was. They say he's distantly related, you know.' Frances learned that Crowfoot had died the year before and Broken Claw had no wish to stay on the reserve if he could avoid it. The government was trying to get them to turn to subsistence farming but he regarded this as women's work and would have nothing to do with it. Pi'taki's opinion on the subject was never aired but Frances detected an aura of resignation about them both which had not existed before. Nevertheless, the reunion was very welcome and they spent a lot of time together. Pi'taki frequently pressed food of her own making on Frances, explaining that it would be good for the baby. She particularly encouraged her to eat the dried meat and berries that had been made into pemmican and, though it took a while to acquire a taste for it, Frances was convinced of its nourishing qualities. Where once she had spurned the very thought of Pi'taki's customs and habits, she now listened and learned and grew in respect.

This relationship, however, was observed with some disdain by the others. Frances began to feel less in tune with the pattern of camp life than when William had been there and her dependence on Pi'taki as a friend increased with the gradual cooling of those around them.

9

The first of June passed and for twelve days thereafter Frances was sleepless with worry and her concern developed into fear as she scanned the horizon for sight of William's return. The stage came and went without him. Night after night she stood at the entrance to the camp, listening for the sound of cart-wheels and the thud of hooves on the dusty ground, and many times it was only Pi'taki's inducements that persuaded her to come back inside.

Frances begged the graders and teamsters to form a search party but the foreman would not allow it. 'Your husband don't work for this railroad no more. We can't go wastin' precious time wandering around them hills.'

'Have a heart,' she appealed, near to tears. 'I still work for ye – surely ye owe me something?'

The foreman looked uncomfortable. 'We don't owe you nothing,' he said stiffly.

'Come on, boss,' someone piped up in her defence, 'she's damn near about to drop that child she's carrying.'

'All right,' he conceded reluctantly, 'guess you can do what you like on your day off – come Sunday you can take the horses and go look for him.'

Frances assumed that William had ignored her advice and tried to bring the cart back across country. There was little enthusiasm for the trip but after prolonged entreaties, she managed to get six volunteers. Then, while explaining the situation and thanking them all profusely in advance, William's cart suddenly appeared and rolled into the camp. Everyone stopped what they were doing and looked up. Frances could not believe her eyes but there he was, large as life, standing up on the buck-board and reining in the horse with a flourish.

Someone shouted, 'It's Bill Munroe! Get him a drink, boys!' William grinned, stretched out his arms and proclaimed, 'Well, folks, I'm a farmer now, what do ye think?' A cheer went up and somebody handed him a bottle. Still standing aloft, he pulled the cork with his teeth and was just about to take a swig when he caught sight of Frances.

She did not share the mood. All the anxiety of the waiting days surfaced in an outburst. 'Where have ye been?' she demanded to know.

'A fine welcome that is when you've no seen your man for a month.' William said it as much to the assembled group as he did to her.

'Six weeks,' she corrected him, the anger welling up inside her. 'Ye were meant to be back on the first of June – or did ye forget that?'

'Och, dinna fuss, woman, what's a few days – how long do ye think it takes to build a house and start a farm?'

'I'm no fussing, William. I've been worried sick about ye.' She was indignant now and did not care who knew it.

'Thought I wasn't coming back for ye, eh?' He tried to make a joke of it and the crowd egged him on, cheering.

'Ye think it's funny, do ye, when you've a bairn on the way and I dinna get sight nor sound of ye for weeks on end?'

He looked embarrassed and his mouth tightened. 'Frances, I've no wish to fight with ye in public.'

'I dinna care where it is, William,' she announced, eyeing the gloating faces, 'but you've some explaining to do. Ye know where to find me when you've finished celebrating.' With that, she crisply turned on her heel and walked away.

William's eyes followed her as she went, then he took a long pull on the bottle. 'Oho, looks like you're in for a hard time,' someone said.

As the evening wore on, sounds of merriment continued to float through the camp. Frances lay, furiously going over in her head what she would say to William when he came back. No doubt, she thought, the worse for drink. The baby kicked inside her and she spread her hands over her swollen belly to feel the tiny heels thud against her palms. 'Aye, you're a bit restless the night too, eh Rory?' she whispered.

Hours passed and her anger gradually subsided as the baby settled. Frances began to think over what she had said and a sneaking guilt crept into her thoughts. Maybe she had been too hard on William after he had struggled alone to get the homestead going. She remembered how drawn and tired he had looked. He had obviously had little sleep and pushed himself to the limits to finish the work in time. They had both underestimated how long it would take him. She stroked her belly again as if caressing the sleeping child. 'Just a few more weeks, Rory . . .' she sighed.

Another hour went by. The camp had grown quiet and she lay alert to every sound, waiting for William's footfall outside the tent. Unable to sleep, she realised how much she had missed him beside her all the nights he had been away and decided there would be no argument when he came back. She thought about what she would say, retracting her harsh words, and how generous he would be once he was alone with her, soothing away the tension that had welled inside her. She smiled. Tomorrow they would set off on their new life together in harmony, the way it should be.

She was dozing with these thoughts going through her head when a shout went up and a loud commotion erupted in the camp. Suddenly the sound of running feet was everywhere. Frances poked her head out. Someone screamed, 'Bear!' and several shots punctuated the night. She eased herself into her boots and pulled a blanket over her shoulders. Outside the camp was pandemonium.

'What's going on?' she asked, trying to make herself heard above the din. Ahead, a large crowd had gathered. With her lumbering gait she could not make her way through to see what had happened.

Then a voice called, 'Somebody better go get Frances Munroe.'

'I'm over here,' she answered tremulously, sensing something was badly wrong. People looked at her strangely. 'What is it? — I'm here!' she yelled, frantically now as she elbowed her way towards the front.

When they brought her round, her head was still swooning and she almost passed out again as the awful vision of William's twisted body loomed back into her memory. He had lain, crouched against the wheel of the cart, his head lolling awkwardly to one side where the neck had been broken. She could see the raw gash in his throat where the bear had struck and his piercing blue eyes were still wide with the terror of what he had seen. Frances gulped back her nausea and looked around. They had removed the body but, at her side, a puddle of blood remained. Listlessly, she rubbed her finger in it and asked, 'What happened?'

The concerned faces bore down on her. Everyone started speaking at once but she managed to piece together the sense of it. When the party dwindled, William had stumbled off. He had got as far as the cart, and curled up to sleep underneath. The smell of food must have lured the bear into the camp, they thought. It was a huge grizzly, though only one or two had actually seen it. Some had come running with guns and a couple had even got hurt in the mad firing that followed. Anyway, they thought the bear was injured and a hunting party had been immediately despatched to finish the job.

Frances slumped forward. They had given her something to deaden the shock and her senses felt numb. Somewhere, in the back of her mind, she knew something terrible had happened. She did not want the awfulness of it to be denied her but to feel the pain of it acutely, as William had done. Still, she could not fight the overpowering effects of the draught she had swallowed and they carried her in a half-conscious state to a boarding car.

The next day was lost to her. When the night came again her sleep was fitful. Several times she awoke in a daze to the muted noises outside and drifted off again. But each time, the dreadful, haunting horror returned clearer and more terrible than before.

The child stirred inside her and Frances opened her eyes. Outside all was quiet and she could see the moon's brilliance through the narrow window of the caboose. Unsteadily, she got to her feet and went out into the night. No one was about as she came past the box-cars and bunk-houses and picked her way heavily between the guy ropes and poles of the tents. All was quiet and a miasma of dwindling smoke drifted in layers over the camp.

Drawn to the edge of the trees, Frances felt the darkness close about her. Shafts of moonlight pierced the canopy above and dimly lit the path where she moved like a silent wraith. Again the baby moved inside her but she ignored it. A dark bulk strung between the trees loomed awesomely ahead and the great chains creaked as it slowly turned in its gallows. She drew closer until the pearly light illuminated the giant snout hanging down against the massive chest and a glint of white teeth showed between blackened lips. Stepping in front of the creature, she stared up. Even in death, an aura of power still clung to the bear. It towered above her, fully the height of two men and wide as a barn door, a heavy musky odour exuding from its glistening fur and overpowering the scents of the night. Frances clenched her fists at her side and her whole body trembled. The sight of the beast evoked both fear and fury in her. She wanted to run at it and thump out her anger on its great bulk but, as she raised her fist, a voice from behind stopped her short.

'Otanimm!' Pi'taki stood, her face carved in sharp relief by the moonlight. She came forward and put her arm under Frances's to steady her.

Frances let her head drop against Pi'taki's shoulder and sobbed wretchedly. 'I wish I was dead too.'

But the brown hand took her own and placed it against her belly. 'The child,' said Pi'taki, 'you must give him life.'

10

The simple funeral took place the next morning. Frances was given one last look at William before the crude coffin's lid was nailed down. They had closed his eyes and his face was now the mask of a stranger. She stared down at the lifeless form and felt nothing. Within her, a stony acceptance had been erected as a barrier against the pain. The anger and despair from the night before had somehow been pushed away, too acute for the moment to contemplate. As the final preparations took place, Frances moved and spoke with an uncanny control and the men watched her anxiously, unsettled by her apparent calm.

Since it was Sunday, many of the railroad gangs had broken from their work and a large number of them attended the service.

They shuffled out on to the plain in a dreary line, scuffing up the dust from the sage-brush as they went. The shrill lark's whistle and the promised heat of the day were at odds with the dour procession. Pi'taki remained at a distance among the shadows of the trees. She wanted no part of a Christian burial but curiosity and concern had brought her along. Frances was proud to see Broken Claw come with the men, though he limped painfully on his injured leg. She had only learned that morning of the bullet-wound he had received in the fracas with the bear.

She too walked heavily now, with downcast eyes, behind the sweating backs of the coffin bearers. How small the box looked, she thought, how insignificant. They stopped where a hole had been dug for the grave. Frances wondered who had chosen the spot, for it seemed an inhospitable place. The priest spoke the service for the dead and she stared ahead as the sound of his clear Irish voice was carried on the light breeze and over the bowed heads of the massed workmen. They made a stilted attempt at the twenty-third psalm, having only a few of the words and she listened, curiously detached, to its message of eternal hope.

When it was over, the coffin was lowered shakily into the grave. As the ropes were loosed, she tried to recall what William had said to her a year ago on the deck of the ship. She strained to bend down and scraped a fistful of dirt from the ground. Trembling, she cast it into the hole and the bitter words broke in her throat. 'Aye, William, what can go wrong?'

Abruptly the service was over and the men began to disperse, muttering words of condolence as they left. Frances stood by with the priest and watched the rich black Alberta soil shovelled roughly into the grave. A crude wooden cross was placed at the head and driven home with the flat end of a pick-axe. The name and date had been burned into the wood but already, as the dust and flies settled, it seemed an insubstantial thing. With their shovels over their shoulders, the remaining men turned to go and she wondered who would come this way again and how long it would stand until it disintegrated like the future, empty before her.

'If you would like me to conduct prayers for you, or if I can be of any comfort, Mrs Munroe . . .' the priest began.

'Thank you, Father, but I have no need of you. Save your prayers for the hopeful.'

'Everyone has hope, my dear,' he said, 'and yours will be renewed again in time. You must not give up, you have the child to think of. We cannot understand God's will but if we have faith —'

'Faith?' she said scornfully, pointing to the grave. 'You buried my faith in that box. Now please, Father, just leave me alone.'

'I know how you must be feeling but trust in the Lord and He will provide.'

Frances clapped her hands to her ears. 'Shut up! I've heard it all before,' she shouted. 'Go and leave me be!'

The priest sighed, crossed himself and hurried away. As the sun crept to its pinnacle of noon, Pi'taki returned to the grave where she found Frances seated on the ground. Her face was flushed and covered in a fine film of sweat, yet her skin was clammy and cold to the touch. She responded vaguely as the firm brown hand gripped hers and drew her to her feet. Then, as she stood up, she choked with a sudden convulsive action and curled forward as if in spasm.

'The baby comes,' Pi'taki said, supporting her.

'Aye,' Frances breathed, gripped with a knot of pain and her knuckles whitened as she waited for it to pass.

Nothing could have interrupted the state of mind into which the two women now retreated. When the first contraction was over, Pi'taki took the situation into her own hands and led Frances back to the camp. Without asking permission, she cleared a space on the floor of the bunk-house nearest the water-barrel. A few men who were off shift lay around on their bunks and were surprised as she burst in unannounced but quickly realised what was happening. Pi'taki dragged her own mat from the tipi and collected water and rags in readiness for the birth. When the last navvy had hurriedly left, she brought Frances in and sat her on one of the makeshift beds. By this time a second contraction had gripped her and, seeing the alarm on her face, Pi'taki waited until it had passed. Then she slipped out again, returning some time later carrying a handful of club-moss. Water was boiled and she crumbled in the foliage, setting it to one side for when it would be needed.

Outside, the sweltering afternoon heat bore down onto the yard. From time to time a couple of the men would stroll by with anxious, curious expressions but mostly they stayed way. Pi'taki covered the windows and within the wooden bunk-house it was dark and relatively cool. Frances, however, was now sweating profusely and she eagerly took the small cupfuls of water offered to her. Pi'taki wiped a wet cloth over her face, neck and shoulders as the spasms grew stronger and more regular. By late afternoon, the sound of desperate, involuntary moans hung on the still air. Pi'taki soaked and twisted a piece of rag and pushed it into Frances's mouth. As she bit down on the knotted wedge, she looked into the face of the old midwife with the urgent need for reassurance. Her eyes begged for it soon to be over but Pi'taki continued to attend to her comforts at a measured pace. She knew it was not yet time.

Later that evening, around eight o'clock, Frances began shifting about uneasily. She was now in a stupor of pain and her voice at times raised itself to a roar. Pi'taki pulled the mat to the floor at the end of the bunk and eased her down on to it. She removed Frances's outer clothing and her drawers, leaving only the thin cotton chemise and petticoat which could be easily hoisted up around the waist when she was ready to deliver. As she washed her down, the room grew dark and Pi'taki swiftly lit a spirit lamp in the corner to give her just enough light to see by. The agonising contractions were lasting longer now and, as Frances suddenly gasped with the urgent instinct to push, Pi'taki encouraged her to come forward into a squatting position and grip the two wooden poles at the end of the bunk. She rucked up the petticoat and watched for the emergence of the head as she murmured the old aboriginal words of inducement.

The head appeared from the opaque bag of water that burst at the moment of birth, flooding the floor around them. Pi'taki did not interfere but watched as the little face revealed itself. Frances was now breathing animatedly with the exertion of the delivery and pushed again with a strength that had been stored up somewhere in reserve, belying the almost total fatigue she felt. The remainder of the body came easily and Frances cupped her hands under the tiny form as it slid from beneath her. She stared in wonder at the child, a boy and, for the moment, nothing of the past interfered with her joy. Pi'taki glanced to check the mother was intact and turned her attention to the baby. He was still blue and breathing irregularly so she rubbed him roughly with a clean cloth to stimulate life and quickly a pinkness tinged his skin. So Rory Munroe came into the world – one month earlier than expected with the goose-greased, loose skin and worried look of the premature. But, most important of all, there was breath in his diminutive body.

Pi'taki then cleared out his mouth and wiped his eyes, helping Frances to lean back and rest as he was put to her breast. Since the death of her own children, Pi'taki had closed her heart to the memory of having an infant in her arms. But now, as she looked on, a vivid sense of her own deliverance returned. How different it had been for her. An aunt took the child and wet-nursed it for the first four days. Indeed now, had she milk in her own dried breasts she would have done the same. The new-born child would have its

114

ears pierced and greased twigs inserted in the holes. There would be a cleansing ceremony for the mother and a naming ceremony for the child. It felt strange that these customs should not take place now but these were not her people and, though she felt a strong bond of love as her eyes rested on the little face, this was not her child.

Frances eased herself back against the bed-roll that had been positioned behind her and relief flooded her features. Pi'taki, however, was now at her most vigilant, knowing this to be the time of greatest risk to the mother. She cleaned the blood and mucus from the mat but remained ever watchful for the moment when the after-birth would come. The waiting seemed endless. It was almost an hour before Frances again was on her haunches and the placenta was delivered. The navel cord, once fat and pumping, was by this time limp and greying. Pi'taki bent forward and, with a practised skill, bit it cleanly away with her teeth. She then poured little scoopfuls of the herbal decoction into Frances's mouth to stop the bleeding, rubbing her belly as she did so, to harden the uterus and make it contract. It was the first time in hours that their eyes fully met and now acknowledged a look from one to the other, inexpressible in words.

The redoubtable task of cleansing the area then began in earnest. As the child sucked voraciously on its mother's breast, Pi'taki scrubbed, mopped up and carried away the blood-soaked sheets. Lights burned outside in the camp and men stood around in a bunch waiting for news of the birth. Pi'taki stopped and regarded their eager faces then she nodded her head slowly to indicate all was well. A smiling sigh of relief rose from the group and they finally dispersed to go about their business.

The priority now was to let Frances rest and rebuild her strength. Pi'taki worked on through the next day, dividing her attentions between the mother and baby and her own ailing husband. Broken Claw's leg had become infected despite her efforts to treat the wound. It pained him more and, though she tried to get him to walk, he was now unable to leave the tipi. Meanwhile, Rory slept in the moss-lined buckskin bag that Pi'taki had laced to a cradle board and from which dangled the navel cord in a quilled pouch.

11

Days passed in the indulgence of her new-born baby and Frances was temporarily adrift in a timeless oasis. The distraction of her infant son would wipe all thought from her mind and hours were passed contemplating the wonder of this new life. And then suddenly the dreadful reality would return afresh, swooping down like a buzzard to tear at her heart and make her cry out in pain. At times, her sorrow gave way to a consuming rage and her thoughts circled in indictment of William. 'How could ye leave me – how could ye do that?' she sobbed angrily, clutching Rory to her as though this part of William could somehow atone for the lost man.

Pi'taki remained by her side constantly. Each time she tried to leave, even for a short period, Frances would grip her hand, pleading with her to stay. The old woman was no stranger to grief and the fear of abandonment that came in its wake. She also knew, only too well, that men die and children are born every day. Everyone in the camp had been delighted at the birth of Rory which had somehow subdued the horror of his father's death. Soon however, Frances and her son would be no longer special and the camp could not remain their home. For the time being, Pi'taki could at least try to ensure that the anguish of loss did not bring calamitous illness on the new mother.

Frances was forced to face harsh facts when after a few days the camp foreman made it clear she could no longer stay. Sympathy had dissipated quickly and her presence was just one more problem he had to deal with. He gave her a week to sort herself out. She looked at the sleeping child and although she was dreading the prospect, she realised a visit to town was now crucial, if only for his sake. Working the homestead alone was out of the question and only by discovering what funds were left could she try to address the future. She thought weakly of how William had always handled their money and she had no idea of what to expect from the account. Whether there would be enough to pay her passage home was one consideration – whether she had the stomach for it was another. Either way, she knew with certainty that she could no longer stay. Pi'taki watched with concern as Frances tied the baby to her chest in a sling, hitched the horse to her cart and headed for Edmonton.

When the Dominion and NorthWest Territories Bank opened its humble front door the next morning, she was the first to cross the threshold.

'Good morning.' Mme Lemieux stammered the greeting, slightly dismayed as Frances thrust past.

'Is your husband in?' she asked impatiently. The manager descended the stairs, acknowledged the look on his wife's face and hurried to open up the counter. Frances explained her business and waited, her fingers thrumming on the polished wood as he riffled through the books.

'Ah yes, here we are Mrs Munroe,' he said at last, 'I see your husband deposited one hundred and twelve dollars on the first of May, to add to the original deposit he made last October. Now this was drawn on over the following six days, leaving a total of, *un moment s'il vous plaît.*' He did a few calculations and Frances waited, holding her breath. '*Oui,*' he said, looking up, 'twenty-two dollars and sixteen cents.'

She opened her mouth to speak but it was a while before the words came out. 'You must be mistaken, Mr Lemieux, please check again.' He sighed but did as he was bidden. The result was, however, the same. Frances stared at him in disbelief.

He tried to help. 'You must understand, Mrs Munroe, to buy what is necessary for homestead life – the cost can be very large. Your husband was in fact quite prudent. He came here first for advice and would not consider a loan, even though I offered it. He wanted to keep a small amount in the account for emergencies as you can see.'

Frances picked up eagerly on this point. 'Does the offer of a loan still stand?'

'Not unless you intend to keep possession of the land and work the homestead – without that security we could not justify it.'

Frances shifted Rory to her other arm and pushed her hair back out of her eyes. The situation was impossible. 'There's no way I can work that land on my own,' she said wearily, 'but I had hoped there might just be enough to pay my passage home.'

Lemieux looked thoughtful. 'Could you not get back the things he took out to the homestead? There must be grain and a plough and what have you – they will have some value. Do you know how much work he achieved?'

'I've no idea. We didn't have time to talk about it before . . .' Frances's voice tailed off and tears came into her eyes.

117

Lemieux flushed with embarrassment. 'I am most sorry, madame,' he mumbled. Her silent tears made him uncomfortable and he fumbled for alternatives. 'Perhaps you could find work?'

'Oh aye, and who'll take care of this one?' she sighed, holding Rory up to his gaze.

'Yes, of course, I am sorry,' he repeated, and started to count out the money in front of her.

Sensing the atmosphere, his wife came forward tactfully. 'Maybe you could ask the railroad for help?' she suggested.

'What do ye mean?' Frances blinked, wiping her eyes.

Mme Lemieux smiled. 'Well, your husband, he worked for the company – perhaps they will make some provision for you. Surely it is worth a try, *non*?'

Frances felt cheered by the suggestion. 'You're right, I never thought of that. This sort of thing must happen all the time on a railroad. They're bound to help.'

Frances left the bank and wandered round to the back of the livery stables where she found a secluded spot and fed Rory before making her way to the rail terminus area of Strathcona. Work on the sidings and platforms was nearly finished now, awaiting the arrival of the last stretch of line from Calgary. A bustle of activity could be seen through the windows of the company offices. She walked with the baby to the entrance in the main building, pushed her way through to a door at the rear and turned the handle.

Angus Dewar looked up from his desk. 'Can I help you, lass?' he asked, removing his spectacles.

'Ye don't remember me then, Mr Dewar?' He shook his head, looking bewildered. She continued. 'I'm Frances Munroe. My husband worked on your survey team last summer.' The effort to mention William in a normal tone left her heart pounding.

'God, of course,' he said, smiling uncertainly in recognition. He motioned her to sit down. 'I – I heard what happened my dear, a tragedy. Please accept my sincere condolences.'

'Aye well, that was nigh on two weeks ago,' she said, keeping her voice calm and without emotion. 'I've no heard a thing from the rail company.'

'What do you mean?'

'Somebody should at least tell me if there's any pay due us – or compensation. I've a child to feed.' She untied the sling and loosed the wriggling infant, holding him forward for Dewar's inspection.

The chief engineer recoiled uncomfortably. 'Oh er, I see. Well, it's a bit out of my hands now. But just give me a minute and

I'll get someone to sort this out for you.' He swiftly left the room before she could say anything else.

It was some minutes before a thin clerk with a twitching mouth came to deal with her. 'Mr Dewar asked me to check the pay records,' he said, sifting through the filing cabinet. He finally pulled out a ledger and laid it on the desk. As he scanned the pages, running his finger down the lines, he spoke the names out loud. 'Mulrooney, Muniavich, ah here we are, Munroe.' There was a pause as he cleared his throat. 'Well, according to this your husband was paid off at the beginning of May.' He looked up at her and his mouth twitched again. 'First of all, there would be no question of compensation. Even if we had such a thing, your husband would not be entitled – he wasn't employed by us at the time of his death, you see.'

Frances glared at him. 'But what about me?' she responded vehemently. 'I worked in the food tent all the time he was away – does that no count for anything?'

The clerk became flustered and her manner irritated him. The railroad was almost completed and he was a busy man. 'I'm sorry, I know nothing about that. I wasn't aware that the company paid wages to women who travelled with their husbands. I assume you got your keep? Frankly, I'm surprised they allowed you to stay once he left the outfit.' He closed the book. 'Now, I really am very busy, if you think you're due anything you should take it up with the foreman at the camp.'

Outrage quickly gave way to rising panic. All avenues seemed blocked to her and she felt completely powerless. 'A lot of good that'll do. He's already told me to get out,' she said, raising her voice as though shouting could drive away the fear.

'Now look here,' he said firmly, 'I think they've been more than generous considering your, er, condition. After all, the railroad's no place for a woman.'

Genuinely angry now, Frances jumped to her feet but the baby began to fret, bringing Angus Dewar back into the room. 'What's going on here?' he asked, dismayed. 'This woman's just lost her husband, Thomas. Have some consideration, man!'

The clerk knitted his brows impatiently. 'I'm sorry, sir, but as I explained, there's really nothing we can do for her. I've checked the records and she's not owed a penny.'

Frances rocked Rory up and down in an effort to quieten him. She fixed both men with a withering look of contempt. 'You've made that very plain mister, your sympathy's touching.' She had

119

nothing left to lose and her acid retort silenced them for a moment.

'All right, Thomas, leave us.' Dewar waved the clerk away and waited till he and Frances were alone in the room. His manner and tone became stiffly paternal. 'He was a good man, your husband. No many around that you can trust like him, remember that, Frances.'

She felt like laughing in his face. Her trust in William had left her begging like a pauper from men who only had platitudes to offer. 'I'll try no to forget, Mr Dewar – it'll be a comfort to me in my widowhood,' she replied cynically, cradling the fractious child.

He would not meet her furious gaze and persisted in trying to keep in control of the situation. 'All right, I know how you must feel, my dear. I just don't want there to be any hard feelings with the railroad.' He cleared his throat nervously and sought for the right words. 'I for one was proud to have worked with William Munroe.' He nodded effusively, as if his utterance somehow explained everything. And, as though in answer, Rory's screaming reached a new pitch but Frances made no effort to quell him.

From the inside pocket of his jacket Dewar pulled out a leather wallet and tried to speak above the squalling noise. 'Here, take this,' he said, passing across a wad of notes. 'It'll pay your passage home. I wouldn't want to see his bairn suffer.'

Frances looked at the crumpled bills. Her heart was pumping with rage and she wanted to throw them back in his face and shout, shame on you! Instead she felt every drop of pride drain from her as her fingers slowly curled around the notes. She tucked them inside Rory's shawl and, with a quiet nod, stepped out into the burning street.

As the afternoon shadows lengthened into evening, Frances steered the cart back towards the camp. Track was being laid at the rate of three, sometimes four miles a day and was almost completed to within thirty miles of Edmonton. She had only a short distance to drive over Boggy Plain to reach her destination and so allowed the horse to amble slowly as she pondered her situation. With William gone and a child to consider, she felt she had no alternative but to return to Scotland. A vague plan had formed in her mind but she could muster little enthusiasm for it. After collecting her possessions from the camp, she would take the cart down to Red Deer and sell it there. Then she would pick up a supply train or the stage going south to Calgary and wait in town for a few days. When she could face the journey with Rory, the Canadian Pacific Railroad would carry her back to the eastern seaboard and the boat for Scotland. Her stomach lurched with apprehension at the idea. But better to be destitute in the familiarity of West Wemyss than to die homeless amongst strangers. When the time came, she would worry about where to go and who might take her in, especially now she had the baby. She looked down at his little flushed cheeks and smiled. The dark hair framed his face and, sleeping soundlessly in the papoose bag, he was hardly distinguishable from a native child. She thought about Pi'taki, how much she had influenced his coming into the world. In the midst of all the misery, she had been the one enduring factor in their lives, the one presence that would be missed. Frances determined somehow to express her gratitude and vowed this time their parting would not be so sudden. Impatient to see her again, she quickened the horse to a canter and let thoughts of the future drift away on the rushing wind.

'Well, doesn't anybody know where she is?' Frances appealed, looking round at their blank faces. 'Shouldn't we go and look for her?' Nobody seemed keen, or indeed interested. She sat down on a log and contemplated the awful news. It was almost impossible to believe that Broken Claw could have died so quickly. Despite the rapid spread of infection, he had resisted all medical treatment they had offered. She wept to think how Pi'taki must have tried with her herbs and root concoctions to stave off the advancing disease, all to no avail. But where was she now? The tipi still stood at the edge of the camp, their meagre belongings inside.

She listened while the men related how Pi'taki would not go near the body once it was confirmed that her husband was dead – neither would she have him buried.

'Had to bring in Indians from the reserve to take him away. Damned nuisance, and cost us a few bucks too,' the foreman complained.

'But those are no her people, they're no Blackfoot,' Frances protested. 'How could you?'

'Just another dead Indian as far as I'm concerned,' came the reply.

She was shaken by his callousness. 'Christ, what's going to become of her now?'

'Dunno.' The foreman shrugged. 'You should've seen her though – went loco, wailing and carryin' on. Cut her hair and I heard said she chopped off a finger too.'

'Jeez, I wish I'd seen that,' someone else contributed.

Frances winced, her heart sank at the appalling news. 'Which

121

way did she go?' she asked, an edge of contempt now creeping into her voice.

'Just wandered off. Ain't no need to bother goin' after her – she'll be back for her stuff.'

'She'll no come back here, you fool!' Frances fought to suppress her fury with them. 'Now come on, tell me which way she went.'

'Hell, how do I know?' He shrugged again.

'One of ye must've seen her.' Her voice had risen to a pitch of desperation and they looked on, astonished. She waited, unwilling to give up.

Then one of the men vaguely remembered. 'Out towards the Bear Hills – thataways, I think,' he gestured.

From that moment, Frances reacted as if driven by some supernatural force. The apathy of only a few hours before was exorcised by a burning determination that she would not suffer another loss so soon. She raced to the bunk-house and collected her belongings. Then she dismantled the tipi, throwing everything into the cart in a mad jumble. Despite the commotion, the baby slumbered on peacefully. She wedged his cradle-board carefully under her feet as she climbed aboard and smacked the reins across the horse's back. Then, without a word she urged it forward, out towards the distant hills where the sun already clung in blazing stripes across the sky.

12

Frances left the baby with Pi'taki seated on a bench outside and went into the Dominion Lands Agency. As she pushed open the narrow door, she fought back the memory of her previous visit there with William, a day that had contained such hope and now seemed inconceivable. The small wooden shack on Edmonton's main street served as the base for all land transactions in the area. It was still a cluttered shambles of papers, maps and ledgers strewn over the tables and the clerk who looked up from the counter as she entered may well have been the same man as before.

'My husband registered for a homestead last year,' Frances began in a cool, level voice. 'He died two weeks ago and I'm here to have the claim put into my name.'

There was a pause while the clerk considered how best to commiserate. 'I'm sorry to hear that, ma'am,' he said, lifting the hatch. 'Why don't you come through here and sit down.' He gestured to the back of the office where there was a comfortable chair and a kettle spitting on the stove.

Frances drew in a deep breath. She could not allow herself to weaken to tea and sympathy. When she had finally found Pi'taki, distraught and wandering in the hills, it had taken all her strength not to fall with her into consummate grief. It had been anger that had kept her in control, rage at the injustice that had rendered them to such a pitiful state and it was that same anger that drove her now.

'Let's just get on with it,' she said crisply, dispensing with the clerk's offer. 'Tell me what I have to do.'

'Er, yes,' he responded uncomfortably, dropping the hatch again and, assuming a business-like tone he picked up his pen. 'If you can just give me a few details, I'll look up the registration.'

Frances briefly outlined what she could remember and he went off to get the appropriate township register. She watched as he flipped through the pages until he found the entry and read it out. 'Yes, here we are, William Munroe, on the seventeenth of October 1890.' He looked up. 'Well, ma'am, the law allows for a widow, as succeeding head of the family, to take over a claim but you do understand that to qualify your husband had to be resident on the land by the first of June this year?'

'We knew that,' she confirmed. 'He was there all through May getting the house built and the well dug before he came to collect me – if ye don't believe me then go and see for yourself.'

The clerk gave an embarrassed little cough to convey that that clearly would not be necessary. 'I take it you've not seen the place yourself then?' he said.

'He was killed the night before we were due to go back. Since then I've had the baby and this is the first chance I've got to go out there,' Frances said, growing impatient. 'Look, does it really matter?'

The clerk was amazed by her candour and could only suppose that she was still in a state of shock. 'Well, I'll need to see the marriage certificate, Mrs Munroe, and – er, your husband's death certificate. You can bring them to me in your own time, when you're ready,' he smiled benignly.

'I'm ready now.' Frances fumbled in her pockets and passed across the crumpled documents.

Everything seemed to be in order and the clerk made the necessary adjustments to the ledger and pushed it forward for her signature. 'Is that all then?' she asked.

He closed the book and thought for a moment before speaking. 'If you don't mind me saying, is this a wise move?' Frances stared back blankly. 'What I mean, Mrs Munroe, is that it's quite an undertaking for a man with a wife and family to start a homestead – but a woman on her own with an infant —'

'I'm not alone,' Frances interrupted, but did not choose to explain. Pi'taki was with her and, where once she could not contemplate working the land herself, now another pair of hands made that seem possible. There had never been any discussion about it or persuasion needed. Frances had sat with Pi'taki until the light faded and her tears subsided. She had bound up the bleeding stump where her finger had been rudely hacked from her hand and pressed the water-bottle to her dried lips. 'Everything we own is in the wagon,' she had whispered in Pi'taki's ear, 'and I have a home for us to go to.' The wet brown eyes had stared at her, mute and world-weary but, when Frances pressed the sleeping child into her arms, she had climbed aboard without resistance.

The clerk gave up his efforts to dissuade her. He offered to draw a map to guide them but she refused saying, 'We'll find it,' and with a cursory nod in his direction she left the Land Office. She was anxious to get away from the questioning eyes, the wagging tongues that she knew had accompanied their arrival in Edmonton. A recently widowed white woman with an infant drew attention in a small community but here they had the added curiosity of her companion, a distrusted and unwanted Indian squaw. This had been vividly brought home to her when, shortly after arriving, they had gone into the hardware store to order supplies. Quite automatically, the storekeeper told Pi'taki to wait outside until he had served Frances. However, he had not quite anticipated her cool response.

'We're together,' she corrected him, 'and I'll thank ye to show some respect.' She flourished a long list in front of his bewildered face. 'We're no in here for just a needle and thread so ye better decide if ye want our custom – or maybe ye would like us both to leave?'

An accomplished salesman, the man knew better than lose a customer, even if these were a little eccentric. When his eyes scanned the list, he wished he had held his tongue. 'No problem, ma'am,' he said, pouring oil on the waters he had unwittingly stirred up, and offered an apologetic smile. 'You homesteaders?' he asked, drawing his own conclusions from the variety of supplies they needed. ' 'Cos if you don't mind my saying, why don't you let the men folk come in and settle this between us? Maybe we can come to some arrangement about the cost – tell your husband I could probably do him a good deal.'

Frances stared at him coldly. 'I'm sure you could, but I doubt he'll be coming in unless he's risen from his grave.'

The storekeeper was momentarily thrown by the comment and mumbled something inaudible to cover his blunder.

She sighed heavily, tired of waiting. Sympathy and concern for her well-being, genuine or otherwise, were of little use to her and she was overwhelmed by a desire to be rid of the place. 'Just add it up please, and tell me how much. We'll come back to collect it tomorrow.'

13

Their departure from Edmonton was delayed because of the time it took to load the cart. Heeding the advice of the local stables, Frances had replaced the wagon that had delayed William and, as she learned, given him so much trouble. Despite the fact that a fairly well-defined trail led out to the west, the ground would be rough and pitted with gopher holes. Stretches near Winterburn were renowned for the unavoidable bone-jarring stumps from felled trees, and a Red River cart with its huge, high wheels would be more suitable to tackle the journey. But these were not known for their spacious capacity. Frances had ordered what she thought they needed without taking the bulk into consideration. The massive bedstead was surrounded by sacks and bundles, buckets, cans of kerosene, lamps, rope, candles. More was then heaped on top: a washboard, bedding, tin bath, table and chairs, not to mention the food supplies. A wooden barrel was strapped to the side and pots, pans and a kettle were slung underneath from the groaning axle. When it was all piled high, a broad tarpaulin was tied over the bulging load and two caged chickens clucked in disapproval as they were slung unceremoniously on the shaft of a projecting broom. Finally, bringing up the rear, a dairy cow was tethered to the tail-board.

There was no room to ride and they accepted they would have to walk alongside the heavy load. One horse pulled the cart while the other dragged Pi'taki's travois, it too piled high with bundles. Ignoring the stares from passers-by, Frances handed the child to Pi'taki and took the lead-rope, tugging the horse forward. It strained in the harness and long seconds passed before it adjusted to the weight. Then, slowly, the wheels were dislodged from the mire, creaking and turning until a gradual, if shaky momentum was achieved. Keeping her eyes fastened grimly on the horizon, Frances led them away from the town.

For what remained of the day, they travelled in a south-westerly direction, the sun's rays spearing down on them and the child fretting in the dusty heat. The trail was easy to follow but, rutted and gouged by heavy farm wagons, it was no quicker than trying to cross virgin terrain. The ungreased wooden axle emitted a high, piercing creak with each revolution of the wheels. The penetrating noise drove all conscious thought from the mind and, whenever they came to a standstill, the silence seemed unnatural.

When darkness forced them to stop, Frances was unsure of how far they had come. The noise of the wheels was replaced by Rory's crying which blew an eerie sound across the empty plains. While Frances fed the baby, Pi'taki unpacked her travois. She produced a bundle of deerskins and with old, practised skills proceeded to erect a small tipi to shelter them for the night. With the child settled, Frances built a fire and quickly heated a perfunctory meal of corned beef and beans. Neither woman spoke as they sat facing the fire to eat, locked in their own private sorrows. Since leaving, most of the few words they addressed to each other were to do with practicalities and the past was not alluded to. Frances understood Pi'taki's grief all too well yet she thought it safer not to acknowledge their mutual pain lest she breach the dam she had built inside and release a flood of emotion that would drown them both.

At dawn they were back on the trail again. Flies and mosquitoes hung about them in clouds and harassed the struggling horses as they continued over the wild grasslands. Parts of the trail passed through marshy ground and it was impossible to detour some of the worst mud-traps. The unceasing flatness slowly gave way to a slightly undulating landscape and for the first time, the rim of the great blue sky was broken by gently rising hills in the distance. The warmth grew oppressive and sweat covered women and animals alike as the air took on a choking quality, heavy and draining with each breath.

Their progress became slower and by dusk Pi'taki saw the distant signs of storm-clouds gathering. She led the cart off the trail towards a small copse of trees already bending in the stiff breeze. They cleared a bit of ground to erect their shelter, securing it with rocks against the worst to come. An early darkness was drawing in fast and the wind had grown to a howling gale with black thunderheads rushing to close up the dimming light above them. The temperature was falling rapidly, and they shivered as they struggled to prepare themselves. Pi'taki found a sheltered spot to tie up the horses. They were still lathered with foam in the chilling air and she rubbed them down with handfuls of torn grass as flickers of lightning in the far west heralded the coming rain. Frances put Rory under cover then hurried to unhitch the cow from the back of the cart. She had to almost drag it to a tree to be tethered, its eyes rolling white with fear as the thunder drew closer. Pi'taki had seen signs of predators as they travelled but there was no option other than to leave the animals exposed.

The two women crawled into the tipi, hoping exhaustion would quickly bring sleep and leave them oblivious to the storm that now broke over the land. The rain started to lash down, running in rivers under the skin tent and soaking everything. There was no more they could do and they held on grimly to the frail structure to prevent it being torn away from above their heads.

In the nightmare of her half-sleep, a roar of thunder jolted Frances into consciousness. It was pitch black and she stretched out her arms, reaching for the body beside her. She gripped Pi'taki's hand and was reassured for a moment. Then a searing flash of lightning briefly lit the interior of the tipi. Rory began to cry in little broken sounds and Pi'taki eased herself up and tied him into a makeshift sling around her neck. They crouched, drenched and freezing in the centre of the tent, clutching at the wildly flapping skins as the howling of the wind rose higher and higher. Suddenly, a grinding crash from not far off signalled the cart had toppled over. Frances looked despairingly at Pi'taki but they were unable to do anything and continued to battle the storm. It was hours before it passed over and began to die away. Freed from holding their pathetic shelter and oblivious to the mud in which they sank down, the two women huddled together. They lay aching and weary, alternating between wretched wakefulness and fitful dozing.

As dawn broke, Pi'taki rose. Frances was not in the tipi and the baby opened its mouth, whining for its mother but still dry within Pi'taki's home-made sling. She looked out from under the tent flap. Behind them, the cart lay on its side, their belongings strewn in a broken jumble. The horses, wet and shivering, were still tethered to the tree but the cow had gone, its broken halter swaying in the stiff breeze. Some way off, Frances stood staring out across the land where the tail-winds of the night's storm still buffeted debris across the plains. Tears cut glistening tracks down her mud-streaked face as she contemplated the disorder around them and, wearied by the thought of what lay ahead, she sank with a groan to her knees.

Pi'taki's footsteps came up behind her and quickly Frances rubbed her eyes. 'Look at this mess,' she shrugged, trying to force a smile.

Pi'taki took in the sight but seemed unmoved. 'Come, feed the child,' she said, gesturing towards the tent and, without pausing for remorse, she began to collect the scattered remnants of their supplies.

They spent the rest of the morning in restoring the cart and its spilled contents to some semblance of order. Nothing had been irreparably damaged although one sack of flour was soaked and spoiled. By midday, all signs of the night's storm had disappeared and once again the sun hung blazing in a clear sky. The storm had been disorientating. As they worked to right the cart, Frances began to worry that they might have lost their way. She had become confused as to the route and had forgotten any distinguishing marks about the landscape. Meanwhile, the cow had to be found. Pi'taki fitted a bridle to one of the horses and set off on the search, riding bareback. Frances stayed behind, stacking everything back onto the cart in an even more unwieldy load than before.

Two hours at least passed before the sound of hooves could be heard in the distance. Frances looked up and was disappointed to see Pi'taki return without the cow. 'You didn't find her then?' she called.

Pi'taki looked animated and she slid from the horse before it came to a standstill. 'I have found the place, Otanimm,' she said breathlessly, 'bring the baby – I have found the place!'

Quickly Frances hitched the cart and set off following Pi'taki's lead. They moved south. The land was growing flatter again with slight rises covered in trees periodically giving way to dips where water settled into marsh. Gophers, alarmed by their passage, stood sentry by their holes and emitted a high-pitched whistle of warning. Overhead a lark bunting soared and the air was filled with bird song. Until then, Frances had suppressed her curiosity about the homestead and she was still wary of giving way to anything like optimism. But the anticipation of seeing the fruits of William's labours and sensing the sweet pain of his presence again now invaded her imagination.

She did not realise they had arrived until Pi'taki pulled the horse up beside a copse of trees. Beyond where they stood was a clearing. 'Is this it?' Frances asked doubtfully. Without looking at her, Pi'taki nodded and started to untie the bundles from the travois. Frances walked ahead into the clearing. Nailed to one of the trees was a piece of wood with the name burned into it, 'MUNRO'. She noticed the cow had been tethered to a stump next to what seemed to be a barn made of mud. Though she looked around for the house, she saw no other building. Then, with a growing sense of horror, she realised that what she took for a cow-shed was in fact the house. Walking up to it, she put out her hand to touch the walls and convince herself she was not still dreaming. It was a turf hut made with great lumps of sod cut from the ground around her feet. There were no windows, just a framed opening for a doorway. The roof was also of turf slabs and the grass was still growing, giving the house the bizarre appearance of having pushed itself up from underground.

Despairingly, she ducked her head to enter. The gloom after the bright sunlight made her squint to see what was inside. Piled in a jumble were all the farming implements – a plough, spades, hoes and a stack of hardware whose uses Frances could not even begin to guess. A cast-iron stove stood in the corner, its smoke-pipe running up into the roof and disappearing through a hole in the turf slabs. Tears came to her eyes. Standing inside made her feel as though she were in her grave. Everything – walls, floor, ceiling – was dirt, with great trailing grass-roots hanging down like streaming cobwebs in a disused dungeon. Slowly she slumped to her knees in what little space there was and, holding her hand to her mouth, whispered pitiably. 'Oh, William, was this the palace that ye promised?'

Once they had placed everything inside, there was little room for them to move about. The large iron bedstead looked particularly incongruous in the surroundings but cramming the limited space with all their gear did make it seem less like a hovel. They got the stove working effectively after a disastrous first attempt when it had merely filled the hut with choking, acrid smoke. Rory's sleeping bag was strung from the ceiling to make more space and the food stores were stacked in unsteady piles against the walls. Much of the other equipment had to be left under a tarpaulin on the cart until they could find time to build a lean-to shelter at the side of the hut for further storage. Not far away, at the edge of the trees, they found the well that William had dug. Obviously he had made this his first priority for the sides of the shaft had been shored up with wood planks and the bucket hung on a rope pulley at the top. Frances was relieved that they at least had a ready source of water, especially with the baby in mind. He hardly made a sound all day, and she checked him regularly to make sure he was all right. Yet Rory seemed contented and they were able to get on with the work of unloading their goods and trying to make some semblance of a home. As night fell, they hung up a blanket in the doorway to keep out the flies, lit the spirit lamp, and, despite everything, slept soundly.

14

In the days and weeks that followed, Frances tried to put out of her mind the crushing disappointment that she had experienced in her first impressions of the homestead. Instead of giving in she threw herself into the tasks in hand, working harder than she could ever remember. There was so much to do, and no time for reflection or self-pity now. The land and the season demanded unceasing activity or they would not survive for already summer was almost past its peak. They had to get a kitchen garden started right away to try and provide some fresh vegetables that would see them through the long winter. On the first morning, Pi'taki began the task of clearing some ground of its sage-brush cover next to the hut. It was the kind of work she knew well how to do, as the women among her people had been forced to adapt to farming on the new reserves. Agriculture was not in their blood and the men still vainly harked after the nomadic life of the plains and the buffalo hunt. But the great herds had dwindled to extinction. Life on the reserves meant new skills had to be acquired and it was the women who learned them.

Frances admitted she knew little of farming methods and her familiarity with the patchwork fields of Fife contributed nothing to the task that lay before them now. She did however avidly read the farming manual and seed catalogues for useful tips and reassurance about their progress. Added to this, she listened and learned from Pi'taki. Each day saw them out working on the land, taking it in turns to carry Rory who remained contented provided he was strapped to the back of one of them.

They decided to keep the small copse of trees around the hut as a wind-break, which they assumed had been William's intention. This meant, however, that they had to go some way off to cut wood for fuel and fencing posts. There was no shortage of timber on their land and when walking round the hundred and sixty acres they discovered an abundance of spruce, willow and tamarac. They could begin breaking a patch not far from the hut for sowing the next spring, but in the long term the clearance of trees would be a major problem.

Learning to fell a tree by trial and error involved some bitter lessons for Frances and there were times when she cursed and swore furiously at her own weakness. But as her strength grew, she came to split logs with alacrity. 'I defy any old timber wolf to try and crack that!' she said of the chicken coop she had made, a tightly-meshed structure of logs and branches. Then, with this new found skill and confidence, she tackled a more ambitious project and with Pi'taki's help, built an enclosure for the cow and horses.

It was not all so gratifying though and the list of chores to be done each day seemed endless. They had to tend to the animals and keep the garden watered. Then there were the back-breaking hours following behind horse and plough. Frances's first attempt at driving a furrow had her red-faced with her own shortcomings. The horse seemed to feel the uncertainty and dragged her and the plough in a winding course, the shaft slipping in and out of the tough grass and leaving a snaking trail behind them. In frustration she would have taken the axe and smashed it, had it not been for the unconcealed amusement that showed on Pi'taki's face. Frances stopped what she was doing and smiled back. It was the first time in weeks that they had shared a moment that was something like happiness and both were slightly self-conscious with the feeling.

With so many new things to learn, it was essential that the two women shared what they could with each other, though Frances knew her own contribution was a poor exchange for the skills she gained from Pi'taki. For the most part she humbly listened and observed. However, not everything Pi'taki suggested was accepted so unreservedly. When it was decided Frances must learn to master a horse, for the first time she exhibited doubt. She knew Pi'taki was right but she had never had much enthusiasm for riding and watched dubiously as Pi'taki, despite her years, swung over the animal's back with ease.

After cantering round in a circle, she slid off effortlessly. 'Now you,' she said, offering the reins to Frances.

'Could we no wait till I can get a saddle?'

'You do not need a saddle,' Pi'taki stated flatly, slapping the broad brown curve of the horse's back.

Frances frowned. Gritting her teeth in determination, she divided her skirt and tucked it into her waistband so she could sit astride the horse. She felt vulnerable with the living flesh of the beast warm against her skin and had little faith in her ability to control it. Pi'taki attached a lead rope to the bridle and walked them round in a wide circle. As it began to move more swiftly, Frances was bounced about remorselessly and slid around on its back. In spite of her initial doubts, she half-expected to acquire the technique fairly quickly and was surprised at her complete lack of competence to ride.

Pi'taki came across and pressed Frances's knee hard against the horse's flank. 'Hold him,' she said and, turning away, added, 'like a man.' Frances stared after her amazed. She opened her mouth to speak but, before she could, the rope was taut again and the animal jerked into a trot. Unprepared for the sudden movement, Frances was thrown off balance and tumbled with an ungainly thud to the ground. This time they allowed themselves more than a smile and the sound of their laughter mixed with the rustling trees.

So it was that slowly they fought back against the wilderness. As they ploughed, the deep, rich, fertile loam was laid open in readiness for the next year. Little by little, the tiny black patches of broken soil encroached upon the blue-green swards of sage-brush and grass, growing bigger with each passing day.

They fitted a proper door to their hut and dug ditches for drainage and to act as a fire-break against the sudden, devastating fires that could sweep across miles of tinder-dry grassland in minutes. Fortunately however, that season brought none of the prolonged rains that could wash away a mud-built home, nor any conflagration. They erected a rudimentary lean-to at the side of their hut which could house some of their supplies and give them more space inside. This was achieved with relative ease and spawned the idea that they could readily build another turf hut, albeit smaller, for the animals to winter in. The reality was grim and Frances rued the day she had laughed at William's efforts. Where his hut may have lacked a certain aesthetic charm, it was however sturdy and symmetrical. Their own leaned awkwardly to one side and needed several attempts to stabilise the door frame. Despite this, they assured each other that it would serve the purpose, even though inwardly neither had much faith in its permanence.

Chopped firewood was stacked up under shelter at the back in readiness for winter and, as autumn arrived, their garden yielded its first crop. A supply of hay had been cut from the prairie grasses before ploughing to help feed the animals in the months to come. Each night Frances tumbled exhausted into bed and fell asleep at once. The bed was big enough for both of them but Pi'taki could not be persuaded to share it and still preferred a mat on the floor, as was her custom. Though they had started out with little in common, a way of teaching, learning and making mistakes together had enabled them to achieve what had seemed impossible on their arrival at the homestead. Frances looked at her rough hands and noticed how the muscles had hardened in her brown arms with the ceaseless toil. But though from time to time her mood was still invaded by her grief, it was a restoring sleep that claimed her every night and very gradually a trace of hope returned.

15

One day Frances saw the dust rise from a distant wagon. She waved but there was no need, for it was indeed coming in their direction. As it reached the homestead, she could see there were three people inside, a man, a woman and a boy.

'We come to welcome you. I am Josef Dutchak.' Tall and bearded, the man wore his trousers tucked into his boots and a belted tunic in the traditional Ukrainian style. He smiled warmly at Frances as he jumped down from the wagon. She gave her own name and held out her hand, unsure of the protocol and he grasped it in a crushing shake. He introduced his wife and son who clambered down to join them. Wasylyna Dutchak was a stout woman with a cloth tied over her head and the usual ruddy complexion of the prairie settler. She turned back to their wagon and brought out a small bundle. Unwrapped, it revealed a loaf of bread, round and still warm as it was handed to Frances. Josef then thrust forward their young son, Nikolai, who murmured a shy greeting.

Frances quickly warmed to the Dutchaks but as they spoke, it soon became clear that they had previously made William's acquaintance and expected to find him there. It transpired that they were immigrants who had only settled a few months before William had arrived at the homestead, indeed Josef Dutchak had helped him to erect the turf hut. He seemed pleased as he looked at his workmanship and, in his broken English, boasted that it would survive anything the winter snows might bring.

Explaining the awful chain of events which had occurred since that time was hard for Frances. She had to be crude and blunt in her description to make them understand and it was almost as painful to see the horror in their eyes. She tried to reassure them that she was all right and called Pi'taki over to show she was not alone. The Dutchaks grew silent and Frances stiffened, seeing the familiar suspicion in their eyes as she appeared. Rory was tied in the usual sling on her back and his sudden waking sounds had Wasylyna rushing over to inspect the tiny infant bundle. She gestured to Pi'taki, asking if she could hold him and the baby was placed in her arms. They all crowded round to admire him and any tension that was there quickly lifted. On his mother's instructions, Nikolai pulled dried apples and corn syrup from her basket and they prepared an impromptu breakfast. Then, sitting in a circle on the ground, they ate the food and talked of the future, letting the past settle until another time.

The seasons changed and autumn gave way quickly to winter. Josef Dutchak regularly trudged the three miles from his own homestead to check on them. He was generous in offering his help, though perhaps this was more to satisfy himself that they were ready for the big freeze. As the temperature dropped below zero and the heavy snows came, outside activity ceased and increasingly more time was spent within the mud walls of their hut. Frances preserved what produce she could from their garden while Pi'taki dried the many medicinal plants she had gathered during the summer. Balanced between tins, the crude shelves they had erected now sagged under the weight of rows of jars, while the sweetly fragrant bunches of dried herbs and roots hung from the roof timbers.

As the blizzards took hold, one night an especially heavy fall of snow precipitated a commotion from outside. Frances and Pi'taki ran out and perceived through the darkness that the inevitable had happened. The turf roof of their makeshift barn had caved in and they were forced to bring the animals into their own hut for fear that they might freeze. Though the close proximity of a cow and horses may have added some warmth, this did not make up for the stench and filth they also brought and, after a few days of this noxious confinement, the women could stand it no more. When Josef next called round, battling through the snow to reach them, they gladly took advantage of his assistance to rebuild the collapsed sod roof. It was an auspicious decision, for no sooner were the repairs completed and he had gone, than the two found themselves completely snowed in. Their only exercise, day after day, was in digging a path from the door to where the animals were stabled and at one point they had had to dig out the roof of the hut to free the stove-pipe, so deeply did the snow lie.

The impossible conditions outside required them to spend long hours together in the warmth. It was a quiet time, often spent in contemplative silence and Rory was usually the main focus of their attention while he was awake. Pi'taki had an inbuilt preoccupation with the child's health and his cradle-bag was stuffed with

134

precautionary medicines to ward off this and that. She hung a bandolier of puff-balls around his chest to ensure he would not catch a cold. Her word for the dried fungus meant 'dusty stars' but Frances thought their pungent odour called for a less fanciful name. Rory, however, thrived on all the attention and grew fatter and more contented with each passing week.

The long winter months afforded them a closeness that eventually made language and understanding easier. The two women talked much more freely, wanting to share the experiences of their lives with each other and to relate stories from the past. Frances listened in fascination to the slow and measured voice which told tales of a way of life that had vanished forever with the passing of the buffalo. In her imagination, she was transported out of their cramped confinement and into another world. Pi'taki spoke of when she was a young woman and of her marriage to Broken Claw. Of when her tribe, desperate for food as the great herds dwindled, had trekked far to the south into Montana. There, they had hunted the last of the buffalo, harassed by the other Indian nations whose land they had invaded. Then how the white men had plied them with whisky, exchanging a bottle of illicit and adulterated liquor for a horse or a bundle of scarce hides. And when they had nothing else to trade, the tribe was destitute and the American army moved them back north. Without horses, without food, they walked eight hundred miles back to the reserves. Hundreds had died on the gruelling journey, not least her children who, one by one, had fallen prey to the measles epidemic. Talking of that time, Pi'taki had rocked back and forth, pulled her hair down across her face and wailed in sorrow.

Frances too had been urged to talk and tentatively she began to unfold something of Scotland. Describing the place she came from was a challenge, especially as it now seemed so remote compared with this vast continent which had become her adopted home. If anything she now felt more alienated from it than before and so her own stories concentrated mainly on the memories of childhood. Hence, her traumatic departure from the old life was related in an abridged version which avoided any cross-examination or painful re-opening of old wounds. But in so doing, she also avoided the truth.

The long winter dragged on. By March they had exhausted their fuel and the trees were becoming unreachable in the deep snow. Pi'taki dried the animals' droppings for use in the stove, but the stench as they burned was overwhelming. Finally, they were faced with a straight choice – they had to have wood to burn or they would freeze. Unless they forced themselves to tackle the blizzard, they would end up breaking the Red River cart for firewood. In the blinding snow, the two burrowed through the drifts to clear a path to the trees. Struggling inexpertly against the driving winds they proceeded to hack off the nearest branches and heave the precious bundles back to their hut. Each day saw hours of back-breaking toil merely to collect enough fuel to prevent them freezing to death in the night and they awoke each morning to face the chilling prospect again. Both women moved about with difficulty, encumbered by the wrappings of every piece of clothing they possessed and Pi'taki was at last persuaded to share the bed for warmth, lying under the very piles of skins that had served them as a tent when first they had set out.

With the first sign of spring, they were out clearing more land for all they were worth, in readiness for planting. Once the thaw came and the snows had melted, the Dutchaks visited more regularly, often bringing their three younger daughters with them. Rory was now crawling around confidently, worrying the hens and getting under everyone's feet. He was no longer the fretful child of his early months and the children loved playing with him.

On the first truly mild day, they arrived as a family and insisted that all work be stopped while they shared a modest picnic with their neighbours. Frances and Pi'taki were persuaded, after some cajoling, to down their tools and join them. A cloth was laid on the ground and everyone sat down to partake of the meagre choice of food that was left after the winter. As they ate, Frances talked longingly of building a wooden house and getting out of the turf hut but did not see how it could be done.

'I couldn't bear another winter in that awful hut,' she said. 'There's plenty wood round here but even if we had the time we could never build a decent house.' She knew their limitations well enough by now and all their efforts had to be concentrated on cultivation of the land which was essential to their survival. 'If only we could afford to hire some skilled labour.'

Josef looked pensive. 'You could ask bank,' he suggested, chewing a mouthful of bread. 'We got a loan for house.'

Frances was cynical. 'A loan? The bank would never loan me money — what have I got as security?'

Josef looked confused and she tried to explain. Then suddenly he understood and raised his hand in a sweeping gesture. 'All this,' he said confidently, 'your land is security.'

Frances remained sceptical, unwilling to believe in such a simple solution. 'But how would we pay it back?' she persisted.

Josef took a deep breath and summoned all the powers of his limited English to explain. 'First, you get loan, yes?'

'Yes,' she said guardedly.

'And when harvest comes, you get money and pay back – easy.' He smiled at her and Wasylyna joined in, nodding effusively, though she for one had not understood a thing.

For several nights Frances thought about it until she was gradually won over to the idea of taking out a loan and arranged to go into Edmonton with Josef once the tracks were passable. She became enthusiastic at the prospect. As the scheme to build a new house took shape in her mind she felt the burden of the past winter slowly ebb away and in its place, allowed herself a little confidence with which to face the coming months.

16

'We sure made a mighty fine job of this, though I say it myself.'

Frances smiled in reply as she stood with Sam Brodie and admired the workmanship of her new home. The log-built house was looking at its best now that she and Pi'taki had fixed it up inside and, to celebrate its completion and the end of a good first harvest, she had invited all the neighbours to come over. Everyone was ready for some relaxation after a summer of hard work.

'Well, you've done all right, I'll give you that.' They were standing in the doorway looking into the spacious kitchen. Stout rafters underpinned the ceiling and the smell of new wood was still pervasive. The grooves between the logs of the walls were caulked with clay and hung around with iron pots and skillets. There was a good-sized window in each wall, something Frances had insisted on after months in the dingy turf hut. Through the back of the kitchen was a bedroom. The end of the bedstead could just be seen through the open door and Rory's sleeping hammock strung above, though it had no permanent resting place and was moved from room to room at will. At one side, a staircase led to two small rooms in the loft where Pi'taki slept. Rory could often be found up there with her and the floor was strewn with home-made toys for the child, hand-drums, willow whistles and little rattles filled with seeds.

Sam took one of the cookies his wife was handing out and

continued to admire the house, even though he had had a major hand in building it. 'Never would've thought it possible but in one year you've sure made this place pay.'

'Hard work, Sam – that's all there is to it,' Frances replied confidently.

'Hard work plus a dollar or two in the bank, I reckon?' he winked.

'Aye, well, it's all spent now.'

'Well, here's to next year's crop yielding as good as this 'un,' Sam said, raising his glass.

'I'll drink to that – I'm depending on it,' she replied. Josef Dutchak had been right. The bank had been persuaded to lend her money – enough to pay a group of neighbours to build the house for her. However, repaying the loan depended on more than one good harvest.

Several of the Ukrainian men stood by the stove and argued about the price of grain and the site of the new grain elevator. Their voices rose and fell with the unfamiliar tongue of their language and Sam shook his head. 'God damn it, Mrs Munroe,' he said, lowering his voice, 'a man gets to feeling like a stranger in his own land sometimes, know what I mean?'

'Can't say I do, Sam, since I'm a stranger here myself.' Frances felt uncomfortable with this turn in the conversation.

'Aw, but we speak the same, you and me. I mean, we belong here,' Sam drawled on. 'And as for the squaw, well I guess you need to have her around for the fetching and carrying and the like, but —'

Frances put her hand up to silence him. 'Don't start on again with that kind of talk, Sam. I've told ye before, we own this house together.' He tried to interrupt but she went on crisply. 'So watch what you say or either one of us might just take a fancy to throw ye out!'

Seeing them argue, Sam's wife came over and joined them. 'That's right,' she said, speaking to Frances, 'you tell him. He's forever getting folks' backs up these days. Ever since we got past the three-year-inspection and the land's ours, he thinks he owns the whole darned country!'

'Now, Hettie, don't come interferin'.' Sam was irked at being put in his place by two women.

But Hettie put her arm round his waist and went on. 'The way he talks, you'd never guess we came west from Ontario three years ago with hardly a bean in our pocket.' She took his arm firmly. 'Now, leave Frances be and come and talk to Josef. He's wanting a barn

built – you could swallow your pride and earn us some money.'
Grumbling, Sam let himself be led away.

Frances watched them move off and sighed. Neighbours were
a necessity of life around these parts but some let the pioneering
spirit go to their heads. Thankfully, this was rare, since most just
got on with the business of survival. She looked around the room
for Pi'taki and made her way towards the door, squeezing past the
animated group of Ukrainians.

Wasylyna looked up. 'You like our food?' she asked grinning
widely. Frances smiled and nodded. It was indeed good, and to
look at the table, you would think they lived a life of plenty.
The neighbouring wives had cooked and brought something to
contribute and the table now overflowed with all manner of dishes,
most of which Frances had never seen before. But it was easy to get
a taste for Wasylyna's cooking, even if she did not always get the
names right. She took one of the *mlyntsis* from the pile of steaming
griddle cakes and went outside.

Pi'taki was feeding the hens while the children kicked a ball
around her feet in the warm afternoon sunshine that flooded
the yard. Frances went over and stood by the well, observing
them play. Rory tottered between their legs squealing excitedly
under the shower of grain as it fell and chased the elusive ball
which seemed always to be out of his reach. Frances leaned back,
watching the scene with obvious pleasure. The garden plot sported
proud rows of pumpkin, beets and corn-cobs. Beans tangled thickly
round the canes and flowers gave an intermittent splash of colour in
between. Beyond them yawned the sprawl of their homestead. They
had managed to cultivate the required ten acres that year and it had
brought in enough to seed a greater area next spring, as well as pay
off the first instalment on the house. Frances looked forward to the
day when their own swaying green prairie would stretch as far as
the eye could see.

She turned her attention back to Pi'taki who was never idle and
always cautious about their progress. She had declined to share in
the harvest celebrations having found the fruit spikes on the blue
grama grass to be thick and abundant that autumn. This signalled,
or so she said, a harsh winter to follow. Frances wished Pi'taki could
share her optimism. 'Won't you come in and join us?' she called to
her. But Pi'taki continued to play with the children, who scampered
around her feet like young rabbits.

Later, after everyone had gone, Frances sat rocking in her chair
on the low wooden verandah that skirted the front of the house.

'What d'ya want a porch for?' Sam had complained but she did not try to explain. Despite the extra cost, she had insisted they went ahead and build it. It had been worth it for the great satisfaction she derived on such evenings when she could sit and gaze in peace at the wide western sky. After two and a half years in Canada she still marvelled at the size of the horizon.

Pi'taki was upstairs putting Rory to sleep. The rhythmical incantation of her voice came from the open window to join the throbbing call of the whippoorwill on the still night air. A spectacular sunset emblazoned fiery streaks across an amethyst sky and the earth smelled warm and yielding.

PART
3

1

The horse walked slowly, struggling as it pulled the wagon over the rutted trail to Edmonton. Four years of increasing farm traffic had not improved the track and in the driving seat Frances shivered and flapped the reins in an effort to speed up the weary beast. But its pace never altered and it plodded on with lowered head into the stiff breeze that had blown since dawn. She sighed, knowing it was as hungry, tired and cold as she was and had not the heart to force it any harder.

It was already the end of April, but the spring of 1896 was late in coming. Deep snows had persisted well into March, their slow thaw delaying all work in the muddied fields. The sky was a grey sheet of threatening cloud that cast a monotonous light on the bleak landscape and the sombre surroundings matched her mood perfectly. Frances was on her way into town to ask for an extension on the loan. In her mind she tried to force herself to go over the arguments she would use at the bank but her thoughts kept wandering and she could not even pretend to feel optimistic. If she got money, what it would buy was anybody's guess. After three successive bad harvests and the slump in the grain market, prices and supplies were as unpredictable as the weather. Already half the farms around the Munroe homestead were deserted, with families leaving for the factories in the east where there was at least the prospect of steady wages. If things did not improve this year, they would be forced to leave too. Frances was depressed by the possibility but could think of no alternative. Two women trying, against all the odds, to create a farm on these inhospitable plains was probably a hopeless undertaking from the start, she thought. Indeed, if it had not been for William's initial outlay and the luck of their first good year, they would not have made it this far. Neighbours had tried to help but everyone was in the same predicament, fighting the unrelenting elements to succeed where success seemed impossible.

She remembered the beginning of their second year – how it had promised to be as bountiful as the first. Then in the late summer, torrential rains and hailstorms had beaten the wheat to the ground, devastating their entire crop. The year after that the rains had not

143

come at all. The sun hung in the sky, a sinister bloated ball of fire that seemed to grow hotter and closer with every passing day. The crops had shrivelled, and prairie fires were common. Dust storms tore up the dried soil and scattered it to the four winds in choking clouds that blackened the molten sky. At the end of the season, an agency inspector had called to see Frances and check if the terms of their land-grant had been fulfilled. Although the house had been built and the required acreage was under cultivation, after three back-breaking years the farm was still a desolate sight. She had almost wished that he had turned them down, made them leave and so released them from their struggle. When he handed her the deeds to the land, freehold and forever, she had stared at them. 'It's all yours, Mrs Munroe. These are the papers to show you now own the quarter.'

She shook her head, disillusioned. 'It's not much to own, is it?'

He tried to smile. 'Oh, it will get better, I'm sure. The past couple of years have just been a bit unusual, that's all. One more good harvest is all it takes.'

But there had been no good harvest and they were at a loss until Pi'taki discovered that a ton of buffalo bones could be sold for eight dollars to a fertiliser company. It was while clearing the land that they had come across many piles of desiccated skeletons and so scoured the fields, collecting the pathetic remains. Even Rory was not spared the wearisome toil and Frances was sometimes reduced to tears seeing his little thin body straining to do the work of an adult. The bones had to be taken to a pick-up point on the railroad, two days' drive from their homestead. Each quarter-ton earned two dollars. It was a ridiculous sum for the effort involved but there was no alternative. Without it, they would starve.

However, this unforeseen source of income had soon dwindled. On the final trip to the railroad, Frances had been alone and, after unloading the last remains of the bones, she found herself taking the road south, away from the direction of home. Often she had thought about taking Rory to show him the place where his father lay. But there seemed no point in filling the child's mind with morbid thoughts and with all the hardship they now faced she had no wish to disturb his young life further. The boy knew how William had died but felt no sense of loss and Frances could see that for Rory it was natural to accept her and Pi'taki as parents.

It was to be the only time she returned to the grave and even then, she had not known why she went. She had followed the old stage trail but when she came to the clearing, there was no sign that a camp of several hundred men had ever been there. Their only monument was the gleaming ribbon of rails that cut the land in two. Leaving the horse and wagon, she had walked slowly in the deepening afternoon through the gold and red trees of autumn, out to the flat land beyond.

The cross was still there, though slightly askew and the letters of William's name could barely be seen. Wild grass, brown and scrubby after the endlessly arid summer covered the mound. Standing before the grave, Frances found herself wondering what had happened to the girl who had come across an ocean and a continent, full of bright hopes. It seemed all the fire inside her had dissipated. She had rejected one life for another but it was a poor exchange. As she looked down at the pitiful little patch of ground, futility overwhelmed any sense of grief she once might have had.

Frances had not lingered at the grave. She left as the shadows of evening fell over the land knowing nothing there held meaning any more.

That was two years ago and the feeling of emptiness had merely hardened inside her. Now, as she was approaching the outskirts of Edmonton, she started to pass other farmers. On every face was the same haggard look of defeat, every cart and wagon was empty, every horse lean and emaciated. Even at the stables, payment was demanded in advance before she could leave her own exhausted animal for the night.

Frances walked to the bank and braced herself before going in. She found the cramped front office deserted apart from Mme Lemieux who was sweeping the floor. 'Frances,' she said, looking up, 'it is so long since we have seen you.' Frances sensed a lukewarm note in her voice and the place seemed grim and impersonal. Mme Lemieux rose and went to the door of the back room. 'Come in, and I will get Claude.'

When he appeared, Frances was shocked at the change in him. His hair was streaked with grey, and his face was thin and lined. He shook her hand warmly, and led her into his office. 'How are you?'

'Well enough, Mr Lemieux.' She eyed the gaunt figure across the desk and assumed she looked as bad to him. 'And yourself?'

'Ah, you know, I should not complain.' He waved his hand dismissively. 'But how is that fine son of yours?'

'Rory's well and right glad that winter's over so he can get outside, thank you,' Frances smiled. 'And I'm glad to get him out from under my feet.'

'Yes indeed, spring is here. Another busy season ahead for us all.' The banker reached for a large account book at his side. Flicking it open, he scrutinised the figures and looked up. 'Now, you are ready to make some repayment on your loan?' He did not meet her eyes as he asked the question.

She shook her head. 'Look, let's not pretend – you've guessed why I'm here.' He was silent, and she pressed on. 'There's no money, I need an extension.'

He sighed and ran his finger down the columns of figures. 'There is still a considerable sum outstanding. To grant further credit—'

'I know I haven't kept up the repayments, but ye can understand. . .' Her voice tailed off.

Lemieux was shaking his head. 'I wish very much I could help you,' he said sadly, 'but there are so many in your situation. The Brodies gave up and left only last week.' His hand tapped the ledger nervously. 'I have not the money to lend, even if I wanted to. Everyone's savings have gone.'

'They can't have,' she said, disbelieving.

He rose, went to the safe behind him and returned to the desk holding a folder bulging with papers. 'This is the security for your loan,' he said, pulling one from the bundle. Frances nodded, recognising the deeds that she and Pi'taki had worked so hard to earn. Lemieux let the paper flutter to the desk. 'And all of these are the same – securities from people who have given up and left. This bank is owed a great deal of money by defaulters.'

'Just enough to see us through to the harvest?' Frances was begging now.

He looked away from her desperate expression and shook his head again. 'I am sorry, I have no other option but to foreclose and recoup what I can.'

'What good are these to you anyway?' she said, waving to the deeds.

He sighed. 'I admit it is not much, but—'

'Then, please, give me a chance – help me, you're the only one who can. Just give us till the autumn, that's not a lot to ask?'

There was a pause. 'But I did that last year, will this be any different?'

'Yes.' Frances tried to sound convincing.

'Very well,' he conceded with a shrug. 'I will extend the term of your current liability this one last time.'

'Oh, thank you—' she began.

'But do not ask me to lend you any more,' Lemieux emphasised. 'All I can say is you will have to keep going. Try and get more grain, sow more fields. Prices cannot stay low forever. There is no more money,' he repeated. 'The only chance you have – the only chance for any of us, is to try and persevere.'

'And how can I persevere,' she spat his words back at him, 'with no money and no food? Where's the seed to come from? Answer me that!' Frances stood and slammed her hands on the desk. She opened her mouth to carry on and then stopped, seeing his defeated face. 'I, I'm sorry,' she muttered, guiltily. 'I'd no right to shout at you, it's no your fault.'

'That is all right, Frances. You are not the first – and you won't be the last.' Lemieux wiped his glasses.

The door opened and his wife entered, carrying a tray with cups of coffee and sandwiches. 'Perhaps you will have something to eat with us before you go?' she enquired.

Frances nodded, realising her stomach was growling with hunger. 'That's kind of you.' She turned to Lemieux again. 'I'm sorry for saying. . .'

'You must not apologise – it is nothing.' He deftly changed the subject. 'You are surely not driving back tonight? There is not much daylight left.'

Frances shook her head. 'No, they're giving me a bed at the church. I'll go back first thing tomorrow.' She shrugged sadly. 'And persevere.'

2

Kelly's saloon was the nearest thing to a wild frontier drinking den that Edmonton could lay claim to. All the itinerant cattle-men, freighters, and trappers congregated there at the end of a long spell away from civilisation to spend their money in a sustained, drunken bout before the next cattle-drive on the prairies or sortie into the wilds. Edmonton liked to think it was growing respectable until the days when the reality of the untamed land surrounding it burst into town and livened things up a little. While the virtuous citizens were scandalised, and editorials in *The Bulletin* preached sobriety and harsher sentences, the local law enforcement agencies found it an annoyance more than anything. There were never any murders or shoot-outs or big fights, just the occasional over-enthusiastic drunk needing to sleep things off in the cells.

The interior of the bar was warm and smoke-filled, contrasting with the clear, crisp night outside that still held a reminder of winter. The initial frenzied burst of drinking had slowed to a more methodical swill. Already, some of the younger men, unaccustomed to the hard liquor and unable to match the staying-power of their older cronies, had dropped out and were snoring in rooming houses along the main street. A few women of the 'dance girl' variety hung around hoping for a bit of business later and watching to see whose bank-roll was likely to last the course. In one corner of the saloon a poker game was in progress, the five men around the table concentrating more on the hands they had been dealt than the drinks beside them.

Leland O'Byrne carefully pulled his cards from the green oil cloth and glanced at them. His face split into a wide grin and he rolled the unlit, half-chewed cigar to the side of his mouth. 'Gonna take all day, Lee?' the dealer asked him impatiently. There was a further pause as Lee made a drawn-out ritual of lighting the cigar. 'I'll open five,' he said, pushing a bill into the centre of the table. His eyes glinted in amusement as the next two men disgustedly threw in their cards. The remaining two matched his stake and the rounds of betting continued until only Lee and the man opposite were left. The pile of money had grown to a considerable size and Lee's opponent was sweating visibly. Lee looked cool and met the other's eyes, his dark eyebrows arching in question as the man hesitated.

'Your bet, pal,' drawled Lee. He laid his cards face down before him and stretched lazily, his large frame bowing back and making the chair beneath him creak in protest. He clasped his hands behind his head and gazed steadily across the table.

'You're bluffin', O'Byrne,' the other man blurted out, pulling a big wad of notes from his pocket and throwing it on the table. 'Okay, I'll see you.'

Lee paused, grinned and rocked the chair upright again. He idly flipped the cards face up before him and the crowd that had gathered joined in his laughter. He had nothing – just five, mismatched cards.

The winner whooped and began to rake the pile of cash towards him. 'Knew you was bluffin', O'Byrne!'

Lee shrugged, raised his drink to the crowing man and tossed the whisky back. 'Well, I guess that's me out. I'll get that back another time, Hank – take good care of it for me.' He then rose and went back to the bar to join a group of the more determined drinkers there.

They gave him a good-natured ribbing about his loss and stood a round of drinks. 'Well, Lee, plenty more where that came from,' said one of the men. 'Another season trappin' and you and Swifty'll have your pockets lined again.'

Lee looked philosophical. 'Yeah, easy come, easy go,' he sighed.

'Come to think of it,' the man continued, 'I ain't seen your partner around. You sell him and his beard to the fur man as well?'

Lee stared into his empty glass. 'No, Swifty's comin' into town tomorrow.'

'You mean, he left you to sell the skins and hold his share?' The man laughed and slapped Lee on the back. 'Well, that's what I call mighty trustin'.'

'Or stupid,' someone else chimed in.

The back of Lee's neck reddened and his eyes flashed up. 'Now, my business with Swifty is between me and him. There ain't no call for that kinda talk.' His voice was ominously quiet and the laughter around him died. He grinned at their discomfiture and patted a large wad in his top pocket. 'Anyhow, his cut's here, safe and sound so who's gonna buy me another drink?'

The tension was broken and they called for the barman to refill their glasses. One of the women detached herself from the group huddled at the other end of the room and walked over to where Lee stood. 'Well, well,' she said, draping her arm across his shoulder. 'Long time no see.'

'Maggie,' he roared, 'where ya been?' He put his arms around her waist and swung her off her feet, kissing her wetly on the neck.

'I've been here all night, if you'd cared to look,' she said, pushing him back, 'but you seemed kinda busy with the poker game.'

He laughed. 'Maybe you should have come over and brought me some luck.' He tried to pull her close again, but she resisted.

'Cleaned out are ya?'

'Naw.' He winked at the men watching. 'I can always borrow a bit from Swifty's share.' This time she showed no resistance when he drew her towards him. 'Why don't you and me go back to your place and talk over old times?'

She smiled up at him. 'That'd be great, Lee. Let me just go get something for us to drink while we . . . talk.'

*

Maggie listened to the breathing beside her until she was sure that Lee was asleep. Hell, he'll be unconscious for hours with the amount of whisky he's drunk, she thought, grinning. Easing herself slowly from the bed, she crept over to where he had dumped his clothes and rummaged in the pile to find what she was looking for. Pulling the bundle from the top pocket, she frowned. The wad felt strange. She edged over to the window where the moonlight streamed into the room, and held up one of the notes.

'Damn!' Maggie hurled the pile of cut-up newspaper to the floor and threw herself at the snoring figure. 'Damn you, Leland O'Byrne!' She shoved him out of the bed and he fell grunting to the floor.

'What the hell?' Lee sat up, dazed.

'You sly bastard! Where's my money?' She tried to hit him, but he managed to grab her hands.

'Oh, peeking when you shouldn't, eh?' He grinned up at her. 'That'll teach you not to go through a man's pockets.' He tried to get back into the bed but she pushed him off again, glaring at him.

'Just making sure I get what's due me,' Maggie pouted, pulling the covers over her. 'Anyway, thought you said that was Swifty's cut?' He did not answer. 'Lee?' Her voice was wary. 'You ain't blown Swifty's dough as well as your own?'

'I'll explain it to him.' He tried to shrug it off but did not sound convinced.

'Jesus, that'll take some explaining!' Maggie shook her head and slithered under the blankets. 'You think you can sweet-talk your way out of a lot of things, but not this time.'

Lee looked grim. 'I don't suppose you could. . . ?'

She snorted angrily. 'Forget it, I'm a poor working girl – specially when I waste my time with guys like you who want it for nothin' – you've got a damned nerve!' She stuck her foot out of the bed and kicked him towards his clothes. 'Get dressed and get out. I don't want you here when Swifty comes lookin' for you.'

He grunted and started to pull on his shirt. As he was leaving, he picked up the bottle of whisky. 'Don't mind if I take this, Maggie, just to warm me up? It's pretty cold out there.'

She made a sound of disgust. 'You never give up, do you?' she said and turned towards the wall.

The street was deserted as Lee made his way back towards the livery stables. Around the saloon, a few diehards had collapsed in doorways and were snoring fitfully but otherwise all was quiet. The night was cool and a steady rain was starting to fall. He shivered and decided he would sleep next to his horse. Then, first thing in the morning, he could be away before Swifty got into town. He pulled his coat around himself and took a long swig from the bottle to warm him on his way.

3

Frances had not slept, lying awake in the hard, cramped cot and watching the stars fade as another day began. She left early when very few people were about and the sky was still flushed with the approaching dawn. Her expression was grim as she drove homewards, muttering to herself about the unfairness of it all. It was easy for Lemieux to tell her to get the farm back on its feet but her spirits had been badly dented and she wondered where she would get the energy from.

The progress of the wagon was hampered by the sogginess of the thawing ground. The wheels clogged with mud and the weary horse struggled to keep going. She gave it no rein, pulling this way and that and shouting encouragement as the cart bumped and swung to avoid the pot-holes. Several times, two of the wheels lifted right off the ground and she had to stand up on the buck-board to keep her balance. As the sun came up and warmed the frozen ground, the mud became worse and eventually, the inevitable happened. Though she snapped her whip across its neck and bawled at the unfortunate animal, the wagon became stuck with two wheels sunk in the mire on the left side. Throwing the reins from her in disgust, she jumped down and hung her arms over the hapless beast, knowing she had pushed it too far and could only blame herself. She walked round to check the damage and kicked out at the cart in a frustrated temper.

Suddenly, a groaning sound came from the back. Frances stopped and listened, thinking she may have imagined it. It came again, a sort of grumbling like someone in pain. Quickly, she jumped up and looked into the back of the wagon. Something bulky moved beneath the sacking and she bent to grab the rifle from under the seat. Her fingers tightened on the trigger in fear as she braced herself. The series of snorting, moaning sounds continued until eventually a stubbly face emerged, eyes tightly closed against the blinding light. A strong smell of stale liquor wafted from under the tarpaulin. 'Damn it, what in hell's going on?' an earthy voice complained. Then, with obvious growing concern the man sat full up and rubbed his bleary eyes. He swung his head around, looking for signs of where he was and an explanation of how he got there. Then he saw Frances. With the sun behind her, she stood above him, the barrel of the gun aimed squarely at his chest.

'Don't try anything,' Her voice was steady. 'I know how to use this.'

'Now just a minute, lady, be reasonable.'

'Get off the wagon.' Seeing him hesitate, she sighted down the barrel.

'Okay, I'm going.' He scrambled over the side and stood uncertainly in the mud. 'Now, will you please calm down.' He made a move in her direction but she jerked the weapon forward threateningly and he backed off, keeping his hands high. 'Look, I don't mean no harm. I just fell asleep in this ol' wagon and before I knowed it, I'm out half-way across the plains.' He paused and scanned the surrounding countryside. 'Where the hell are we headed?'

'*We're* headed no place, mister. This is as far as you're going.' Frances gestured back down the trail with the gun. 'Now, get moving. Edmonton's that way.'

He looked around dubiously and his eyes came to rest on the wagon. Then, realising her predicament, he gave a broad white flashing smile. 'Well now, looks like you ain't goin' far with this wagon,' he said with satisfaction.

'I can wait for help.' She did not let down the gun. 'Now, get away from here.'

The grin remained on his face and he lowered his hands. 'Seems to me, ma'am, that I've as much right to wait here for a lift back into town as you.' He hunted around for a dry spot and sat down heavily. Grasping his head in pain as if the effort had been too much for him, he peered up at her. 'I don't suppose you got a spot of whisky in that wagon?' He gave her a wink of cheerful familiarity. 'For purely medicinal purposes, you understand.' Frances continued to glare at him, the gun still pointed at his chest. 'Jesus,' he sighed. 'Let's at least be civil and introduce ourselves. Leland O'Byrne, ma'am, pleased to make your acquaintance.' He smiled at her. 'You can call me Lee.'

She ignored the smile but he saw the gun droop in her hands. 'Frances Munroe,' she said, flatly. 'You can call me Mrs Munroe.'

Lee shook his head. 'Hell, I should've known a pretty woman like you'd be married already. Just my luck.'

'Cut it out, O'Byrne,' she snorted. 'That kind of talk may work back in Edmonton, but it's wasted on me.'

He jumped up, looking offended. 'Look, Mrs Munroe, I'm sorry I gave you such a fright and all, but I am tryin' to be friendly here, and you ain't making things easy.' He pointed to the wheels sunk in the mud. 'Now, if you'd quit being so high and mighty, the two of us could shift this and you could be on your way.'

Frances wavered. With his grizzled unshaven features and tousled hair, he certainly did not look threatening. She knew he was right, it was pointless to wait here hoping another wagon would pass. Throwing down the gun, she jumped to the ground. 'All right. Let's get started.'

In an instant, he produced a knife and Frances flattened herself in horror against the side of the wagon. Lee saw her reaction and sighed in exasperation. 'Oh, for Chrissakes, lady. I gotta cut some branches to put under the wheels.' He walked off towards the trees. 'Go get your gun if it makes you feel better.'

Annoyed with herself, she waited for him to return carrying a large armful of branches. 'Look, Mr O'Byrne—'

He gave her a wide grin. 'Lee, please.'

'Mr O'Byrne,' she insisted. 'I'm sorry but you did give me a fright.'

'That's okay, no need to apologise.' He threw down the bundle, and rubbed his back. 'I noticed a spade in your wagon – think I must've slept on it. We'll need that to dig out the wheels.' Pulling off his jacket, he explained to her what they had to do and, while he cleared a space around each wheel, she jammed the cuttings under them.

'So, where are you headed?' he asked while they worked.

'Stony Plains area. We've got a homestead out there.'

'Homestead, eh?' He looked at her questioningly. 'Not a good time to be in the farmin' business.'

Frances grimaced. 'Is there ever a good time for farming?' The despair showed in her voice.

'Sure there is. I was born and raised on a spread in Montana. Great times there, when I was a kid.' He smiled. 'Kids love farms. They don't see the heartbreakin' side of it till they're grown.'

'Are you still farming?'

He laughed. 'Hell no! Once I was growed, couldn't wait to get away from it – left home when I was thirteen and seems I've been movin' ever since.' He stood up and grasped the spade. 'I've done a few things in my time. I even went gold prospectin' in the Cariboo, for all the good it done me. Mostly trappin's my trade, working the wild country north of Edmonton.' It was warm work and streams of sweat were pouring off him. 'This sure is one way to kill a hangover,' he said, stripping off his shirt.

Frances glanced up. 'The best way to avoid a hangover, Mr O'Byrne, is no to drink in the first place.' He made a face and they resumed the digging out of the wheels. 'Is there money in trapping, then?' she asked, 'I thought there wasn't much call for it these days.'

'Sure there is – big money if you can get the skins the traders want.'

'Then why were you sleeping in my wagon?'

Lee leaned on the spade and looked abashed. 'Well, to tell you the truth, I'd lost all my pay in a poker game and I didn't have the price of a hotel room.' He shrugged. 'I'm flat broke.'

She laughed. 'Well, O'Byrne, that makes two of us.' Frances thrust a branch into the mud with venom. 'Even the banker claimed he had no money when I went to see him.' Remembering his words, anger spread through her. 'Try harder he said!' She slammed the earth with her hands and pulled up two great sticky clods. 'We've tried for five bloody years!' She flung the handfuls of soil from her and sat back on her haunches.

'As bad as that?' Lee looked at her thoughtfully then straightened up and wiped his hands. 'Well, I think this should do it.' He told her to lead the horse by the bridle and he would try to lift the wheels from the mud. She urged the horse, slapping it on the flanks while he strained to help dislodge the wagon, the muscles in his back and arms bulging with the effort. Slowly, it was raised from the slime as the wheels were able at last to find some purchase on the path of branches they had spread beneath.

With the horse and cart safely tethered to a stump on dry ground, they stared at each other. Both were covered in mud. Frances looked down at her ruined dress as she tried ineffectually to dislodge some of the grime. Lee chuckled and pointed into the trees. 'There's a stream just over there. You can go wash up.'

'Thanks, but I'll wait till I get home.'

He pulled on his shirt. 'Mrs Munroe,' he began hesitantly, trying to gauge her mood.

'Yes?'

'Look, I've no real cause to be goin' back to Edmonton.' He was acutely aware that his partner would already be looking for him. 'Thought, maybe we could help each other out?'

She eyed him suspiciously. 'I thank you for helping me get the wagon free, but I've already told you – we've no money.'

He waved his hands, trying to keep the desperation out of his voice. 'No, I know that. What I mean is, if I could work for you on the farm, then you could pay me after the harvest.' He smiled at her uncertainly. 'You'd get an extra pair of hands when you need it, I'd get a place to stay for a while, and somethin' to set me up for next season.'

Frances shook her head. 'We've had no decent harvest to speak of for three years. If we fail again this year, that's it – we're finished.'

'I'll take the chance.' He could see she was still unconvinced. 'It's a gamble for me, but you've nothin' to lose. If the farm don't pay this year, you won't owe me a cent. Is it a deal?'

She started to refuse again, but paused. What he was offering might indeed be the solution to her problems. And he was right when he said the risk was all on his side – at this stage, she had absolutely nothing to lose. She gave it some thought for a while, then nodded and held out her hand. 'It's a deal.'

He grabbed and shook it enthusiastically. 'Well, that's just great, ma'am. You won't be sorry.'

Frances pulled her hand away and looked at him steadily. 'I know I won't,' she said as she walked back to the wagon. 'And just to make sure, we'll have some rules.' Lee looked at her puzzled, as she continued. 'Even though I can't afford to pay you yet, you'll be the hired hand. That means the house is off-limits and you'll sleep in the barn with the horses.' She eyed the back of the wagon and smiled coldly. 'Well, you're used to that. I expect hard work – there's no place on a farm for a drinker and gambler. You'll take your meals apart from us and any attempt to become familiar with me or my family will mean you're out. Do we understand each other?'

Lee scratched his head. 'Are you sure it's a farm you're runnin' and not some kinda mission?' he asked.

Frances ignored the remark. 'Those are the terms, O'Byrne, ye can take it or leave it.'

'Gee, Mrs Munroe, you sure are one hard woman. But – I guess I'll take it.'

All the way back, she let him do the talking, fending off questions about herself and the homestead. 'You'll see it soon enough,' was all she would say. Taking the hint, Lee concentrated on himself and expanded on the story of his life. Clearly a subject in which he had an inexhaustible interest, Frances thought. She did however, enjoy listening but it was hard to separate fact from fiction. She gathered he was older than her by about ten years, he had certainly been around and, if even half his stories were true, he had crammed a lot into those years.

By sundown they reached the homestead. On the porch, Pi'taki stood watching as the dark smudge on the horizon drew closer. From a long way off, she could see that Frances had company and her eyes narrowed with curiosity. She had been worried by the lateness of her return and had concealed this from Rory as she put him down to sleep. Stepping off the porch, she walked slowly towards the approaching wagon. As they came into the farmyard, Frances waved and called out in greeting. Pi'taki did not respond and she eyed Lee suspiciously. He nodded curtly but she gave no sign of acknowledgement. 'Ain't too friendly, the help around here,' he murmured under his breath.

Frances ignored the remark and jumped down to embrace Pi'taki. 'I'm sorry we're so late,' she said and breathlessly tried to explain about the wagon.

Lee pushed his hat back on his head and looked around him. He admired the farmhouse with its wide front porch and the out-buildings surrounding it. 'Yep, Mrs Munroe, you got the makin' of a mighty fine farm here.'

Pi'taki's voice cut the evening air. 'Who is this man?'

'This is Mr O'Byrne,' Frances said, 'he helped me get the wagon out of the mud and he's agreed to come and work for us for a while.' She tried to sound matter-of-fact but was met with a stony expression.

Lee jumped down from the wagon and doffed his hat in a sweeping gesture. 'Pleased to meet you, ma'am.' He held out his hand.

He was so excessively polite that the rudeness could not be missed and Pi'taki turned away from him. 'You got the money from the bank?' she asked bluntly. Frances shook her head, embarrassed, even though Lee knew the financial situation. 'Then how do we pay him—'

Before Pi'taki finished speaking, Lee cut in. 'Is Mr Munroe around? Maybe I should have a word with the boss,' he said, returning Pi'taki's stare with equal animosity.

Frances had been nervously waiting for that question, but her cool voice did not betray it. 'There are two bosses around here, O'Byrne – myself and Pi'taki. We run the farm together. My husband is dead.'

He gave her a startled look and scratched his head. 'Ain't you got no men folks about the place?'

'William died before we came out to the homestead. Pi'taki and I have built this up from nothing.' She held his gaze. 'If you don't

156

think you can handle working for two women, then you had better go now.'

Lee was visibly shocked. 'Well, I'll be damned,' he said as he walked about surveying the scene, 'if this ain't the strangest thing I ever did come across!' Pi'taki walked away from them and went into the house. 'Well, I'll be damned,' he said again as she disappeared through the door.

'So you said.' Frances was annoyed that she had been unable to speak to Pi'taki privately without O'Byrne swaggering about. She felt guilty at imposing her decision on the other woman before first consulting her and hoped she could make amends. Leaving Lee to his disbelieving inspection of the farm, she went indoors and returned carrying some bedding. 'Here, take this. You can settle yourself in the barn over there and I'll bring you something to eat in a minute.'

Lee rubbed his arms and shivered. 'It's mighty cold now the night's drawing in,' he said. 'Sure would appreciate warmin' myself by your stove first.'

Frances kept her voice level. 'The barn's warm and clean and it's one step up from the back of a wagon which is where you slept last night. We made a deal, O'Byrne, and we're going to stick to it.'

'Okay, only kidding,' he smiled and took the blankets.

'Glad to hear it.' She turned to go back to the house and then stopped. 'By the way, if you have any ideas about taking advantage of two poor, defenceless womenfolk, I'd remind you that I have the gun.' She pulled it from under the wagon seat, 'And Pi'taki has a deft touch with that knife.' She gave him a wide smile. 'Now, get the horse stabled and make yourself comfortable.'

He gave her a searching look and then shrugged, leading the animal away. Frances watched him disappear into the barn and went indoors. Pi'taki stood by the stove. Two rabbits hung from the beam above her head and the rich smell coming from a bubbling pot conveyed she had already cooked another.

'Did you catch these?' Frances asked the obvious, knowing at once that her light manner would only signal how defensive she felt. She waited for some sort of reaction but Pi'taki remained bent over the stove, stirring the stew. When no words came, she sighed and sank into the chair at the side of the stove.

'Pi'taki, I went to the bank and Lemieux wouldn't hear of extending the loan. He knew before I even opened my mouth what I was going to ask. We're broke.'

'I know.'

'Then what's the matter? Don't ye agree, we must have help?'

'Yes.' Pi'taki paused. 'Not this man.'

Frances fought to keep her temper. 'Look, he's offered to work for a share of anything we make on the farm this season. If we don't make any money, we get him for nothing. What's wrong with that? – it's a good deal.'

'Ask yourself, why does he do it?'

Frances looked puzzled, annoyed that she had skirted this question herself and shrugged her shoulders. 'Plenty of men around here without work. He gets free board and lodgings for a while, I suppose.' She saw Pi'taki's expression and jumped up. 'Look, I don't really care why he's doing it. I'll take all the help I can just now, no questions asked, all right?' Pi'taki turned back to the stove and Frances gave up. Maybe things would look different after a night's sleep, she thought and she went off to the bedroom to change out of her filthy clothes.

Later, she realised with a jolt that she had forgotten to take food to Lee. Guiltily, she slipped over to the barn with a plate of Pi'taki's stew and found him already snoring in the straw. Damned if he hasn't got a smile on his smug face even when he's sleeping, she thought.

4

Frances was in a deep sleep when she felt herself being roughly shaken awake. 'Quick, come! He takes the horse and wagon.' Pi'taki's voice was urgent and the words snapped Frances into full awareness. She leapt from the bed and ran to the window. In the early dawn light, she saw the dust rise in the distance as Lee made off. She cursed herself for her own stupidity. It was obvious he would take the first opportunity to steal the wagon and leave.

'Damn!' She pushed up the window and screamed, 'O'Byrne! Come back here!' but the disappearing figure never turned round or gave any indication he had heard her. Enraged, Frances swept up the gun from the side of her bed and swung to aim through the window. Trying to fix him in her sights, she found herself trembling too hard to hold it steady and realised what she was about to do. Throwing the gun down with a sound of disgust, she turned to Pi'taki who still stood by the bed. 'Could you no stop him?'

Pi'taki shook her head and gazed steadily at her. Then she

turned to leave the room. 'I will take the other horse and go after him.'

Frances caught her arm. 'No. If he's that desperate, he might hurt you.' She slumped down onto the bed. 'I'm sorry, I should have listened to you. This is all my fault.'

Pi'taki sat beside her and put her arm around her shoulders. 'We can borrow a wagon if we need it. It is good he has gone.'

Frances sighed and wearily got to her feet again. 'All right. Go and find Rory. I'll get the breakfast and we can talk this through.' While she quickly washed and dressed, the frustration of their situation boiled up inside her. Things had been bad before, but to have their wagon and a horse stolen from under their noses was the last straw.

She was busy making pancake batter in the kitchen when the door burst open and Rory tumbled in. 'Na'a!' he yelled. Frances tried to lift her flour-covered hands out of the way but he threw himself at her and ended up with white streaks across his brown back.

'Look at yourself – away out my road and wash your hands.' She smiled as he pulled a chair up to reach the bowl, and watched him fill it from the giant water jug. At five years old, her son never ceased to surprise her. At times like this, when he was boisterous and overpowering, she could see the part of him that was William. His sun-streaked hair flopped over his eyes and he pushed it back in exactly the same way, just as if he had learned it from his father. He was independent and free-spirited and Frances was proud of that but, in his occasional bursts of anger, she saw all too clearly her own worst failings. Pi'taki's influence had kept this at bay and the child had learned tolerance which showed most strongly when he was with her, listening and learning the Blackfoot ways. With his dark skin he looked more like a native child, but the clear blue eyes spoke of another heritage.

Pi'taki came in carrying more water from the well. Rory started to chatter away to her in her tongue, speaking so fluently that Frances could only make out the occasional word. Pi'taki, as she always did in her presence, replied in English. 'Ask your mother, Issohko.'

'Na'a, who was that man?'

Frances kept her voice steady and beat the bowl of frothing batter with increased agitation. 'He was going to do some work for us, but . . . something came up and he had to leave.'

'But he's took the wagon.'

She started to pour the pancakes on the griddle pan. 'Oh, he

159

needed it to get back to town so I sold it to him.' She spoke casually, dismissing the subject. 'Now, come on, no more questions. Away out and fetch me some eggs!' Rory was confused but he did as he was told and dragged his feet out the door.

'Why do you not speak the truth to the boy?'

Frances ignored the question, busying herself with the pancakes, but Pi'taki waited for an answer.

'Och, why bother him with it? He's too young to understand.'

'He is too young for lies, Otanimm.'

Frances was flustered. 'You're right,' she sighed, 'I'll explain to him later. But not now, please?'

The sun was already well into the sky by the time they went out to the fields. Frances felt drained and exhausted but Pi'taki insisted that she ignore what had happened and try to carry on. Moping about the loss of the wagon would not bring it back. She concentrated on the work to be done, letting her mind go blank and feeling the warmth of the sun on her bare arms. The day was promising for ploughing but still it was hard not to be downhearted. Even if they ploughed, there was little seed left to plant. Rory seemed to sense the tension and alternated between helping and running in front of the plough, shouting encouragement. Frances was touched by his simple concern and she raged inwardly all the more against Leland O'Byrne.

'Na'a!' Suddenly Rory's piercing shout roused her out of her depression. He was pointing to the wagon that had appeared and she stared in disbelief. It was Lee. Rory started to run towards the cart, and Pi'taki grabbed him, holding him close to her. Frances seethed with renewed fury, flung down the hoe and marched out to meet him. Lee pulled the wagon to a halt in front of them and jumped off, grinning widely.

'Mornin', Mrs Munroe,' he said, tipping his hat politely.

'What the hell have ye been doing?' she demanded. 'What right did ye have to take my horse and my wagon—'

Lee held up his hands in mock surrender. 'Whoa, lady! I'm sorry, but on a farm you gotta get up with the sun and get goin'. I couldn't wait all day for you women to stir your stumps, there was things to do.'

She seethed at him through clenched teeth. 'Why you, you. . . We've put more hours of hard work into this farm than you'll ever know.' As she spoke she became distracted by the sight of a few sacks in the back of the wagon. 'And what's that?'

He grinned, walked round to the tail-board and dropped it

down. 'You told me yesterday you had no seed. Well, now you do.' He patted the bulging sacks.

Frances stared at him, suspiciously. 'Where did ye get them?'

'Some of the other quarters around you is empty. They've up and gone.' He grinned again. 'Most left nothin' behind them, others. . .' He shrugged his shoulders. 'Well, seed corn's no use in the city, is it?'

She was appalled. 'You mean you stole it?'

He shook his head. 'Nope, I took what somebody else left as useless to them. It's of use to you.' He looked at her. 'You don't want me to take it back?'

'Yes I most certainly do!' She glared at him defiantly.

Lee did not move. 'You mean that?'

She wavered. 'No. . . Oh, I don't know.'

'Well, Mrs Munroe, make up your mind.' He waved at the work they had done. 'But there's not much point in ploughing fields if you ain't gonna seed 'em.'

Frances knew he was right. No one was coming back to the empty farms and she might as well get the benefit from what they had left behind. 'All right,' she sighed in agreement, and Lee grinned at her, insolent and unabashed. 'But next time, O'Byrne,' she insisted, 'you ask my permission before you do anything – anything! Ye understand?'

He nodded in an off-hand way and went to lead the horse and wagon to the barn. As he did so, he noticed Rory for the first time, standing clutching Pi'taki's hand. 'Well, hi there little fella,' he called. Rory peered round Pi'taki's legs and stared back blankly. Lee shrugged. 'Guess he don't speak English, eh? He your boy?' he asked, addressing Pi'taki. 'Naw, thought he was a mite young – what is he, your grandson? Looks like a bit of a half-breed.'

'He is *my* son, Mr O'Byrne,' Frances curtly interrupted, 'and you'd better watch your runaway tongue because I can assure you he understands everything. Rory, say hello to Mr O'Byrne.' The child muttered a greeting in Blackfoot, the irony of which was not lost on any of them and Lee led the horse away feeling suitably chastened.

Frances felt Pi'taki's disapproving eyes on her. 'Don't say it, I know what you're thinking but we've no choice. I dinna care now what we have to do to survive. Reckonings can come later.' Pi'taki sniffed loudly and went back to the ploughing.

'Na'a?' Rory was tugging expectantly at Frances's skirt. 'Why's the man come back?'

She sighed, and started to explain. Pi'taki had, as usual, been

161

right. Telling a lie before now made this explanation even more difficult.

5

'No water.'

'What do ye mean, no water?' Frances stopped hitching the horse to the wagon and turned to meet Pi'taki's eyes.

'In the well.'

'Oh no, that's all we need. . .' She pulled off her gloves, walked over to the wooden-framed structure and peered down into the blackness. As she hauled on the tackle, the bucket came up lightly with only a small deposit of sludge in the bottom of it. 'Jesus, I hope it's no dried up.' She spoke her thoughts out loud. 'Was the lid left off – maybe Rory's been chucking things down it?'

'No, the lid was there. It was not the child, something is wrong inside.'

Frances groaned. 'Oh, I don't think I could bear it if the well gives out on top of everything else. We canna afford to get somebody out here.' The two women stood looking thoughtfully down into the dark abyss. She made a decision. 'I'll get Mr O'Byrne to climb down and take a look,' she said emphatically, pulling her gloves back on. 'I'll send him over on my way out.'

'You are going then?' Pi'taki asked in a flat, unemotional voice.

'We've been over this already.' Frances sighed in exasperation. 'You know I'm going. The doctor's calling at Fred and Mary Olsen's place today and it's bound to be busy. I've got to get there by noon if Rory's to see the doctor.'

'He's not sick.'

'Maybe so, but we're as well to be on the safe side. It's just a check over and he only comes once in a blue moon.' She called to Rory who was jumping in and out of a pile of straw. He had already got his clothes covered in dust and stalks of hay stuck out from his dishevelled hair.

Pi'taki sucked her teeth contemptuously. 'Look at the boy,' she said as he raced over to them. 'He is like the a'sinnoka. He needs no doctor.'

'He needs a kick up the shirt.' Frances tried to restore some semblance of order to Rory's looks. 'I'm not going to discuss it any more,' she said, losing her patience. 'You're only saying this because you don't want us to use O'Byrne's help but you know fine that we canna survive without water.'

'We could do it – you and me.'

'We could – if I had the time.'

Pi'taki folded her arms and turned away. Rory jumped into the back of the wagon as his mother climbed aboard. 'We'll be back by sundown.' Getting no response, she gave up and snapped the reins. 'I'll send O'Byrne back,' she called over her shoulder.

She found him clearing a new field some distance from the house. Two weeks had passed since she had brought him to the farm. His skill and knowledge meant that the work had moved quickly with the three of them spending every day in the fields. The weather was a blessing, neither too hot nor too wet and, for the first time in months, she dared to hope that things would start to improve. Burning and clearing had already added two acres to those under cultivation from previous years and now Lee was starting another field. Despite the chill in the air, his shirt stuck to his sweating skin as he put his back into the work. He looked up as he heard the wagon approach. 'Howdy! Well, what do you think?'

'But we'll never be sowing as much as this, not in the time we've got.' Frances gazed at the land, unconvinced.

'Just you wait and see. It's your land. You might as well grow on it – no point in leaving it barren another year.'

'Well, I'll believe it when I see it. Right now, Mr O'Byrne, we've got more pressing problems.'

Lee leaned back against the well and rolled himself a thin cigarette. 'You don't like me, do you?' he said squinting into the sun. Pi'taki remained with folded arms looking into the distance without speaking.

'What's the matter? – not got a tongue in your head?' He licked the paper and spat out some loose tobacco. 'Well, I guess we got nothin' much to talk about anyways,' he went on. 'Blackfoot, ain't ya?' There was a barely perceptible nod. 'I ain't had much dealin's with Blackfeet. Cree, mostly, up this way.' Pi'taki snorted in disgust and Lee grinned. 'That's right ol' lady, you and them don't get on too well.' He lit the cigarette and dropped the guttering match down into the shaft. 'It's a mite dark down there. Go get me a lamp from the house.'

'I am not your servant.'

He grinned. 'Never said you was. But Mrs Munroe said I ain't to go in the house.' He held her stony gaze. 'You sayin' I should?'

163

Pi'taki strode off huffily and returned with a lamp. He laughed and trod the cigarette butt into the ground. 'Okay, Pocahontas, now we understand each other, let's get to work.'

He took a stout plank and laid it across the mouth of the well. To this he knotted a long rope which he twisted around his body before carefully lowering himself into the shaft. The channel was narrow and claustrophobic and he plunged deeper with only the small pool of light from the lamp to guide him. The wooden sides gave way to earth walls as he dropped deeper still and the air grew dank and cold. Once or twice he looked up and high above him saw the face of Pi'taki watching vigilantly from the rim of the well.

Suddenly, Lee's feet hit upon something hard. It felt secure and he loosened his grip on the rope to get a better footing. It was a mistake. The obstruction gave way beneath him and he toppled over. The lamp hanging on his belt shattered, plunging him into darkness and his legs were sucked into a sludgy hole. Desperately, he fought to retrieve his hand-hold on the rope but as he sank further into the mire, it was beyond his reach. His anguished voice echoed up through the well shaft to where Pi'taki stood. 'Help me! More rope, I'm sinking!' He barely made out the bronze moon of her face from where he struggled but could only guess at its expression. 'Dammit!' he cried. 'Help me!'

Precious seconds ticked by and Pi'taki listened as Lee squirmed pathetically in the mud-logged snare. His voice was at fever pitch by the time she eventually reacted and slowly fed out more rope until it reached him. He clung on for his life and with all the strength in his body he heaved himself, bit by bit, to the top. As he surfaced, mud smeared, cursing and collapsing with fatigue, she was nowhere to be seen.

When Frances returned that evening, she could sense that the tension between Pi'taki and Lee had intensified but neither would admit anything was wrong. He had unblocked the well, although the water was still too muddy and churned up to be used, so Pi'taki and Rory went off with buckets to a stream at the edge of the homestead.

Frances changed out of her good clothes and donned her old working dress again. She poured two cups of coffee from the pot that always bubbled on the stove and took them out to the yard where Lee was chopping firewood.

'Thanks,' he said, taking the cup from her. He wiped the sweat from his face and drank deeply.

'So, what was the problem with the well?' Frances asked after a while.

'Part of one side had caved in – whoever dug it didn't shore it up enough.' He handed back the empty cup and placed another log on the cutting block. 'I've put more planking in and fixed the sides. Shouldn't be no more trouble to you.'

'And Pi'taki?'

He stopped swinging the axe. 'What about her?'

'Look, O'Byrne, I'm no daft. I can see the two of you don't like each other but if this kind of bad feeling goes on,' she faced him squarely, 'I think you'll have to go.'

'Mrs Munroe, I've knowed Indians since I was a kid. Trapping up north, you see a lot of them. They're different from us – I don't interfere if they leave me alone.' He swung the axe down viciously, shattering the log. 'But her! I ain't even said boo to the woman, and she's dead set against me.'

Frances smiled. 'Pi'taki has very firm ideas that are difficult to shift, I know. But if you'll just try to get along, it would make it easier for everyone.'

'Well, I'll be trying, Mrs Munroe, you can depend on that.' He started to lift the cut wood to the stack at the side of the house. Frances helped him and they worked in silence for a time. 'Rory's a funny kid, though.' Lee's remark was unexpected and her back stiffened.

'What do you mean?'

'I dunno. He's a bit wild – ain't like other kids. I suppose not havin' a father an' all makes a difference.'

'You think so? Well, of course life doesn't always go the way ye expect it to.' The residue of bitterness in her voice surprised her and she rushed on. 'But all things considered, I'm proud of how Rory's turned out. He's as loved and cared for as any child I know around here – probably more so.'

'Well sure, don't get me wrong, he's a bright kid – sharp as an Arkansas toothpick, just . . . different. I ain't criticising, just sayin' he could maybe do with a bit of male company, that's all.'

'Oh, I see. A bit o' drinking, gambling, womanising male company like you could provide, eh? Ye think that would be better for him? Dinna try to tell me how to bring up my son, O'Byrne.' Frances was unsettled yet vaguely persuaded by his comments so her response was harder than she had intended.

Lee held up his hands. 'Forget I mentioned it. Ain't nothin' to me how the kid grows up. You're his mother.'

165

'Aye, and don't you forget that.' She brushed down her clothes and briskly turned and walked back into the house.

His eyes followed her as she disappeared indoors. Then he raised the axe and swung it home to rest in the chopping block. 'Gee, Frances Munroe, you sure do try a man's patience,' he breathed.

Frances thought about their conversation and as her anger subsided she began to wonder if he might have had a point. In the time that Lee had been with them, he had tried to be friendly but Rory had kept away from him, torn between curiosity and the distrust he shared with Pi'taki. When the two of them returned with the water, Frances found herself telling Rory to go and help Lee stack the wood.

'Why?' he asked. The boy looked uncomfortable and glanced at Pi'taki.

'Because he needs help and I'm tired.'

Pi'taki moved towards the door. 'I will go,' she said.

'No, you're tired too.' Frances gave her a warning look. 'Rory can help him.'

Going out to the back of the house, Rory stood some distance from the wood stack and watched. Lee found the scrutiny unsettling. Finally, he stopped and walked over. 'What do you want, kid?'

Rory backed away slightly. 'Momma said I was to help you.'

'She did, eh?' Lee grinned. 'Well, that's mighty nice of your momma. C'mon then, it won't take no time with two of us doin' it.' He could hear raised voices from the house and he put his hand on Rory's shoulder, leading him away. 'Let's go get us some more logs. Sounds like they're busy.'

At the enclosure where the horses were penned, he stopped. 'Say, kid, can you ride – want me to teach you?' Rory squinted up at him, then his face split in a wide grin. With a leap, he was over the fence. He put two fingers in his mouth and gave a shrill whistle. The horse lumbered up to them and sank forward onto its front knees. In a trice, the boy was over its neck, clutching handfuls of the mane and urging it up. It set off at a gallop round the enclosure. Lee watched in astonishment as Rory guided the animal, changing direction and fearlessly waving his arms aloft.

The horse slowed to come alongside Lee. He scratched his head and smiled. 'Well, I guess you don't need me to show you how to ride, little fella,' he said as he lifted him down.

'Want me to teach you?' Rory asked cheekily and Lee laughed as he ruffled his hair.

Slowly then, with each passing day the two grew more friendly.

166

Rory overcame his distrust and Lee was able to win the boy's confidence, spending more time alone with him. Occasionally, he was allowed to take him to check the traps he had set. It was an area where he had superior knowledge and used it to draw them closer, though even here the child's skill was already developed. Sometimes on Sunday afternoons, leaving the two women back at the house, they would ride out beyond the homestead and Rory discovered new sights and sounds to capture his interest. It was on these long rides that Lee talked of when he was a boy, relating improbable adventures that left Rory wide-eyed and begging for more.

Gradually, these stories became interspersed with gentle questioning. Frances gave away few personal details when they talked, and Pi'taki never spoke to him at all. Rory was his sole source of information and, in his frank and honest way, he had a surprising store of it. Lee's problem was in sifting truth from the boy's confused recollections but, even so, it was astounding to learn what the two women had achieved on their own. At times, riding home after a day out, Rory's drowsy speech would slip into Blackfoot as he responded to the casual probing. It was then that Lee had to restrain himself from shaking the boy and telling him to speak in a civilised tongue.

But Pi'taki's influence was a strange and powerful one that could not easily be dismissed. Once Lee told a wild tale of how his friends had been ambushed by Indians and had fought them off, gunning them down one by one. After that, Rory had grown silent and for the rest of the afternoon was listless and withdrawn. When they had got back to the farm, he had jumped down from the horse and run straight to Pi'taki, burying his head in her skirts. The old woman had stroked the boy's head, silently staring into Lee's eyes, her expression giving nothing away. But he had felt naked under her gaze and unable to summon his usual air of superiority.

'Come on, kid, help me stable the horse.' Lee tried to cajole the boy but got no reply. Leading the tired animal back to the barn, he swore under his breath. 'OK, Pocahontas, round one to you.'

It was a while before Rory would speak to him again. And by then, Lee had learned to keep quiet on any subject that might result in a similar rift between them.

6

It was some weeks later when a horse-drawn buggy drove up to the house. Frances could see it was Fred and Mary Olsen and ran out to greet them. 'Good morning,' she called.

'Howdy there, neighbour,' Fred shouted back cheerfully. He drew the horse to a stop and helped his wife down. As the two women hugged and exchanged greetings, he looked around at the fields that were green with the sprouting wheat. 'You're looking well – and so much land under the plough! Think it'll be a good year?'

'Could be, Fred.' Frances led the way to the chairs on the verandah. 'Sit down and I'll make us some coffee. Are you away into Edmonton?'

Mary sat and pulled off her cotton bonnet, wiping the dust from her face. 'Yes, we're going in for some supplies. Do you need anything?'

Frances laughed, heading towards the kitchen. 'I need plenty, Mary. But I've no money to pay for any of it.' They laughed with her. A year ago they would not have been so light-hearted about it. Yet now the possibility of a good crop had everyone cautiously optimistic. When Frances returned with the coffee, the discussion continued in the same cheerful vein as they exchanged news. Mary detailed all the latest births in the vicinity, throwing in a few morsels of gossip as she did so. As they relaxed in the gentle sunshine, dawdling over their coffee, the pressures of working the land for once seemed less immediate. Frances found her attention wandering from the conversation as she idly fantasised on what few luxuries she might allow herself if the harvest was as good as they hoped.

'It's the same story everywhere,' Fred was saying as she came back to the present. 'Them as are still farmin' are seeding every square inch. Never seen so much wheat planted.' He waved at the fields beyond the yard. 'You and Pi'taki must've been workin' non-stop to get so much done. This is quite a sight.'

Frances shifted, uncertain what to say but just then, Lee strode around the corner of the house. He gave the Olsens a most winning smile and offered his hand. 'Howdy. I saw the wagon draw up, and thought I'd come and be neighbourly. Name's Leland O'Byrne.'

Fred rose and shook hands, introducing himself. Mary shot a glance at Frances. 'Nice to meet you, Mr O'Byrne,' she said.

Frances felt her face reddening as they looked at her expectantly. 'Mr O'Byrne has come to work for us for a while.' She waved vaguely. 'That's how we got so much planted.'

'Oh? You never mentioned this when you came over with Rory the other week.' Mary was finding it hard not to smile at Frances's discomfort. 'Where is the little lad, by the way? And Pi'taki – how's she keeping?'

'They're around some place,' Frances explained, glad at the turn in the conversation, 'I'll go and call them if you like.'

Fred finished his coffee quickly and rose. 'Now come on, Mary, these folks got things to do and we gotta get to Edmonton.'

'All right, maybe another time.' She followed him to the wagon, turning to call back, 'Oh, Frances, I almost forgot. The Dutchaks are planning a barn-raising after the harvest. They said to invite you all.' She nodded to Lee. 'I'm sure you'd be welcome too, Mr O'Byrne.'

Frances flushed uncomfortably. 'That's kind of you, Mary. See and thank Josef and Wasylyna for me and tell them I'll be there.' She took a deep breath and frowned at Lee. 'Of course I can't speak for Mr O'Byrne.'

'Sure, I'd be delighted to come,' he chipped in cheerily, 'and look forward to seeing you folks again.'

'Good then, that's fixed.' Mary smiled sweetly and allowed herself to be lifted onto the wagon by her impatient husband.

After waving the Olsens on their way, Frances turned on Lee. 'What do ye think you're up to?' she demanded, hands on hips.

He looked confused. 'What d'you mean?'

'I mean, acting like you owned the place.' She squared up to him. 'You're the hired help, O'Byrne, and don't ever forget that. I dinna need a man to act as host when my neighbours call round.'

He pulled off his hat and flung it to the ground. 'You dunno what you need,' he yelled back at her. 'Every time I try to be nice, you act like I was some kinda leper.' He stamped on his hat in a rage. 'You trample on me and my feelings, just like that,' he said angrily, giving it one more kick.

By now, the hat was ruined. Breathless, he stopped and glared at her. She tried to hold his gaze, but the absurdity of the situation suddenly made her want to laugh. 'O'Byrne,' she said, folding her arms, 'what do you look like?'

Lee stopped frowning and smiled back. 'A fool,' he said softly.

He picked up the flattened hat, jammed it on his head and slowly walked away. Frances stood watching, still giggling quietly to herself but unsure of what she really felt. Sometimes she found herself liking him, though in many ways he was still a stranger and the little she knew of his past was hardly a reference for trust. There was also Pi'taki's implacable dislike of him and, if Frances could not understand the intensity of Pi'taki's feelings, she still would not lightly dismiss them. As far as she was concerned, though Leland O'Byrne worked well and gave no cause for complaint, she was not to be lulled into a false sense of security. The gun, for the time being, remained beside her as she slept.

The next morning, Frances stirred in her bed as the first light filtered through the curtain. Suddenly, the floorboards creaked and she felt the closeness of another body bearing down on her. She opened her eyes and was startled to find Lee's within inches of her own and the cold steel of the gun-barrel protruding from under his arm. He jumped backwards, the gun still pointing in her general direction.

She fought to control her fear. 'So this is your game, O'Byrne!' Her voice was as loud as she dared make it, hoping to attract Pi'taki's attention. 'I might've guessed it would no be long before ye tried to take advantage.'

'Look, I can explain,' he began nervously, placing the rifle against the washstand.

'I would pick that up if I were you.' Frances said as she tried to judge the distance to where the gun stood. 'There's no way you'll get into my bed without a gun at my head – that's for sure!'

Lee's face changed. His eyes flashed and a thin smile spread across his lips. 'You got me all wrong, ma'am – nothin' coulda been further from my mind. Not that you ain't a fine lookin' woman and all, but dammit, Mrs Munroe – how could you think such a thing?' His voice was raised in indignation.

She continued to keep an eye on the rifle. 'If ye had no intentions towards me then what the hell are ye doing in here?'

'Now, hold on just a minute. Before you go jumpin' to those conclusions of yours and condemnin' a man before he's even got a chance to speak up for hisself, let me just put you right on a thing or two.' He jabbed his finger at her to emphasise the point. 'First, I never had no dishonourable intentions towards you and I ain't never had to put a gun to a woman where that's concerned.' Frances tried to interrupt but he continued. 'Second, I wasn't taking the gun – I was returning it.'

'Returning it?'

He nodded and moved over to the bedroom door which stood ajar. From behind it, he slid three plump prairie chickens across the floor towards her.

Frances looked at him, bewildered. 'You shot these?' she asked in a small voice.

'I surely did,' Lee replied, triumphantly folding his arms. 'Was up before daybreak as usual, and I could hear them over in the dip behind them trees in the southwest quarter. Knew I couldn't catch 'em, I needed a gun. So I came up here and took yours.'

At that moment, Pi'taki appeared in the doorway. She had heard the raised voices coming from the house and run over. She looked questioningly at Frances, ignoring Lee and the fallen birds. 'It's all right, Pi'taki,' Frances reassured her. 'Mr O'Byrne and I have a bit of a misunderstanding here. I'll be out once I've had a few words with him.' Pi'taki looked at his gloating face and seemed reluctant to go. When she eventually did so, she left the door open behind her.

'You had no right coming in here and stealing the gun,' Frances said, not meeting Lee's eyes.

'I know,' he admitted softly, 'and for that I apologise. But don't you see, I really did it to make a point with you. Ever since I came here you've treated me like some kinda fugitive. I have to sleep and eat in the barn like one of the animals – well, I'm a man, and I got feelin's too, y'know. I just wanted you to trust me.'

'And how am I going to trust you now, O'Byrne?' she said.

'Cos now you know I coulda taken that gun any time I chose to.' He leaned forward with one eyebrow raised. 'Now look here, Mrs Munroe, ain't it about time we started treatin' each other a bit more civil?'

Frances had to admit he could be right, although she found the whole episode unsettling and wanted time to think. 'We'll talk about it after breakfast, O'Byrne.'

He glared back at her. 'And you can start by calling me Lee.'

'All right, Lee,' she sighed. 'Now would you mind leaving so I can get dressed?'

Pi'taki would not enter into a discussion on the matter so Frances took the decision alone. Lee was allowed to eat with them in the house, although she insisted he continue to sleep in the barn. The first few meals were embarrassed, stilted affairs and only his playful banter with Rory kept long silences at bay. Watching him with her son, Frances realised what a change had taken place in Rory over the past weeks. All Lee's talk of the world outside the confines of the farm held the child spellbound and he had begun to ask his mother if he could go with her on her next trip into town.

Lee's infectious good humour gradually overcame her initial discomfort at having him eat with them and Frances slowly began to warm to his company. Pi'taki however, did not budge in her opinion of him and remained silent and brooding through every meal. Despite this, or perhaps because of it, Lee gave his full attention to Frances, asking about the hard times she had had, nodding and sympathising, coaxing her to talk. She responded cautiously at first, but gradually found herself telling him more and more. As a listener, he had a charm and appeal she found hard to resist. And, though she would never have admitted it, for the first time in years she remembered how good it felt to be paid attention to as a woman.

7

As summer passed its height, the wheat in the fields stood tall with the fat ears of grain bowing the stalks and promising a bumper harvest. Work on the farm was slacking off and there was a pause before the right moment when they would embark on the next major task – that of cutting the wheat. One night, as they ate supper, Lee suggested a picnic the next day. He winked conspiratorially at Rory who ploughed in with enthusiastic support. Frances could see they had been scheming and she looked doubtful. 'We've no time for playing.'

'All work and no play makes Mrs Munroe a pretty dull lady.' Lee mimicked her disapproving frown, drawing peals of laughter from Rory. 'Come on, it's no big deal to take a day off when there ain't so much to do. We all need a break before the harvest.'

'Na'a, *please*.' Rory jumped up on her lap and gave her his most appealing look.

'All right, you win,' she laughed, 'It's like having two bairns instead of one.' She looked over to Pi'taki. 'Where do ye think we should go?'

'I will not come.'

Rory ran round to her. 'You must come, Na'a, you *must*.'

He reverted to Blackfoot and began whispering endearments in her ear.

Lee interrupted. 'Pi'taki, the boy's right. Won't be fun for any of us if you don't come. It's only a few more weeks till harvest, and then you can be rid of me for good.' He gazed at her beseechingly, 'Come on, what d'ya say?'

Grudgingly, she nodded and Rory whooped in delight. Long after supper was over, they were still making plans and Frances was busily preparing food for the outing. The next morning, they set off in the wagon and headed for one of the many small lakes that dotted the land to the south-west. The weather was bright and warm and by the time they reached the place, the sun was burning fiercely. The horse was tethered in the shade and Frances began unpacking the wagon. She watched as Lee tore off his hat, shirt, and boots and ran towards the water. 'I'll race you, Rory,' he challenged and the child could hardly contain his excitement as he bolted after him.

Frances walked to the edge where she sat, pulling off her shoes and letting her feet dangle in the cool water. She watched the two figures splashing around and called to the bobbing heads. 'Be careful, Lee. These lakes can be deep and dangerous.'

'Aw, he'll be safe with me.' He swam over, heaved himself out on to the bank and sat beside her. Together they watched as Rory tumbled and ducked under the surface, spouting water and making squealing noises that echoed around the lake. 'Great kid,' Lee observed, shaking his head wistfully.

Frances was going to speak but thought the better of it. She glanced at Lee out of the corner of her eye. The months of hard work on the farm had trimmed his body down to a lithe, tanned leanness. He had lost the debauched look he had when she first saw him crawl from his hiding place in the back of her wagon, and he seemed to have changed in other ways too.

Lee twisted round and lowered himself back into the water. 'Coming in for a dip?' he suggested, grinning.

Frances was momentarily flustered. She would dearly have liked to plunge into the fanning ripples and play with Rory but she felt strangely inhibited by Lee's presence. She laughed to cover her embarrassment and lied to answer him. 'I can't swim,' she said quietly.

He moved closer towards the bank, his chest almost touching her feet in the water. 'Maybe I can teach you?'

Frances shivered and rubbed at the goose-flesh that had appeared on her arms. 'No, it's too cold,' she said, jumping up. 'I'll away and sit over there.' She walked quickly back to where Pi'taki was under the trees. The two women sat in silence for some time, watching Lee and the boy take turns at diving. 'Rory seems to like him well,' Frances mused.

'The child does not know – he is too young.'

'Know what, Pi'taki?'

'He is cunning like the timber-wolf – more so, for he traps the wolf and kills it.'

Frances sighed, nervously pulling on a strand of grass. 'I'm sorry you still feel that way. He's made such a difference to our lives.'

'Yes, you are different when he is there.'

'Dinna be ridiculous,' Frances said, feeling uncomfortable.

'I have eyes, Otanimm. I can see.'

It was pointless trying to deny it. 'Well, he'll be going soon.'

Rory interrupted them as he came rushing up, dripping water over them both and shouting, 'Look Na'a – I caught a fish!' He tossed the squirming prize into her lap and Frances pushed it away, feigning disgust.

'I think ye better throw that back, it doesn't look like something we can eat.' Rory grabbed it again and made off down to the lakeside. 'Fetch Lee back with you,' she called after him. Lee returned with Rory riding high on his shoulders and they stretched out in the sun to dry themselves. Frances then laid the food on a cloth and watched as they ate hungrily.

'Can we do this again soon?' Rory implored of Lee. They had finished eating and the child leaned across his chest looking around and watching for grasshoppers.

Frances saw his expression change. 'I dunno, son,' he replied sadly, 'we'll see.'

By the time they reached the homestead, the stars were out. Rory had long since fallen asleep in Lee's arms in the back of the wagon. 'I'll put him to bed so's not to wake him,' he offered, and Frances nodded. Pi'taki went to her room and said nothing but her disapproval was obvious.

Frances stood alone on the verandah, leaning against a post and gazing at the hazy constellations, their brilliance subdued by the summer lightness of the night sky. Eventually, Lee emerged and joined her. 'He's beat – sleepin' like a lamb,' he said softly. 'Take more than a thunderbolt to wake him now.' He followed the direction of her gaze. 'Sure is a fine night.'

Frances looked at him gratefully. 'It's been a fine day,' she said. 'Thanks, Lee, it was a great idea, the picnic.'

'My pleasure,' he smiled. His arm rested on the post just above her head, uncomfortably close.

They stared at each other for a moment and Frances cleared her throat nervously, searching for something to say. 'About when you leave. . .' she began.

'Oh, I meant to talk to you about that,' Lee looked down at her. 'Thought I'd go after the Dutchak barn-raisin' – then you can give me a ride into town and we can settle up. Would that be all right?'

'Oh, right. . .' She picked up her things from the rocking-chair, 'that would be fine. Just fine. Well, er, I'll say good night.'

''Night,' he whispered, paused for a second and strolled off towards the barn.

8

The harvest was all too soon upon them. The glorious weather held out and the wheat was bone-dry as they cut it from the fields. Everyone in the vicinity took turns to have a group of neighbours come and work their farm. Later, the threshing machines would come with their crews to turn the stacks of sheaves into a mound of golden grain ready to be transported to the elevators for sale. The work was hard and had to be done as quickly as possible. No one knew how long the good weather would hold and recent memories of hail-flattened fields gave them all a sense of urgency.

Shortly before the Dutchak celebrations were to be held, Rory got sick and for a few days he was confined to bed. When the measles spots appeared, Pi'taki became alarmed and, although the fever had passed, she slept beside him each night continuing to administer her own natural remedies. Despite vociferous attempts to demonstrate how well he felt, there was no question that he would be allowed to attend the party and he complained loud and long about the injustice of it.

Frances smiled down at Rory's pouting face. She had closed the curtains to block out the early sun and the room was cool and dark. Smoothing the sheets around him, she sat at the edge of the bed and felt his brow. There was no longer a trace of fever but, though it saddened her to disappoint the child, she was not prepared to take the risk.

'I'll be back before ye know it. Dinna be a nuisance to Pi'taki while I'm gone.' He shook his head dolefully and she bent to kiss his cheek. 'I've to get dressed now, so lie quiet.'

'Can Lee tell me a story?'

'All right, I'll go and ask him.'

As she rose he tugged her sleeve. 'Does he have to leave us, Na'a?'

Frances paused in the doorway. 'Ye know fine that he does, son. He only came to help through to the end of the harvest. Now he's got better things to do than bide here with us.'

Going out on to the porch, she found Lee seated on the step polishing his boots. 'I'll not be long getting ready,' she said, 'but Rory wants a story, do you mind?'

'Course not,' he grinned ruefully, 'I'll miss him – best audience I ever had.'

She smiled back at him. 'I should think so too. Give him another year and he'll be old enough to recognise nonsense when he hears it!' Frances disappeared through the screen door and gathered her new dress from the back of the chair. The blue calico cloth had been a gift from Wasylyna Dutchak and long evenings had been spent in making it into a dress to wear to their harvest thanksgiving.

As she washed herself in the bowl on the bedroom dresser, Pi'taki came in. 'How is the child?' she asked, passing Frances a cloth to dry herself.

'Oh, he's still moping but I think he'll be all right once we've gone. Lee's in there now giving him a story.' Pi'taki helped pull the dress over her head and fix the buttons at the back. Frances studied her reflection in the mirror. It was a long time since she had worn anything other than her patched and threadbare working clothes and she was pleasantly surprised at the way she looked. Pi'taki picked up the hair brush and, soothed by its languorous stroking, Frances closed her eyes and thought of the coming party. From the comments already passed around as they went from farm to farm, she guessed Mary Olsen's tongue had been working overtime. Everyone knew of Lee's presence and was eager to meet him. Knowing looks from the women implied that they already considered him to be more than just a hired help. She smiled to herself – let them think what they wanted. His unstinting efforts had turned things around on the homestead and she would always be grateful.

Opening her eyes, she became aware of Pi'taki's face beside her own in the mirror. 'What is it?' she asked, catching the rough brown hands and holding them still. She addressed the image in the glass rather than turn around. 'Ye don't want me to go, do you?' There was no answer, and Frances searched for words to mitigate her slight feeling of guilt. 'Dinna worry,' she pleaded. 'Tomorrow it'll just be the three of us again.'

When they returned to the kitchen, Lee was waiting. His eyes widened and he gave a low whistle of appreciation when he saw Frances. 'Well, Mrs Munroe, will you look at you!'

'Thank you.' She blushed at the compliment and busied herself with her shawl and gloves. 'Did Rory go down quietly?'

'Yep, fell asleep right in the middle of my best story.' Lee paused and looked down. 'Still, I guess it saved me havin' to say goodbye.'

'Goodbyes are never easy, Lee, but Rory's only five. Children quickly forget and no doubt you'll forget us too, soon enough.'

He looked at her steadily. 'No, I don't think so.' Before she could reply, he went off to fetch round the wagon and team. Pi'taki said goodbye to her on the porch and watched as Lee drove up to the steps. He put out his hand and helped Frances aboard, then looked back. 'Well, Pi'taki, I'll be seeing ya.' She gazed at him coldly, saying nothing. He looked away and muttered under his breath. 'Good to know I'll be missed.' Then he flapped the reins and the wagon pulled away from the house. Pi'taki stood motionless and watched until long after they were out of sight.

As they drove along, taking their time in the lazy morning sunshine, there was a companionable silence between them. Occasionally, Lee would remind Frances of her responsibilities by pointing out some work that needed to be done before the winter set in or musing on which areas should be cleared for next season. She listened carefully but it was hard to worry about next spring when for now she had money in the bank, seed and fodder in the barn and life was good.

Not far from the Dutchak home, they met up with another wagon-load of people on their way to the gathering. Greetings were exchanged and some of the children jumped down from their own wagon to clamber aboard beside Frances and Lee where there was more room. The adults tried to shout their news to one another but this was drowned by the squeals of laughter as the children played. On arrival at the front of Josef and Wasylyna's fine white-washed home, they could see more families were already helping to lay the long line of trestle tables with piles of food. All the Dutchak children were dressed in colourful Ukrainian costume, looking very pleased with themselves, apart from Nikolai who blushed furiously when Frances marvelled at how tall he had grown. Josef stood holding an earthenware platter on which sat an ornately shaped loaf of bread and a mound of salt. Each arriving guest was greeted with this token offering of the essentials of life. He shook Lee warmly by the hand and embraced Frances.

'Where's Wasylyna?' she asked.

'Inside, cooking,' Josef laughed. 'She thinks all the Ukraine comes here today, so she cooks too much!'

Lee led off the wagon and horses to be stabled in the old barn and Frances slipped into the house to add her contribution to the feast. Wasylyna rubbed her hands down her apron and gave her a rib-cracking hug. They chatted about Rory until they were interrupted by Josef coming in with two great earthenware jars clutched under his arms. Wasylyna clucked disapprovingly and spoke to him briskly in their own language.

He laughed and turned to Frances. 'Wasylyna says we should not be drinking before the priest has blessed the harvest.'

'Quite right too,' said Frances. 'You men are all the same.' She took the flagons from his grasp and shoved them under the table. 'Plenty of time for getting drunk later.'

'You are just as bad – like another wife!'

Wasylyna clicked her tongue reproachfully but Frances laughed. 'Think yourself lucky it's Wasylyna you have and no me – I'd no put up with ye!'

By midday, there was a sizeable gathering at the homestead. The priest finally arrived with other Ukrainian families and it was agreed the feast could begin at last. Everyone formed a large procession and they made their way to the nearby wheat fields. A small corner was still unscythed and, as they gathered around the swaying stalks, Josef tied the stems together in the middle with their heads bent downwards and scattered the seed around him. The priest uttered the benediction, 'Lord, thou hast given us a good yield. Give us a bountiful harvest in the coming year.'

Wasylyna and the other Ukrainian women then wove the wheat into a huge wreath, intertwining the golden stalks with red and white flowers.

'We need a "hospodar".' Josef lowered his voice and turned to Frances and Lee.

'What's that?'

'The master of the harvest.' He looked at Lee. 'We wonder if you would. . .'

'Why, that's an honour, I'd be proud to.'

Josef announced in both Ukrainian and broken English that Lee would be the harvest master and the crowd cheered as the wreath of wheat was presented to him. The youngest Dutchak daughters, arm-in-arm with Lee and Frances, led the procession back to the house. They crowded into the yard and Josef led Wasylyna to the centre of the circle and raised his arms for quiet. 'Bless you all for coming,' he roared. 'Let us now eat what God has given us.'

There was a stampede to the tables, and everyone was anxious to sample the wonderful variety of food. Plates were piled high with *pyrohy* dumplings to be dipped in bowls of creamy *smetana* and platters of steaming *lokshyna* noodles stood next to mounds of *holubtsi*, the traditional stuffed cabbage leaves. The drink was at last brought out. The women and children took the sweet cider Wasylyna had made, while the men praised Josef for his distilling success. People spread themselves across the grassy space in front of the house, eating and exchanging news. Everyone had experienced a good year and they swapped stories of more fields planted, thriving livestock and new barns raised. Frances and Lee sat with the Dutchak children and were soon joined by the Olsens.

'So, Lee,' said Fred, 'I hear you're leavin' us. And what'll you be doing now?'

Lee shrugged. 'Back to trappin', I guess. Maybe I'll head out British Columbia way again. It's easier now we got all these railroads.'

'That must be a mighty lonesome life – trapping?' Mary asked, looking first at Lee and then Frances.

'You get used to it.'

Frances tried to divert the conversation. 'I read in the paper how this recession is supposed to be over. We should get an even better price next year for the grain.' The men picked up the theme and the talk continued, mainly complaining about the extortionate charges of the grain elevator companies. Fred was keen on forming a co-operative to build their own elevators and enthused about his idea to Lee. Then he turned the talk to Edmonton's latest news.

'I heard tell in town last week that they've found gold in the Saskatchewan river.'

Lee pulled a face. 'There's rumours of gold strikes every year, Fred. I reckon they say it to sell newspapers.'

Fred shook his head emphatically. 'No, I'm telling you —'

'Lee used to be a gold prospector,' Frances interrupted.

'You don't say!' Fred was impressed. 'I'd sure like to hear about that. They say there's good money to be made.'

Mary leaned over and kissed him. 'Go for a walk and sober up, Fred,' she laughed. 'You'll need a clear head for the barn-raising.'

He got to his feet. 'Come on, Lee, I can see we're not wanted. It'll be women's talk now.' They walked off.

'Pity that Lee's going,' Mary said, non-committally.

Frances smiled, knowing she would not be allowed to dodge the issue any longer. 'Aye, he's been a great help. But we'll manage fine now.'

'Won't you miss him?'

'I'll miss the help. And Rory'll miss his stories and his games – he was good to the boy.'

Mary shook her head. 'You must be crazy lettin' him get away, Frances.' She looked coy. 'I mean, he's a good-lookin' guy – don't tell me you ain't noticed.'

Frances laughed. 'I haven't had the time, Mary.'

'Well, he's sure noticed you. It's writ all over his face – all you gotta do is say the word. You've been on your own long enough.'

'Och, ye're imagining it, Mary, there's nothing between us. You must have a touch o' cabin fever!' She stood up and brushed down her dress. 'Come on, they'll be ready for the barn-raising by now.'

Her brusque tone did not invite further comment and conversation moved to other matters as they joined the crowd. At the site of the new barn, men were organised into teams and the lumber, nails and tools were already stacked and waiting. Josef gave the signal and with an enthusiastic rush forward, they began. The work went quickly and smoothly, for barn-raisings now were a regular occurrence in the area. The afternoon wore on and people circulated from group to group as the walls rose and took shape around them. Bargains were struck for other barn-raising efforts, livestock swaps were arranged and there was talk of trying to start a school. The listening children all wailed at this suggestion and Frances wondered if Rory's reaction would be any different. A school was a good idea. There was only so much she could teach the boy and she had seen a big change in him since Lee had been with them. Rory needed more than the confines of the homestead. He was self-contained and independent beyond his years but she thought it would be good for him to mix with other children his own age.

By evening, when the air had grown cooler and the sky was dark, the new barn stood complete. Lamps were strung from the rafters and cast a warm glow on the honey-coloured wood. The air was rich with the heady smells of pine resin and freshly mown hay. Bales of straw were piled in great mounds at the sides but the centre was left clear as a dance floor. The older children had refused to go to bed and many now lay half asleep in the straw. But the adults found renewed energy as they prepared for the dancing after the effort of the work. At the far end of the barn was a makeshift platform of crates, barrels and planking. The impromptu band stood self-consciously with their ancient fiddles and wheezing concertinas at the ready. Josef led Wasylyna to the middle of the floor and waved to them. 'Play,' he roared. There were a few false starts and much laughter before the band swung into a fast-moving polka. Josef swept Wasylyna into his arms and they were off, dipping and spinning to the cheerful melody. Soon, other couples joined them and the barn was a swirling mass of colours as the women's dresses fanned out like gaudy parasols on a summer's day. The men too were changed out of their drab old overalls into bright new shirts and neckerchiefs. Their wildly stamping feet cast up faint flecks of straw to glint like gold dust in the lanterns' light.

'Looks like fun.' Lee's voice was close beside her and Frances turned. She had been lost in thought, watching the mesmerising wheel of dancers before her.

'Aye,' she answered quietly. 'I was wondering where they got the energy.'

'It's relief,' said Lee. 'The grain's been sold, all's well – for this year anyway. It's like men coming out the hills after trappin' a winter. You forget the hard times, just bent on spendin' what you got in your pockets before next season.' He looked down at her but she did not seem to be listening, still watching the people move around the floor. 'Like to dance?'

She returned his gaze, but it was a while before she realised he had spoken. 'What? Oh I'm sorry, I was miles away.'

'Mind tellin' me exactly where? I'd sure like to be there too.'

Frances got to her feet. 'Did you say something about dancing?' Her eyes sparkled and she grabbed his arm and pulled him into the well of the dance as the other couples happily made way for them.

One dance followed another and Lee was indeed hard pushed to keep up with her. 'It ain't fair,' he pretended to moan, 'you must've had plenty of practice.'

'You're wrong – it's years since I was dancing.'

'Well, you sure ain't lost your touch,' Lee said breathlessly, 'but I think I'm about ready for a rest.' Fortunately, the band thought so too and demanded time for a drink before continuing. More cider and corn whisky was brought in and Frances and Lee sat together on a bale of straw. She frowned as he swallowed his drink.

'You'll be falling down drunk.'

He shook his head. 'I can handle this stuff.'

'Plenty of practice, eh?' she teased.

'Won't touch another drop, if you say so. Anyway, you'll have it sweated out of me in no time. You're quite a dancer – never have believed it if I'd not seen it with my own eyes.'

She shot him a look. 'That's an awful thing to say. . .'

'But it's true. You're so cold, so hard all the time. Always thinkin' about the work to be done, never time for enjoyin' yourself. You need more fun like this, or you'll end up like Pi'taki.'

She looked at him reprovingly then managed a laugh, seeing the twinkle in his eye. 'Och, I wish you'd got on with her. Things would've been even better. . .'

He was gazing intently at her now. 'So they were good then?' he asked, his fingers faintly brushing against hers.

'Well, there's no denying that.' She patted his hand, her matter-of-fact response defusing the charge his touch had sparked. 'I should have said this before: I can never thank ye enough for all you've done.' She let her eyes drift casually away from his and saw that the band were returning to their places. 'I've had enough o' these polkas,' she said decisively. Squaring her shoulders and putting down her empty cup, once again she encouraged him to his feet. 'Come on, it's time for some real dancing.'

Grabbing the arms of the people around her, Frances started to organise them into the sets for an eightsome reel. She explained the steps and showed them the turns and soon had everyone back on the floor. Clapping her hands to give the band an idea of the rhythm, they quickly came up with a Ukrainian tune that suited the reel. It was a great success and afterwards they called for another. Frances danced and was the centre of attention, everyone delighting in the carefree disposition she so rarely displayed and, as time went on, Lee reluctantly surrendered her to a succession of partners.

When the band took another break, one lone fiddler stayed to serenade the crowd and couples started to circle in a gentle waltz. Lee took Frances's hand. 'Come on,' he said, 'this is more my style.' She did not pull away, as he had expected but instead seemed drawn to the music, a far-away look in her eyes.

'Wasn't that your husband's name?'

Frances stared at him. 'What?'

'You just called me William.'

Frances was shaken to her senses. She tried to tug her hand away but he held it tightly. 'It's all right,' Lee said softly. 'It don't matter who you think I am. Like to dance with you anyway.' She shook her head but he insisted, encouraging her out onto the dance floor. She could feel the power in his arms turning her this way and that, spinning and swaying with the lilt of the violin's tune. She allowed herself to be pressed against his body and, gradually surrendering, let her own respond. At last, when the music ended, he slowly let her go saying, 'I'll be damned. You sure are full of surprises, ma'am.'

Frances felt flustered and uncomfortably aware of the eyes that followed her as she walked back to the edge of the dance floor. Mary Olsen had been watching. 'Well, Frances Munroe, if that's how you dance with the hired help, I'm keeping Fred out of your way!'

Lee came towards them. Sensing Frances's embarrassment, Mary tactfully grabbed his arm as he approached, 'C'mon, Mr O'Byrne, we can't let this woman keep you all to herself. My turn now.' Frances was relieved as he let himself be led away but wondered still at what indiscretions Mary might tease from him while they danced. She sighed and walked out into the coolness of the night air. The sky was ablaze with stars and in the north a strange green light played across the blackness. She stood watching the shimmering colour strengthen then fade almost away. After a few minutes, hearing footsteps behind her, she turned and Lee was there.

'There's a funny light over yonder,' she said.

He looked up. 'That's the northern lights. It's the time of year for them.' He came closer to her. 'Surprised you ain't seen them before.'

'Aye, and how often do I stay up till all hours of the night to gaze at the stars?'

He was perceptibly touching her now. 'Not often enough, I reckon.'

She moved casually, just far enough out of reach. 'That's farming, Lee, you live and breathe it. You know yourself how it just takes over your life.'

'Only if you let it. You gotta make some time for yourself.'

'That's easier said than done.'

'Well maybe things'll ease up now, after the good year you've had and all. You should think about getting out more. It'd do you good.'

Frances took a deep breath. As he spoke, he had circled in on her again. He was standing very close to her now and there was a hinted intimacy in his manner. She was confused and alarmed by the sensations that he aroused in her and hoped the morning's light would restore sanity. Meanwhile, there was safety in numbers. 'Come on,' she said, turning sharply and making for the barn. 'We're missing the fun.'

The night wore on, filled with music and laughter and it was dawn when Josef called a reluctant halt to the proceedings. They were all still farmers, he reminded them, and they had cows to milk and a daily routine to attend to. Wasylyna started to serve coffee and warm, newly baked rolls on the tables outside. People moved around slowly as a quietness descended, broken only by the occasional fragment of wakening bird song. The encroaching actuality of the new day did not seem real enough to break the night's magic and the chill of morning could not quite dispel the heady intoxication of the last few hours.

Everyone dawdled, reluctant to return to the confines of daily life, unwilling to relinquish this unaccustomed sense of freedom. But one by one, farewells were exchanged and the crowded yard began to empty. While Lee fetched the wagon, Frances went round her neighbours, promising to attend the forthcoming christenings and other celebrations that punctuated the months ahead. At last, she climbed aboard and he steered the horses out of the homestead, setting off for Edmonton at an easy pace with the echoes of their goodbyes clinging to the stillness of the air.

The sun was not fully up and there was a lingering coldness. Frances pulled the blanket from the back and slipped it over her knees. Neither of them said much. The slow rumbling of the wheels in the fresh morning air and the shrill whistle of a lark overhead were the only sounds on the vast plain. Far away, violet hills stood against the first flush of roseate sky and a sense of splendid isolation enveloped them.

As time passed, the light slowly flooded the plains. Frances wanted to talk to break the quietude but could not think of anything to say. Lee usually had a ready way with words that could easily turn the conversation round to his advantage and she would almost have preferred this to the silent brooding that now accompanied their drive. She wondered what he was thinking and could see his body swell with the heavy intake of breath. Their legs touched but only slightly. Yet, in that touch she felt a searing contact, a heat that penetrated her whole body. She closed her eyes and swallowed. Lee let the reins slip through his fingers and the wagon slowly trundled to a halt. He sighed, took off his hat and leaned forward, spinning it between his hands before letting it fall to his feet. The gentle clink of the harness was barely audible. Frances waited but he did not move.

Trembling, she put out her hand and stroked his head. Still, he did not stir and the smouldering ache within her flared to an edge of excruciation.

Suddenly, she tugged his hair vehemently and jerked his face up to meet hers. He gasped as her mouth bore down on his, her breath exploding in his ears, her lips rubbing over his skin and bruising his neck. She tore at his shirt and the buttons burst in a spray, rattling around at their feet. He groaned as she buried her face in his chest, grabbing little mouthfuls with her teeth while her hands fumbled for his rough hide belt, pulling it through the loops. Hours of hand stitching were ruined in a second as they tumbled backwards into the cart, tearing the seams of her dress. The frenzied ripping and flinging aside of impeding garments continued until at last she had him inside her. Her legs clasped him in a grip that sent them rolling down, crashing against the tail-board. It sprung open and still clutching each other they slid to the dusty ground. The axle of the wagon creaked as they kicked out, their bodies moving rhythmically between the wheels and their breath catching sharper. Frances's hair fell free covering his face. Then as they turned over again Lee felt her fingernails score tracks across his back. The horses snorted nervously, shifting their weight, lifting their hooves. A raven rose in squawking commotion from the ditch. And, at the same time as these sounds subsided, their voices came gasping feverishly to a risen moan.

Lee rolled off her, panting. The sun cast slanting shadows through the cart that striped her glistening skin and Frances felt his hot breath on her as he idly licked the sweat from between her breasts.

'Well, I'll be damned, Mrs Munroe – you sure are full of surprises.'

Her face was rough with the burn of his stubble and her hair clung damply to her forehead. 'I think ye better call me Frances,' she said.

It was very late next evening when Rory heard the sound of the wagon wheels trundling across the hard-baked ground of the yard. He leapt excitedly from bed and, running out to the kitchen, he flung open the screen door to join Pi'taki. She stood stock-still, staring at the approaching wagon. Surprised that she had not scolded him, Rory followed her gaze. On the front seat of the wagon sat not one person but two.

'Lee,' he cried in delight. 'You've come back!' He ran to meet them as they pulled the wagon to a halt.

Frances jumped down and swung Rory in the air. 'We've a

surprise for ye!' she laughed. Then, catching sight of Pi'taki, her voice faltered for a second. 'Lee and I are married, son. He's come back to stay.'

PART
4

1

The brilliant moonlight reflecting from the thick covering of snow outside the farmhouse made the night seem almost as bright as day. Peering out anxiously at the cold white landscape, Frances could see no sign of Lee's return and she grew increasingly agitated. She let the curtain drop back over the window and returned to the warmth of the stove.

'When's he coming home, Na'a?' Rory yawned, struggling to keep awake.

She forced a smile and tried to seem unconcerned. 'Och, he'll no be long now. But it's getting late and there's no point in ye waiting up – away to your bed.' He pulled a face but she was unmoved. 'When he gets back I'll send him through to see ye, I promise.' She ruffled his hair and drew him close to her, kissing his forehead. For a moment they held each other tightly then a small voice came from the folds of her shawl.

'I miss Pi'taki.'

It was weeks since he had last mentioned her name and Frances was surprised that he too was thinking of her. It was at times like these that she missed Pi'taki most of all. 'I know son, so do I.' She gathered him in her arms and hugged him again, trying to ward off the familiar sense of desolation. He gave a shaky sigh and she stroked his back. 'Come on, don't get sad thinking about her now or you'll no sleep.' Still holding him pressed to her, she carried him upstairs to the small bedroom and laid him on the bed. It was much colder away from the kitchen and she tucked him in snugly under the mound of furs. 'Do ye want a story?' she asked, relieved when he sleepily shook his head. Sitting on the edge of the wooden frame, she stroked his hair and watched the drooping lids fall heavily across his eyes as she softly hummed an old cradle-song.

Once he was asleep, she went back to sit by the stove and brooded on Rory's words which had rekindled a storm of unresolved feelings. She tried unsuccessfully to force the anguish to the back of her mind, but the pain was as fresh now as it had been three months previously. On that night when she returned to the homestead as the wife of Leland O'Byrne, she had hoped that Pi'taki could be persuaded to accept him as a member of their family but the look of despair and disbelief on the old woman's face had quickly given way to a stoic withdrawal. Lee had diplomatically gone to put Rory to bed so the two women could talk. Frances tried to be placatory but quickly grew impatient as she found herself getting nowhere. 'Pi'taki, you're making it difficult for all of us. What's so bad about Lee? Look at the farm, we never could have done without him. . .'

'You are a fool,' was the only response.

'A fool to want to be happy?' she burst back. 'A fool to want a better life after five years of scratching a living out of this bloody land?' They were standing facing each other across the kitchen table. 'Think I don't know what I'm doing? Oh, I know all right. Lee may not be perfect but he's good to me and Rory. He makes us happy and he'll look after us. Is it so wrong to want that?'

For the first time that Frances could remember, Pi'taki had repeated herself. 'You are a fool,' she said and went upstairs to her room, refusing to discuss the matter any further. Even so, at that moment it never occurred to Frances that she would leave them.

The next day was one that lived on vividly and agonisingly in her mind. Rory and Lee had gone out early to hunt and she could hear the gun popping in the distance as she slammed around the kitchen in a thoroughly bad temper. Lee's contradiction of her expressed wish that Rory should not use the gun was the first thing that had upset her. They had argued about it but he was adamant. 'This here's pioneerin' country, honey. If he's gonna be a man, he'll have to learn to use that thing.' She had gone on protesting till he interrupted. 'Listen, don't take it out on me and the kid just because you and her have had a bust-up.'

As Frances had gone to draw water from the well, she was confronted by the sight of Pi'taki preparing to leave. Without a word, she loaded her belongings onto a travois, donned her old shawl and set off across the fields. Frances had dropped the bucket and gone running after her, weeping and calling for her to stop. But the bowed figure just kept determinedly walking, dwindling to a shadow until it disappeared over the crest of the rise. The repeated hollow crack of the rifle continued to sound in the distance, making Frances jump and provoking a swing from grief to frustration. Swatting the tears from her reddened eyes, she stormed back to the farmhouse telling herself that Pi'taki would soon be back with her tail between her legs. When Rory returned and found her gone, he had begged them to take the wagon and go after her but his mother would not allow it. 'She's just being stubborn, son, she'll be back soon enough.'

But the days had slipped into weeks and there had been no sign or news of her as autumn turned to winter. Now, as Frances crept upstairs again to look on the sleeping boy, she remembered how he had cried and cried, and how she herself had realised with shocking finality that Pi'taki was not coming back to them. At least Rory seemed happy enough with Lee, she thought. But the sadness that Pi'taki was no longer a part of their lives still clung acutely to the homestead.

Returning to the kitchen, she shoved another couple of logs into the stove and decided to wait up a little longer before going to bed herself. Idly, she sat twisting the ring on her finger and thought over the last few months. There was money in the bank and the house and barn were fully paid off. Things were fine but she would be glad to see the back of winter because they had often been cooped up in the house for days on end. Lee regularly went off hunting, returning with furs that would fetch a good price and supplement their income. On short trips he would take Rory and once Frances had gone along too, glad to get out. But mostly, they were confined indoors. Lee spun rambling stories of his past to entertain them through the long nights. These had Rory wide-eyed, always asking for more. Even Frances, sceptical of just how true they were, found herself intrigued by the man she had married. He knew how to fire their imagination and whenever they grew bored with the inactivity, he could enthuse them with a rosy picture of the coming season and their lives together on the farm.

It was this optimistic vision of the future that Frances clung to. Although Pi'taki's departure had left a great void in her heart, there was the security of Lee's presence as husband and father to reassure her. She still found it difficult to allow herself to be looked after by him but increasingly she deferred to his decisions about the farm, the house, and Rory. In letting him take some of the weight from her shoulders, for the first time in years she had found a relief from the constant, nagging worry of day to day survival. In the late evening, after Rory had gone to bed, they would spend hours together in the comforting warmth of the kitchen making plans and discussing the coming season. While Frances baked or sewed, Lee would be busy whittling another toy for Rory or mending one of the farming tools. Though neither of them mentioned the fact, the loss of Pi'taki meant that work would be slower next year. Still, they reckoned that they could clear a few more acres and if the harvest went well, their savings could be almost doubled. They vied with each other to devise

191

shopping lists of what they considered essential: with her, it was always something practical like a better plough or another horse. Lee would listen and then recite his own catalogue of requirements: a new dress and perfume for Frances, a proper saddle for the boy, a pair of fancy silver spurs for himself. This was done in absolute seriousness, and she inevitably let herself fall for his trick.

'Och, Lee, we don't need all that. You're so impractical.' She would look up then to see the grin on his face and know she had been caught out again.

His laughter at her discomfort would gradually soften to leave a questioning smile on his face. 'Bedtime, then, Mrs O'Byrne?'

He never had to ask twice. Frances was an enthusiastic partner in their love-making and had learned not to be shocked by the boldness of their intimacy. After their frantic coupling following the Dutchak barn-raising, coy demureness in bed would have seemed out of place. Lee was a skilful lover and could coax forgotten responses from her body that seemed to fuel their joint passion rather than quench the desire for each other. In the quiet aftermath, sprawled across each other's bodies, Frances often wondered how long it would be before the baby she hoped for came along. Lee never alluded to the subject directly, but she assumed he would want a child of his own flesh to seal their union.

Lately however the tranquil happiness of their lives was marred by Lee's occasional periods of restlessness. He dismissed it as cabin fever when she accused him of being bad-tempered. A visit to town to sell the skins always cured him and he usually returned in high spirits. On this latest occasion, he also promised to get the few essential things they needed and that would delay his return. Nevertheless, Frances was worried now. He should have been home long ago and she feared that with the heavy snow, he may have lost the track and gone astray. Haunted by the prospect, she drew a blanket round herself and dozed off into a fitful half-sleep.

After midnight, she awoke with a start. The logs were dying embers and the room had become chilled. Shivering, she blew on her fingers and tried to revive the fire. Suddenly, a rumbling of cart-wheels could be heard in snatches through the sound of the wailing wind. With her hand still gripping the poker, Frances moved towards the window and peeled back the curtain. She recognised Lee's sheepskin and the thick muffler he wore against the cold and breathed a sigh of relief. Lifting the latch, she rushed out into the yard to welcome him, pulling a heavy shawl around her shoulders to keep off the freezing wind.

'Oh, Lee, I'm so glad you're back, I've been worried sick.'

'Stop frettin' and fussin' woman', he said, his arms swatting the air as if to fend her off. He stumbled as he climbed down from the buck-board and she put out her hand to support him. 'Leave me be, I can manage,' he insisted. He walked unsteadily into the house, leaving the horse and wagon for her to see to and she knew he had been drinking. When she returned to the kitchen, she found him leaning back in the rocker with his feet up on the stove. His boots and jacket were scattered over the floor and she gathered them up as she approached.

'What kind o' state is this to come home to your new wife in,' she said in a half-scolding, half-teasing voice.

'Well, I gotta admit I have had a drop or two,' Lee said, producing the bottle, 'but with good reason – I was celebratin', see?'

'Oh aye, and what were you celebrating – you've no got married again without telling me?' she joked.

'Honey, come and sit down, we gotta talk.'

'I'll just fix ye something to eat.'

'That can wait.' He grabbed her hand and pulled her on to his knee. 'There's somethin' I gotta tell you.' His eyes were bright with excitement. 'I met a guy I know, name of Mike Duff. He's one of the old-time trappers, been in the area for years. He was tellin' me a story you'll never believe.'

'Och, I never believe your blethers, why should I believe his?' She tried to rise but he held her on his lap.

'Listen. He's just got back from up north and he heard that the whole of the Yukon is buzzin'.'

'What about?'

Lee lowered his voice and almost whispered. 'Only the biggest gold strike ever.' He was trembling as the words tumbled out. 'Not ounces of gold, *tons* of the stuff. They're just dragging it out by the shovel-load.'

'So?' She was not sure where all this was leading, but already had an uneasy feeling.

'So, he told me the news hasn't got out yet. Not many people know about it, apart from the prospectors already up there and the likes of Mike. They're all frozen in for the winter, but he reckons the minute the thaw comes, the whole country'll be swarming up to the gold-fields. He was getting ready to leave hisself, to go back north, just as soon as he got supplies.' Lee looked pleased with himself. 'He weren't gonna tell me nothin', but I knew he was up to somethin'

193

so I bought him a few drinks and it all came out.' He took a long pull from the bottle and grinned. 'Think we should go too, honey. We could be there before anyone else and make our fortune.'

'Och, away with you. You're drunk.' She prised herself from his grip and started to prepare some food. 'You'll think different after you've slept it off.'

He came and stood behind her, nuzzling her neck. 'Leave that a minute,' he said, turning her round to face him. 'I know I've had a few, but I can still think clear.' She made to interrupt him but he silenced her. 'I've had plenty of time to work it out, and we'll never get another chance like this – never!' His voice was compelling. 'I've told you about when I went prospectin' in the Cariboo Rush. When I got there, it was well after all the big strikes had been made. I never so much as saw gold. But I learned something, listening to them as had made it big – you gotta be the first to arrive when there's a strike or there's nothin' left worth having.'

Frances was confused and wondering if she was still half-asleep. 'Lee, ye don't seriously mean we should just up and leave. It's the middle of winter. What about me and Rory? What about the farm?'

'We'll need all we can get to buy supplies so I — I found a buyer for the farm.' For the first time, his voice had lost confidence and he hesitated over the words.

She dropped the pan she was holding. 'You did what?'

'Now don't get all upset.' He was trying to placate her but she would have none of it.

'Tell me this is just another one of your silly stories, Lee – tell me you're just making it all up.'

The sound of her voice carried through the house and brought Rory running into the kitchen. 'What's the matter, Na'a?' he asked, rubbing his eyes and squinting at her. Then he saw Lee and rushed forward to jump up into his arms.

Lee gave him a hug. 'It's nothin', son. Your mother and me, we're just makin' a few plans, that's all – now you go back to bed.'

'No.' Frances pronounced firmly. 'Rory, you stay right where you are. I want you to hear what your so-called "Daddy" wants us to do.' Lee cleared his throat uncomfortably.

'What? What?' Rory squirmed down onto the floor, standing uneasily between them.

'He's only talking about selling everything just because o' some cock and bull rumour about gold in the north.' She addressed her remarks more to Lee than the child and wrung her hands, pacing about the floor.

'It's more than a rumour. There's always been gold minin' up in the Klondike.'

'And just where the hell is that, may I ask?'

'Yukon Territory – a bit north of here. I'm tellin' you, the gold's just there for the takin', honey. We're gonna be rich!' Lee's eyes widened at the thought and Rory jumped about in excitement imitating him.

'We're gonna be rich! We're gonna be rich!'

Frances was speechless with rage. 'Get back to your bed,' she shouted at him.

'But you said—'

'*Now*.' The boy became glum but reluctantly obeyed. When he was gone, Frances rounded on Lee again. 'Did you even once think about me and Rory when you made up your mind? This place represents years o' work. It belongs to us. What right did ye have? What right?' Angry tears came to her eyes.

'Belongs to me too now, honey, or were you forgettin' that?' He pulled her back down on his knee. 'Oh, Frances, this is the kinda chance comes once in a lifetime – if that. We could spend forever breakin' our backs on this land and just barely scrapin' by.'

'But things are getting good now, Lee.' She protested, trying to reason with him. 'The farm's picking up. We have friends, Rory can go to school. . .'

'They've only just started talking about buildin' a schoolhouse. It'll cost money and you know how long that'll take.' He shook her in gentle exasperation. 'Everything depends on the next harvest – then the next, and the next. It never stops when you work the land. A couple of bad years and you're back to square one.'

'But all the plans we've made for next year – you said we could double the money we have in the bank.'

His face glowed with excitement. 'But this would be better than that. We could make our fortunes in a month and never have to work again. Just think about it. And think what it would mean for Rory.'

She sat without speaking, reflecting on his words. Till now, Rory's young life had been marked by loss and deprivation. If there was another run of bad summers she would be condemning him to more of the same. But what was Lee offering in return? She sank into his arms. 'What in God's name do we need to sell the farm for? Don't we have enough saved in the bank?'

'We'll need a lot of supplies. Ain't many stores up north, you gotta take everything with you.' His voice grew coaxing. 'Look,

195

I know all of this is kinda a shock, but you have to see when somethin' like this comes along and grab it with both hands.'

'It's such a gamble, Lee.'

He squeezed her affectionately. 'Look, didn't you say yourself you took a big risk in marryin' William Munroe and emigratin' over here?'

'But I was younger then and didn't have a child to think about.'

'The boy'll have a great time – a real adventure for him at last.'

'And what about the farm?'

'Oh, Frances, think big! This could be our only chance. Where would you be now if you'd never come to Canada? Or if you'd gone home after William died? Take another gamble, Frances, this time on me. But honey, don't take for ever to think about it – even dallyin' a week means some other guy steals a march on us and he gets the gold.'

Frances was silent for a few minutes, thinking it over. 'Look, Lee, I've taken enough gambles in my life. I understand what ye're saying, but now, for the first time, I'm settled and happy. I don't want to leave here.'

He started to speak, then stopped and sighed heavily. 'Yeah. Okay.' He squeezed her shoulder. 'You're right, sweetheart.'

'Oh, thank God.' Frances kissed him. 'So we'll hear no more about it?'

He looked at her askance. 'No, I mean you can stay here – look after the farm and the kid. I'll go alone.'

Frances was shaken. 'Lee, ye canna mean that – just go off and leave us!'

He laughed. 'Don't worry. I'll come back for you.' He stood, lifting her with him. 'I'll be back with sacks of gold to buy you all them fancy clothes and perfumes.'

She struggled in his arms. 'What if ye don't find any? How can me and Rory work here. . .'

'All right, all right, just forget it.' He silenced her with a kiss. 'We can talk in the mornin'. For now, well, I ain't seen you in days and we got some catchin' up to do.'

The next morning, Frances woke to find the bed empty. As soon as she opened her eyes, the panic from the night before returned in full force. She was suddenly anxious about Lee's absence and hurriedly arose and dressed. Through in the kitchen, Lee and Rory sat together at the table but the reassurance she felt at seeing them quickly turned to anger. From the child's flushed face and sparkling

196

eyes, she knew his head had already been filled with this gold non-sense.

'Sleep well, darlin'?' Lee smiled at her.

Frances nodded and turned to Rory. 'Have ye done the chores?'

His face fell. 'I thought—'

'Well, ye ken what thought did.' From her stony expression he could see there was to be no argument and went to fetch his jacket. Frances waited until he had gone to feed the chickens before turning again to Lee. 'Ye've been winding him up with all this talk of gold.' She went to the stove and poured a cup of coffee.

'Of course I have. I'm excited, and so is the kid. Ain't you? The least little bit?' Lee looked hurt when she did not answer. 'I know you've had a hard life, but can't you see when something good drops in your lap?'

She sipped the scalding, bitter coffee and nodded slowly. 'Aye, I can, Lee. Probably better than most.'

'Then come with me – we can do this together. . .'

She put down the cup and noticed her hand was trembling. 'I've too much to lose.'

He leaned across the scrubbed table. 'Look around. Take a good, hard look around you and tell me what you have to lose.' He waved his hand. 'All this stuff, either you made it or I made it. Ain't half a dozen things in this whole house been store-bought.'

She gazed at the room. Familiarity had dulled her perception of how utilitarian and worn the furniture was. Makeshift utensils and rusted pots hung round the stove. The once-bright curtains hung threadbare and dull, filtering the drab light of the winter morning. The despair inside her was intensified by the sight but still Frances would not give in. 'There's the land,' she protested.

He held up his hands in exasperation. 'Right. Then you stay and work the land. We went through all that last night.'

'Lee, don't go.' She spoke softly, but the words were heavy with pleading. 'Rory and me can't manage all this alone.'

'You managed before, didn't you?'

'Aye. We did.' She shook her head wearily. 'But I had Pi'taki to help me then. The way I need you now.'

'If it's that important to you, we can get another homestead if it don't work out but I won't give this up, Frances. I've been too close, too often, and then suckered outa what coulda been mine.' Lee's voice was hard and uncompromising. 'Stay if you want but I'm gonna start packing some things.' He rose and went through to the bedroom.

Frances almost ran after him, revisited by the pain of abandonment and she suddenly wanted to scream. Then the door opened and Rory trudged in, snow frozen in his long fringe and his little face white from the cold. Shivering despite the heat of the house, his fingers were too numb to unfasten the buttons on his coat. Frances watched him fumbling for a moment then rising, she went to help but inexplicably found herself clutching him very tightly, pressing him to her in a long and desperate embrace. Still holding him, she turned and called through to Lee. 'How far is it?'

Lee raced from the other room, grinning at the tentative question. 'With an experienced trapper like me, we'll be there in no time.'

A week later, Frances stood with Lee and Rory beside a team of laden pack horses on Edmonton's Jasper Avenue. She still found it hard to believe she had gone along with this mad scheme, but Lee was so convinced of success and had so meticulously planned the trip down to the last detail, it seemed they could not possibly fail. The farm had been sold for a good price, and their savings were gone. Everything they now owned was strapped to the backs of eight horses. With all the feverish preparations behind them, they were at last ready to leave. Lee untied the lead horse and grinned at them. 'Let's go!' he shouted, tugging the rein. Frances took a deep breath, gripped Rory's hand tightly and prayed that she had made the right decision.

2

Fort Assiniboine was little more than a collection of shacks drawn together by the presence of the Hudson's Bay Company trading post and a division of the North West Mounted Police. It was the first major stop on their journey and they made it comfortably in five days travelling along a well-established trail out of Edmonton. A recent snow fall had kept all but the hardiest souls off the road, hence their progress attracted little attention. In different circumstances, a man, a woman and a child, swathed in furs against the winter chill, with a train of eight laden pack-horses might well have excited some curiosity along the way. For these were no homesteaders. They proceeded without a wagon, without the furnishings of settlement, and headed in a northerly direction towards the most inhospitable terrain. Close inspection of their baggage would have revealed that they carried with them over three thousand pounds' weight of food supplies to sustain them for a year, chopped feed and hay for the horses, strong tents, long-handled shovels, snow-shoes and many other bewildering items.

Once in sight of the fort, Lee grew cautious and he stopped and knelt down to Rory. 'Now, son, we're gonna stay here a couple of days, so when we go in it's real important you don't tell anyone – anyone, mind you – where we're headed.' Rory looked perplexed and shifted uneasily as Lee held him tightly by the shoulders. 'Well now, don't you see, if they hear we're after gold they'll all be racin' to get there first and there won't be none left for us – it's our secret, okay?' Rory grinned and nodded. Lee looked up at Frances. 'Now leave this to me, honey. I'll go in and check things out. You and the boy wait here – and remember, don't talk to no one.'

Frances watched as Lee disappeared inside the trading shed. She and Rory busied themselves tightening the strapping on the packs and inspecting the horses. Lee had spent days training them in the skills they would need to meet the challenge of the journey that lay ahead. He had shown them how to pack and unpack a horse, how much they would need to carry in the way of supplies, clothes and footwear. He knew when the rivers thawed and where hidden pastures could be found for the horses. Frances felt secure in the belief that they were well prepared and Lee's confidence was unshakeable. His optimism made light of the hard work each day's travel involved. If Rory started to lag behind or Frances grew quiet, he would soon have them laughing at his wild boasts of what he would buy when they had struck gold. His knowledge of the country also set her mind at rest. The trip out to the fort had been quick and uneventful, and he assured them that the rapid settlement of the past few years meant they should find many more well-worn trails to speed their journey.

In the trading shed, Lee was greeted as an old friend. He had often brought in pelts to Fort Assiniboine when he was a trapper and was no stranger to the assembled men.

'Well, look what the wind blew in boys – if it ain't Leland O'Byrne!'

Lee peered through the dim light and recognised the faces between the furs and skins hanging aloft. 'Abe, Foxy, Dan! How long's it been – a year?'

'More like two,' Abe replied with a friendly slap on the back. 'Get this man a drink!' A bottle was pulled surreptitiously from beneath the counter and passed across. Lee took a welcome swig and wiped his mouth with the back of his hand.

199

'So, where you been hidin' out?'

'Long story, Abe,' he replied. 'Got me a wife and kid now.'

'Shotgun weddin', eh?' They all laughed raucously.

'Naw, nothin' like that,' he protested. 'We've been homesteadin' west of Edmonton but we're headed north now.'

'You farmin'? Can't see it, Lee – no wonder it didn't last long.' Foxy shook his head in disbelief as the bottle was handed round.

Abe took a pull on it and thrust it back. 'So, how long you here for?' he asked.

'Coupla days if you can fix us up?'

'Sure thing ol' buddy. An' meantime, maybe we can arrange a little poker game?'

Lee smiled. 'You read my mind.' The bottle went around again until it was almost drained.

'So, what plans you got up north?'

'Well, I'm thinkin' about gettin' back in the old business again,' Lee lied, stroking a pile of beaver skins that lay close by. 'Guess trappin's just in my blood.'

'Yep, you said it. We'll drink to that,' Abe agreed. 'Trade's sure fallen off since you dropped outa sight. And I know one man who'll be glad to hear the news – that's Swifty Maguire – never stops askin' for you.'

'Swifty?' Lee looked uncomfortable at the mention of the name. 'He's hereabouts?'

'Sure. He's just up east at Athabasca river. I guess if you're wantin' to avoid them Swan Hills you'll be headin' that way anyway. See and look him up.'

'Er, sure thing, Abe. I'll do that. Say, thanks for the drink but I better git goin'.'

'So soon – what's your rush?'

'Gotta see to the wife an' kid. I just remembered somethin'.'

'Ain't ya gonna stay? What about the poker game?'

'Sorry, boys, some other time.' Lee strode to the door leaving the bewildered group staring after him.

'Ain't never seen him like this before,' Abe observed, scratching his head. 'Must be some woman he's got there.'

Meanwhile, Frances, Rory and the horses had not gone unnoticed. An old trapper came over and raised his fur-tailed hat to her. 'Afternoon, ma'am.' His grin exposed black and rotted teeth. 'Looks like you're fixed up for a long hike?' He gestured to the horses but Frances looked away, ignoring him. Grimacing, he bent down to the boy. 'Kinda stand-offish, your ma. Where ya off to with all that?'

Rory backed away. 'It's a secret.'

'Hush, Rory,' Frances drew him to her side but the man was even more fascinated now.

A detachment of Mounties was drilling on some flat ground near by and one of them left the group and came over. 'This man bothering you, ma'am?' he asked.

'Well, er. . .' Frances was anxious at all the attention they had attracted and could see Lee's face darken into a scowl as he emerged from the shed.

'C'mon old timer, move along there.' The Mountie despatched the inquisitive trapper and turned as Lee joined them. 'That's a lot of supplies you're carrying, sir. Can I ask where you're headed?'

'North,' Lee answered vaguely.

'North? At this time of year? By what route exactly?'

In an indeterminate gesture, Lee jerked his thumb towards the hills that lay behind them.

The Mountie shook his head. 'That's mighty irresponsible, if I may say so, sir.'

'What d'you mean?' Lee snapped, his irritation growing.

'I mean, to try and take your wife and child through the Swan Hills, not to mention the horses. There's no proper trail – you'll never make it. So, if I might suggest —'

Lee was angry now but tried to control himself. He did not want trouble. 'Listen, son, you ever been through them hills yourself?' he asked.

'Not personally, sir, no,' the Mountie replied, a little embarrassed.

'Well, let me tell you something, I been through them a hundred times.' Lee stabbed the other's chest with his finger to emphasise his point. 'I know them better'n you know the inside of your own pants, mister. I ain't about to endanger the lives of my own kin, now am I?' He put his arms protectively around Frances and Rory.

The Mountie shrugged but remained polite. 'Well, no, I understand that. But it's not often we have families passing through at this time of year. May I ask the purpose of your journey?' he enquired.

Lee thought quickly. 'Goin' to stay with my cousin up at Slave Lake.' He turned his back and started checking the packs on the horses. 'Now I think we've answered enough questions. We're law-abidin' folk and we got a right to go on our way – it's a free country.'

The young officer was reluctant to let them go without a last warning. 'If you take my advice, you'll wait till the thaw and go by boat. Remember there's bears in those hills.'

'Thanks pal,' Lee called as they prepared to move out. He patted his rifle. 'But ain't no grizzly gonna argue with this!'

This turn in the conversation had made Frances uneasy and once they were out of earshot she tackled Lee about it. 'You didna say anything about bears. And I thought we weren't going to go through the Swan Hills?'

Lee put his arm round her shoulder again. 'People are gettin' just a bit too nosey here – that's why we ain't stayin'. And it's the Mountie's job to warn newcomers who don't know any better. But I'm no stranger to these parts. If we head straight into the hills we can stay clear of any settlements till we get further north. It'll be a bit tougher going but just remember what I taught you – keep the loads balanced and watch the horses. We'll make it,' he said, squeezing her reassuringly. 'And as for bears – honey, I know how you feel about that, but don't worry – I made my living puttin' bears outa their misery so just relax. Anyway they're all sound asleep this time of year. I'm tellin' you, if anyone can get us through this country, I can.'

3

When Lee hinted the going might be tough Frances could not have guessed from the mildness of his tone that it was in fact to be the foretaste of a nightmare. Where there was the semblance of a trail, it was blocked by fallen timber, often concealed under treacherous snowdrifts. For every mile they covered, it felt like they had traversed five more as the horses fought their way, stumbling over the broken deadfall and crashing into holes. After days of arduous travel, Frances realised they could still see the same landmarks, were still flanked by the same hills and had made little progress. Hour after hour was spent watching the horses' brittle legs and hooves picking their way between the tumbled logs or testing the soft snow for a foothold. It was back-breaking work for they had to be vigilant at all times. But it was hard for three pairs of eyes to keep account of sixteen pairs of hooves and inevitably injuries occurred. Raw wounds began to appear on the animals' legs and their backs became blistered with the chafing of the packs. Daylight hours were still short and it sometimes seemed as if they had hardly loaded up the train before they were unpacking again and pitching their tent. At other times they were holed up for days waiting for blizzards to abate. Despite this, Lee somehow managed to keep their spirits up. The obstacles of the detour were explained as a temporary hindrance and they remained inspired by his sense of adventure. Frances was heartened by this unwavering confidence, and as they passed through the most inhospitable of terrains, his protective strength created an encircling sense of security.

He was scrupulous about care of the horses. Every night there was a ritual of grooming and tending to their sores, feeding them and melting ice for watering. A tarpaulin shelter was erected to stable them during the snowstorms. The hay was running desperately low and major detours had to be made in their journey in order to seek out the pasture-land that he had spoken of.

'Sometimes I think ye care more about those horses than us,' Frances observed one evening after they had been going about two weeks out of Assiniboine. She was watching him tear strips of rag to bind the sores on a fetlock.

'Well, honey,' he replied, 'anything happens to them and you gotta haul that gear yourself – how d'you feel about that?'

Rory heaved a sack of flour on to his back. Bent double he stumbled around under the weight. 'Look, Lee, I can do it,' he yelled. 'You try Na'a, see how strong you are.'

He dropped the sack and Frances picked him up under one arm, swinging him round as he giggled and squealed. 'Will ye carry your poor old mother like this when her legs give way?' she laughed.

A twig snapped. 'Shh!' Lee waved at them to be silent and reached stealthily for his gun. 'Don't move.' Frances slid Rory to the ground and they stood stock-still while Lee crept around through the trees. After a while he came back. 'Sure I heard somethin' – must've been mistaken.'

'A bear?'

'Don't think so,' he mused. 'Gone now, whatever it was.'

Frances slept only fitfully that night. Every sound in the forest provoked terror-filled dreams that jerked her awake to dwell on haunting memories. By morning she was exhausted. Dark shadows hooded her eyes and she found it difficult to focus her attention. As she tried to lift a pack onto one of the waiting horses, her weariness overwhelmed her and she slumped to her knees.

'Na'a!' Rory ran to her, throwing his arms around her neck protectively.

'What's wrong, Frances?' Lee helped her rise, half-carrying her back to the tent.

'I'll be all right, I'm just tired.' The words were mumbled with difficulty, and she threw herself on the pile of furs. 'If I could just sleep a wee bit. . .'

'We have to pack up and get movin', sweetheart.' Lee tried his best to persuade her but after a while knew they would have to stay put or she would be of no use to them. 'I guess an hour or so ain't gonna make no difference.' He quickly arranged the blankets and furs around her, then turned to Rory. 'Go pick up some of that wood for the fire. You know what to look for, son, just like I told you.'

Rory bounded off pleased to be given some responsibility. Periodically he came back, his small arms straining to hold a big load of twisted branches and soon they had a roaring fire on the go. Though Frances was overwhelmed by a wave of fatigue, she could hear Lee's voice speaking in low tones to him. 'Now you go off and play over there, son, by those trees. Your momma needs to sleep for a bit so we don't want to disturb her.'

The child willingly complied. It was the first chance he had had to play since they left and he disappeared before Frances could call a drowsy warning after him. 'Dinna go too far now!'

'Let him be, Frances, the kid can look after hisself. Besides,' he said softly, 'when was the last time you an' me was alone. . . ?' He undid the buckles at the front of her fur-lined jacket and slid his hand inside.

Light-footed, Rory crept between the frozen limbs of the trees. He was a fearless warrior, his eyes wide to any flickering movement, his ears alert to the briefest fragments of sound. Noiselessly he skipped over the frost-stiffened undergrowth, darting into holes and pressing himself against the silvered bark of trunks, his tiny form unseen by the unwary prey he stalked. Deeper he penetrated, following in his imagination the spoor of some great moose whose winged antlers loomed ahead through misty branches. Suddenly a little muffled crack assaulted the shrouding silence of the forest. Rigid as rock, Rory halted in his tracks. This was no dead wood felled by a slide of snow but unmistakably the sobering sound of a large and living thing. He stood motionless but his heart fluttered wildly with a mixture of anticipation and fear as he gauged the distance between them. Inch by inch he mustered the courage to go on, drawn forward by a need to at least behold the creature now he had come this far.

Ahead the trees parted into a small clearing. This dismal little dell was bereft of the thin light which elsewhere filtered through the trees and Rory feared to enter in case he became trapped. Heedless of the frozen ground beneath him he lay flattened and waited for a movement to betray his quarry. Lifting his head his breath shortened as he discerned the brown pelt of an elk or similar animal merely yards from where he lay. Rory waited for a movement, sure that its delicate nose would seek him out and send it scampering off in alarm. But nothing happened. Minutes slipped by, though to him the time seemed endless. He was trapped, immobilised by his own indecision. Then he heard a rustling issuing from the hollow and he opened his eyes wide, expectant, every sense acute.

'How long will you lie there waiting, Issohko?'

The words were soft but they carried clearly on the silent air. Rory stood, forgetting the fear, drawn like a magnet to the warmth of that familiar voice; an expression of disbelief spread across his little features. Below him in the dip he could see that the elk skins were nothing more than a shelter for the simple staples of life. And beneath them the face that looked up to his sent a spasm of joy through his body.

'Pi'taki!' His scream resounded through the woods as he stumbled headlong towards her open arms. She held him close to her breast feeling the small and trembling frame yield beneath her. 'Why did you go away, Na'a? How did you find us?'

'But it is you who found me.' She smiled and raised his face up. 'I see you remembered well what Pi'taki taught you.'

Rory looked at the ground and screwed up his nose. 'I thought it was a moose,' he admitted in a small voice. For a while he was speechless then the questions formed in his mind and rushed out in a jumbled torrent. 'Why are you hiding? Are you following us?' He gripped her again, filled with the hope that she would not leave him. 'Are you coming with us – to find the gold?'

Her voice darkened. 'I know nothing of gold. All I see is a child alone in the forest. Should he not be with his mother and his father? What if he got lost?'

Rory knew better than to argue with her. 'I'll take you to them,' he said, pulling her hand.

'No, Isshoko, I will take you,' she declared firmly. Quickly she gathered her belongings and hoisted the boy onto her back.

When they reached the tent, Frances and Lee were not there. Their urgent voices could be heard some way off calling to Rory and he responded with a shout. This brought them racing back into the

205

clearing and both were visibly shocked to see Pi'taki standing there shielding him.

Rory ran to Frances and she knelt down, holding his shoulders and looking into his eyes. 'Oh thank God ye're all right!' Then she turned, all thoughts of the past forgotten, and instinctively her arms opened to the old woman.

But Pi'taki was not in a welcoming mood. 'Well, you may thank your god, Otanimm! Where is the mother when the child needs her, why do you not watch over him – has this man poisoned you so soon?'

Frances felt a sob rise in her throat. She wanted to rush forward and embrace her, but Lee stayed her arm. 'Now don't go gettin' yourself all worked up over nothin'. The boy's okay.' But he had misjudged her reaction and she glared at him, roughly pulling herself free.

'No, she's right, Lee, we should be ashamed. He could have been killed.' Tentatively she again moved towards her. 'Forgive me, Na'a?'

Pi'taki's eyes softened as she received her. The two women held each other without speaking and Frances felt something of her old self return as the solid strength enveloped her. 'Oh Na'a, I thought we'd never see you again.'

Lee pushed his hat brim back off his face. 'Well I'll be damned,' he said cynically. 'Knew there was somethin' following us and it sure weren't no bear!' He looked at Pi'taki. 'Ain't nobody gonna ask what she's doin' here? Seems mighty strange she just turns up in the middle of nowhere.' There was silence.

'She's going to come with us and find the gold.' Rory was breathless with excitement and did not notice the angry expression whip across Lee's face. 'And she's going to stay with us and not go away ever again!'

'What you go tellin' her about the gold for boy – didn't I say to keep your mouth shut?' he snapped.

'But Lee —'

'No buts kid.'

'I did not come for your gold,' Pi'taki spat the word back at him with disgust.

There was an uneasy pause but Lee's patience had been tested to the limit. His frustration burst to the surface. 'Look, nice of you to visit, ol' lady, but we gotta be movin' on now.'

Frances was outraged. 'Is that all you can say? She's risked her life to follow us all this way, saved my boy from near death and you're just going to turn her away?'

206

'Well, she ain't gonna tag along with us, that's for sure,' he said emphatically.

'Now just a minute,' Frances butted in, 'what about the rest of us — don't we get a say?'

'It ain't a question of takin' a vote. We got supplies for three — it's another mouth to feed.'

'I will feed myself,' Pi'taki said and dragged forward her rawhide bundle which was stuffed with packs of pemmican.

Lee shook his head with finality. 'It don't matter. Ain't no way you're comin' with us,' he said flatly.

All this time Rory had stood looking up at the adults, his eyes darting anxiously between them. Suddenly he found the nerve to intervene, going up to Lee and tugging at his sleeve. 'If you send Pi'taki back, I'm not coming with you,' he said quietly.

Lee looked at Frances, anticipating her response. She moved across to where he stood and took his hand. 'I want her with us too,' she said softly. 'Don't you see she's part of this family, she belongs with us.' He seemed unmoved and she tried to reason with him. 'Besides, we could do with the extra help — the three of us can hardly watch the horses on the trail as it is.' He gave an exasperated sigh but she held his eyes persuasively. 'Admit it,' she said. 'We need her.'

Lee remained moody for several days but the arrival of Pi'taki had lifted the spirits of the other two. This was propitious, since the full horror of navigating the Swan Hills was yet to descend on them. Weeks passed in their stumbling slow progress. The horse-feed dwindled to nothing and they spent more time locating pasture grounds than moving forward. The poor animals became weak and emaciated, less sure-footed and more prone to slipping and injury. The sores on their backs began to fester and their pace slowed to a staggering gait. Lee was desperate to get out of the region before the thaw or they would have to sit it out, holed up in their tents waiting for the run-off to end.

Pi'taki's presence made a significant difference and it was she, more than anyone else, who kept the horses alive. When no grazing could be found, she led them to patches of larkspur weed. Lee said it was poisonous but she argued that only the roots were dangerous and if closely watched, the horses could chew on the tops of the plants. Her knowledge saved their lives and so an uneasy truce developed between her and Lee as he reluctantly acceded to her better judgement.

Having established a way of working together, the group now negotiated the remaining fifty-mile stretch to Peace River Crossing. As the ground melted and became boggy with the onset of the thaw, a horse would often sink to its shoulders in mud and the strength of all four of them was required to heave the poor creature out. Gradually however, the tangled mass of deadfall underfoot became less dense and the ground opened up into a hilly wilderness.

4

Lee was now resigned to the fact that they must make a stop at Peace River Crossing. After the encounter at Fort Assiniboine, he had vowed not to go near another settlement but this time there was no choice. The horses were wasted and starving, they needed grazing space and time to recover. Equally, the party's food stocks had to be replenished, if possible, at the post. Inwardly, he was deeply worried about the adequacy of their supplies to see them through to the Yukon but betrayed little of this to Frances. His main hope was that they could proceed with all speed as soon as possible. Time was of the essence for he knew that at the very most they had six months left before freeze-up in the north and still a thousand miles to go.

As expected, their arrival at the Mounted Police post at Peace River Crossing did cause a few raised eyebrows. Weary and footsore, the four led their straggled train of scrawny animals into the enclosure and presented themselves to the officer in charge.

Inspector Powell listened to their request. 'Gold prospectors, I presume,' he said with an edge of contempt in his voice.

Lee's head jerked up. 'Whatever gave you that idea? I'm just taking my family here up to Fort Nelson – we've a cousin there expectin' us.'

'And your cousin's name?'

Lee fumbled for a convincing reply but the Mountie was one step ahead of him. 'Look, Mr O'Byrne, it makes no difference to me what the purpose of your journey is as long as it's lawful. Every so often we hear the whisper of a gold find in the north and there's always one or two idiots who think they can make the trek without a damned idea of what they're up against. I must say,' he said, eyeing the others, 'this is the first time I've seen anyone mad enough to drag women and children along this route with them.'

'Now look here —' Lee interrupted, but Powell silenced him.

'No, you look here,' he insisted. 'When you get in sight of those mountains you'll know what I mean. Do you think those wretched animals of yours will survive – let alone yourselves? We can only release a small amount of provisions to you here and you will definitely not be able to stock up beyond this point. If you do not die of injury or exposure, starvation will claim you all. It's my men who have the unpleasant task of bringing in the bodies of fools like you and I don't want them to be coming back with yours.' He turned to Frances. 'I've no wish to alarm you, ma'am, but I must implore you not to attempt this folly. Try to persuade your husband to turn back – or at least to let you and your family stay here.'

The Mountie's warning affected Frances deeply and, for the next few days, she did indeed try to reason with Lee. Hitherto, she had not understood the true danger of their journey and was now faced with the dilemma of whom to believe.

'Did I ever tell you this would be easy, honey?' Lee said in his defence. 'You're forgettin' we're goin' after gold. It's gonna make us rich, remember? I thought that's what you wanted – a better life for us and the boy.'

'I know, but it's not worth it if we all get killed in the process.'

Powell had agreed to put them up in the visitors' lodge for a few days in the hope that its comforts might dissuade them from their onward journey. But, as Lee lay back on the straw mattress, nothing was further from his mind. He laughed. 'He's just tryin' to scare us off, Frances. It's jealousy, see?'

'What do ye mean?'

'Aw come on, honey – I saw the way he looked at you. When d'you think was the last time a pretty woman came through these parts?'

'I've no idea but the state I'm in nobody would look at me twice.'

'You're wrong. Believe me, I know what I'm talking about. I've been stuck out in the wilds for months myself – does somethin' to a man.'

'Oh Lee, don't try to fool me with that kind of talk again, I've just about had enough. The inspector said it wasn't safe and I think we should listen to him.'

'Well, believe what you like, Frances. But truth is that we're over the worst now. Remember Swan Hills – you want to go back through them? You could take the long way round but even if ol' Pi'taki does know a thing or two, women and children travelling alone is mighty dangerous.'

Frances looked at him. 'You mean you'd let us go back alone?'

Lee grabbed her by the shoulders. 'What's there to go back for? Everything we own is in them horse-packs. We'd have to start all over again with nothin' – you want that? All our hopes are pinned on gettin' to the gold-fields. We've still got a chance, Frances, and you're willin' to throw it all away. Think what you're sayin', honey. Don't let the words of some hard-bitten old Mountie hold us back now we've come this far. I'm tellin' you, there ain't nothin' in them mountains we can't handle, sweetheart. Believe me, I know.'

5

Within two weeks of leaving Peace River Crossing, the once distant phalanx of snow-streaked blue mountains now loomed before them. Frances was beginning to have a growing respect for the police inspector's warning but the others took no heed. Lee was a driven man, fired with the quest for gold. Pi'taki walked with the calm dignity of one who had accepted whatever the journey might bring, while Rory bounded ahead like a jack-rabbit, diving behind trees and jumping out on them unawares. The air was fierce and cold with the late season frosts but tall spruce and poplar stood out against a cobalt sky and everything was new and throbbing with the coming of spring. For days they trekked through birch copses on the slopes and over wild little streams that had burst into life with the thaw but all the time their tread was growing harder and the gradient steeper. Where recently they had been able to discard their fur wrappings, now, as they advanced into colder altitudes, once again the nightly encampment was a ritual of unpacking as more warm clothes and bedding became necessary. Stout willow staffs were cut to help aid their progress and they tied muslin cloths over their wide-brimmed hats to fend off the clouds of mosquitoes.

Lee walked ahead. Frances watched his iron-cleated top boots striding on redoubtably and wondered why she alone felt a gnawing lack of faith in their venture. She could no longer even discuss it with him, so convinced was he of their success. Yet, as she moved among the laden train of wretched pack-horses, their chances seemed ever more remote. Flanked by the animals where the path was wide enough, she checked the loads and glanced back regularly at Rory and Pi'taki bringing up the rear. She smiled. They seemed distracted by the happiness of having found each other again. The child ran about making little sorties into the forests and discovering new sights and sounds in the abundance of wildlife that proliferated there. Then he would rush back to Pi'taki wide-eyed, bringing gathered treasures for her inspection.

The terrain was changing rapidly now and the climb became steeper. Terrifying precipices of slippery slate had to be negotiated with extreme care. The horses whinnied and snorted with the effort of breathing in the thin air. Razor-sharp rocks tore at their flesh exposing bleeding wounds and running sores as they squeezed through the narrow gorges between the infinite basalt walls. Lee urged them on. His concern for the defeated animals seemed to have dissipated with the climb and often his stick would come down mercilessly on their flanks. Grimly, Frances watched this cruel display but was helpless to do anything, concentrating more and more on the hazard that lay beneath her own feet. Precariously they stepped over splintered shale, displacing stones to send them spinning to abysmal depths. Although the freezing air numbed their skin, the sun's glare reflected off the snow and simultaneously burned their faces. As they inched their way upwards, skirting the rim of unfathomable dark canyons, their breath became shorter and their backs bent further under the ponderous loads.

Higher and higher they climbed, each day bringing them closer to the snowy summits. In places the danger of slipping was increased by the thickening slime brought on by the thaw. Sometimes ankle deep, their feet pulled on sucking holes and the damp seeped up through the tops of their boots. Still Lee hollered at the straggling horses and pelted them with his stick and soon Frances could not stand any more.

'What's got into ye?' she whispered, trying to keep her voice low so the others would not hear.

He pulled her to one side. 'I know this looks bad,' he said, 'but there ain't no place to stop here. If we don't keep movin', the horses will give up on us. We'll find a place to rest just as soon as we can.'

'Lee they're half-dead already – if ye push them any further they'll collapse.'

'Trust me, honey. I know what I'm doin',' he said, resuming his position at the head of the train.

Frances looked on impotently as he thrust ahead, driven now by a stronger force than she could bring to bear.

They came to a narrow rock fissure beneath which yawned a black sunless ravine. The gap was small, wide enough to step across, but as a precaution the horses were unhitched and pulled over one at a time. Lee organised this procedure as the others looked on from behind. 'Get up there, you lazy, good fer nothin' mules!' he bawled at the pathetic creatures as they stumbled across, slithering with mud-clogged hooves on the slippery shale. The heavy burdens became displaced as the horses tried to make the leap and the final one lost its footing and stumbled backwards before it could regain its balance. Horrified, the three watched Lee's grip tighten on the lead rein as the horse's neck strained forward in jerks, its front hooves desperately scraping the edge as its hindquarters became wedged deeper in the gap. With flaying legs, it neighed in high-pitched terror, thrashing about and splintering off bits of rock which plummeted into the black vaults of the canyon. Rory grew silent watching the gruesome spectacle. Frances tried to cover his eyes but he pushed her hands away.

'God damned animal,' Lee breathed angrily, his grip slowly loosening on the reins. The horse's eyes were wild with pain now. Its whole body convulsed in spasms as it fought with the inevitable gravitational pull that sucked it downwards to its fate.

'Quick, unloose those supplies!' Lee's shouted orders jolted the stunned group to their senses. 'Don't stand there staring,' he commanded, 'do as I say or we'll lose more than one dumb animal. . .'

'But can ye no do something?' Frances was dismayed and felt her hands shaking uncontrollably. Rory touched her skirt in an effort to comfort her but he too was trembling to witness such suffering. Pi'taki moved forward. Deftly she cut free the sacks and cartons throwing them across to Lee who waited with outstretched arms.

'Now over, all of you,' he yelled. 'We've wasted enough time here already.'

As each of them leapt over the hapless creature a circling eagle screamed, soaring against the rock face. The horse continued to fight the air with despairing haunches and an awful tremulous moan now issued from its throat.

Frances looked back. Lee put his arm around her shoulder and she buried her face in his chest. 'For pity's sake,' she wept, 'do something!' He strode to the lead pack and unsheathed his rifle. One clear shot rang out, the beast gave a jerking movement and then was still.

Sighing, he wiped the sweat from his head. 'All right, all right, it's over now. I guess it's time we took a break.' They sat in silence for a while. Then Lee got to his feet and said what was in all their minds. 'We gotta figure out how we're gonna carry the rest of this gear.'

They loaded what they could onto the remaining pack-horses who shifted about uncomfortably under the extra weight. Now grossly overburdened, they stood with heads hanging resignedly. The rest of the stuff was unpacked and distributed into back-packs. Frances was now grimly reminded of how they had joked and laughed about such an eventuality. She watched as Rory shouldered the sack of flour and made off uncomplaining under the weight. The straggling group moved on. Deeper and higher into the mountains they penetrated with the doleful wheeze of the dying beast still a haunting echo behind them.

Days rolled by and the fatigue of the relentless climb wore them down. Rory had moments when he became uncharacteristically subdued and did not lift his small head from the course of the path. Lee pushed on with a resolution now lacking in the others. Sure-footed, his great boots crushed over the shattered rock and broken deadfall and, occasionally, the space between them grew as Frances found herself lagging back with Rory and Pi'taki. Each continued to carry their own pack for camping at night in addition to the supplies that had been distributed and though Rory did not ask for it, Lee shouldered him too when he grew tired.

It took a few days before they returned to a semblance of normality but with the downhill trek towards the river gorge of the Liard, some energy returned. As they descended slowly, discarding their furs and mufflers, they felt again the warmth of the summer air. From a distance they could see the tumbling cataracts, white water rapids and swirling pools of the wide Liard and their eyes scanned up and down for a suitable place to cross. The afternoon sun blazed onto their backs as they reached the water's level and flopped down for a welcome rest. Flies buzzed over the surface and waterfowl spluttered along the bank. The current in the river was fast moving and it was difficult to decide on a safe location at which to ford it.

They searched for days tramping along the bank but the turbulent foaming surface of the water did not abate. By late afternoon on the fifth day, they came to rest at a place where the river was still swift but without rapids. Lee insisted that here they must take their chance. He tried to persuade them to attempt a crossing that evening but Frances argued that their exhaustion would only add risk to the venture.

'It's light till late, honey. Ain't as if we can't see what we're doing,' he protested but she flatly refused.

'Ye canna sweet-talk me out of this one, Lee. I see the water

213

as clear as you and I know it's dangerous. We'll make a start first thing. Right now we need sleep.'

They made camp and built a huge fire to fend off the chill of the night. Frances bathed Rory's blistered feet while Pi'taki made fur-lined skin bags to tie over his hole-worn boots. The child's face was bronzed and there were white rings around his eyes where he had been made to wear snow-glasses against the glare. Frances looked at the other two faces. Pi'taki, impassive as ever, now seemed drawn and wearied. Lee lay propped on one arm outside the tent, his mackinaw coat hooked on a tree above his head. In the light of the fire she could see his beard had grown thick and grizzled over the deep brown weather-beaten face and he stared at the moonlit river with a far-away look.

'Can we really get across safely, Lee?' she asked. 'Tell the truth.'

'Yeah,' he replied vaguely and smiled at her.

'Seven half-dead horses and four worn-out people?' She gestured to the rushing water. 'We can't swim that.'

'It's okay, I'll swim across with a rope. Then all we have to do is pull ourselves across.'

'And the horses? And the supplies – what about them?'

'I've thought about it, for Chrissakes!' Fatigue made his anger half-hearted. 'We can make a raft, and tie on the supplies. The horses can swim over – they can stem the current better'n us.' He lay back and settled down to sleep. 'Piece of cake.'

Early the next morning they stood anxiously on the bank and watched as Lee fought the currents to the other side, hauling the huge rope with him. Once it was secured, his return was made easier as he hung onto it and heaved himself back across. Soaked and exhausted, he threw himself down on the ground. His chest was rising and falling with the effort of the swim and droplets of water clung to his beard. Frances kneeled down beside him and he rolled over on his back to face her.

'Ye could have killed yourself! We'll never make it.'

'Bullshit. 'Course we can make it. Keep your voice down or you'll frighten the boy.'

Frances jumped to her feet and stepped back a few paces. 'I'm sick of ye telling me everything's all right,' she said, looking down at him. 'I can see with my own eyes, Lee, we'll drown in the effort. And I dinna care if Rory hears me, for so he should be scared – it might save his life.'

Lee rose up angrily and faced her. 'And I'm getting sick of you

214

naggin' me and grumblin' every step of the way —' She swung out her hand to slap his face but he grabbed her wrists. 'Now listen here,' he said through clenched teeth, 'we could walk for days, maybe weeks lookin' for a better crossing place and there ain't no guarantee we'll find one. We can't waste any more precious time, d'you hear?'

Pi'taki spoke. For once, she addressed herself directly to Lee instead of through Frances. 'Take the boy and cut wood for the raft,' she said. There was a moment of silence till Lee did as he was bidden and she turned to Frances. 'We must cross the river. The child will be safe – I will watch him.'

The two women arranged the packs and crates into piles while Lee lashed small trees together into a makeshift raft. Rory ran excitedly from one task to another, impatient for everything to be done but it was well past noon before they were ready. Flanked by the unladen animals they waded into the icy water holding the rope and floating the gear across. Once submerged, they were quickly aware of the swirling undercurrents that could suck them down. Rory clung to the rope and watched the neck of the foremost horse as it fought to keep its head above the freezing water. Pi'taki swam alongside him uttering reassurances and urging the beast forward out of their way. When one made it to the opposite bank and vigorously heaved itself ashore, the other horses were encouraged by this and with a renewed thrust pushed on. Suddenly, two became tangled with a floating train of cartons that had detached itself from the raft. Vainly Lee watched the poor creatures being sucked away dragging the boxes after them into the swirling currents.

'Somebody grab those boxes,' he shouted back down the line. Rory reached out to try and grasp the strapping on the nearest box as it swirled past him but, as his hand caught hold, the other was immediately wrenched from its grip on the rope.

'No,' Frances screamed, watching in horror as the child tumbled sideways into the water and surfaced, gulping and spewing in his terror. Away downstream the brown heads of the drowning horses disappeared in a whirlpool only to reappear fighting for breath again. Rory was being pulled inexorably towards the same churning spot. But a firm hand caught him under the chin and Pi'taki raised his head above the current. Her knife flashed, cutting the strap the boy still clutched tightly and the crates swept off. Then, holding him to her, Pi'taki struck out for the bank.

When they reached the shore Rory was choking and coughing but alive. Frances looked again at the whirling well of water but the horses were gone. Only the wooden supply boxes swung down-river moving faster over rapids and eventually disappeared out of sight. She dragged herself ashore, numb, chilled and with hardly the energy to breathe. Lee came towards her but she merely stared at him and said. 'Don't come near me. Don't even talk to me.'

Pi'taki fed the bonfire that night and they all sat staring vacantly into the flames, their meagre baggage strewn around as a hopeless silence descended. Lee moved apart from them and laced himself into the sleeping-bag. Frances watched him fumble about and discreetly pull out a bottle. Sickened, she turned her attention to Rory who slept curled in her lap. His breathing was fitful and the light from the fire highlighted the sweat on his forehead. She felt the burning little face and glanced anxiously at Pi'taki. The fire was kept ablaze and Rory was smothered in the warmest furs and skins they had to hand. All through the night they bathed his feverish brow until eventually they too could keep their eyes open no longer and slumped beside him in weary sleep.

Just as dawn was breaking, Lee was roused from his bed by a wild commotion. He leapt from his sleeping-bag and grabbed for the rifle. A pack of wolves had descended from the mountains and raided the camp. He fired the gun setting off a thunderous echo that sent them in all directions, but not before they had scattered the horses and plundered and ripped apart some of the gear that lay around. Incensed, Lee tore after them cursing and firing at anything that moved. He recovered four of the horses but vainly searched among the trees for the fifth. The wolves left a waste ground of chewed and burst sacks, damaged crates and mangled clothing. 'That's the last straw!' Lee flung the rifle to the ground. 'The final goddam straw.' Restlessly he began to shout orders. 'We gotta move – now!'

'No,' Pi'taki countered, 'the child is sick.'

'If we don't move him he's gonna die of starvation anyway – we all are!'

'But it's impossible,' Frances implored. 'Have a heart, Lee.'

'Heart don't come into it, use your head woman,' he shouted. 'There's barely enough food to see us through to the Klondike now, let alone survive once we get there. Can't afford to hole up here any longer wastin' time – we got four horses and less'n half what we set out with.' He turned to her with a cold stare. 'Even if you never listen to me again, Frances, hear this. As God is my witness, that boy ain't gonna make it if we don't keep movin'.'

Alarmed by his words, she dragged herself out of the tent and began to gather the scattered remnants of their gear. Pi'taki gripped

216

her hand and searched fearfully into her eyes but Frances averted her gaze. 'Sorry,' she mumbled, 'but I just can't take the risk. We've got to do as he says.'

Pi'taki reacted with fury. Though she spoke in Blackfoot, the invective she shouted at Lee needed no translation. He ignored her, silently continuing with the task of packing until at last she stopped and returned to sit by Rory.

With so little of their supplies left, it was not long before Lee and Frances had repacked everything. Lee came across to the old woman. 'I'll carry the boy,' he said, reaching down.

'No!' Pi'taki struck him full in the face. He raised his arm to strike her back, but Frances intervened.

'Stop this.' She thrust Lee back. 'Come on, we must go.'

Pi'taki would not let either of them near the boy. She laced Rory's swaddled body into a bag and fixed it to her back. Then heaving up her own pack into her arms, she moved off slowly, burdened under the excessive load.

They walked with bowed heads and a defeated air, all pioneering spirit doused. The weary horses shook their heads vainly at the maddening blackflies that swarmed about their eyes and scabious flanks. Their flesh hung thinly, exposing bony ribs and haunches. Frances looked on, weakened by a growing sense of hopelessness.

Sensitive to her mood, Lee came up level with her. 'You done the right thing back there, honey.'

'Did I?' she said vaguely. 'I don't know what's right any more.'

'Least this way we still got a chance for the gold.'

She stopped abruptly. 'I was thinking about Rory – I assumed you were too.'

He reached out to touch her. 'I didn't mean. . .'

But she had already moved away to catch up with the shuffling figure of Pi'taki ahead.

6

May turned to June and the daylight lengthened into the nights. Moving between the high, columnal, basalt faces, the weary party often remained shrouded in cold, grey shadow only to round a steep bluff and be plunged in vibrant light again. As the higher zones quickly thawed, the rocks became sieves to the turbulent mountain streams and the sound of crashing water now accompanied their trail. The mosses sponged up the moisture and tiny pink campion sparkled in patches on the slopes. In the early morning, the lark's throbbing chirp hung on the air and the rasping crack of the jay echoed up from the lower forest reaches. But the beauty and magnificence of the jagged mountains was lost to the dejected travellers. Despite the warmth, their progress was slow. Flanked by the sheer volcanic crags, there were few resting places and sometimes they went for days without making camp due to the lack of level ground.

Frances watched the dragging feet and hunched shoulders ahead of her and knew defeat. Their boots were all worn, patched and strapped around with leathers. Clothes clung in the shape of their bodies like a second skin, never having been off their backs in weeks. They were lean and sinewy, brown and blistered by the sun, chafed by the heavy packs and bitten by the flies. Above all, they stank of urine, of sweat and of fear.

The sun brought a little colour to Rory's face, though the grippe had weakened him so much that he still had to be carried. It was some days before Frances could persuade Pi'taki to share the burden with them. But the old woman had ceased to argue, her own resolve wearied by the long trek. They now all took it in turns to shoulder the child, but inevitably Lee carried him most of the time. They devised a harness for the cradle-board to keep Rory in place on his back since the boy usually slept, oblivious to the passing of the days. On the rare occasions when he eased himself out and stretched his emaciated legs he looked like a new-born foal and Frances was shocked to see his bony rib-cage and fragile limbs. He needs good food and plenty of restful sleep, she thought. But the hope of that had diminished long ago and now she could see no end to their torment. Though Rory had stumbled over the rugged floor in his attempt to prove he was fit, she knew he would still have to be carried for a long time to come.

The summer months brought with them an additional unforeseen hazard. Rains made the higher slopes impassable. They often streamed with mud and shale, drawing earth and rubble down with them and reducing the ground to a quagmire. The scrawny horses slithered about on the slimy scree, regularly losing a foothold, stumbling and falling. Everyone became alert now as the animals plunged their fetlocks into waterlogged sinkholes that brought them to their knees.

One day, after their route ended abruptly at a canyon flooded by the run-off, they were forced to tackle a steeper incline. Retracing their steps took hours before they started the slow ascent of the same towering, black moraine they had previously tried to avoid. As they struggled to gain a purchase in the slurry of gravel and water, it soon became obvious that they were stationary and had been for some time. Lee vehemently thrashed at the horses in a furious effort to get them to move.

'Mind the bairn!' Frances called to him as he forgot the sleeping child on his back.

'Okay, okay,' he answered. He shifted the weight of the boy, trying to ease the cutting edges of the board from his hips. Digging his heels into the mud, he hauled once more on the reins but the beasts were unable to climb. The track had now disintegrated to a swampy porridge and he gave up, leaning wearily on the lead horse. As he waited for the two women to catch up, Lee unstrapped the cradle-board and laid the sleeping boy to one side. Looking up ahead, he realised there was more to come, with the slope stretching on, climbing for some distance into the mists. 'God dammit,' he muttered, and sat down to light a cigarette.

By the time Frances and Pi'taki drew level with him, a brown silt had begun to slide towards them, gathering momentum as it smeared the mountainside. Everyone was spattered by the slime as it sparked over stones and foamed up through fissures. They stood dismayed while they were showered by the precipitous gumbo, and the gentle rumble turned into a gathering torrent above them. Bubbling, soupy cataracts tumbled downwards, uprooting trees and dragging the topsoil in a violent mud-slide. The bolting horses reared around them, snorting in terror and Frances was thrown off her feet. With a horrified cry, she perceived through the brown drizzle the boulders crashing in the wake of the first surge. The ground gave way beneath them and they were plunged into darkness, swept down the slope in the thickening mire. Thousands of gallons of melted water were unleashed in the flood before the avalanche of gravelly scree finally slid to rest in a heaving swamp of debris.

Frances moved an arm. Battered and bruised from the pelting stones and cut by flying flints, she slowly dragged herself from the cloying hole into which she had sunk. Time had passed and everything was silent now. She could see Pi'taki and Lee moving amongst the twisted trees and deadfall like spectral figures in a greying, slimy skin. The horses lay motionless, their eyes still open with the terror of the fall, their bodies horribly mangled. Suddenly Frances came to her senses.

'Rory?' The question came out in a tremulous whisper. Pi'taki looked over, alarm and concern on her face. 'Rory!' Frances's voice rose to a roar of desperation as she hauled herself up and began feverishly pulling at the logs and rocks around her. With bleeding fingers she tore at the boulders and scooped up armfuls of the squelchy clay, searching for the child. Her scream filled the silence of the canyon as she frantically threw aside boxes and sodden sacks.

Lee walked about in a daze, pathetically urging the dead horses to get up and muttering dementedly about the need to move on. It was he who found the harness. Quite by chance, as he heaved aside the collapsed and waterlogged supplies, he looked again at the thing before him. The upturned cradle-board was covered in mud and he reached out nervously and sucked it from its squelchy grave. Like a carving in stone, the child's body lay trapped in its own grey coffin. Confused, Lee looked at it. Then he drew off his muffler and wiped the tiny face. As he did so the dead blue eyes stared sightlessly at the sky and he felt a hard knot bulging in his chest, almost choking him as the awful truth dawned.

Frances caught sight of Lee and came scrambling over, pushing him aside as she did so. For a moment she stood still, looking down at the child then stooped to unloosen the belts and gathered the small, wasted body into her arms. 'Come on, Rory,' she said. 'Wake up now.'

'Frances. . .' Lee tried to make her look at him, but she kept turning away.

She jiggled the bundle in her arms. 'All right, you just sleep, then. Your mammy's here.' She walked up to a ridge, clear of the mud and sat there cradling the boy as she slowly rocked back and forth.

Pi'taki came over, wrapped the plaid shawl around her shoulders and moved away again. She had loved Rory as her own and, though death was no stranger to her, the sight of Frances pressing the dead child to her breast, seemed a pain too private to witness. She consumed her grief, suppressing it for another time.

The afternoon wore on in silence and a deep heat penetrated the site of the carnage. Mud dried and cracked around them and the only sound was Frances's hoarse voice, softly singing lullabies. Pi'taki lit a fire and its thin pall of smoke rose up through the dust as the mighty shadow of the golden eagle glided over the sun-splashed rock face.

By evening, Lee had cleared some of the ground and erected a makeshift tent. He moved cautiously, afraid to distract Frances, yet equally afraid of the moment she faced reality. Quietly, he stacked their belongings in a pile and slumped beside it. He felt vacant, useless and sat mute, awaiting a sign that might prompt him to take up the lead again. As he watched, unnerved by the pathetic sight, he was wise enough to know that it was too soon yet.

Frances continued to rock with the child, urging him to feed from her breast in an effort to bring back life. The little body grew stiff in her arms and silty water seeped from the corner of his mouth and nostrils. She rubbed his skin to try and restore colour to the stony flesh and drew the blanket in closer.

Meanwhile, Pi'taki set about cutting the young branches from the uprooted trees. Hours passed and she was absorbed in preparation for her task. As evening fell she began to construct a simple platform with a small tableau to take the body. The night merged into day and the sun was fully up again by the time she was ready. Then moved by her own ancient customs she walked up through the smoky atmosphere and confronted Frances. 'Give him to me,' she said softly.

Frances shook her head. 'No, leave him, you'll wake him.'

'Otanimm.' She cupped her hand under Frances's chin and forced her head up. 'His body is dead. You must let his spirit go.'

Slowly, the vacant look in Frances's eyes cleared as she focussed on the familiar old face. Pi'taki leaned forward to prise the little corpse from its mother's grip and as she did so, Frances's arms gradually unlocked and yielded up the bundle. Their eyes met in consummate grief and Pi'taki drew Frances towards her. The two women stood, their arms around each other with the dead form of the child held between them. Then as the pathetic weight was lifted from her, Frances felt the anguish welling inside, rising inexorably until it broke as a tormented cry in her throat. Finally admitting the irrevocable truth, she slumped to her knees and wept inconsolable tears for her son.

The high wooden frame was covered with the old tipi skins and Pi'taki placed the body on top. She set small fires at the base poles and kept them smoking throughout the day and into the next night. But when the sun came up again, she was gone.

A predatory squawk resounded in the canyon and Frances stumbled through the tent-flap at a run. Aiming the rifle randomly in the air, she fired off a volley of shots. High above, the golden eagle soared away, the rhythm of its sweeping wings uninterrupted by her distracted shooting.

Lee came up behind her. 'Okay, honey, leave it be.'

'I've got to keep that eagle off my boy,' she shouted, her

wild eyes scanning the sky for any other approaching scavengers.

Lee eased the gun from her hands and put his arm around her shoulders. 'Let's go,' he urged, leading her back to the tent. They crossed the clearing, still strewn with debris, and a broken crate caught Frances's eye.

'That needs fixing.' She pointed it out to him.

'Okay, I'll do it in a minute.' He tried to get her to move to the tent.

'Do it now, O'Byrne.' She shook off his arm and walked away. This was how it had been for the last five days. Frances was disorientated, her mind moving between the present and the past, and Lee was never sure where she thought she was. One certainty was that she was not ready yet to leave the child. He tried to be patient and bide his time, but increasingly, he feared that Frances would never recover enough to move on. A hard shell had clamped around her since Rory's death and she seemed bereft of emotion, unaware of anything apart from a fierce need to protect her son's body. Lee even had to push the food into her mouth to get her to eat.

Later that night, the smoke still wreathed the camp in a macabre half-light and the two sat opposite each other inside the tent.

'Guess it's just you and me now, Frances.' Lee tried to get her attention though her eyes were blank, her expression empty. 'Honey, you gotta listen. Staying here ain't gonna bring the boy back – more likely it'll kill us too.'

'I don't care,' she said, looking directly at him for the first time.

'Well I do. I reckon we got four, maybe six weeks if we're lucky. We gotta get down to the river before the big freeze.' She looked beyond him again. He grew exasperated and shook her by the shoulders. 'I hate to do this to you but I'm tellin' you now – we're movin' on tomorrow whether you like it or not.'

'I'm no going without Pi'taki.'

'Aw come on, what do we need her for? We'll have a whole new life when we get to the gold-fields.'

'I dinna care about the gold,' she spat at him, pulling free.

'You say that now, but when we're settled you'll see things different. We can have more kids and. . .'

She stared at him, her eyes clear with hard anger. 'It's all just a game to you, isn't it?' she said acidly. 'Life's a big gamble to Leland O'Byrne. Well, I was the loser this time – your gold can never replace my bairn.'

He tried to pacify her. 'I understand that, but we can't afford to wait any longer. We gotta move on.'

'No. Not till Pi'taki comes back,' she shouted.

Lee was confounded and frustrated by her obstinacy. 'What if she don't?' he said.

'She will. I know she will.' The words were jumbled by her mounting hysteria. 'She won't leave me like the rest.' Frances pushed him out of the way, suddenly certain that if she searched one more time then she would find her. As she crawled from the tent, she was immediately distracted by the strange brilliance that flooded the plateau. Her urgent quest was forgotten and she stood immobile, looking up at the coruscating green fire of the northern lights that had consumed the sky. Spasmodic beams shot overhead, their reflections glittering like emeralds in the muddied pools and she was lost in wonder as the little funeral plinth was bathed in the auroral glow.

Beyond their sight, miles down into the foothills of the mountains, Pi'taki stood. Her eyes strained against the thinning light and searched the sky for stars. For two days and nights she had walked without food or water, her hair bristling in the wind now the braids had been bluntly chopped off. The blood dried in tracks down her arms where she had scored them with her knife, re-opening old scars first cut in grief for her own children. Wailing the old ancestral words of mourning, she laid the spirit of her dear Issohko to rest and now as she sat cross-legged facing the north, the sky, as if in acknowledgement, filled with a brilliance of flashing, shimmering lights.

With the dawn she awoke, suddenly aware of her discomfort. The cold and dampness of the ground had seeped into her clothing during the night yet there was a haze over the lowlands, a prescient hint of warmth in the atmosphere. She scanned the distant valley and, as her eyes adjusted to the morning sun, she saw what she had come to find. There, snaking far below, rushed the mighty Yukon river. Pi'taki turned and made her way back up into the mountains.

7

It was another week before the three were walking more easily on the lower slopes that brought them nearer to the river's level. From time to time Pi'taki would turn and cast a glance back up into the dark jagged mountains where the child now rested but Frances never

223

raised her eyes from the ground before her. She focussed ahead without optimism, just a driven impulse to keep going, feeling nothing and thinking herself the safer for it. Lee too remained subdued but inwardly his spirit had lightened with the prospect of finishing the journey.

The sun blazed mercilessly during the day-time and they welcomed the respite of darkness when it fell. Their faces were blistered and they tied rags over their necks and foreheads to protect themselves from burning. All that was left of their supplies, one box and two bundles, were now tied on to their backs with home-made slings or dragged behind on ropes. As they came silently down between the trees, they looked like the defeated fugitives of some ancient civilisation, unapproachable and only half human.

The river was a vast, wide swathe that gathered its swell from the mountain tributaries. By boat, the easy current would sweep them all the way into the Klondike region. Demoralised, they sat by the shore and examined their paltry collection of tools. There was no hatchet or saw, only some coils of rope and Pi'taki's knife. Hardly adequate to build a strong, wide raft to take them the five hundred miles down river. Ironically, the gold pan and a long-handled shovel still stuck out of the gunny sack. Lee could have saved weight by discarding them long ago but, still fired up with the dream of finding gold, he could not bring himself to throw them away.

The sun beat heavily on their backs and they withdrew into the shade of the dense overgrowth of poplar that reared up behind them. There was no shortage of timber but after months of ordeal they were wise enough to know their limits. A strange torpor now descended on them. The trees swayed and a gentle breeze combed the river before them. They made a fire, boiled water and Pi'taki added the torn up leaves she had collected along the way, using a twig to stir the herbal infusion. She then shared out the last meagre berries that were to serve as their meal. Frances took hers and scooped them up hungrily with both hands and Pi'taki was heartened to see that her appetite had returned. Lee grimaced and picked distastefully at the fruit. 'This is for the birds,' he complained, tossing the remainder away. 'I ain't eatin' any more. Gonna get us some real food.'

With that, he walked down to the lapping water at the shore's edge, pulled off his boots and waded in. He rolled up his sleeves and flexed his fingers as he leaned forward, staring into the depths. 'See if I can't catch us a fish,' he said, scanning the water as each flash of sunlight tormented his imagination.

Frances looked doubtfully at the old woman but she was preoccupied. Pi'taki made her remove the makeshift boots and began to
ease her feet by massaging them with the leaves. Hard callouses had
cracked into running sores and Frances had suffered greatly with the
relentless treading over uneven ground. For the most part, however,
she had been unaware of it and now looked on surprised at the sight
of her wounded feet. There was little talk between them and a mutual
disinterest in Lee's ineffectual attempts to fish.

Frances lay back, lulled by the soothing ministrations. Momentarily she caught an image of Rory. He had loved the water. When she
called to him on the homestead and he did not answer, she knew she
could always find him wading in the creeks and streams that freckled
their land. Fearlessly he explored the mud, sinking his arms into holes
and returning to her proudly with unspeakable things squirming in
the bottom of his tin. Tears pricked her eyes. She imagined if he were
here now he would be lying on the bank, deep in concentration, with
one arm reaching over into the water foraging the secret places. She
could see his little drawn brows slowly flatten and a smile spread over
his features as he gently stroked the underbelly of the unsuspecting
fish.

Pi'taki nudged her and pointed over to where Lee squatted in the
water. He was waving his arms and shouting to them and gesturing
towards a spot beyond their line of vision. Frances straightened up,
shading her eyes. They walked down to the river's edge to take a
look. The yellowing, swollen hand was the first glimpse they had
of the man's weed-entangled body. Frances felt her stomach turn
as she came closer and saw the bloated cadaver wallowing in the
slough at the water's line. The eyes bulged hideously and swarmed
with blackflies and a necrotic stench filled the air. Lee already had
his hands inside the pockets and she could not understand why he
was excited by such a find.

'Don't you see,' he said with uncontrollable delight as he rescued
a wad of sodden bank notes and a watch and chain, 'where there's
a drowned man, here in the middle of nowhere – well, there's gotta
be a boat!'

Pi'taki looked downstream for other debris. She walked further
along the bank to an inlet where the remains of split-open cartons
bobbed on the eddying tide. A huge rudder-paddle was jammed
among them and she waded in to retrieve it. As she hauled the
long pole up on to the bank, the others came running, their
eyes frantically searching the shoreline for the precious boat. The
corpse was of a white man, a man from the south who had surely

come to grief in the narrow course between the Five Finger Rapids which they had caught sight of back upstream. If so, then Lee was right and it could only mean one thing – a boat. That was what he hoped and a fierce urgency now gripped him as he ran faster in his excitement, feverishly scanning every runnel, every sluice and calling encouragement with each sighting of another piece of evidence.

Finally, he found it, upturned and wedged against a fallen tree that overhung the water. It was a wide snub-nosed scull, hand-built from green lumber planks and caulked with spruce pitch. The mast pole was shattered but the base was sound. Two other bodies floated face-down in the wash and Frances, unwilling to witness another plundering by Lee, guided them out into the mainstream with the pole and they were quickly swept away.

'Dammit, Frances, what you do that for?' he complained. 'They won't know any different – they're dead.' Then he realised it was a sensitive subject and turned his attentions to the boat.

Righting it proved to be a mighty task requiring ropes in a pulley system tied to the trees. It took them over an hour of straining until the huge raft was sucked up and over. As it came, boxes and crates loosed themselves from their housings and floated free. Lee plunged in to retrieve what he could, shouting to Pi'taki to hook them from the shore as he pushed them towards her.

The work was exhausting and all had to find some residue of strength, one final burst of energy to complete the task. When it was done, shattered with fatigue, they dropped to the ground where they stood. Frances lay on her back and stared up at the tall spruce that fringed the sky overhead. Lee beside her turned his head and looked at the rescued cartons, wondering about their contents. Grabbing Pi'taki's knife, he split open the first crate. It was watertight and the contents remained unharmed. Drums of salt, tinned beans and black-eyed peas lay packed in a rubberised lining. The next layer revealed yeast, flour and sugar and a couple of pots and pans. Lee tossed them all out one by one, and the two women stared, fascinated by the array of goods and utensils that had long since left their memory. Wedged in the middle of all this was a bottle of whisky. Lee's eyes lit up. Frances ignored it and continued to look spellbound into the depths of the treasure trove. Pi'taki came forward and tried to prise it from his hands but he danced back from her laughing as he pulled the stopper with his teeth.

'What's the matter, ol' girl? Don't deny a man a drink now surely?'

'Whisky makes a man slow. Then he is good for nothing,' she declared, frowning.

For once, Lee's obsession to push on at all costs began to dwindle. 'Well, guess we can rest up a bit now. One more day ain't gonna matter.' He ambled off into the trees hugging the bottle to his chest. 'Don't know about you, ladies, but I aim to have myself a little shut-eye.'

Frances and Pi'taki sat together re-examining the contents of the crates. The next was waterlogged but in it they unearthed a sealed tin box containing an array of little jars and packages. Pi'taki listened bewildered as the labels were read out one by one: tincture iodine; chlorate potash; laudanum; quinine; mustard and belladonna plasters. Carefully Frances packed them back in their container to be preserved for future use. Then, as she replaced it in the bottom of the carton, her fingers brushed against a small hard object. Initially she did not realise what it was but as she brought it out into the daylight, Pi'taki reached across and pulled the string that was attached. The little wooden horse nodded its head and the realisation that there had been a child amongst these folk weighed heavily on the air. Snatches of Lee's tipsy singing wafted through the trees towards them. As if it burned her fingers, Frances flung the toy from her, sending it spinning over the water where it landed with a plop and drifted downstream.

The next morning Pi'taki found Lee snoring on his back, the empty bottle by his side. She shook him vigorously but could only exact a low moan in response. Leaving him to sleep off his hangover, she and Frances prepared a new mast-pole for the boat by chopping off the longest branch from the fallen tree. Then, fitting some ragged and tattered remnants of clothing to it, they hoisted a rudimentary sail.

When Lee recovered, in disgrace, he helped them load the goods aboard. 'You shoulda woke me,' he said examining their efforts. 'Even so, you ain't done a bad job.'

Pi'taki settled herself at the middle of the boat. Lee took the rudder-pole and, with Frances ahead at the bow, he pushed off from the bank. Once they were out in the central current of the big river they moved swiftly downstream. As the momentum of the flow carried them on effortlessly, they sat back in the steaming air and each was lost in their own private thoughts.

For days the craft slipped along with barely a word from its occupants. Lee could not believe their luck at the discovery of the boat, but the thought was double-edged and he was uneasy with the knowledge that other prospectors were clearly on their way. He sweated for the want of a drink but inspection of the crates yielded no secret cache and he could only sustain himself with the thought that they were now so close to the end of their journey – almost close enough to reach out and pick up those nuggets of gold that surely lay on the ground for the taking.

The great Yukon ploughed on, swelled and muddied by its tributaries. Gradually the mountains opened up and the land on either side became marshy, enveloping their boat in a steaming mist. Then one day, while the other two slept, Frances steered the boat round a rocky bluff. As she did so, the mist cleared a little and she blinked into the hazy sunlight. Up ahead was a mountain bearing a great sliding scar and, at its feet, lay Dawson City.

8

Front Street of Dawson overlooked the Yukon River and the mud-flats where dozens of boats were lined up. They found it difficult to navigate their own craft into any sort of recognisable mooring and it was more chance than skill that finally saw them safely beached on the black shore. Dazed and bewildered, they had spent the first night huddled under furs, disorientated and drifting in and out of restless sleep. Lee was agape at the eternal bustle of activity that was going on mere yards from where they lay, astounded by the shock of the masses that had got there before them. But there would be no more coming in their wake. Although it was still only September, further north the freeze-up had begun and the river was already impassable. The sub-Arctic winter blocked off the overland routes and those who had arrived had no choice but to stay. For the Klondikers there would be no way out now until spring.

Dawson City stood where months before there had been little more than frozen muskeg. Now a sizeable town of some fifteen hundred souls, it was an improbable mixture of sprawling tent settlements circling Front Street on which new wooden buildings seemed to erupt from the mud overnight. To feed this insatiable building demand a sawmill was located right in the middle of the main street, working non-stop twenty-four hours a day. More basic human demands were met by the stores, saloons and dance-halls which never closed and swarms of men wandered up and down Front Street at all hours.

Frances awoke suddenly and jerked out of her nightmare. She

228

struggled to free herself from the furs which in sleep had become the suffocating mud-slide once more. Again she had tried desperately to reach Rory but his face, calm and peaceful, had slid beneath the surging wet earth. Jerking upright, she sat gasping and blinking at the thin early sun, realising it was morning. A great wave of fatigue had engulfed her once they arrived and she had slept for longer than she knew. She looked around. Pi'taki still snored beside her but Lee had disappeared. A group of drunks staggered from one of the saloons and she guessed where he would be.

One of them spotted her. 'Hey there,' he drawled as he lurched across, sliding in the thick mud, 'looks cosy in there. Mind if I just climb in beside you darlin'?'

'Go to hell.' Frances's voice was flat and her face composed but a hint of dark and dangerous anger reached the man through the fog of a night's whisky.

'Well pardon me, ma'am,' he muttered, moving off to rejoin his carousing cronies.

Gently Frances shook Pi'taki. 'I'm away to get us some bread and see if I can find Lee, I won't be long.' Pi'taki nodded, her face still heavy with exhaustion, watching through red-rimmed eyes. Frances pulled on her torn boots and Lee's mackinaw to ward off the piercing cold of the early morning. Easing herself from the boat, her legs sunk calf-deep in cold, slimy mud and Frances found it took all her concentration to keep upright as she struggled to reach the wooden pavement opposite. After months in the isolation of the wilderness, she found the sight and sound of so many people more of a threat than a comfort. Nervously, she backed out of the way when anyone approached, afraid they might pass through her as though she were a ghost.

In a gap between two wooden buildings was a large tent with a sign advertising fresh bread. A woman stood behind a plank set across logs that served as a counter and eyed Frances curiously.

'How much for a loaf?'

'Four dollars or a quarter ounce of dust.' The reply was given in a matter-of-fact tone and Frances could not believe her ears.

'Christ, I could buy a sack o' flour for that!'

'You could if there was any for sale – but there ain't. You want the bread or not?'

Nodding, Frances handed over the crumpled notes and received a stale-looking loaf in return. Then she cut through the gap next to the bakery tent and headed away from the river. Hundreds of tents were pitched in haphazard confusion behind the main street.

The nearest clear space was some way up the slope that rose at the back of the town and Frances sighed as she imagined the effort it would take to move everything there from their boat. She had to find Lee and prevent Pi'taki from wearing herself out any further. In the weeks since Rory's death, she had aged before their eyes.

Wearied by these thoughts, Frances continued to look for Lee. Nervously she peered through the open doorways of the saloons but he was nowhere to be seen. She thought he might perhaps have gone to find out about staking a claim but it was impossible to know where to begin looking. After a while, she found herself in a narrow passage at the back of Front Street. The mud was thick here and there was nowhere to walk except on the little wooden steps which led to the row of huts. Above was a sign that read PARADISE ALLEY though nowhere less enchanting could be imagined. Buxom women in voluminous cotton smocks sat preening themselves in the open windows or leaning languorously in the doorways. Frances felt ill at ease as their eyes followed her. She pulled a lump from the loaf and began chewing on the dry bread, hunger making it seem more palatable than it was. Then, in the dim light at the end of the alley, she saw Lee. Furtively he slipped out of one of the huts. He looked around, buttoning his trousers and pulling his braces over his shoulders.

'*Tot ziens, geliefde*!' a female voice called after him as he disappeared round the corner. Frances stood stock-still with the crust half-way to her mouth and stared.

When she got back to the boat, she found him curled up against the boxes, half-asleep. He rolled over dreamily and looked up. 'Where you been, honey?' He rubbed his eyes and the smell of liquor came off his breath as he spoke.

'Where have *I* been?' she asked coolly, trying not to wake Pi'taki.

Lee put his hands up defensively. 'Okay, so I've had a drink.'

'And that's not all you've had.'

'What d'you mean?'

'Shh, keep your voice down. And don't pretend ye don't know what I mean – I saw ye not ten minutes ago coming out one o' those stinking cribs in Paradise Alley.'

His face darkened and he stood up unsteadily. 'All right, I was there, but what d'you expect, Frances? You ain't come near me in weeks.'

'Ye think I care about that?' she hissed under her breath. 'Where did ye get the money? I thought I was holding what little cash we have but you're managing to have yourself a spending spree.'

230

Pi'taki shifted in her sleep. 'You're wakin' the ol' woman,' Lee said with his finger to his mouth. 'Think we better leave this till another time, eh?' He sat down heavily and pulled the covers over him. 'Need a bit of shut-eye myself.'

'Not now. We have to move. We canna stay here in this boat for ever. Get up and find us a space on the hill where we can take the stuff and pitch the tent.'

'Aw come on, honey, I'm tired.' He turned his back on her and made himself comfortable. Frances tried again to persuade him but it was not long before he was asleep and snoring drunkenly. With nothing to do but wait, she started to rearrange their supplies. Some of the medicines in the wooden case were missing and she realised this had to be the source of the extra cash. She was angry with Lee for wasting it on himself, but relieved to know they had some re-sale value. She packed up everything else in readiness for the move and waited for the others to awaken. Pi'taki opened her eyes first.

'Are you all right?' Frances asked.

Pi'taki nodded but her movements were slow and her voice cracked when she spoke. She looked across at Lee. 'You found him,' she said, with an edge of contempt.

'He came back about an hour ago. I'll wake him now because we've got to get all this moved out of the boat before dark.'

'Leave him, we can get on without him.'

'No, we need his help, Pi'taki. I don't want you lifting these boxes any more.'

Pi'taki waved her off dismissively but Frances insisted on Lee's help before they could begin. For hour after hour they hauled and dragged the crates and sacks from the boat, across the churned mud and up on to the slope among the other tents. All the trees around the township had been cut down and the stumps left behind created an obstacle course that had to be negotiated with care.

Lee worked reluctantly as, still suffering the effects of the drink, he stumbled over the uneven ground. Finally they got the tent pitched and left Pi'taki to build a fire while they returned to retrieve the last of the supplies. As they were leaving the mooring, they were approached by a man who enquired if the boat was for sale.

'No,' Frances retorted flatly.

'Yes,' Lee countered, 'she's for sale – how much you give for her?'

Frances gripped his arm. 'It's no for sale,' she whispered ardently but the man continued to conduct his conversation with Lee.

'No use for a raft this end of the river. Give you ten dollars.'

'Twenty.'

'Fifteen and it's a deal.'

'Done,' said Lee and pocketed the bills.

Frances tore at his mackinaw to try and reclaim the money. 'You'll waste it away,' she protested.

He danced around her. 'Just lookin' after it,' he said. 'You go back to the tent – I got some shoppin' to do.'

When she reached the tent Frances was too tired to think about food but Pi'taki pressed her to eat something. Lee returned later, as expected, clutching a bottle.

'What's got into ye?' Frances said despairingly as he slumped beside her. 'You're useless.'

'Oh yeah, useless am I?' He staggered to his feet. 'And who got you here, eh? – you'd never have made it without me.'

'Aye, and what was it all for, Lee? I don't give a damn about the gold but it was your big dream, remember? Since we got here you've done nothing – except get drunk.'

He sat down again and looked vacantly through the gap in the tent and down over the river. 'Tomorrow,' he said. 'I'll go into the land office tomorrow and get us a licence.'

All this time, Pi'taki had remained uninvolved but once he was asleep, she leaned towards Frances and spoke with a lowered voice. 'Go with him, Otanimm.'

'Aye,' Frances nodded wearily and knew she must make the effort. She looked across at Lee and, as if seeing him clearly for the first time, she wondered how much lower he would bring them.

9

The next morning, Frances realised why the man had been so eager to buy their boat. With the hillsides stripped bare of trees, wood for fires had to be bought. Cursing Lee for his stupidity, she paid across the couple of dollars that was left and received in exchange a small bundle of logs that would last them no time at all.

Despite his hangover, Lee awoke with a burst of renewed enthusiasm and stood up, anxious to get away. 'Well, I'm off into town,' he said.

Frances was ready. 'I'm coming with you.'

'No honey, this is man's business – no need for you to tag along.'

'I'm coming anyway,' she said. He tried to say something but she overruled him. 'We're going together, Lee. Now you need rest, Pi'taki. Stay here and keep the fire going. Don't worry about the wood, we'll be back as soon as we can.'

Grudgingly, Lee set off down the slope into the town with Frances following. Hundreds of people milled around the muddy thoroughfare between carts and dog sleds and she was hard pressed to keep up with him. In time, they became separated. She was not sure if they had just lost each other or if he had slipped away deliberately. But, whether by accident or design, Frances now found herself alone. For half an hour she wandered about looking for the land office, presuming that to be where Lee had gone. Nervously she approached some of the men who passed but they either ignored her or thought she was soliciting.

'Not having much success, dearie.' A stout woman of enormous proportions blocked Frances's path. Her gaudy dress and fur-trimmed coat were a bizarre costume for the dirt streets of Dawson. They eyed each other, and the woman snorted. 'Not surprising. Some o' these men never wash from one year's end to the next, but they like their women smellin' sweet.' She looked Frances up and down again. 'And young.'

'Get out of my way.' Frances tried to walk past her but she blocked her path.

'Aw, come on – no offence meant. I can fix you up at the Golden Slipper – a bath and a new dress, you'd do okay.'

Frances sighed. 'Please, I just want to find the land office.'

The fat woman shook with laughter. 'Honey, you gotta be kiddin' me!' She looked into Frances's face and stopped. 'No, I guess you ain't. Well, I seen it all now.' She stuck out her hand. 'I'm Bella Gibson.'

Frances hesitated, then took the offered hand awkwardly. 'Frances O'Byrne.'

Bella looked her over once more. 'Well, Frances, if you don't mind my sayin', you look like shit.' The laugh bubbled up again. 'How 'bout you and me have a cup of coffee?'

Suddenly, Frances found herself softening towards the woman and the thought of a hot cup of coffee made her mouth water. 'All right,' she said, smiling.

'You should smile more often, kid. Takes years off you.' Bella linked her arm with Frances's and led her to the door of a saloon. 'It's okay,' she said, 'I got a room at the back. We can have our coffee there in private.' Frances let herself be taken into the dim bar-room. She glanced around nervously, fingering her worn coat.

233

There were a few men sitting around at tables and they called over as the women entered.

'Hey, Bella. That a new one for us? Needs a bit of meat on her bones.'

Another voice joined in. 'Sure looks like she could do with a bath – want I should scrub her back?'

Bella never slackened her pace. 'A woman's no use to you, short-dick! Try a chicken – it's a better match.' The men roared with laughter. She shouted to the barman, 'Ernie, bring us through some coffee. And make it fresh.'

Closing the door and taking off her coat, Bella sat down. 'So, Frances O'Byrne,' she said, facing her across the table, 'what do you know about minin' for gold?'

She was taken aback by the question. 'Me? well, nothing. . .'

Bella saw the confusion on her face and leaned over to pat her. 'You ain't the first cheechako to turn up here with no sense and you won't be the last.'

'What's that, cheechako?'

'What the old boys call all you gold rushers. Means greenhorn, innocent . . .' she waved her pudgy hands vaguely. 'Useless.'

'We're no' that bad.' Frances sighed. 'My husband's been prospecting before, I think he knows what he's doing.'

Bella raised an eyebrow. 'You don't sound convinced.'

Frances shrugged. 'We were on our way to the land office and I lost him in the crowd. It's strange, but you know he was crazy to get here and now I don't think he's really bothered. I can't understand it.' She was surprised at how readily she had confided her fears and looked down self-consciously.

Bella shook her head. 'Happens all the time, sweetie. The street's full of them. Men who got all fired up with the dream of findin' gold and broke their backs comin' over the passes to get here – now they just sit on the sidewalks squintin' at the sun.'

'But why?' Frances looked confused.

'Search me. Just the way it is.'

The barman came in with a pot and two tin mugs and Bella poured the coffee. Frances gulped it down gratefully. 'So what do we have to do?' she asked.

'Easiest thing in the world. You walk outa town till you find the next bit of land that ain't been had and you claim it. Then you prays to Almighty God that the bit you claimed has gold in it, 'cos one claim's all you get.' She refilled Frances's cup. 'The old-timers here say the best has long gone already. Nothin' left worth stakin' now.'

234

Frances stared into her cup. 'I thought as much,' she said dismally. 'Och, I wish we'd never come here.'

Bella sighed. 'Well, the river's iced up north of here by now so you ain't gonna get out this year. You might as well give it a try. Now, go find that man of yours and quit frownin' – that's better!' She returned Frances's smile and walked over to the door. 'Is Duke Summers still out there?' she bawled into the bar-room.

Somebody shouted back, 'He just left, Bella.'

'Well, what you waitin' for?' she ordered. 'Move your scrawny ass and git after him!'

Within minutes, Duke Summers appeared in the doorway. 'What you wantin', Bella? I was half-way down the street, dammit!' He was a small man with wide grey whiskers from ear to ear. He wore a brocade waistcoat and gold fob-watch over otherwise shabby clothes and a neat little bowler sat snugly on his head.

Bella gestured to Frances. 'This here girl needs you to show her where the land office is. Take her down there in your buggy.'

He grimaced. 'Aw, Bella, don't waste my time. What's a woman wantin' with that place anyway?'

'We're good for more than just one thing, Duke.' Bella slapped him on the back. 'And if you won't help out, I'll see to it you don't get that one thing for quite a while.' Her eyes were gleaming.

He looked at her appealingly. 'Bella, I'm your best customer. . .'

'Plenty more where you came from, Duke.'

'But I should've been out at Grand Forks by now,' he complained.

'Well, then take her with you, man, let her see the lie of the land – now the pair of you git goin'. I gotta get my beauty sleep.'

All this time Frances had stood in the background, amused by the scenario but equally impressed. It was the first act of kindness a stranger had shown her for a long time. As she followed Duke from the bar, Bella's voice called after her. 'Mind you come back and let me know how you get on.'

Frances explained the situation to Duke as they came out into the chilly morning sun. She climbed into the cart beside him and they moved off.

'Well now, if your husband's serious 'bout lookin' for gold, then the first thing he's gotta do is get a licence.'

'For what?'

'Miner's licence. You can't stake a claim till you're licensed – that's the law. I guess this is where he'll be.'

They drew up before a small wooden shack at the far end of Front Street where a queue of men stood in waiting. Some of them nodded to Duke, others eyed Frances curiously. She looked around for Lee but he was nowhere to be seen. Duke went inside and, by some means that she was not privy to, he engineered her position to the front of the queue.

'This here's the lady, McBride,' Duke said by way of introduction. The man behind the desk looked up at her, his eyes questioning.

'Can you tell me if a miner's licence has been applied for in the name O'Byrne?' Frances asked. There was a pause while McBride looked through the register.

'Nope, nothing here in that name.'

'Are ye sure?'

'Like I said, ma'am, no O'Byrne's been in here.'

Frances cursed Lee under her breath. She hesitated, unsure of what to do next.

'If you're all done, lady, we'd like to get on with business here.' The clerk was waving the next man in line forward.

'All right, I'll take the licence myself,' she said decisively.

McBride laughed, joined by the men in line behind her. 'Well, I just about seen it all.'

'What's wrong?' Frances asked, reddening.

'Don't you think you better square it with your husband first, lady?'

'Is there a law says I can't?' She was angry now and knew if she waited for Lee it would never get done.

'C'mon man, the girl's got as much right as anyone,' Duke intervened, remembering Bella's words.

McBride shook his head again, then he shrugged and drew out a paper. 'Sign here – or make your mark,' he said sarcastically.

Frances pulled the pen from his hand. 'It's all right,' she said, scrawling her signature on the form. 'I can write, I'm no completely stupid.'

'Yeah, but will you last a winter in the creeks?' one of the men behind joked cruelly.

'I'll give her three days – five at most,' another piped up and they all joined in laughing.

'All right boys, that'll do. For Chrissakes, McBride, just give her the card.' Reluctantly it was handed over. 'This here's your licence,' Duke said. 'When you've staked your claim, you gotta come back here and register.'

'Right,' she said, 'well then, let's get going.'

Duke looked around at the blank faces. 'Ain't nobody gonna wish her luck?' he said.

'Needs more'n luck, Duke – needs a goddam miracle that 'un!'

On the way out to the creeks, Frances managed to deflect Duke's questions away from herself by getting him to tell his own story. He had been prospecting in the north for years making a bit of a living with small finds of gold and silver. As a result, when the first big strike was made in Bonanza Creek he got the news early and came over fast. By the time he arrived the richest streams were already gone, but his claim was close enough to be pulling out a sizeable fortune.

Frances was sceptical. 'But, if you're so rich, why are ye. . . ?' She stopped, realising she had not meant to be rude.

'Why am I a bum?' cackled Duke. 'Yeah well, gold is only good for one thing – buying a man a good time. What do I want with fancy clothes and a fancy house? Hell, ain't many of them around here anyhow.' He shook his head. 'No, once in a while I go into Dawson and have myself a jamboree. Then, when my poke's all gone, I come back out and dig me some more.'

'But what about when the gold runs out?' Frances asked.

'Then we'll all move on somewhere else. That's the fun – tracking it down, finding the big strike. Once you've found it,' he shrugged, 'well, a man can only spend so much.'

The ride out from Dawson followed a well-worn trail. Every five hundred feet, a numbered claim stake was driven in the hard ground. The land had been torn up as though a giant explosion had ripped across the hillsides with mounds of gravel and spoil littering the boundaries of each claim. Long, winding water-channels ran from the hills to the panning beds where wooden sluices and rocker cradles sat. There was a feverish activity everywhere with men working ceaselessly to pan as much gold from the gravel as they could before the winter freeze stopped the essential supply of running water. Already, shaded pools were covered with a crust of thin ice despite the feeble warmth from the sun hanging low on the horizon.

They travelled quickly, the horse fresh and well-fed, unlike the poor pack animals Frances had seen die on the trail. They were twelve miles from town before Duke pulled in the reins. A small creek flowed down from the hills to join another, bigger one already marked out with a claim. 'This here's Hunker,' he said with a sweep of the hand. He took out a stake and wooden shingle he had brought. 'Guess you got as good a chance here as any place now.'

237

Frances jumped down and snatched them from his grasp. 'No, I'll do it.' She drove the post into the frozen ground, banging it home with a mallet. On the shingle, she wrote her name, the date and her miner's licence number.

Claim 79 Below Discovery
—

I lay claim to five hundred feet up here for mining purposes.

F.O. Byrne 16/9/97

Licence 2047

'Once you register back in town, the inspector will come out to measure and mark the boundaries,' Duke explained, 'but it's all yours now.'

Frances looked around at the desolate landscape. Each plot of land was a rubble-strewn mess with a ramshackle hut in the middle. Here she was laying claim to five hundred feet of Yukon permafrost, after giving up one hundred and sixty acres of fertile Alberta farmland. Somehow, it did not seem a fair exchange.

It was late by the time she got back to the tent. Frances had thanked Duke and tramped back into Dawson, leaving him to make his way to Grand Forks. In town, she had gone straight back into the land office and registered. McBride was surprised to see her so soon. This time he was cool but courteous and noted the particulars of the land she had staked, saying he would come out in a couple of days to mark it out. Back at the camp, as she had expected, Pi'taki had allowed the fire to go out rather than use up their sparse wood supply. Instead, she had occupied herself sorting out their stores.

'You've been busy,' Frances smiled. 'Where's Lee?'

'He did not come back with you?'

'I lost him in town – at least I think that's what happened. Well I suppose we'll no be seeing him tonight.' She sighed and started to build the fire anew. 'Ye should've kept this going, Pi'taki – you're frozen.' She blew on the green wood, trying to get it to catch and once there was some heat coming from it, they sat back, huddling into the furs for warmth. 'Well, I've staked our claim – tomorrow we can make a start.' Frances looked down at the glinting lights of the town. 'With or without him.'

10

It was late October by the time they started to sink their first shaft. Frances sold the remaining medicines to the local druggist and used the proceeds to eke out their supplies. Lee was tardy and sluggish about making a start on the claim but, with no more obstacles to the work and no money left for drink, his enthusiasm was for the time being revived. With a makeshift travois they had dragged their cumbersome belongings out to the creeks. For the first few days the work had concentrated on the hurried erection of a crude log cabin that would house them through the winter. The tent was bitterly cold at night but in the day-time the physical effort of cutting and sawing kept them warm in the rapidly cooling temperatures. The Yukon river was freezing over quickly now and they realised how narrow the margin had been between getting through to Dawson during the thaw and perishing, trapped in the ice.

In contrast with the situation back at the town, timber was plentiful on the slopes behind them so, after felling trees for the hut, they were able to cut the huge supply of firewood needed to sink the shaft. The ground was permanently frozen, even in summer, and to drive down through the gravel it had to be thawed. Each evening the valley was covered in a man-made fog of wood-smoke drifting up in the still, cold air and hanging in a low cloud that turned the setting sun a garish blood-red. Fires were built into the shafts and left to smoulder all night. In the morning, the resulting mud of thawed gravel was scooped out in buckets to be piled in mounds that immediately froze again in the sub-zero temperatures.

Without a stove, they were forced to build a fire-pit in the centre of the tiny hut, which was only ten feet square. The pit had to be well lined with rocks or the heat melted the ground around it, turning the floor into a quagmire of slimy mud. There was no chimney, just a hole in the roof to let the smoke escape. Water for drinking and cooking had to be chipped from ice pools and melted in cans. Washing their clothes or indeed their bodies was a luxury and the stench in the cabin grew worse over the long, dark winter months. Each day, there were only a few hours of sunshine in contrast to the eternal lightness of summer and once their supply of candles was finished they had to make do with the glow of the fire as their only source of light.

Frances kept a strict eye on their food supply. She knew they would only make it through to spring by rationing what they ate and she had to watch Lee at all times. When his moods descended, he was morose and unreasonable, complaining that they were trying to starve him to death.

The long dark months dragged by and Frances lost all sense of time. One day merged with the next into an eternal black night of cold and hunger. There was now little talk between them and work on the shaft was pitifully slow. The freshly cut wood was green and hard to burn. Only a few inches a day could be thawed but the tunnel had to go down thirty feet. They found their first shaft was useless, hitting bedrock without the hint of a fleck of gold. There was no proven method that could be followed in deciding where to dig. Shafts were sunk at random and gold could lie a few inches to either side and never be found. Lee would have bursts of enthusiasm for the digging when he would be under the ground for hours on end, hacking away at the rock and heaving the buckets of gravel to the top. Then, quite suddenly, he would fall into a fit of gloom and remain in the cabin, lethargically staring across the hoar-whitened landscape. At those times he was immovable and Frances and Pi'taki had to continue the back-breaking toil alone.

Winter turned and as the days at last began to lengthen again, their second shaft was well under way. There was a hint of the coming thaw in the air. Around them, the other miners were growing daily more optimistic that the water would soon be running from the hills, allowing them to pan the gravel. For most it would be a fruitless exercise. Tons of rock and grit would pass through the sluices and riddles, leaving no trace of gold behind.

The women had been diligent about maintaining their supplies but by April these were dangerously low. They had counted on Lee's ability to supplement the stock of food by hunting but he could rarely be persuaded to make the effort. One day, he refused to get up, and Frances and Pi'taki worked outside on their own. When darkness fell, they returned to the cabin, frozen and hungry. It did not look as though Lee had moved since morning, but when Frances searched through the battered crate, she found the last of the rusted tins had gone.

'What's happened to the food?' she asked. Lee sat mute, avoiding her gaze. 'Lee, look at me,' she demanded. 'We only had enough for one day – two at the most.'

'Dunno about food but I could sure do with a drink,' he drawled in reply.

Suddenly she was across the room, towering above him and trembling with all the pent-up rage she had harboured over the months. 'So, you're just going to sit there and let your family die?'

'Call this a family?' he mumbled.

'It was once,' she shouted. 'All this time we've been scrabbling in the dirt. And for what? Your greed! Your greed brought us here – that's what killed Rory. And now it's killing us.' She beat at him with her fists, venting her feelings at last with all the vitriol she could muster and screaming, 'You bastard! Bastard! I hope ye burn in hell for what you've done to me and mine!'

Stunned by the outburst, Lee was caught off guard and barely tried to defend himself, though his mouth was split from her blows. 'You don't mean that,' he said, fingering the blood as he watched Pi'taki pull her down on to a seat to calm her.

But Frances's face was set in bitterness. 'Oh I do,' she sobbed. 'I mean it, every word.'

That night Frances was tormented by their looming fate. Restlessly tossing under the weight of furs, she considered what few options were left to them. Her rage at Lee had been replaced by the dull ache of hunger and she gave in time and again to despairing tears. By morning she knew she would have to go into Dawson, it was their last hope. 'I'll see what I can get on credit,' she said to Pi'taki as she prepared to leave. 'Dinna let him give ye any trouble.'

'No trouble,' the old woman assured, gesturing over to where Lee now worked. The incident of the night before had provoked him into a burst of activity and with first light he had been back down the shaft again.

'Aye, but for how long?' Frances sighed cynically. She left just after dawn, walking down the trail into town wrapped in the tattered remains of the mackinaw. Though her boots were a patchwork of rotted leather and strips of fur she kept up a brisk pace to try and keep warm.

Pi'taki watched her go and walked over to the head of the shaft. A wooden windlass had been built to haul the buckets of melted ice and gravel from the bottom. This second dig was already beyond thirty feet and there was no sign of bedrock. Normally, two of them worked up top at the hard job of winching the loaded bucket

241

and carrying the slopping contents to the pile near the frozen creek. Without Frances, Pi'taki would have to do it alone. She grunted and watched as Lee swung himself over the edge.

The long morning's labour began. Lee filled the bucket and yelled to her when it was ready. With aching arms, she hauled the load up and carried it to the side of the creek. For the first time in months, a slow but steady trickle of water ran under the sheets of ice. The thin sun made it perceptibly milder and, as the morning wore on, Pi'taki trudged back and forth in a daze of fatigue. The track from the shaft-head to the creek was slowly churning into mud and she twice slipped and fell with the heavy burden. She was thankful that Lee took so long to dig out the thawed gravel at the bottom, giving her time to rest.

But by midday her exhaustion was total. The bucket slipped from her grasp and, as if in response to some inner voice, she dragged her feet wearily to the cabin. Inside, she slumped on to the sleeping bench and lay looking up at the dismal rafters. Her eyes were glazed and her stomach hardened with the unremitting knot of hunger. It was a pain that had visited her many times in her life but now seemed an abiding presence. Minutes passed. In the eerie calm of the little hut a cold stillness descended on her, slowly dulling the ache and her thoughts drifted timelessly. Her body stiffened but her spirit seemed unwilling to revive as, consumed by a terrible isolation, she felt herself drawn to the brink of hopelessness. She watched her breath swirl in little vaporous fragments, fading on the air and let her eyes close in defeat. The shadows embraced her and drove away the cold. She had only to welcome the blackness to be free of the pain for ever. But even as she sought to cross the threshold, another's ravaged face invaded her mind. She saw quite clearly the pitiable, hollow features and reached out her hand as if to touch, to reassure the illusion that was Frances.

The ennui that had settled gently lifted from her and she opened her eyes again. Nothing had changed but her resolve. From somewhere she found the strength to drag herself to her feet and, with one last effort, went outside.

'Where you been, ol' lady?' Lee's harsh voice echoed from the head of the shaft. But she said nothing and merely retrieved her bucket to resume the back-breaking toil.

Over the winter, Dawson had gone on growing. Some of the saloons had added a second storey and now proclaimed themselves hotels. A new line of buildings paralleled Front Street and the mass of tents had been displaced further up the hillside. There were few people about, however, and an air of defeat and neglect hung over the town. The ceaseless bustle of summer had given way to a more sedate winter pace. Frances made her way to the general store and went in. Looking around as her eyes accustomed themselves to the dimness, she saw that the shelves were bare. The storekeeper came from the back room and eyed her warily.

'What do you want?' he asked.

There was no point in long explanations. 'My family is starving and I've no money,' she said directly. 'Let me have some food and I'll pay ye as soon as I can.'

He stared at her in astonishment. 'Are you kidding? Even if I gave credit, which I never do, I've no food to sell let alone give away.' He waved to the empty shelves. 'You ain't the only one starvin'. If the river don't thaw in the next few days, we'll all be dead.'

Frances was frantic. 'There must be food somewhere,' she said.

'Dare say the Eldorado Kings ain't goin' hungry. They can afford a hundred dollars for a sack of flour or twenty for a wrinkled old orange to keep the scurvy at bay.' He shrugged. 'But the rest of us are in the same boat as you.'

Shaken, Frances left the store. The mention of scurvy had troubled her. It explained their bleeding gums, their weakness, their lassitude. The need for food – the right food – was crucial now. She stood on the wooden sidewalk and gazed across to the river. Its mass remained in rough disordered layers of packed ice despite the promise of warmth in the spring sun. The steamers would be waiting downstream for the thaw to work its way to them before the much needed supplies could be brought in. But their immediate situation was desperate – she had to do something now.

Further up the street was a saloon. The chink of glasses and raised voices could be heard against a background of music. Frances made her way towards it, pushed open the door and peered in. A handful of men stood at the dimly lit bar while others wheeled around the floor with their florid partners, whom they had paid for at a dollar a dance. Oblivious, she walked through them and all conversation stopped.

'I need food,' she said quietly to the barman. 'Can ye use me as a dance-girl?'

He stared for a second then roared with laughter, the men joining in. 'When was the last time you saw yourself?' He stood to one side and pointed behind the bar. 'Take a look. Take a long, hard look and then tell me who'd pay to dance with that.'

Frances went to the mirror and slowly raised her eyes to her reflection. Her clothes were a jumble of fur padding, strapped around with rags. A gaunt face stared back at her through bruised eyes and her skin, now dry and scaly, had lost all its bloom. She pulled the blanket back off her head revealing a matted mess of hair that had once been her crowning glory. Tears bulged in her eyes but the assembled drinkers were unmoved. They slapped the bar in uncontrollable laughter and rained a hail of comments after her as she quickly turned to leave.

She was overwhelmed by the need for a kind word and, remembering Bella, she rushed across to the Golden Slipper saloon. The doors were shut and the place was deserted but going round the back she saw a light and knocked on the window.

'We're closed,' a booming voice shouted.

'But, please . . . it's Frances O'Byrne.'

Bella's surprised face appeared at the window. 'My God,' she exclaimed. 'What in heaven's name?'

'Help me, Bella.' Frances started to weep.

'Go round to the door.' Bella rushed to open it. 'Come in child, come in.'

Frances almost fell into the room and sat heavily on the bed. 'We've been out on the creeks all winter and now we've no food. No money, no gold, nothing.'

'Same all round.' Bella handed her a cup of weak lukewarm coffee. 'I ain't had no liquor for a month. Closed the bar. Only ones making money are the girls in Paradise Alley – and even they can't eat gold dust.' She sat at the table. 'Listen, go get your people and bring 'em back here. Give up this foolishness about gold. When the river thaws and the boats come up, take the first one outa here – I'll find a way to get you on it. You can stay with me till then.'

Frances nodded and knew she was right. It was time to end the senseless suffering and go. Maybe they could work their passage back, she thought. If not, she would find some way of leaving this freezing hell Lee had condemned them to. She would take Pi'taki and they would survive somehow, anyhow, and nothing could ever be as bad again. Lee could stay or go as he wished but whatever he did, from now on it would be without her.

Though worn out and hungry, Frances felt vaguely relieved as she made the long walk back to the claim. Several hours passed and she noticed her feet were slipping in the melting mud. Water was running down towards the river and cracks were starting to appear under the boulders of ice. The sky gradually blackened and thunder rolled ominously in the distance. Coming up through the gravel piles of the creeks, she saw distant figures feverishly working on the claims. Pi'taki could just be discerned, straining over the windlass of the shaft and pulling ineffectually on the rope. Frances felt a sob rise in her throat at the pathetic sight and quickened her pace.

As she reached the edge of the claim, from over the hilltops dark storm-clouds unleashed a sudden downpour. Resting the heavy gravel-filled bucket on the edge of the shaft, Pi'taki looked across to acknowledge her arrival and could tell the news was not good. Frances shook her head solemnly. There was no need for words, the failure of her mission was written all over her face. She reached out to hold the old woman for a brief intense second and said, 'We're leaving here.'

The rain gathered strength and Pi'taki turned her face up, as if to let it cleanse away the misery of the day. All around them on the other claims, men whooped and threw their hats in the air as the first real water started to pour into their sluices. Above the creek beds, miners were frantically shoring up the long water-carrying sluice-runs as the flow from the run-off increased. In their own creek, the sheets of ice were breaking and being pushed along by the steadily mounting rush. Pi'taki bent down and struggled to lift the bucket again when Frances heard a warning shout from behind. Turning, she saw the network of fragile aqueducts had collapsed and a surge of water was sweeping down the stream-bed. In no time, the ground around her feet was awash in a muddy swirl as the waters poured from the creek and into the shaft. She had forgotten Lee's presence until his scream echoed up from the depths. She heard him choke convulsively as the torrent cascaded over the sides of the shaft and drenched him. In the dim light, she saw his fingers scrabbling uselessly at the streaming walls, trying to claw himself up from the rapidly rising water. His eyes met hers from the darkness far below. 'Help me, Frances! For Chrissakes get me up!'

Pi'taki leaned over the hole and stared implacably into Lee's terrified gaze. Slowly, the heavy bucket slid from her grip until, free of her trembling hand, it plummeted downwards, striking him full in the face and driving him under. Then, almost as suddenly as it came, the flood abated. The water in the shaft slowly settled and there was no sign of the man underneath the muddied scum.

In the wake of the deluge, large drops of rain spattered the grey ground around the two immobile figures and a strange silence followed. Pi'taki lifted her head and turned away from the dark opening. She searched deep into Frances's eyes and the look was returned with an empty composure. At last Frances spoke. 'I'd better get some help. We canna pull his body out ourselves.'

The Mountie pushed through the knot of miners flanking the cabin doorway and came forward to where the two women sat. In the opposite corner, Lee's body lay stiff and soaked on the makeshift bed. The young officer assumed a placatory tone. 'Mrs O'Byrne,' he said, squatting down beside her, 'it was an accident – a flash flood. There was nothing you could do.'

Frances was trembling and her fists were clenched. In the instant when the body had been pulled from the shaft, it was not Lee she perceived, but Rory. She was haunted again by the image of his little face, the mouth bulging with the mud that had drowned him, the blue eyes cloudy and smeared with silt. She choked again at the memory and her hand gripped Pi'taki's.

Misunderstanding her grief, the Mountie continued. 'I'm sorry, ma'am, perhaps now's not the time for talk. When you're ready we can take care of the details.' He looked across at the bed. 'Ain't no reason to move him right away, we can leave him here a while if you want?'

'No!' Her voice cracked with vehemence.

He paused. 'Well, if you're sure?'

'I'm sure. Take him away, I don't want him here.'

There was a short uneasy silence before he complied. 'Just as you wish.' He glanced around at the other men and signalled for volunteers to carry the body out. Two of them stepped forward and heaved Lee's lifeless frame off the bed. Frances continued to sob wretchedly with her head in her hands, Pi'taki beside her. Both knew the tears were not for Lee, they were the final edge of despair.

Some of the men mumbled condolences but most were glad to be away as quickly as possible from the numbing presence of the tragedy. Frances followed them to the doorway and watched while the body was unceremoniously dumped in a cart, a blanket thrown over it in an ineffectual gesture of respect. The wheels threw up splashes of mud as the cart rumbled off down the track. Taking up the rear, the Mountie rode in escort, the red of his coat sharply at odds with the drab landscape. Men doffed their hats in a sullen line as the pathetic cortège passed between the creeks, their elation at the thaw now dampened by awesome reality.

When everyone had left, Frances wandered outside. She gazed at the shaft-head, still full of water. 'He got the easy way out,' she muttered bitterly, now more acutely aware than ever of their utter dejection. The bucket, still full of gravel had been recovered and placed at the side of the windlass. Filled with rage, she lashed out at it viciously with her foot, cursing through clenched teeth. 'Damn you, Leland O'Byrne! Damn you to hell!'

The bucket lurched forward and the contents were spilled over in a sodden heap. The late evening sun caught a sudden sparkle in the muddy gravel and Frances was momentarily distracted. She knelt down curiously, looking closer. There, between her feet, a nugget as big as a baby's fist lay glinting on the ground.

11

News travelled fast in the gold-fields. Lee's death and the subsequent sudden upturn in the fortunes of his wife fuelled the rampant gossip. There was endless speculation about Frances's token appearance at the funeral but, like everything else it was soon superseded by other Dawson dramas. From the time of the perfunctory burial, Frances denied any pretence at grief and did not care who knew it. There was no room now for false sentiment and she had decided that life would no longer have the power to wound her. She cared nothing for the impression created by her bluff and determined manner; if people were offended then that was too bad. As she found herself having to take control of a successful and sizeable gold-strike, she quickly achieved a reputation as a woman to be reckoned with.

The week after the funeral, she was browsing in the joinery examining the sluice-boxes that were for sale. Chisholm the store-keeper appeared from the back room. 'Don't touch unless you intend buyin' it – I'll need money up front for one of those.'

'Did ye no hear, I made a strike,' Frances replied curtly.

'I'd heard a whisper but you get that kind of story all the time round here.'

'Well, it's more than a rumour,' she replied in the same matter-of-fact tone. 'It's the biggest pay-streak seen on Hunker.'

Chisholm was incredulous. 'Well, you sure ain't been advertisin' it,' he said, scratching his head.

Frances turned to him irritated, 'And what do ye expect me to do, eh? Take a bath in champagne? Or maybe I should gamble it all away? No, you'll no see me throwing it down the drain like most of the idiots who've made their fortunes round here.'

'Okay, okay, keep your hair on lady. So, what are you gonna spend it on then?'

She was losing her patience. 'If you're no careful, I might just take a fancy to buy this joinery out from under ye!'

'Ha! Like to see you try. This here's part of the sawmill – you'd have to buy the whole damn lot. Think you can pull enough gold out the ground for that?'

'Shouldn't take much to buy out this dump,' she said looking round.

'Hmm, you're takin' on some pretty high an' mighty airs for a woman that was a pauper not more'n a few days ago – an' your poor husband lyin' in the frozen ground an' all.'

'Dinna talk to me about husbands – I need something I can rely on. Look, I can't stand around here all day,' she snapped. 'Are ye going to serve me or not?'

'Sure thing, lady, one sluice comin' up.'

'Correction, Mr Chisholm, I'll take six.'

'Six? You'll need help to work that many.'

'Well, if you'll keep them for me I'll send one of the men to collect them later.'

'I told you, I need money up front. When exactly is later?'

'When I've hired them. Give me a plank o' wood.' She stared him down until he went to fetch an off-cut. 'Ye'll get it back, never fear,' she said, tucking it under her arm.

Outside, Frances chalked up her message and wedged the sign in the mud at her side.

MEN WANTED FOR SLUICE WORK
$10 A DAY AND RATIONS

She knew the money was good. If you had ten dollars left after feeding yourself, you were living well in Dawson. She did not think she would have much trouble getting a work-force together.

Gertie Lowe came out of her laundry-tent wiping her raw hands on her apron. She read the board and turned to Frances. 'Mrs O'Byrne, can't you get a man to do the hirin' for you – I mean you can afford it now. Why go to all that trouble yourself?'

'I want to know who's working for me, Gertie. I'll no take shirkers or wasters. The only way is to hand-pick them myself. Besides, they might as well know who they're dealing with right from the start.'

'Oh, they'll know that soon enough,' Gertie said, raising her eyes to the heavens.

'Tell ye what, loan me a table and chair – I'd as well sit down while I'm waiting.'

Too astounded to argue, Gertie went and fetched out a small table and battered chair. Frances nodded her thanks and made herself comfortable. A few stragglers walked by and stopped to read the notice. These were the unlucky ones. All too soon they had found the streets of Dawson were not paved with gold and the claims were already staked. Vacant and disillusioned, their only means of survival now was to dig out another man's fortune. Or in this case, a woman's. They peered cautiously at Frances.

'What are ye gawping at?' she challenged, 'If you're looking for work, step forward. Don't be shy.'

The first one approached the table and stood uneasily before her.

'Name?' she asked briskly, with the pencil poised.

'Er, Jed Hennessy, ma'am.' He pulled off his cap. Frances looked up into the young face. His vivid blue eyes shone out from the stubble and grime and she caught the trace of a blush as he spoke.

'How old are ye, boy?'

'Seventeen – nearly eighteen.' He sounded young too but there was a frank honesty in his face that endeared her to him.

'Well, it's straightforward work, shovelling and panning – think ye can handle it?'

He smiled, 'No trouble, I'm good and strong.'

'You'll need to be, it's no Sunday-school picnic, ye know.'

'Yes ma'am, I know.' He looked at the ground dolefully.

'All right Jed, you've got yourself a job,' she said and noted down the particulars. 'Be here on the dot at five tomorrow morning. If you're late you get left behind.'

'Yes ma'am,' he brightened up and they shook hands on it.

'Next,' she called and the line that had formed moved forward. 'Willi Kruger.'

'Do I smell liquor on your breath, Mr Kruger?'

'It's hours since I had a drink ma'am, honest.'

'Get going.' She waved him off dismissively. 'There's no job for ye here.'

'But I need it,' he protested.

'If ye can afford to be drinking at this time of day, you're no needing work – be off with ye.' He shuffled off muttering abuse under his breath but she ignored it and called for the next in line.

Two large fists implanted themselves on the table in front of her and a gruff voice boomed, 'Vic Lewinson.' Frances was about to speak but he interrupted her. 'I got a question first,' he insisted. 'Who exactly will we be working for – who's the boss of this outfit?'

'You're looking at her,' Frances said with a steady voice. 'Does that bother ye?'

Lewinson threw back his head and laughed, turning to the bunch of men behind. 'Hear that, fellas? This here's the boss!' They joined in the mirth. 'Think you know a thing or two about minin', do you?'

Frances stood up and fixed him with an angry stare. 'I know enough to tell me that I'm hiring ye for the easy part. I've been up at those creeks through the winter burning fires and digging shafts.' She pulled off her gloves. 'Do these hands look as though I've been embroidering all my life? I know as much about what's under those hills as any one o' ye!' By this time the laughter had subsided. 'Now, I aim to get the gold out of the ground with or without ye. But if you're needing the work, you'd better ask yourself first – are ye man enough to work for me?' She held their gaze and looked around. One or two drifted off with Lewinson but she was pleased to see a substantial number stood their ground.

Frances interviewed them all and picked what she thought were the best of them. At five the next morning she sat on her horse and surveyed the motley little band she had recruited. Ten bedraggled men stood before her, and a more pathetic crew she could not imagine. Their spirits broken, their dreams shattered or forgotten, now all they hoped for was to save enough for the ticket home.

'Two things I won't tolerate,' she shouted over the heads, 'and that's fighting and drinking.' There were a few uneasy mumbles in the group. 'Work hard and I'll treat ye fair,' she continued, 'but dinna try to cheat me or you'll regret it.' This statement was met by silence. 'Right, then, I take it ye understand. Let's go.' With that she dug in her heels and set off with the rag-bag bunch trailing behind.

Up at the diggings there was much to be done. Frances split the men into two groups. 'You lot start by repairing the flume and get those sluices fixed up by the shafts,' she said to the first. 'And the rest of ye take the whip-saws over to those trees and start on the cabins. Build two. I'll see ye get stoves put in once they're up.'

For the rest of the day they toiled while Frances supervised a trail of supplies from the town. It took two more days to finish the cabins but by the end of the week they were in business and not one man had walked off the job.

*

250

Frances knew organising the work was the first priority because the summer season was short. Only three months were free of frost and could be used to wash out the gold. They had to move fast and she drove the men hard. In her distinctive breeches and high boots, she became a familiar sight as she walked between the flumes supervising the work-force and shouting encouragement. But there were no complaints. She kept her side of the bargain, treating them fairly, and they responded with enthusiasm.

Dawson was surprised at this frenzied activity, and not a little sceptical. Twice a week she rode the few miles into town for more supplies. The men who stood at the counter of Liza Browne's tobacco store threw back their whiskies and laughed when she entered.

'You buyin' smokes for those diggers now, Mrs O'Byrne? Next thing you'll be bringin' in women for 'em!' Someone else joined in. 'Spends so much time out there on those hills, maybe she's providin' that service herself!' Frances glared at them as another great burst of laughter went up but she managed to restrain herself and place her order. These incidents had become common occurrences. They knew she had a fiery temper and used any opportunity to provoke it.

Back at the claim the men worked relentlessly, winching the piles of pay-dirt that came from the shafts and shovelling the gravelly clay into the rushing waters of the sluice. As it was washed through, the gold remained trapped in the riffles of the box. Every couple of days the water was stopped to lift the matting and the work of panning out the gold began. It was tough work and Frances offered them little respite in the long day yet it was the most efficiently worked claim for miles around and the rewards were beginning to pour in.

All this time Pi'taki remained in the rough-hewn log cabin they had built the previous year. She had never fully regained her strength since their trek north and had deteriorated further during the hungry winter. Frances insisted that she do no more work now the gold was discovered and had warned the men to keep an eye on her. 'If she makes a move out of there or tries to lift one bucket of dirt, I want to know,' she demanded. As a result, though she was bored and not a little bewildered, Pi'taki's health slowly recovered. But Frances noticed a change in her. She really was an old woman now, less steady on her feet and no longer walking with her easy loping gait. Stooping, she seemed diminished in size and her skin had wizened and dried.

When Frances entered their cabin and found Pi'taki huddled next to the stove struggling to thread a needle, she knew it was time for a change. Frances took it from her. 'Forget that,' she said, 'we don't need to mend clothes any more. This place is cold and cramped. Don't ye think we should move and get a little comfort in our lives? God knows we've earned it.'

The old woman looked up. 'Move where?' she asked.

'Into town. We could get somewhere decent instead of this draughty old shack. What do ye think?'

'But the men, they need you here. . .' Pi'taki made a vague protest but Frances could see she was inwardly relieved.

'They know what they're doing now and I can still come out and supervise. Why don't we just start packing up now. I'll go over and have a talk with them before we leave.'

At the first log bunk-house she rapped loudly on the door and went in. The men sat around the stove in the dim, oil-lit interior. From the rafters above hung a jumble of steaming underwear and boots and the stifling smell of sweat filled the room. They looked up and rearranged themselves abruptly as she entered.

'Mrs O'Byrne, er, this is a surprise. Will you sit down?' They cleared a space on the cluttered bench but she declined.

'I won't stay, boys – just wanted to let you know I'm moving myself and the old woman into town.'

'Well, that's fittin' – you'll be better off there,' said one and the others agreed. 'Don't you worry about us, we can get along just fine.'

'Maybe so,' Frances replied archly, 'but just so there's no squabbling, I'm putting a foreman over ye.' They looked at each other blankly. She continued, 'Jed Hennessy, where are you, boy?' He jumped to his feet. 'You're in charge. You'll report directly to me from now on – all right?'

The youth was overwhelmed. 'Yes, ma'am,' he said beaming.

Frances knew she had made the right choice even if the rest of them were disgruntled. Though Jed was young, she had his loyalty. He would make a good foreman. 'Any complaints, gentlemen?' she asked, looking from one to another but they held their tongues.

12

The two women spent a few days in Dawson taking stock of the place from a different perspective – one in which money was no object. They stayed in a rough hotel but ate well from the varied choice of food that now flooded the markets. They bought new boots and unceremoniously dumped their working ones on a bonfire. Pi'taki's choice of clothes still retained its unique style. She purchased moose-hide from the Alaska Commercial Company and made leggings to replace the old tatters, wearing them under a new calico skirt. The plaid shawl, however was rarely off her shoulders.

It was a strange time for both of them. Frances had a few vague ideas about what they might do with their new-found wealth but she hesitated, hoping for a sign from Pi'taki. She worried that the old woman might be unhappy in these unfamiliar surroundings. 'Do ye want to go back home, south – anywhere just say,' she would ask but got little response. Pi'taki was clearly bemused by all that was happening around her.

One day, Frances had some business with the bank and agreed to meet up with her later. Passing the Grand Imperial saloon that afternoon, she caught sight of Pi'taki sitting at the faro table, deeply engrossed in the game. A mounting stack of chips amassed beside her and she was clearly on a winning streak. Frances entered and walked through the dimly lit bar-room. As she watched, her curiosity turned to astonishment. For the first time in months, Pi'taki looked content. Conversely, the proprietor, Pete Mallory looked anxious. He gestured to the dealer, drawing the edge of his hand across his throat.

'Game's over, lady,' the dealer said, retrieving the cards and returning them to the metal box, 'you've cleaned us out.'

Frances walked over. 'How much did you win?' she enquired, smiling. Pi'taki shrugged and pushed forward the pile of chips.

The dealer turned and took a slip of paper from the rack behind him, assessing the total. 'One thousand, three hundred and twenty one dollars,' he admitted ruefully.

'Christ!' Frances stared at him as he weighed out several pokes of gold and pushed them across the table. Pi'taki heaved herself off the stool, brushed herself down and made for the door.

'Here, what about these?' Frances called after her. But it was clear she was not interested and Frances quickly scooped the little bags into her own pockets and ran to catch up, bewildered. 'Look, you've won all this.' She tried to hand them over but they were ignored. 'If you don't want it then why did ye play?'

Pi'taki smiled. 'In my people, only men do this. I wanted to try.' She headed off down Front Street weaving through the crowds with Frances in pursuit.

'Well, ye certainly had beginner's luck,' she said.

253

The old woman sucked her teeth dismissively. 'No luck. I used my eyes.' She turned in through the swing doors of the Golden Slipper. 'Come. I will show you.'

For the next hour, Frances watched spellbound as another small fortune accumulated in front of them. There was no system or logic that she could follow but she could see Pi'taki was engrossed. Only the darting flicker of her eyes as they scanned the cards betrayed the energy of thought that absorbed her. Fascinated by all this Frances became intrigued by an idea that was developing in her mind. And as she thought about it she sensed that this unforeseen possibility could offer a glimmer of hope for the future.

Later that night, she talked long and hard with Pete Mallory in his office at the Grand Imperial. It was an outrageous name for what was a very basic construction. Apart from the painted façade, which suggested a three-storey emporium, the reality was a grim saloon where the girls did a turn on the floor for a dollar a dance. Behind this was the gaming-room and upstairs the cramped and dismal living quarters.

Pete lit a thin cigar and split the match with his thumbnail. 'You drive a hard bargain, Mrs O'Byrne,' he said.

'Aye, I do. But you've had time enough to think about it Pete, what do ye say?'

His face broke into a smile. 'Okay, it's a deal,' he said and they shook hands on it. 'So, when will you want to be movin' in?'

Frances casually picked up her things. 'Why right away – did I not make that clear?'

'Well not exactly, no.'

'The steamer leaves tomorrow for St Michael, Pete. Start packing now and you can be on it. No point in hanging around here now I'm the new owner or I might start charging you for your room!' The smile on his face quickly disappeared.

Downstairs the usual noisy uproar filled the crowded saloon. Everything was paid for in gold. Along the bar the men stood in groups clutching their little pokes of dust. A whisky changed hands for a dollar and the grains were weighed out on the sets of scales that punctuated the long mirrored bar. The mirror was about the extent of Pete's improvements around the place and, as Frances stood in the doorway observing the rabble, she thought of the changes she would make.

'If it ain't Frances O'Byrne,' said one old-timer, catching her around the waist. 'Give us a dance for half a dollar, girl – you

254

got more chance makin' your fortune here than scratchin' the dirt on that hillside!' he laughed drunkenly. Another grabbed her arms and twirled her round but she pulled away from them.

'That's just where you're wrong,' she declared, jumping up on the bar. A big cheer went up but she gestured for silence and the shouting dropped to an inquisitive mumble. 'Listen here all of you —' Frances began.

'Better get down before Pete sees you,' called one heckler and a roar of laughter went up again.

She waited until it had subsided and continued. 'Pete's no running the show round here any more. I am.' The place went quiet and they stared in disbelief. 'That's right, you're looking at the new owner.' Frances walked down the bar with her hands on her hips, 'And I aim to turn this foul-smelling byre that calls itself an "emporium" ...' she paused for effect, 'into the smartest saloon in town.' They looked from one to another, flabbergasted. 'Of course,' she went on, 'that means some of ye will have to change your attitude, not to mention your underwear. But, just to show there's no hard feelings and, since it's the last time some o' ye will be in here, tonight the drinks are on the house.' She jumped down again amid cheering and clapping and a mad rush to the bar.

Later, while the drinking continued below, Frances and Pi'taki stood in the doorway and peered into the first-floor suite of rooms which was to be their new home. These were Pete's 'best' rooms but from what they could see there was little to commend them. The floor-boards were bare and the curtains were merely rags tacked over the broken windows.

'We'll fix it up,' Frances said, more to reassure herself. Downstairs the bar room had grown quiet while a tinkly piano accompanied visiting artiste, Bella Gibson, as she sang 'Only a bird in a gilded cage'. Pi'taki frowned and put her hands over her ears while Frances continued to look around, shaking her head doubtfully. In a second their eyes met, at first worried, then questioning. And finally, months of pressure and suppressed grief found a spontaneous release as they succumbed to the aching need to laugh before they cried.

13

Within a few short weeks, Dawson had transformed from a rough, frontier camp site into a boom town. Stores, hotels, theatres and dance-halls were springing up everywhere and the streets were alive with signs and banners advertising the common currency:

GOLD DUST

Bought and Sold

they bawled out. Banks were opened, newspapers began circulating and the town was being wired up for a telephone service. With the building of the new docks, the river was swarming with colourful paddle-steamers and stern-wheelers dumping tons of freight and hordes of newcomers. The news that thousands of gold-seekers were on their way down-river, having made it across the terrible passes from Skagway, brought inroads of dancing-girls, vaudeville acts, businessmen, gamblers and swindlers. There may have been gold in the hills but now the real money was to be made in town.

Almost as a matter of principle, Frances began by taking over the sawmill. There were several springing up in town now but the one incorporating the joinery was still the most profitable. Sam Chisholm threw down his hat and was speechless when he heard the news. The need for prepared wood had never been greater and she knew she was making a good investment. What with that, and the takings at the Imperial, they could live comfortably without touching the profits from the claim.

All this time, the gold was rolling in from the creeks. Detachments of soldiers from the Yukon Field Force guarded the priceless wagon-loads with their cargo of sausage-shaped hide pokes. Thousands of dollars' worth was deposited in the Dawson banks and still it kept coming. For the first time in years, Frances found her thoughts turning back to Scotland and her family. The pain and anger and resentment had dulled to a vague curiosity about how those left behind had fared and she felt she should do something with her new-found wealth. Her father would now be of an age when work would be difficult and it seemed uncharitable of her not to offer to share her good fortune.

The Dawson City end of the Canadian Postal Service was chaotic to say the least but mail eventually did get through. Hoping to impress, Frances drafted a letter to her father on the remains of Pete's stock of headed stationery. Her eye was taken with the gaudy lettering at the top of the page advertising the delights of the Imperial and she tried to make her own writing match its opulence. Her note was brief, explaining only that she was now in a position to help out financially and wanted to effect a reconciliation with the family. If her father would reply with news of himself and her mother then Frances would make arrangements to transfer funds to Scotland. Sealing the envelope, it gave her a strange feeling to see her old family name and home address set down in black and white. She sat motionless with the letter gripped in her hand while she wondered how the unexpected news would be received. At last, she summoned one of the barmen to post it for her and, knowing it would be months before she could expect a reply, she put the matter to the back of her mind.

Frances had quickly developed a taste for business. She spent hours in the little office that used to be Pete's and kept a strict reckoning of their affairs. Her time was taken up with visits to the creeks, checking the daily record of gold in the ledger and sorting out minor disputes amongst the men. Then there were production figures to be looked over at the sawmill and the endless ordering and receiving of stores and materials at the docks. However, far from being overburdened by the efforts to hold all the strands of their business interests together, she thrived on it. For the first time she felt in control and despite a deserved reputation for bluntness, those who had dealings with her gradually developed respect.

If the day-time hours absorbed all Frances's energies, the nights belonged to Pi'taki. After spending some time getting to know the ways of the gaming room, she set about improving it. She had the place decorated and well-lit to discourage chicanery. More tables were installed for poker, dice and roulette and new dealers recruited. She had a nose for a trickster and could sniff him out at twenty paces. Many was the night when she would personally oust a gambler from his stool and send him packing, much to the amusement of the crowd at the bar.

To begin with, there was an uneasy mistrust of Pi'taki amongst the staff at the Imperial. Whereas Frances was too busy with accounts and stock-taking, Pi'taki noticed their little peccadillos. It was the habit of some unscrupulous barmen to heavily grease their hair. Then, when serving drinks and weighing out the gold dust in exchange, they would run their hands through their hair, thus leaving a princely deposit to be collected later. Equally popular was the underweighing of the dust and the fixing of scales so as to short-change the customer. Pi'taki put a stop to both these practices and any other dubious intentions on the part of individuals in her employ were quickly forgotten.

Dawson was an enigma, a burgeoning cosmopolitan town where men and women from all walks of life came with one common dream. As a result, it produced more than its share of colourful characters. A once indigent creek miner might now be seen sporting a diamond stick-pin and thinking nothing of spending two ounces of gold on a bottle of champagne. Thousands were won and lost on the turn of a card and for many, gambling became the focus for the precipitous spending of their hard-won pokes of dust. It was therefore not so surprising that Pi'taki should find her niche in this strange melting-pot of humanity. She was successful as a gaming-room hostess and, in time, her reputation for running an honest house secured her an affectionate place among the unique personalities that the gold rush had spawned.

14

One morning in that mad summer of '98 Frances returned to their parlour at the Imperial to find a calling card. It had been left in the hope that she would receive the visitor later that afternoon. She read the card.

> *Christian Ballantyne*
> *Ballantyne & Sons*
> *Bankers and Financial Agents, Edmonton*

The hapless Mr Ballantyne had been despatched by the bank to make the trip to Dawson and tout for custom among the nouveau riche. Troubled by the mosquitoes and unused to the steamy heat, he had endured a river-boat journey of immense discomfort to be of service, as he later said, 'to people of such distinguished standing in the town as your good self'. Frances was amused by the flattery but intrigued by the distinctive style of the banker, a very different breed of businessman to the raw-edged characters with whom she dealt in Dawson.

Receiving him in her narrow office she called for tea to be brought up to them. Ballantyne dusted off the chair before sitting down. The air was stifling and as he dabbed his brow with a silk handkerchief and smoothed back the silver hair at his temples, she could see that he was unused to conducting affairs in such conditions.

'Why don't you take off your jacket,' Frances said, thinking he must be extremely uncomfortable but he declined such informality.

When he had collected himself he buffed his fingernails against his lapel and began, 'May I enquire as to where you keep your gold deposits, Mrs O'Byrne?' He asked the question casually.

'Why, in the Dawson Bank, of course.'

'And what is it doing in there?'

'Doing? Well, nothing, just sitting there.'

'Exactly,' Ballantyne said with a satisfied smile.

Frances looked bemused. 'Is that no what a bank's for? To keep your money safe?'

'Hmm, yes of course but it can do so much more.'

'Like what?'

'Well, let me first explain that I approached you because I heard you hailed from Edmonton and I'm assuming you will return there eventually.'

'I'm in no hurry to move, Mr Ballantyne. Things are going very well for us here.'

'Quite so, ma'am, but let's face it, this cannot last for ever.' He dismissed Dawson with a wave of his manicured hand. 'Sooner or later the gold will run out.'

'Aye, you're right there,' Frances admitted.

He continued. 'It's never too soon to think about the future. Now, we don't just offer the usual banking services but pride ourselves on the high standard of financial advice we can give our clients. I mean, have you thought about investments at all?'

'Well, I've got the sawmill – that does all right,' she replied. 'And then there's the Imperial. It brings in a tidy sum.'

'Hmm,' he mused, looking around as if unconvinced. 'Maybe, but you don't seem to realise you're in possession of a fortune now. These are mere playthings compared to what you could do with your wealth. Carefully managed and with, er, a little humble advice and guidance,' he offered, self-effacingly, 'well, you could remain a very rich woman throughout your life.'

259

'You talk as if I don't keep good records but it's all up to date and it all balances.'

'Of course, and I have to say I'm impressed. You've been extremely shrewd,' Ballantyne assured her. 'I've seen many a fortune slip through the hands of those who got rich quick. A fool and his money are soon parted.'

'Well, I'm no fool,' Frances interjected.

'My dear Mrs O'Byrne, I can see that and may I say that's exactly why I'm making this proposal.' He tapped his fingertips together. 'Deposit your money with us and we'll make it work for you.'

She smiled. 'You're very persuasive,' she said. 'I'd no really given it much thought.'

'But look ahead. No doubt you'll be glad to settle somewhere, er, more suitable eventually. I mean, I realise you have to endure some discomfort at the moment but in time —'

'It's no so bad.'

'Oh come, come, Mrs O'Byrne, Dawson's a rough diamond of a place, you've got to admit.'

'Well, Edmonton wasn't so grand when last I laid eyes on it.'

'But things have changed – the town's booming. Banks, hotels, factories – of course the railway brought much of the wealth but we now find ourselves in the centre of the gold rush with everybody passing through on their way north. The stores have done a fine trade, I can tell you. Maybe you should think about investments in Edmonton – or round about. There's a lot of coal-mining in Alberta now. So much going on, it's just the beginning. Why, I'll wager we'll be the provincial capital before long.' He paused. 'I've said enough. But I encourage you to give it some thought before my next visit.'

Frances was impressed. 'All right, Mr Ballantyne, I think you've made your point. Let me say that I'm prepared to let your bank handle the account but I can't make any decisions about the future until I've talked with Pi'taki.'

'Er, yes, you mentioned her earlier – well if you think it's necessary.'

'I must warn you that I couldn't consider moving to Edmonton if she was opposed to the idea.'

'Perhaps I should have a word?'

She smiled. 'No, I think that's best left up to me – somehow I don't think you two will have much in common.'

He gave a hint of a bow. 'If you say so.'

'There is one thing you could tell me.'

Ballantyne looked expectantly at her. 'Of course, anything.'

'My family. . .' The words were unfamiliar and she paused before continuing. 'I have family back in Scotland, and I'd like to send them some money.'

'Nothing easier, Mrs O'Bryne. If you let me know the details, I can arrange a transfer at once.'

'Good, that's all I need to know for now. I've already written to them and I'm expecting a reply any day. As soon as I hear, you can do what's necessary.' She stood to indicate the interview was over. 'And I'll get in touch once I've spoken with Pi'taki about the other matter.'

Ballantyne offered his hand. 'It has been a great pleasure to talk with you and I shall eagerly await our next meeting.'

Still smiling at his effusive flattery, Frances went in search of Pi'taki. Though she patiently explained everything that the banker had said, the old woman showed not the least interest. 'If you want it, I agree,' she said, distractedly as she watched a new croupier on the roulette table.

Frances persisted. 'It's your money as well.'

Pi'taki nodded, but as always she had made her decision and saw no point in debating the issue. 'As you say,' she said, patting Frances's hand. Then, her attention still on the trainee, she marched over to the table and pointed out a dubiously placed bet the nervous employee had missed. Frances sighed and went off to write a note to Ballantyne.

A few days later, the deal was struck. Arrangements were made to move the capital to the new bank and Ballantyne said he would personally supervise the transaction. 'I'll draw up the papers tonight,' he promised, clearly delighted with his achievement, 'and you can sign them tomorrow. I'm staying on the *Pioneer Belle* – do you know it? Charming steamer, a little haven of refinement in this lawless swamp, wouldn't you say?'

'I've never been on it.'

'Why, my dear, you must visit. Come and take coffee on deck in the morning. I'll introduce some delightful travelling companions – two sisters from England, the Staniforths. If it wasn't for them, I think I might have expired in this dreadful place.'

'Why, Mr Ballantyne, I declare you are a snob,' Frances smiled with mock effrontery.

'Maybe,' he demurred, 'but can't you see what's all around you? This really is the most God-forsaken hole on earth.'

She laughed. 'Ye wouldn't last here a week.'

'You're probably right, but equally all these roughnecks who got rich quick would stick out like a sore thumb in polite society – they may be at home here but wait till the gold runs out.'

After he had gone, Frances thought about those words. She looked at herself and glanced around the office. A few additional comforts had been introduced since Pete's departure but there was still little to commend it. She wondered if Mr Ballantyne counted her among the uncouth of Dawson, though he would hardly have expressed it to her face. Momentarily she felt a little unsure of herself and thought morning coffee on the paddle-steamer could be more than she bargained for.

Hermione and Cecile Staniforth belonged to that unique breed of females from the Victorian upper classes who, for reasons best known to themselves, chose to relinquish the assured comforts of their homes. Instead, they sallied forth into remote corners of the globe with an insatiable curiosity, an unshakeable superiority and a little England packed inside their trunks. Cecile wrote her journals and Hermione organised their trips. They were a fount of knowledge about timetables; how to rent camel trains in Khartoum; dhows in the Gulf of Arabia; native packers in the jungles of Ceylon; or house-boats on the lakes of Srinagar. So it was little surprise that these two pioneers had arrived in galleon-state up the Yukon River to contribute to the motley ferment of Dawson society and drink in the atmosphere of the gold rush.

Scores of stern-wheelers now plied the river bringing all the accoutrements of modern life to the thriving town. Their multifarious cargoes ranged from fine linens to horse-feed and their passengers were just as diverse. Many bunked down among the cords of wood fuel and stacks of crates in the hold. Others more fortunate occupied the first-class cabins and dined with the captain in silver-service style.

The next morning, Frances picked her way carefully along the river front. On a strange whim, that surprised even herself, she had decided to wear a hat. Not a wide-brimmed serviceable sun shade, which was her habit, but a decorous fuss of feathers perched uneasily on her head. To fend off the sun, she carried a parasol. And so it was, in this state of slight discomfiture, she kept her appointment.

The *Pioneer Belle* gleamed in the sunlight, its flags and pennants fluttering against the bluest of skies. The velvet-curtained windows on the upper foredeck screened a curved sun lounge with polished wood floors and rattan chairs. People sat around in little groups playing cribbage or chatting in discreet voices. Mr Ballantyne was there too, poring over his papers. As Frances approached, she gave a little cough and he looked up.

'Ah, Mrs O'Byrne, I'm sorry I didn't see you board – please, do take a seat. As you can see, I'm just finalising these for you to sign. I won't be a moment.' Frances waited then he took out a gold pen, unscrewed the top and handed it to her. While she went through the forms, Ballantyne excused himself and exchanged a few words with the two women who were seated at a window table.

'Those are the Misses Staniforth I was telling you about,' he said when he returned. 'They agreed that we could join them.'

Frances looked across. Hermione gave an exaggerated smile in her direction and swatted the air with her fly-whisk. Cecile meanwhile, wrote busily in a small leather-bound book. Ballantyne folded away the papers in his briefcase, retaining copies for Frances and they moved across. He made obsequious introductions to the sisters by whom he was clearly impressed. Then Cecile removed her glasses and Hermione clapped her hands to summon the bringing of refreshments. Frances observed that they seemed to live in a world of their own with an aloof disregard for the backdrop of life around them and she felt strangely subdued in their presence. Coffee was ceremoniously poured from a silver pot into fine bone-china cups. She held hers uneasily, afraid she might crack the delicate porcelain.

'A little cream?' they asked. The whole scenario had a formal quality to it. She watched the others, unsure of the correct procedure and did as they did. Biscuits were nibbled, coffee was sipped and napkins were used to dab the corners of the mouth. Frances thought the formality of it all was ridiculously cumbersome and was relieved when Ballantyne began to make conversation.

'Mrs O'Byrne has worked a very successful claim out at Hunker Creek. She's the new owner of the Grand Imperial now – is that not so?' he said, smiling at Frances.

'Yes,' she confirmed with pride. 'Why don't you two come down and have a wee flutter. You'd be very welcome.'

Two pairs of eyebrows were raised. Hermione coughed. 'Er, I hardly think such a gaming establishment would suit us, my dear,' she said and quickly changed the subject. Frances felt diminished by the remark and could only assume it had been unintended. Her face reddened and she looked down at her hands. Ballantyne noticed this but said nothing.

Meanwhile the other two had become involved in an animated discussion about their guest. Without even looking in Frances's direction, Cecile turned to her sister and said, 'You know, I believe she is not an American as we had falsely assumed but this is in fact a Scottish accent.' She tapped her fingers excitedly on the table. 'I would divine it's from the region of Fifeshire or thereabouts – tell me, dear, am I correct?'

'Aye, er, yes,' Frances replied awkwardly.

'There you are, Mr Ballantyne,' said Cecile slapping her lap. 'Never been wrong yet – I have a natural affinity with languages you see. Give me a subject such as this, and I can pin-point its origin to within a few miles.'

Frances put down her cup and saucer. She turned over the words in her mind to confirm she had not misunderstood. 'Excuse me,' she said quietly, facing them, 'but I thought we spoke the same language. I'm no a subject – no some curiosity for your amusement and I didn't come here to be insulted.'

'What do you mean, my dear woman? No one has insulted you.' Cecile looked genuinely surprised, and turned to the others for confirmation of the fact.

'The Imperial's an honest saloon.' Frances fumbled for her gloves and stood up. 'We have high standards there – is that not so, Mr Ballantyne?'

The banker looked distinctly uncomfortable, suddenly caught between two camps. 'Oh, most certainly,' he agreed enthusiastically. 'But I'm sure Miss Staniforth did not mean. . .'

Hermione tried to save the day. 'Of course, dear,' she said, 'and we'd be delighted to visit as you suggested, wouldn't we, Cecile?' She nudged her sister.

Frances did not wait for the answer. 'Forget it,' she said curtly, collecting her parasol. 'The offer's withdrawn. As I said, we do have standards to keep.'

With that she left the astounded group. Ballantyne caught up with her as she stepped down the gang-plank. 'I, I'm so sorry,' he said hurriedly, 'I hope this doesn't affect our arrangement.'

'Why should it?' she replied, crisply. Her face was flushed and he could see the beginnings of tears in her eyes. 'It's no your fault, Mr Ballantyne, after all ye did warn me.'

When she got home, Frances rushed indoors, not wishing to speak to anyone but she was intercepted by a member of the saloon staff.

'There's a letter here for you, Mrs O'Byrne,' he explained.

She snatched the offered envelope and scanned it. The stamp was British and she recognised her father's scratchy, cramped writing.

Her mood changed at once and she hurriedly smiled her thanks to the young barman before running up the stairs to her room. She tore open the letter with trembling hands and started to read. As her eyes rapidly swept over the slanting, irregular lines, her face gradually crumpled until at last she flung the page away. The blood drained from her cheeks to leave a white mask of despair. 'I want no whore's money.' She could hear Henry Rintoul's blunt, sanctimonious voice in her head. 'If you are reduced to working in a den of vice. . .' A bitter laugh caught in her throat. So much for the fancy notepaper she had used, thinking to impress him. 'I considered you dead the day you left – and to me you are still dead. Do not write again.' Bending to retrieve the letter, she saw her reflection in the mirror and stood up, holding herself erect to face the image squarely. Her eyes were bright but she refused to let the tears come. The anger and frustration brought on by the episode on the steamer had returned and she felt powerless to deal with them. Neither world fitted her now and neither seemed to want her. Her hand clenched as if in reflex action and screwed her father's letter into a tight ball. So be it. If she were dead to her family, then they would be dead to her. And Ballantyne had been right, she thought. Her encounter with the Staniforths had given her a glimpse into another way of life that made Dawson seem rough by comparison. She pulled off the hat. It looked so inappropriate, and her clothes were too. She stared in the mirror – all this money and you can't even dress properly, she told herself angrily. The standards of so called polite society may have eluded her but she had enough to feel shamed by her own reflection. 'You're right, Father. I do look like a bloody dance-girl!' It was said out loud and Pi'taki overheard as she passed the open doorway. She paused but did not go in.

Frances was tearing the dress into shreds, scattering the room with streams of colour. 'And you're right too that the daughter you knew is dead. But believe me, Frances O'Byrne is very much alive, and nobody – nobody! – will ever look down their noses at her again!'

15

After that, the transformation began with a vengeance. The interior of the Imperial was completely gutted, and the original walls of rough planking replaced by scrolled gilt plasterwork. Crates and cartons began to arrive from Seattle bringing all the embellishments needed for this metamorphosis. Frances meandered between them, examining the contents. She pulled ornate light fitments of etched glass from their sawdust packing and supervised the positioning of engraved mirrors and polished mahogany handrails. She ran her fingers over bolts of rich brocade and velvet and took stock of the porcelain dinner service, silver plate and napery. Bella Gibson passed by one day and caught sight of her through the window.

'Well, strike me down!' she exclaimed as she walked into the room, 'You fixin' on opening a bazaar?' She guffawed loudly.

Frances continued checking the order. 'You can laugh, Bella, but I'm going to turn this into a place with a bit of class.'

'Save your money, honey,' Bella said, looking sceptically at the glass ashtrays. 'These guys don't want fancy bits and pieces – just give 'em a bottle and somethin' to spit into and they're happy.'

'Well, that's all going to change. I'm no having those society types laughing at me again.'

'You're taking it too much to heart,' Bella said sitting on one of the crates and unpinning her huge feathery hat. 'Just 'cos two tight-assed old biddies put your nose out of joint – this is Dawson, not Buckingham Palace – you can't make a silk purse. . .'

'We'll see about that,' Frances said flatly as she continued sorting through the jumble of goods.

'This here's just a crazy waste of money,' Bella went on, gesturing round the room. 'Jesus, girl, I bet you don't even know what to do with this stuff.'

'What do ye mean by that?'

'Oh, come on – I wasn't born yesterday.' Bella picked up a handful of forks and knives. 'Answer me this. What order do you arrange these in when you're layin' your fine table?' She waved a napkin at her. 'And how do you fold one of these, lady?' Frances looked glum as she finished. 'See, you ain't got a clue. I ain't trying to insult you, honey, but you've got a deal of learnin' to do before they let you into their precious high society.' She folded her arms with finality across her large bosom.

Frances bit her lip. She stopped what she was doing and flopped down next to her with a defeated sigh. Bella pulled a small hip-flask from her cleavage and removed the stopper. She took a swig and handed it to Frances. 'Here, have a drink, and don't you worry none. Help is at hand. Now, I ain't saying I know any better'n you but I think it ain't too late for you to pay a visit to Cad Wilson – she'll put you right. Got all the refinements of your élite but she ain't had it all easy – just like you, I guess. She may be a singer and a dancer but she's a class act. One of the richest women in Dawson – got maids and butlers and God knows what. She'll put you right.'

Bella made the necessary introductions between the two women and Frances was soon a regular visitor to Cad's salon where the cream of Dawson society flocked. For a few weeks in the late summer of '98, Miss Wilson's parlour became a second home to Frances. Cad was amused by her urgency to better herself but did not ridicule her and was soon teaching her all she knew. Frances was a good pupil, listened well and did her homework. She walked the boards of the Imperial with a book in front of her nose and recited the words over and over again, rounding her vowels.

Pi'taki, however, was amused at these new-found refinements and often made fun of them at her expense. Sometimes she would hold her cup with her little finger cocked, or step over the duck-boards of the muddy streets, carefully raising her hemline. The men drinking in the lobby bar too colluded with her japes and Frances occasionally lost her temper. It was at times like those, when her guard was down, that she resumed her old turn of phrase and demeanour, much to the mirth of everyone around.

Cad was nevertheless pleased with her efforts. 'You'll do,' she said one day, as Frances tried on the new outfits that had been ordered for her.

'Ye think so?' Frances asked, unsure.

'I'll just fix up your hair before I let you see yourself,' Cad said as she went to work with the heated tongs.

'Ouch!' Frances yelped as another hairpin was secured.

'Hush up, honey, it takes time to put a big pile of hair like yours in place.' Cad stood back and surveyed her handiwork. 'We've got a ways to go yet,' she sighed. 'Pour her a gin, Bella. It'll dull the pain.'

'Cad, it's only ten in the morning.' Frances tried to sound scandalised. 'How can ye drink at this hour?'

'Because I'm with friends, that's how.' She bent to resume her attack on Frances's hair. 'Now, if you were the preacher's wife, I'd be serving weak tea and pious thoughts,' she said, accepting the glass that was handed to her. 'You have to learn to match yourself to your surroundings.'

Bella flopped into a large, overstuffed armchair. 'That's what I keep tellin' her, Cad. She thinks she has to be a goddamn lady in Dawson.' She snorted and took a good swallow from her own tumbler.

'Oh, Bella,' Cad laughed. 'We all have to make an effort – excepting you, I suppose. Not a lot in the way of good raw material to build on in your case.'

'What d'you mean?' Bella slapped her ample thighs. 'You could build a hell of a lot on these legs, sweetie.'

'Now, in Frances's case,' Cad went on, ignoring the crude gestures, 'there's an innate sense of propriety. A little twist here, a new outfit, the right turn of phrase and *voila*! – the real Mrs O'Byrne!'

'Bullshit!' Bella rose and went to refill her glass from the drinks trolley in the corner of the luxurious salon. 'Where did you learn all them big words?'

'By keeping my eyes and ears open and my mouth shut when I didn't know what all them big-shots were talking about.' She finished Frances's hair with a flourish and brought forward a tall cheval mirror for her inspection. 'Well, what do you think?'

Frances stared in disbelief. The reflection in the glass was an impostor, a beautiful stranger wearing a pale green dress, bordered with a darker green trim. The neckline was deeply cut, revealing the pleated bodice of a high-necked blouse, the lace cuffs of which protruded from the end of the sleeves. This other woman watched Frances with cool assurance, the serene face framed by soft curls at either side and the remaining hair piled in a sweeping chignon at the back. She moved slightly, letting the heavy richness of the dress swirl around her and for a moment, she forgot everything she had learned. 'My god, Cad, I didna ken mysel'!'

'Good gracious, Cad, I did not recognise myself! For heaven's sake Frances, listen to what you're saying.' Cad busied herself clearing away the brushes and scissors. 'You don't need to be lah-di-dah when you speak, just say the words properly. A hint of an accent is attractive and interesting, yakking away like a fishwife most certainly is not.'

Frances toasted Cad with her glass of gin. 'Whatever you say, Miss Wilson. You're the teacher.'

As her confidence grew so the Imperial changed and people with money started frequenting the establishment. The saloon bar was transformed with glittering style and the stage area, though small, was newly refurbished and began to attract much sought-after vaudeville acts. Cad often dropped by from her regular spot at the Tivoli and did an impromptu turn herself. This was a very good advertisement for the Imperial and she never asked for pay, nor did she need to. Her act was the most popular in town and it was not unusual to see the stage littered with nuggets thrown by the men as they shrieked for an encore. Dawson's social élite, the Klondike and Eldorado Kings who had made their fortunes over-night, now flocked to the roulette tables in the Imperial's gaming room.

Dick Milligan, a local Mounted Policeman, was brought in to supervise the wheels and keep order throughout play but Pi'taki remained strict about the standards in the place and he often said he was wasted there.

'You gotta allow a bit of trouble, Miss Pi'taki, or I ain't got a job,' he said one night. She had just thrown out the famous Arizona Charlie Meadows for taking bets while he shot spots off a playing card at thirty paces.

Pi'taki had responded in characteristic manner. 'Hmmph,' she said, 'one day someone will get shot – I want no blood on my floor!'

In addition to the changes in the saloon, the suite of rooms upstairs was also transformed. There was a small parlour with curtains of Belgian lace and sumptuous rugs adjoining two bedrooms, each filled by a four-poster bed with feather mattresses and drapes. If at first bemused, Pi'taki now took it all in her stride. However, she was unable to acquire a liking for the mattress and it was days later when Frances discovered her sleeping on a mat as usual at the side of the bed.

Pi'taki's presence in the Grand Imperial had long since gone from being a source of suspicion to something of a novelty and, strange as it might have seemed, she liked the life. She became a familiar face around the place. In the day-time, people hailed her cheerily as she sat on the board-walks of Dawson and watched the world go by. At night she would move between the roulette wheels and faro tables, shouting encouragement at the turn of a card and slapping the backs of old regulars.

As her eyesight weakened and she eventually succumbed to the need for spectacles, Pi'taki's general demeanour slowed to an elderly pace. She was still a woman of few words but now laughed more readily. Her greying hair never grew back to its original plaited length and was fastened in a knot at the back of her head but the ubiquitous plaid shawl rarely left her shoulders. Tailored clothes now concealed her shuffling gait and floppy moccasins had long since given way to button-up boots. From time to time, however, her raised skirts still revealed a glimpse of old leather leggings when the biting frosts of winter could be felt. Frances looked on fondly but with fascination to think how much had changed since that first night they met in the dim light of the tipi. How close now their dependence on each other, how different their trust. And how distant seemed the memory of that desolate little railroad camp.

16

In the early months of 1899 Dawson was gripped in the usual hard rime of winter. Frances spent much of her time immersed in books and letter writing. She was communicating regularly with Ballantyne now and he had become useful as an adviser and something of a friend. He was wary of Pi'taki, however, and on his occasional visits she teased him remorselessly for it. Despite this, she seemed equally satisfied, indeed relieved, to leave the money matters with Ballantyne & Sons.

On the evening of April twenty-sixth, the two women sat around a crackling fire in their parlour enjoying a short respite from the night's entertainment which was in full swing below. Recently they had received news that work on their claim out at the creeks was slowing down. This was not entirely unexpected but, even so, it put a breath of change in the air, as if the future had a need to be addressed. Pi'taki seemed more aware of it than Frances and spoke her thoughts out loud as she watched the flames dancing.

'Soon we should go, Otanimm.'

'What, and leave Dawson – I thought you were happy here?'

Pi'taki pulled the shawl around her shoulders. 'Too cold here,' she said.

Frances gave a little sighing laugh. 'You're just getting old.'

A knock on the door interrupted them. It was the foreman, Jed Hennessy. He stood in the doorway, looking embarrassed and holding his cap in his hands. 'I'm sorry to intrude on you like this, Mrs O'Byrne.'

'Not at all, Jed. Come in.' Frances drew up a chair for him to warm himself and he nodded to Pi'taki before he spoke.

'I don't quite know how to say this. . .'

Frances patted his shoulder. 'Save it, Jed. Don't worry, I think we know what you've come to tell us.'

Jed sighed and looked at both of them. 'We followed the pay-streak as far as we could but it's disappeared now, I'm afraid. There's a fair bit of dirt to sluice out this summer but apart from that – well, I guess we're through.'

'All right, Jed,' Frances smiled. 'No complaints. That creek bed made us rich – it couldn't last for ever.' She poured him a drink from a crystal decanter on the dresser. 'Anyway,' she continued, 'it's time you men came in from those hills and got back to your families. I'll see you're all paid off well as I promised. Meanwhile, I think we should have a party for you all at the Imperial, what do you think?'

'That would be just fine!' Jed looked enthusiastic.

Pi'taki rose and went over to the dresser. Opening a drawer, she gestured to Frances. 'Give him this,' she said quietly, placing something in her hand and, with another nod to Jed, she left the room.

He drained the remainder of his glass and stood up. 'Well, I guess I better get going too, ma'am.'

Frances took his hand and he felt the hard pebble pressed into his palm. He looked down at it in amazement as she spoke. 'This was the first nugget we took out of the ground, Jed. We want you to have it.' He started to protest but she silenced him. 'No buts – you've earned it. Now go home and marry your sweetheart or whatever it is you dream of doing. That will just help you along a bit.'

Jed was speechless and the firelight danced in his eyes giving the blueness an intensity that made her strangely sad. Something in his awestruck, innocent expression seemed to strip the last years away, releasing a poignant nostalgia for another time, when the riches of life had been counted in days of hope and love rather than pouches of gold dust. She felt aged beyond her years, wearied by all she had endured. The future was this young man's and something akin to jealousy made her look away.

Suddenly from outside there came a crashing sound accompanied by panicked screams. Frances rushed to the window and looked out. Far down the length of Front Street, flames could be seen licking the sky. 'Looks like a fire at the Bodega,' she said. 'We'd better get down there.' She called for Pi'taki and they evacuated the bar downstairs but, by the time they were out in the street, the inferno had swept through the flimsy façades of the dance-halls and saloons and a blazing conflagration now threatened the Imperial.

Pi'taki dashed back inside before they could stop her and minutes later her face appeared at the first-floor window as she threw blankets out into the street. Frances quickly jolted herself into action and organised the crowd outside. She watched as her fine bed linen was dragged in the mud and hung over the timber frames. With Jed shouting orders to co-ordinate the mad scramble, they draped the

271

wooden slatted walls and doorways, even the roof, until the building was shrouded with slime.

People were screaming and running about in a frenzy as their property collapsed like a tinder-box. The firemen were on strike for better wages and helpless individuals fought in vain to work the hoses. But with the boilers off, the water froze in the pipes before it reached the nozzles. In the freezing stillness of the night, the blast of heat caused clouds of steam to condense and smother the town in an icy fog. The flames leapt higher and men could be seen dropping to their knees in despair as they watched the crackling structures crumble into charcoal. Half-clad girls ran screaming from the cribs of Paradise Alley, the famous Opera House clattered to the ground in a smoking ruin and the gold in the strong-boxes of the bank burst out in a molten mass.

Jed organised a crowd to set fires alight on the frozen river to thaw the surface and pump water in from there. Others began blasting with dynamite to halt the advance of the fire but, by the time it petered out, over a hundred buildings had been reduced to ashes.

Quick thinking had saved the Imperial and the next morning, as they peeled off the mud-soaked drapes, the damage was found to be minimal. Scores of homeless men and women had spent the night in the lobby as Frances and Pi'taki moved among them distributing food and keeping the stoves burning. They woke to a town in a daze. Half of Dawson was laid bare and the scale of the damage was unaccountable. They stood in the street looking down at the crashed telegraph poles, the piles of charred wood and steaming clay and felt a definite sense of finality.

It was to be three more months before Frances and Pi'taki had worked out the claim, settled everything and sold up but it was that moment after the fire that had precipitated their decision to leave. Curiously, others around them took a different view. Within hours of the fire petering out, the determined spirit of the Klondikers was re-building a new town from the ashes. But time was running out for Dawson. Stragglers who made it over the route from Edmonton still trickled in but they were too late and their expressions betrayed only gaunt disillusionment.

The men who had worked the O'Byrne claim celebrated their departure before they moved out of town. Frances was left running the Imperial and sawmill with ease and as a consequence had more time to devote to entertaining. Once Front Street was restored with an even grander façade than before, with it came a new sophistication. Dawson acquired its own social élite and for a short period Frances relished her position as the focus of this privileged circle.

In June, Ballantyne arrived again on one of his biannual visits to Dawson. He came in on the paddle-steamer, damp and ruffled by the journey as usual. However, the frown on his face was replaced by a look of astonishment when he encountered Frances in her refurbished parlour.

'Do sit down, Mr Ballantyne,' she said, indicating the sumptuous armchair. 'Would you care for tea?' When he heard her speak he was taken aback even further and momentarily forgot the heat and the flies. 'May I say, Mrs O'Byrne, this change in you is most — most charming!'

'Why thank you,' she said, returning a winning smile. 'Let's make a start then. A great deal has occurred since last we met.' She explained about the closure of the mine and he brought her up to date with the state of the account in Edmonton. The discussion then moved on. Frances had given some thought to their previous conversation and was now ready to consider the investments he had originally proposed.

'And before I forget,' he said, drawing a paper from his brief-case, 'I have prepared a transfer deed for you.' Frances looked at him blankly and he continued. 'During our first meeting, you asked me about sending some money to your family in Scotland.' At first, he thought she had not heard him. Then he saw the vein beating furiously in her brow and the clenched set of her jaw. 'Are you all right, Mrs O'Byrne?' he asked solicitously.

Frances tried to smile. 'I'd forgotten all about that.' She searched for something to say. 'You see, I didn't want to wait till you returned to Dawson – time was pressing and, well, I just went ahead and made the arrangements myself. Through the bank here.'

'Oh, I am sorry you were inconvenienced. You could have written to me in Edmonton.' Ballantyne poised his pen over a blank page in his notebook. 'If you give me the details, I'll just make sure. . .'

'It's all been taken care of. There's no need to talk any further of it,' Frances interjected, making it obvious that the matter was closed. 'Now, we've a lot of business to get through.'

Ballantyne winced and coloured slightly. Clearly her acerbic tongue had not suffered in the transformation and, though he admired Frances, she remained a little too unpredictable for his taste. 'Very well,' he concurred, recognising when it was politic to defer to her mood.

They discussed further the arrangements for selling up the Imperial and the sawmill and agreed on a date for the move. Ballantyne offered to find somewhere suitable for them to stay in Edmonton, albeit temporarily until an appropriate property could be purchased. He was delighted at this upturn in events and looked forward to having the bank's major client within easy reach. It would be a coup for him and would thankfully bring to an end these ghastly sorties into the frozen wastes of the north.

Everything was sold up and settled by the end of July. The mill had fetched a tidy sum and there was no shortage of cheechakos willing to pay good money for the chance to re-work the old O'Byrne claim. Frances handed over the keys of the Grand Imperial to Bella Gibson saying, 'It's yours now and you're making a sound investment.' Then added with affectionate good humour, 'Just try to keep up the good name, will you?'

'Trust me, honey,' came the reply. 'You tell Pi'taki she ain't to worry none – this place is gonna be safe in my hands!' Frances shook her head and smiled. Though unconvinced, it did not matter. She hugged Bella warmly for all her kindness and left before the tears came to her eyes.

And so it was with a myriad trunks and baggage stowed below, the two women waved to their friends and boarded the *Eloise*. As they stood on the deck, the speckled slopes of Dawson receded into the steamy mists of summer and the high Arctic sun burst across the mountains, flinging their shadows over the milky water.

PART
5

1

It was before six when Frances mounted up and headed for the trail running north out of Edmonton. Baines, the groom, had risen early to get the horse ready as she had requested and was still bleary-eyed when she appeared in the stable yard.

'Fine mornin' for a ride, ma'am,' he said, adjusting the girth strap on the tall black mare.

Frances looked up. The sky was pale with a light brushing of thin clouds and the air was fresh with a hint of the coming autumn. 'Yes, I'll take advantage of it now – looks like we'll have rain later.' She raised her foot into the stirrup and swung herself onto the horse's back, gathering in the reins as it lifted its hooves and turned in anticipation. Then she dug in her heels and the animal reared twice before setting off at a gallop. Baines watched her go down the sweeping drive and out into the grounds of the O'Byrne estate. He had checked himself from warning her to take care for he knew her to be an accomplished rider but he could not understand the surfeit of energy that caused her to race out alone on the plains at such an hour. He shook his head and with a yawn, turned and padded back to his quarters.

The horse gained ground as it hit the well-beaten trail to St Albert. No one else was about and only a few nervous gophers scuttled into holes as the pounding hooves disturbed the calm. Soon Frances passed the junction where the track led out to Stony Plains and the farmlands to the west that had once been her home. Frances thought about her old neighbours and how they had prospered in the five years since her return from Dawson. The Olsens and the Dutchaks were big landowners in the region now and very successful in the farming community. There had been a lot of rain that year but one bad season could no longer alter the course of their lives. Though they remained a good day's ride from town, she was pleased to think she saw them more now than ever before. Her own house, in its sprawling grounds above the river, was a wonderful accommodation for large gatherings and she enjoyed the opportunity to receive several families at once, filling the place with bustle and noise. Weekend parties at the O'Byrne spread had become renowned throughout the district.

Stones were sent spinning and the dust rose in clouds behind as Frances urged the horse on northwards, her face glowing with the exhilaration of the gallop. The sun was fully up when at length Mission Hill that overlooked the settlement of St Albert rose into view and she slowed to a trot to enter the town. It was impossible for her to come here without remembering their passage this way on the fateful trek north. That was nine years ago but what had once been a small huddle of dwellings surrounding the church had now given way to a burgeoning downtown development. The morning's activity was already under way in the streets as she sauntered towards the Livery. There, she dismounted and left the horse to be watered and rubbed down before contemplating the return journey. Going into the hotel dining-room, she found a seat and ordered coffee. The proprietress came over personally and filled her cup. 'Keepin' well, Frances?'

'Never better, Janette, how's business with you?' Frances smiled. She liked the easy informality with which she was accepted. When approaching Edmonton, she would make a show of riding side-saddle before entering the town, but here the sight of her in divided skirt and high boots was no longer considered unusual.

'Oh, we can't complain. Been a lotta folks passing through for the Dutchak weddin' – they got relatives all over the place. It's gonna be a big affair. You goin'?'

Frances smiled. 'Of course, I wouldn't miss it.'

As they chatted, the room began to fill up and Janette moved off to serve the other customers. A few of them who knew Frances stopped at her table to swap news and it was well into the morning before she noticed the weather outside had changed. After a hurried round of goodbyes, she retrieved her mount and was out once more, heading back along the trail for home. There were more people about and she had to slow her pace to avoid collision with the various goods wagons and buggies that now plied the roadway. Some of them waved and shouted a greeting, recognising the distinctive Mrs O'Byrne as she sprinted past on her elegant horse.

Gradually the skies grew ponderous as grey clouds threatened from the west and soon a fine sprinkling of rain had muddied the track. It was driving heavier by the time the spread of her own acreage came into view and Frances had to rein the animal in to a gentler trot to prevent it slipping. Two English setters bounded out to greet her as she came between the trees and through the vast gateway arching across the drive. From the flat landscape that characterised the area, there was a gentle rise up to the front of the house. It stood gracefully bordered by a vast two-tiered verandah that afforded expansive views all round. On the other side, green lawns swept down in a curve till they met the edge where the rock fell away steeply and the North Saskatchewan river moved like rippling brown silk, many feet below.

This had been a factor in selecting the location for the house whose elevated position overlooked the valley and Edmonton. The town had developed and, in the five years since taking up residence, Frances had achieved prominence as a member of its thriving community. Though she had been urged to choose a more central spot on which to build, still she wished to remain at some distance from the mainstream of city life. It had taken nearly three years to complete all the special features she and Pi'taki desired. First and foremost was the impressive double verandah that skirted the entire house with carved handrails and curlicue newels at each corner. A bank of french windows opened out onto these twin decks so that the sun could be seen from the moment of rising to the last trails of light in the sky. And for the darker months they had insisted on the latest innovation in modern heating systems. In addition there was a fine stableyard with accommodation for a dozen thoroughbreds plus a sprawling collection of barns and stores which serviced the farmlands beyond. While all this was being built, daily they had driven the mile out to observe its progress and only these visits had enabled them to tolerate the unfamiliar town house in which they were forced to live for the first twelve months.

Dismounting, Frances saw the old woman watching at the drawing-room window, urging her to come in out of the rain. She waved back and smiled, realising she had allowed herself to become soaked through. Baines hurried out of the stable-yard and looked from the mare, lathered in sweat, to Frances in her mud-spattered riding habit. 'You all right, ma'am? The weather sure did turn like you said.'

She laughed and dismissed his concern. Then her eye caught sight of the familiar buggy parked under shelter to the side of the house. 'How long has Mr Ballantyne been here? I wasn't expecting him.'

'Oh, he arrived more'n an hour ago, I'd guess. I told him you was out ridin' but he said he'd wait.'

Briskly she went inside and was stopped in the hallway by Pi'taki, who looked down at her damp apparel. 'Go and have your bath. He can wait,' she said quietly, gesturing with her eyes towards the study.

Frances went quickly up the curving staircase and met the maid on the landing. 'Dulcie, draw the water, would you?' she said, unbuttoning her jacket.

279

'It's all ready, ma'am. Miss Pi'taki asked me to do it a while ago.'

In the steaming bathroom, Frances lay back and let the soothing water relax away the exhaustion of the vigorous ride. All around the polished wood floor, her clothes lay in piles where she had dropped them. As she listened to the rain spraying against the glass of the verandah doors, a draught swelled the filmy curtains and she wondered what had brought Christian Ballantyne out on such a wild October day. In recent years, he had made sweeping changes in the running of her business empire. When she offered him the exclusive job of handling her interests, it was as if this had been the opportunity he had been waiting for and it had proved to be a wise decision on her part. Their twice-weekly meetings now enabled her to keep a hold on all the developing strands of her investments while his shrewd management allowed her to make necessary visits to other provinces without fearing that urgent matters might be neglected at home. An easy friendship had grown from their working partnership. Recognising the value of an escort at the various functions she was called upon to attend, she was often seen in public with her trusted counsellor. As a rich widow, Frances had been a source of relentless speculation for the local gossips though she made no secret of the fact that another marriage held no allure for her. On a social level her friendship with Ballantyne was a convenient arrangement, purely platonic and uncomplicated by emotional entanglement, it suited them both well. Even so, she was still his employer and as such would, in some sense, retain the upper hand. Sometimes she took undue advantage of this. The bedroom clock could be heard chiming the half hour of eleven and a sneaking guilt crept into her thoughts as she realised she had kept him waiting far too long.

As she crossed the hall, Frances quickly checked her appearance in the mirror. Here and there, strands of grey now interspersed the deep brown of her hair which was swept back into a broad roll, giving an elegant frame to her face. Fine lines around her eyes enhanced her expression, still reminiscent of the fresh openness of her youth. At thirty-four, she carried herself with an assurance that, if anything, made her more attractive than before. She opened the study doors. Despite the modern warm-air heating system that had recently been installed, a large log fire still crackled and sparked in the grate. The setters lay sprawled sleepily before it and the smell of their damp coats permeated the room. The accountant was seated by the desk, perusing some papers and he looked over the rim of his gold spectacles as she entered.

'Forgive me for keeping you so long.' Frances smiled warmly and held out her hands to him. Ballantyne rose to greet her with his customary politeness. Regardless of the prevailing style for moustaches, he was still clean-shaven and the silver in his hair had intensified over the years, adding to the dignified charm which had first endeared him to her.

'Of course,' he said, observing her. 'I must say you do look well, my dear.'

'Why thank you. I take it then, you're not angry with me?'

'Not at all, a woman is entitled to spend as long as she likes in her bathroom.'

'Oh, is she indeed? Well, I don't think I could be bothered to wait this long.'

Ballantyne gave an embarrassed little laugh. 'Yes, well, had you been expecting me . . . but I did, after all, come unannounced.'

Frances seated herself on the large spoon-backed chair behind the desk. 'Oh, before I forget,' she said, 'it's the big wedding at the end of the month. Just imagine, Nikolai Dutchak getting married – it seems only yesterday he was a young boy.' She looked up appealingly. 'You will come, won't you? I can't persuade Pi'taki, she rarely ventures out these days.'

'Frances, it hardly sounds like my sort of weekend – all that roistering and drinking they get up to. I'm too old for that. Besides, to tell you the truth, I've been feeling a bit off colour lately . . .'

'Nonsense, Christian, it should be a lot of fun. It will do you good.'

He looked vaguely irritated but decided not to argue. 'Oh very well, if you insist.'

'I do,' she smiled. 'Now that's settled, what was it you came to see me about?'

Ballantyne produced the relevant papers and laid them before her. 'I need some signatures,' he began. 'It shouldn't take long.' He waved to the disordered sheets on the desk. 'We're still trying to sort out the Ramsay shares you've acquired. The family was so anxious to liquidate his assets, they didn't know the half of what was there – Indian Railways, Malayan Rubber, you name it, he had his finger in it.'

Frances turned up her nose. 'Forget those. Any mining interests?'

'A few. Small investments here and there, mainly tin it seems. The only thing he owned outright was the lease on this.' He passed her a summary sheet. 'We got the rest for a song but had to pay a tidy sum for that particular mine. It seems the one thing the family did know about was the value of coal. It could be a useful contributor to your own company's ability to generate earnings, as you can see . . .' He looked up as Frances scanned the paper. 'Are you all right?'

She had grown pale and gripped the curled wooden knob on the arm of the chair. 'Christian, this is in Scotland.'

He glanced briefly down at the report. 'Yes, Fife – does that mean anything to you?'

'Mean anything?' she said, continuing to run her eyes over the page. 'This pit is in Thornton – it's only a few miles from where I used to live.'

'Really? What a fortunate coincidence.' He still knew little of her early life before Canada but something in her tone touched a warning chord in him.

'It's not fortunate,' she said with sudden sharpness. Jumping to her feet, she let go of the paper as if it was something vile that had stuck to her fingers. 'Get rid of it!'

'What on earth's the matter?'

'Never mind,' she said. 'Just do as I say. I don't want to hear or speak of it again, is that understood?'

Ballantyne was stunned by the outburst and shook his head in bewilderment. 'But why?' he asked. 'This is a profitable little mine, it's a good asset for —' But her urgent look halted him in mid-sentence and he raised his hands in frustration. 'Fine, if that's what you want, I'll see that it's sold.'

She turned. 'Good, I'd like you to get on to it straight away – and make sure it's done quickly.'

'Well, I'll do what I can.'

There was a perfunctory knock on the study doors. They opened and the maid wheeled in a small brass tea trolley. Pi'taki followed behind, moving with difficulty and resting shakily on her stick. 'All right, Anna, take out the dogs. I will see to this,' she said, dismissing the girl. The accountant got to his feet and nodded politely to the old lady. He was still marginally uncomfortable in her presence and was usually glad to have Frances present when they were together. However on this occasion he was distinctly relieved by the interruption.

'How are you, Mr Ballantyne?' There was an ageing frailty in her voice though her understanding of English was fluent now.

He coughed slightly. 'One mustn't grumble, I suppose. And you?'

'Ah, what do you expect at my age?' she sighed vaguely, pouring from the coffee pot and passing him a wobbly cup.

'Mmm, quite so. Thank you.' He settled himself in one of the armchairs facing her.

'So, have you finished your business?' she asked.

'Well, er, more or less.'

'Then are you staying for lunch?'

'I doubt it,' he replied grimly.

Pi'taki glanced across at Frances, then leaned forward conspiratorially. 'What have you said to upset her?' she whispered hoarsely.

'I'm not sure.' He looked back to the figure who remained standing motionless at the window, staring out at the dismal gloom which the greying afternoon was bringing to the landscape.

Pi'taki shrugged. 'She is just tired. I heard her ride out before the sun this morning.'

'Oh I see.' Ballantyne was not convinced.

'Yes, that horse will fall dead from under her one day.' She shook her head with dramatic weariness, and called over to Frances who was oblivious to their conversation. 'You want a drink, Otanimm?' There was no reply. 'See what I mean?' Pi'taki's voice held a hint of exasperation as she poured a cup and handed it to Ballantyne. 'Give it to her.'

He rose and crossed the room. 'Can't you tell us what this is all about?' he asked, placing the cup and saucer in Frances's hand.

She looked up at him. 'I'd prefer not to talk about it.'

'Very well,' he sighed with growing irritation. 'Obviously you need time to think it over. I presume, when you have given it some consideration, you will come to your senses and realise it is a good investment.'

But her tone changed again and she raised her voice to him. 'Then you presume wrong, Mr Ballantyne.'

'But if you are originally from those parts —'

'You are to keep that fact out of any dealings. Now I meant what I said, I want the Thornton Pit out of my hands as soon as possible – do I make myself clear?'

Pi'taki intervened with a voice as hard and loud as she could muster. 'You need not shout, Otanimm. We hear you well enough. Now, what is wrong with you?'

Frances looked contrite but sorry was all she said.

The old woman gestured to Ballantyne. 'Help me up,' she told him sharply and he came forward awkwardly to offer his hand as she slowly eased herself out of the chair. 'I will speak to her myself.' She pulled a cord to summon the maid. 'Now, I think you should go.'

There was an uneasy silence. Ballantyne looked piqued by the summary dismissal but had no inclination to remain while this mood prevailed. He addressed Frances. 'Very well, I'll take my leave while I still have the manners not to answer you back.'

Her expression softened and she came over to him. 'I'm sorry, Christian, it was unforgivable of me to speak to you like that. Please don't ask me to explain. I don't want anything to do with this mine and I wouldn't want it known that I had any previous connection with the place. I beg you, contact someone reliable in Scotland and get them to handle the sale in person on my behalf.'

He hesitated but did not resist her wishes. 'Of course, if it is so important to you.'

'Oh thank you,' she said relieved and kissed him briefly on the cheek. 'I know I can be difficult at times, but please understand, I need someone thoroughly dependable to deal with this – you're the only one I can really trust.'

'That's very reassuring,' he said flatly. The maid entered and he allowed himself to be helped into his heavy topcoat. Then, dispensing with any pleasantries, he drew up his astrakhan collar and made his exit.

From the window, Frances watched his carriage leave. A shuffling noise behind her indicated that Pi'taki had re-entered the room. She stood still, leaning heavily on her stick and waited, her silence demanding more than words could ever expect. Frances turned and looked at her and knew she had not the right nor the inclination to continue the charade. Today's news had left her reeling from the power of the past still to hurt her. After all that had been buried by the passage of years, there was still pain and the shame that accompanied it. She felt her self-assurance crumbling, giving way to an irrational fear, a strange and unfamiliar vulnerability. Pi'taki coughed slightly and Frances knew it was time now to tell her the truth.

'Come over here and sit down,' she began. 'I want to explain to you about what happened.'

The old woman took her seat and folded her hands in front of her, looking up with a mild, yet critical expectation in her eyes.

Frances felt uncomfortable. 'I haven't been entirely honest with you,' she began. 'When I told you about coming to Canada, I left out —' She broke off and seized the old woman's hands. 'Pi'taki, I'm sorry. There are things I should have told you. The things which happened in Scotland that made me run away from home.' She paused, then tried again. 'No, that's not exactly true – when I decided to come away with William, my family disowned me, turned me out. Now do you understand?'

'You have told me nothing, Otanimm. Why do you still fear them?'

Frances glanced out the window again. 'I brought shame on them, I did something very bad,' she added in a quiet voice, going on to reconstruct the events of fifteen years before. This brought renewed distress and she was disconcerted at how easily old wounds inflamed again. It was the first time she had spoken of them to a living soul yet far from being purged by the revelations, she felt more threatened than before. 'Don't you see,' she said in conclusion, 'it's just an embarrassment. The sooner I rid myself of this mine, the sooner we can all get back to normal. I just want to put the past behind me – is that so wrong?'

Pi'taki sat motionless throughout it all and when the confession was out she merely said, 'All the time you take your trouble and wrap it in bundles and put it in the ground. But you forget it will grow like the prairie grasses.'

Frances was unwilling to accept the truth of the remark. Though she was glad to have finally shared her burden with another soul, her heart was already hardening with the need to avoid its consequences.

2

For two weeks relations between Frances and Ballantyne continued to be strained, mostly because she would not budge from her intractable stance over the sale of the pit and he was still wounded by her abrupt treatment of him. They saw little of each other and at their meetings the vexed question of the Scottish mine was not raised. However, as the wedding drew closer, Frances went out of her way to be conciliatory and he eventually relented and agreed to be her escort. The weather that weekend was glorious and their companionship was restored as they were absorbed into the colourful chaos of the celebrations. Frances was never happier than when she was amongst these people. Despite her perceived standing in the provincial hierarchy, with these old friends from her homesteading past, she could relax and be herself.

The Dutchak spread was swarming with guests and Frances was in great demand as people she had not seen for months sought her out to catch up on the latest news. Briefly extracting herself from an animated conversation about the prospect of a new telephone exchange, she wandered over to sample the tempting *zakuska* on the buffet table. She helped herself to some of the tasty appetisers and observed from a distance the bride and groom in the midst of the assembly. Nikolai had grown from a nervous and retiring youth to a tall, confident man. He positively beamed with pride, standing next to his young bride. How splendid Zoyka looked in her brightly embroidered costume with the medallions around her neck and head-dress. Frances mused on what a different start in life this young couple would have, compared to the travails that their parents had endured.

Ballantyne joined her. 'There you are! I've been looking for you everywhere.' She hardly acknowledged his arrival, her mind still lingering in the past. 'A penny for your thoughts?' he laughed.

She smiled self-consciously. 'You know, I can't remember being that young, Christian.'

'Nonsense, you don't look a day over twenty. And the way you were dancing earlier on! I just don't know how you do it, my dear.'

'It's fun, you should give it a try.'

He put the flat of his hand against his chest. 'No, it's probably not a good idea. I've had these pains lately. Nothing serious, but I've been told to take it easy. I'll leave the exertions to you young things.'

'God, you're such an old flatterer,' she laughed. 'And a hypochondriac, too – you'll see us all off!'

He laughed with her. 'It's good to see you happy, Frances. You gave me quite a turn the way you reacted to that Scottish business . . .' He paused tentatively. 'Since you're in a better mood now, perhaps this would be a good time to bring you up to date on that?'

Her face clouded. 'I hope you're not going to spoil our fun, Christian.'

'Hmm,' he frowned. 'I see it's still a sore point with you. I had hoped to avoid mentioning it again but unfortunately there has been a small hitch.' He shook his head. 'Well, actually, quite a considerable one.'

'What kind of a hitch?' She looked slightly alarmed and forgot the food, placing her plate back on the table.

He braced himself, wishing he had not re-opened the subject. 'We're up to our neck in legal wrangles over probate on the Ramsay will. Apparently, the family have questioned the legality of some of

286

the bequests. You can't hope to sell off the lease on the Thornton Pit until it's sorted out and frankly that could take months, if not years.'

'But can't you put pressure on them to hurry things up?'

He shrugged lightly. 'Frances, I can't work miracles. It's bad enough trying to communicate at this distance. There's only so much can be done by post and telegraph.'

Suddenly her face brightened. 'Of course, that's it.'

'Er, I'm not with you?'

'Obviously you should go over there and deal with it personally. Don't you see, Christian, they're just playing for time, hoping they'll get more out of us. If you were there it would cut the time in half.'

'Frances, for goodness' sake, it's not going to make that much difference. I'm not up to a journey like that. Besides, I won't go traipsing across the world just to satisfy a whim on your part.'

'Why not?' she snapped. 'That's what I pay you for.'

People were beginning to stare in their direction and he guided her to a window alcove for some privacy. The muscles in his aquiline face tensed perceptibly as he spoke. 'My patience has its limits and I will not have you talk to me like that,' he declared quietly. 'Now, I've been a loyal member of your staff for eight years – but if you want my resignation, it will be on your table in the morning.'

Frances swallowed hard as a sudden convulsive sob threatened. She gripped Ballantyne's sleeve. 'Christian, please forgive me. It's not a whim that makes me react this way. You see, I'm afraid . . .'

He passed her a silk handkerchief from his jacket pocket. 'Then for heaven's sake be honest with me and tell me what's going on. I like to think I'm more than a mere employee. Aren't we friends enough to share this problem?'

Frances wiped her eyes and nodded. 'Do you remember I once consulted you about making provision for my family after the gold strike in Dawson?'

He nodded. 'Yes, but then you told me —'

'Never mind what I told you, it was a lie.' She interrupted, fighting to control her voice. 'What I never revealed is that they disowned me when I left. When I tried to re-establish contact I was informed that as far as they were concerned I was dead to them and always would be.'

'But that's dreadful! What could have possessed them to treat you like that?'

Frances took his hand in hers. 'That's something I still can't tell you, Christian, so please don't press me to explain. I hope now you will forgive my behaviour and understand why it is so necessary for me to have done with this transaction as quickly as possible.'

He considered her words and nodded. 'Yes, I do see.'

'And do you also see how important it is for me to send someone I can trust to deal with this on my behalf – someone in whom I place the deepest confidence?' She looked at him appealingly. 'I'm not asking, Christian, and I'm not telling you as an employer. I'm begging.'

Four weeks later, the two women sat deep in thought before a blazing fire-grate. Only the chiming clock and snoring dogs broke the gloomy silence in the drawing room. The cause of their desultory mood was a telegram which lay on the rug between them. Frances picked it up and despairingly re-read the message:

CHRISTIAN BALLANTYNE ESQ ADMITTED
KIRKCALDY GENERAL HOSPITAL 21ST OCTOBER
FOLLOWING HEART ATTACK STOP NOW RECOVERING
AND REQUEST YOU COMMUNICATE DIRECT TO
INFORM INSTRUCTIONS STOP
PROF HECTOR LEACH FRCSE MD STOP

She put it in her pocket, went over to the window and peered between the heavy corded drapes. The rain drove puddles into the gravel and hammered on the roof of the vast porch that bounded the house. A curtain of droplets fell from its carved awning and soaked the wooden boards beneath. 'Poor Christian. I feel wretched about this, I shouldn't have pushed him to go.'

Pi'taki did not contradict her but shivered as she listened and pulled the footstool round to the fire to warm her toes.

'Of course, I can't keep him out there, he'll have to come home,' Frances continued. Once he had given his agreement, Ballantyne had been despatched immediately and since his departure there had been a tense period while she waited for news. She sighed as she gazed out of the window. All the anxiety had been wasted, since it seemed there had been no time to achieve a breakthrough in the legal wrangling. 'Who can I get to handle this business now? There's no one else I can trust.'

The old woman sniffed loudly from behind. 'You must go yourself,' she said decisively.

'How can I? People have long memories back there.'

'And here too, Otanimm. You do not forget.'

288

Frances wrung her hands. 'God, I can't believe this has happened,' she said. 'I wish I could wake up from it. It's like a bad dream that's come to ruin everything.'

'No, it is a sign and you must heed it.'

'But I can't possibly go. It's out of the question.'

Pi'taki raised her voice. 'Ballantyne is sick, he might die – while you think only of yourself!'

'How can you say that?' Her temper flared, eager to find a target for the frustration straining within her. 'You know I have good reasons for not going there. It's ridiculous to even suggest it!'

Frustrated in turn, Pi'taki slapped her palms on the arms of her chair. 'Why will you not see what you must do?'

'But it's not my fault!' The response slid from an angry shout to the whine of a despairing child.

'But it is your problem, Otanimm. Only you can solve it.'

Frances was humbled and chastened by the quiet authority. 'Aye, you're right.' She looked across and said in the same child's voice, 'If I went, would you come with me?' But she already knew the answer.

'Ach, I am too old – look at my legs. And the winter comes.'

It had been a pointless question and only half-meant, since she was even less willing to risk Pi'taki's health on such a journey. Frances suspected she was somehow destined to make the trip alone, whatever the circumstances. She watched a raindrop trickle down the pane and merge with the one before. Then she turned and her own face was tear-streaked, her voice weakened. 'I'm scared.'

'Of your own people? What can they do?' The old woman gestured for her to come over. 'Sit down by me,' she said, gently pressing her with stiffened fingers to rest against her lap. 'You are strong and changed in many ways.'

Frances raised her head. 'Maybe they won't recognise me?'

Pi'taki sighed and continued stroking her hair. 'That is for you to decide. Just go and finish your business.'

Frances stared into the flames as a flood of old memories assaulted her imagination. Since leaving Scotland, half of her life had been taken up with the business of survival, and the rest so absorbed in preoccupation with her work and the O'Byrne estate that there had been little room for retrospection. It was true she had found happiness in this place and it had been deeply unsettling to be suddenly provoked into the painful reality of the past. But already there was a small yet compelling force working within her, irresistibly drawing

289

her away and she knew she would have to yield to it. She clung to Pi'taki's knees.

'I will be here . . .'

Frances smiled. 'You can always tell what's in my mind.'

'I read your face, Otanimm. I see where your thoughts are.'

Frances cabled to Scotland the following morning and made all the travel bookings. Somehow, once the decision had been made, she became more collected, allowing her thoughts to be distracted by the practicalities of such a major trip. However, parting from Pi'taki was strangely disturbing. In the otherwise busy flurry of activity before her departure, she was suddenly aware of her own vulnerability, something not experienced in years. They had often been separated for short periods but never like this, she thought. Though she confidently expected to be back by Christmas, there was an unknown quality about this trip and it rankled that she could not overpower it. She went out of her way to make all sorts of special and unnecessary arrangements to ensure the old woman's comfort while she was away and even organised a clerk from one of her company offices to come regularly and read her the profusion of correspondence she promised to send. Pi'taki took it all in her stride and largely ignored it.

They rode together to the station and, in the swirling steam of the waiting engine, held each other close. Frances's embrace was almost desperate, her face wet with tears. 'Oh Na'a,' she breathed as the word involuntarily escaped her lips, 'keep well for me.'

Pi'taki hugged her, then gently disengaged herself. 'It is you who must take care,' she said.

The journey by rail to Montreal took four days and on 6th November, 1905, Frances Rintoul Munroe O'Byrne took passage on a luxury liner bound for Southampton, travelling back across the Atlantic in first-class style. She remained in her cabin for much of the journey. On the few occasions when she strolled on deck she drew admiring glances from the other passengers. But little they knew how her poise and sophistication belied the anticipation and uncertainty with which she viewed the horizon.

3

Kirkcaldy General Hospital stood at the foot of St Clair Street, on the same headland of rock as Ravenscraig Castle. Adorned with turrets and cupolas, the buildings mimicked the ancient keep beside them, giving the impression that here was a medieval armoury rather than a place of medicine and healing. In the wing to which Frances was directed, the iron bedsteads were arranged against the circular wall of the domed ward. Between each bed was a tall, narrow window and shafts of weak sunlight played across the floor in a criss-cross of spokes. A nurse in a long white apron and frilled cap moved between shade and light like a benign ghost, bending to check the patients as she passed. Seeing the aristocratic-looking lady in the doorway, she came across quickly. 'Can I help ye, madam?'

'I've come to see Mr Ballantyne. Dr Leach told me I might find him here.'

'Yes of course, this way please.' Frances followed her across the room, her eyes scanning the pale faces of the patients. The warm air was heavy with the taint of sickness, overlaid with the pervasive odours of carbolic soap and lye. At his bedside, though she had expected to see a deterioration, Frances was still not fully prepared for the change in him. Ballantyne lay propped against the pillows, his face drained of colour, a wan mask emphasised by the white in his thinning hair.

'Christian?' she leaned across and whispered. 'It's me, Frances.'

He opened his eyes and paused a moment before his smile showed recognition. 'Good gracious, I don't believe it – you've come all this way?'

'Of course I have,' she said briskly, kissing him on the forehead. 'How are you?'

'Oh it's all right now – no recurrence, thank God. I'm just tired. But it surely wasn't necessary for you to turn up in person, my dear?'

'Someone has to look after you and see you get home safely. Besides, it's my fault you're in here now.'

'What nonsense!' He made an effort to raise himself but she gently restrained him and he lay back. 'When did you arrive?' he asked.

'I came here straight from the station. I left Edmonton the moment I got the telegram to say you were ill.'

'Well, I'm most flattered by this attention.'

'It's the least I could do. If I hadn't pushed you into making this trip, you'd probably never have had the heart attack in the first place. I've been over-working you, Christian, but I'm going to make up for it. You're to go home and rest up – for as long as it takes to get better. I'll stay and handle things at this end.'

'But I thought you wanted nothing to do with it?'

'Never mind about that now. The main thing is to get you well again. I've been so selfish over this whole affair.'

Ballantyne patted her hand. 'Don't blame yourself. I know you had good reason. Before all this,' he waved vaguely, 'I did at least manage to sort out the dispute surrounding the will.'

'Oh that's a relief. I'm really grateful.'

'But there's much to be done yet,' he cautioned. 'We've still to find a buyer for the pit. And perhaps, if I stayed, I could also be of some help with your family?'

'I have no reason to see my family – they've made that clear enough. I'm here only to settle the business.' Frances checked the annoyance in her voice and smiled. 'Now, I want no argument, you're going home on the next available ship. I have already spoken to the doctor and he says you're well enough to travel as long as you rest. A nurse will go with you. You'll have the best of everything, I promise. As for the sale of the mine – you know me, Christian, I'll have it done and dusted in no time.'

'Well, if you're sure?' There was relief in his voice.

'Indeed I am. All you have to do is get better.'

'Will you be staying on at the house I rented in Fergus Place?' he enquired.

'I should think so,' Frances replied. 'It seems comfortable enough for the purpose and it won't be for long. Hopefully I shall be back home before Christmas.'

'There's an automobile and chauffeur at your disposal too, did you know that?'

'Really? How exciting.'

'You may think so, personally I've no time for the confounded things – a danger to life and limb I say.'

She laughed. 'You mean you've not even given it a try?'

'What me? I wouldn't go near the thing. Anyway,' he said, tapping his chest, 'to tell you the truth, this started to trouble me almost as soon as I got here. I've not had a chance to do much except work.' Ballantyne reached into the cabinet at the side of the bed and handed her a small brass key. 'This is for the bureau in the study. You will find some of the relevant papers there although the solicitor, Robert Moskow, has most of them now. Since they took me in here, he's been entrusted with the negotiations. I've not seen him lately, so you might pay him a visit, Frances.'

'Right, I'll do that straight away. Now please, don't worry, everything is going to be fine.'

Ballantyne continued to fill her in with all the minor details she might need to complete the business. Then, with the initial concerns taken care of, the two fell to talking of more mundane things. Frances gave him the latest news of Edmonton and delivered all the messages from well-wishers. By the time they were finished she was relieved to see a little colour restored to his face and could tell, in spite of his mild protestations, that he welcomed the prospect of a return home.

Robert Moskow was an immensely fat man, barely able to rise in greeting when Frances entered his tiny office. Oily hair clung to his skull and sweat shone on the swollen face. Sitting by the searing fire like a roasting pig, he offered her a chair but it was uncomfortably close and she declined. 'No thank you, Mr Moskow, I cannot stay long.'

Undeterred, his thick lips curled in an unctuous smile. 'Mrs O'Byrne, may I say what a great honour it is for our humble company to act on behalf of such an esteemed client as yourself. And such a pleasure to have you here in person.'

Frances nodded curtly, avoided shaking his hand, and pulled some documents from the leather attaché case. 'I need this matter brought to a satisfactory conclusion as soon as possible. The delay over the settlement of the will was unfortunate but that's behind us now. My main concern is the sale of the pit. As Mr Ballantyne suggested, I've looked over the terms of the mining lease and royalty payments made to the landlord on the tonnage raised. The earnings forecasts, costings and profit ratios are all summarised, and these are the figures he has prepared. Our selling price will be a minimum of twenty thousand pounds.' He beamed at her, inwardly calculating his commission on such a sum. 'But I expect you to negotiate up from that amount.'

'Of course, of course,' he said in a thick, rheumy voice, hardly able to keep up with her flow of information. He leaned back and vigorously wiped his nose with a large, stained handkerchief. 'Have you been out to look over the mine yet?'

Frances shook her head. 'No. I do not think that will be necessary, Mr Moskow, I have all the information I need here.' She tapped the file in front of her. 'I acquired this mine as an asset amongst others purchased in Canada. To try and manage such a small operation from across the Atlantic is not worth the return on my investment. Goodness, you only have to look at the costs I have incurred thus far in trying to sell it. That is why I am anxious for a quick settlement. Now, have you had any potential buyers so far?'

'Well, the Fife Coal Company have shown some interest but they've made no bid as yet. Naturally I haven't approached them because I wanted to gauge the interest in other quarters first.'

'Don't waste any time. Remember, I want a quick sale. If the Fife Coal Company are keen, find out their offer and get back to me as soon as possible.'

'Whatever you say, right away, Mrs O'Byrne.'

Frances fastened the clasp on the briefcase. 'How soon before I can expect a decision?'

He pulled his lumbering frame from the creaking chair. 'I'll do my best to let you have something within two weeks,' Moskow said, extending a pudgy hand. 'Let me say, Mrs O'Byrne, what an honour it is to act on your behalf. And my wife and I wondered if you would further grace us by coming to dinner on Friday?'

Frances smiled. Her face was impassive as she briefly held the flaccid fingers. 'That really is most kind, but I'm afraid I must sadly decline. I have several other pressing commitments to deal with before I return to Canada and my free time is very limited. Please explain to Mrs Moskow and offer my apologies.' She walked smartly to the door and stood, waiting for him to open it. Wheezing, he made his way awkwardly round the desk but before he had reached her, she smiled sweetly and was gone.

4

It was a relief when finally Frances waved goodbye to Ballantyne and his escort as the carriage moved off on the first leg of their long journey home. For two days she had sustained the pretence for his sake that everything would be all right but in reality she had dreaded the very thought of mixing too closely with others, of being exposed. Now she let the heavy blue velvet curtains fall back and turned away from the dismal scene outside the window. A cold, steady drizzle had been falling since morning and the chill seeped through into her bones. The hiss of the gas lamps was matched by the spatter of raindrops blown in gusts against the panes of glass that streamed with condensation. It was early closing day in Kirkcaldy, and few people were about. The dull, sombre weather muffled the distant noise of trams rumbling up and down White's Causeway and along the High Street. The clatter of the occasional passing carriage was deadened by the thick carpet of leaves strewn across the cobbles. After the dry climate of Edmonton, the dampness of the Scottish east coast winter was hard to endure. No one in their right mind stayed on if they could afford a few months in Monte Carlo or Biarritz. Frances felt separate and withdrawn, somehow detached from a world that had once been her home.

There was a discreet knock at the door and the maid entered. 'Are ye receiving callers yet, madam?'

'No, Maisie. Ask them to leave their card and I will return the visit.' Frances dismissed the girl and wondered again at the efficiency of the Kirkcaldy grapevine. She had only been in town a couple of days and already the local worthies were falling over themselves to make the acquaintance of the rich, unknown Canadian. The silver tray in the hall was scattered with a variety of visiting cards but she had not yet returned one call.

'Grandtully' was an imposing residence standing on the corner of Fergus Place. It would be dwarfed by her own home back in Canada, yet still it was cold and cheerless. The massive, grey stones seemed to take their colour from the metallic sky. Inside, the heat rose to the high ceilings, leaving feet frozen in the perpetual draughts that swirled across the floors, creating eddies of dust. To the dismay of the housekeeper, Frances had ordered every fire in the house to be lit and kept going twenty-four hours a day.

'But the cost!' Mrs Heggarty was scandalised by the extravagance.

'Since I own a mine, I hardly think supplies of coal will be a problem,' came the blunt response. The sarcasm was lost on the bewildered woman who went off to give the order to the house-maids. We'll hae a' the lums up, she thought, muttering to herself about the extraordinary behaviour of foreigners.

The short days were sunless, drawn in by lowering clouds that blocked any view of the moon and stars. Gas street lamps cast pools of dim, shadowy light in the darkness, making the nights even more inhospitable and lonely. Frances was besieged by memories. Every-where she went, each thing she saw conjured up feelings and images she would rather forget. The changes to the town only emphasised her sensation of alienation. On the morning after her arrival she

295

had walked up to the hospital through heavy fog, climbing from the Port Brae to Ravenscraig. Standing before them, she shrank in the shadow of the immense linoleum factories. In sixteen years they had proliferated, spreading along the shoreline and back into the countryside behind. Great chimneys dominated the skyline belching out huge black clouds into the freezing November air, obscuring the already darkened sky. Watching from a safe distance she had seen the women come streaming from the gates at the end of their shift. But she need not have concerned herself. If there were any there that might have known her once, her appearance only emphasised the huge gulf that now divided them. Chatting amongst themselves and seemingly oblivious to the dank coldness that set her own teeth chattering, they ran past her unaware.

The next morning Frances escaped the heavy stone walls and close proximity of the neighbouring houses to walk along the familiar seashore. She did not venture far, aware that now Ballantyne was safely gone, she must act swiftly, finish her business and be rid of the place. Before retracing her steps, she pulled her wrap closer round her shoulders and glanced back down the Firth of Forth. It was as grey and threatening as the sky overhead with waves crashing onto the beach, the heightening tide driven by fierce east winds to a churning frenzy. Beyond Pathhead and Dysart, hidden by the curve of the coast and the perpetual mist that whipped from the rolling waves, was West Wemyss. She shivered, and not just from the cold.

Frances knew the next few days would merely be a matter of waiting for a decision on the transaction and ironing out the minor details. She now had time on her hands but was still reluctant to re-acquaint herself with old memories. She was not enthusiastic either about participating in the less familiar high society of Kirkcaldy, despite considerable pressure for her to do so. Nevertheless, after a further week of languishing in the confinement of the house, boredom soon encouraged a little recklessness. Her own visiting cards had now arrived from the Edinburgh printer's with the heavily embossed, gilt-edged design she had specially ordered. Idly she flipped through the pile of less distinguished-looking cards that lay in waiting on the hall table. Many of the names she recognised as owners of local businesses or people she had only ever read about in the paper as a girl. It brought a wry smile to her face as she played with the idea of entertainment at their expense. Anxious to learn about the mystery woman in their midst, they were now paying court to her and it was hard to suppress some amusement at the thought.

After an initial few calls had been made, Frances came to enjoy the charade. Politely deflecting enquiries about her past only served to increase the curiosity and intrigue that her presence had created. Speculation heightened and she did nothing to dispel the myths that sprang up around her. Within a few days, she had crammed her life with a round of receiving and returning visits, from which she accepted three dinner invitations and joined a concert outing to the Adam Smith Hall. Once it was established that, in addition to being very rich, this newcomer was also a widow, local mothers with unmarried sons went to great lengths to engineer a meeting and a handful of eminent older bachelors also sought her company. Soon the gossip columns of the local papers took up the scent and, within days, the enigmatic Mrs O'Byrne had become a feature of the conversation at every social gathering.

Early in the third week of her stay, Frances was surprised to receive an urgent note from the solicitor asking her to call into his office without delay. Irritated by the tone of the demand, her first instinct was to put him off until he called upon her. But the thought of receiving him in her own home, and being forced to maintain polite conversation during what was bound to be a protracted visit, was enough to change her mind. She did, however, arrive at his office in optimistic mood, assuming there to have been a development in the negotiations at last. As she was shown through into the small oak-panelled room, she found him in an extremely agitated state and his expression was less than encouraging. A tall, sombre gentleman in a black frock-coat sat to one side of the desk. They both rose as she entered.

'Mrs O'Byrne, it was good of you to come so quickly.' Moskow held a chair for her, puffing at the effort of remaining upright in the confined space.

'What seems to be the trouble?'

'May I introduce Mr Garston, general manager for the company up at the Thornton Pit. Perhaps he can better explain our predicament.'

The tall man extended his hand and allowed her to settle before he began. 'Mrs O'Byrne, I'll not beat about the bush with you. As has been said, we do have something of a problem on our hands. On the question of the purchase of the lease on the Thornton mine – it would appear the Fife Coal Company are holding back.'

Frances raised her eyebrows in surprise. 'And why might that be, Mr Garston? – the asking price is hardly unfavourable, considering what I paid for it.'

'Well, you may not be aware of it, madam, but the pit is currently in the grip of a dispute.'

'Whatever do you mean?'

'There's been a good deal of discontent among the work-force ever since they learned of the decision to sell to the Fife Coal Company.'

'I can't imagine why. What difference does it make to the men which company manages the pit?'

'Yes, I found it hard to understand myself. It seems they have a rather low opinion of the F.C.C. and they're worried that bargaining conditions will be swept aside in the takeover.'

'I am sure that won't happen. Come, come gentlemen, don't let's get carried away by a storm in a teacup.'

'Forgive me, Mrs O'Byrne, but I think it's a little more than that. It has reached quite serious proportions now with talk of strikes and so forth.'

Frances was disturbed by the thought of another obstruction to the conclusion of the sale. 'Oh, that's nothing new,' she said dismissively. 'Surely, there has always been a measure of dissatisfaction among miners. Really, Mr Garston, you are the manager. Can't you deal with this yourself? Explain the situation to the men and I am sure they will understand.'

Garston glanced uncomfortably at the solicitor before he resumed. 'With respect, madam, it's not that simple. Their organisation is strong – in recent years the Fife and Kinross Miners Union has won some significant ground in conciliation with the coal companies. Frankly, we don't have the luxury of ignoring their grievances any more.' He shook his head resignedly. 'It just leads to further unrest, loss of production – you know the story.'

She knew the story only too well. Frances was distinctly uncomfortable with the situation but it was impossible for them to understand what she felt inside. A wave of acute guilt now tormented her. She had just heard herself colluding with this man, sharing his regret at the gradual erosion in the wholesale power of the coal-owners by the introduction of what she knew to be paltry concessions to their workers and families. Frustrated, she got to her feet, the threat of hot tears angrily stinging her eyes as she faced them.

'Look, I don't want this problem, do ye hear? Do what it takes to push the sale through and let the Fife Coal Company sort it out once they are in ownership.'

Moskow pulled at his collar, trying to ease the constricting rolls of fat that hung over the celluloid strip. 'Forgive me for interrupting but that is just it, you see?'

'No, I don't see.'

'In view of this unrest, the Fife Coal Company are now reluctant to enter into negotiations on the – er, original terms.'

Frances looked from one to the other. 'Oh, now it's clear as day. And I don't suppose they would consider a lower price?'

He coughed awkwardly. 'Well, it was mentioned that they might be prepared to . . .'

'I see,' she retorted archly. 'Well, Mr Moskow, I told you my terms. If you are to be led around by the ear by the other side, then you are obviously not the right person to be negotiating on my behalf.' She stood up briskly and turned towards the door.

The solicitor practically ran to stop her. 'No! Oh dear me, no. Good lady, you have misunderstood me completely.'

'I think the misunderstanding is yours, Mr Moskow.'

Garston interjected. 'Might I make a suggestion here, Mrs O'Byrne? Perhaps if you would agree to meet with the men – say a small delegation of union officials and management? I think a personal appearance would set their minds to rest, reassure them there will be no problem in the sale.'

'You're not serious?'

'Oh indeed I am. Far be it for me to advise you, dear lady, but I think in this case it would not do for you to distance yourself from the issues. To remain too aloof could foster a sense of disaffection in the work-force and might further entrench their hostility. We cannot risk a full-blown strike at this stage – the implications of that would be disastrous for the sale of the pit.'

'Aye, and disastrous to the security of your job too, no doubt?' There was an uncomfortable pause. Then Frances sighed deeply with the recurring knowledge that she had gone too far. 'All right, Mr Garston, I take your point, and you were right to advise me so – after all, that is what I pay you for.'

Garston held the door open for her. 'I'll make arrangements for the meeting and let you know,' he said. 'I am sure we can come to a successful resolution.'

'Hmm, well if we do it will be through my efforts alone, gentlemen. Good day.'

When she had gone, the two men looked at each other and Garston shook his head ruefully. 'I see what you mean, my friend.'

5

With its headlamps gleaming and the trees overhead reflected in the sleek, royal blue of its bodywork, the Daimler chuntered agreeably down the east road out of Kirkcaldy. The meeting had been arranged for the following Tuesday and Frances was agitated by the fact that it was now the second week of December and there was still so little progress. She sat well back to avoid the stares from passers-by and drew her fur wrap closer around her shoulders. Even the thick rug over her knees did little to fend off the bitter frost of the morning and put her in an unsettled mood. 'Please, Donald, just ignore them,' she said to the chauffeur who persisted in blasting the horn at the throng of children who scampered behind in pursuit.

In time they reached the muddy roadway that led in through the gates of the Thornton Colliery. It was not a colliery she knew, being some miles from West Wemyss, but still it looked much like any other. As the car trundled over the uneven ground, Frances raised her eyes to the dismal spectre of the pit-head – the engine house and protruding pump beam, the headgear pulleys and the massive furnace chimneys. She was moved by the familiar sight. Groups of men walked past holding their collier's pick and hammer over their shoulders, their safety lamps and piece boxes swinging in the other hand. But there was no reciprocal familiarity in their gaze when, black-faced and white-eyed, they stared into the vehicle as it passed.

Garston welcomed her into his office where she removed her outer garments. Formality dictated that she keep on her wide plumed taffeta hat though it did seem inconsistent with the surroundings. They drank coffee together before the meeting commenced. 'I don't think you will find this too intimidating, Mrs O'Byrne,' he promised. 'There will only be six of us. Myself and another for the management, and three from the union side.'

At ten o'clock she was ushered into the boardroom. It was dominated by a heavy table with gadrooned edges, the shining expanse of mahogany like a bulwark dividing the opposing groups. Garston stood up to make the necessary introductions. 'This is Mr Hammond, my deputy. He's been with the Thornton seventeen years now.' The small bald-headed man half rose and gingerly offered his hand. Frances shook it and nodded politely. 'And across the table, so to speak, we have Arthur Moffat, Colliery Representative for the Fife and Kinross Miners Union – here to present on behalf of the men some of the issues raised by the proposed sale.' Moffat stood, gripped her hand decisively without expression and resumed his seat. 'And next to him,' Garston continued, 'we have Mr Gavin Douglas, Executive Member and regional representative to the board of the M.F.G.B. who'll say a few words first.'

'M.F.G.B., what's that?' Frances blurted out the words, trying to conceal her shock as she faced him. She had known it was Gavin from the moment she laid eyes on him but felt compelled to hear him speak as if to erase any possible doubt.

'It's the Miners Federation of Great Britain, Mrs O'Byrne. I thought you would have known that,' he replied tersely and sat down without taking her hand. Frances was amazed that he had not recognised her. She was thrown off balance by the unexpected encounter and though she felt her hand grasped by the third delegate was unaware of his name or rank.

'First of all gentlemen, I am sure you will all join me in thanking Mrs O'Byrne for taking time out in her busy schedule and devoting her attentions to the pit.' She did not listen while Garston meandered on with his opening remarks and her heart thudded anxiously as she glanced across at Gavin's seated form. It was almost impossible to believe that such a trick of fate could bring them into confrontation after sixteen years. Now in his late thirties, he had thickened out a little but still retained the mannerisms that seemed to make apologies for his tall, wiry frame. He sat hunched over the table and scribbled down a few notes. Once or twice he too looked up but no sign of recognition showed on his face. His grey eyes remained distant, lost in concentration under the dark drawn brows and his wide mouth was concealed beneath the great brush of his moustache. He wore a suit and seemed comfortable in the role of negotiator and with the boardroom surroundings. There was a new-found confidence about him though he clearly identified only with the men and their grievances, betraying little empathy for the Company élite. Frances looked at his hands. No more did the black intrude into tiny cracks and folds and she knew it was a long time since Gavin had hacked at the coal face.

He stood to speak. 'Just to set the record straight, Mrs O'Byrne, we've no come cap in hand to ye. But if you're the woman of principle that we've heard ye claim to be, then you'll give heed to some of the points we want to make.' He cleared his throat with the effort of maintaining a polite façade and fixed his eyes somewhere beyond her. 'Last year we – er, that is the Federation, spent months in negotiation with the Scottish Conciliation Board trying to enforce agreement on the minimum wage. The Fife Coal Company was the only member of the coal-owning fraternity in this area that refused to participate or give any assurances to the union that the agreement would be upheld in their own collieries. I therefore don't need to tell you how the men view the prospect of this takeover. I must warn you that we abhor the relationship between wages and the market price of coal and will resist any attempt to destroy the principle of the minimum wage.'

'And by resist, you mean strike?' Frances interjected. Mesmerised by his presence, she did not think about what she was saying.

He looked across, for the first time focussing directly on her. 'Anything it takes . . .' As he spoke, his voice tailed off and grew faint. His eyes scanned her clothes then examined her face quizzically. Suddenly his expression changed and he leaned forward, supporting himself on the table as if he might fall.

His comrade quickly grabbed him by the arm. 'Are ye all right, Gavin?' he asked but was shrugged off.

'Aye, leave me be. I just need some air.' He refused to look again at Frances but she knew now he had recognised her and could see him breathing heavily as he made for the door. Arthur Moffat followed. The rest of the group seemed startled by the unexpected turn of events and waited in silence for some news.

Eventually Moffat returned, looking somewhat embarrassed. 'I'm afraid we'll have to abandon the meeting – at least for the present.'

Frances tried not to sound too concerned. 'Is Mr Douglas all right? Is he sick or something?'

'Och, he'll be fine, it's probably just overwork.'

Garston was on his feet. 'I am sorry this unforeseen circumstance has brought things to an untimely close.'

'Wait a minute, let me have a word with him.' Frances stood up and walked across the room. 'I wouldn't want to think that one meeting with me is enough to put the health of our delegates at risk,' she smiled. There was a ripple of laughter and Arthur Moffat came forward to open the door for her. 'That's all right, Mr Moffat, I'll speak to him alone, if you don't mind.'

'Er, right – you'll find him down there in the lamproom.'

Frances went quickly down the corridor. She pushed open the creaking door and caught the intrusive smell of oil and wicking as she peered into the dimness. Lamps were hooked to the rows of shelves that lined the walls of the little room and tags hung on their chains from the empty spaces between. In the corner, Gavin leaned against the narrow window frame, his hands in his pockets.

'Don't worry, I'm alone,' she said, acknowledging the look of alarm on his face when he saw her. She walked in, shutting the door behind. 'Are you all right?'

He remained speechless but his eyes followed her, astonishment gradually superseded by contempt. It was as though an exquisite bird had flown in, so incongruous with the dismal setting. She wore a crêpe day-dress of dull Prussian blue with a high collar edged in finely pleated gauze, the yoke and gimp covered in ivory lace. The smothered quiet of the little room was somehow invaded by the rustle of her satin underskirt, its little crossways frill flouncing at the hem when she moved.

Frances felt very uneasy with the silence. 'I'm sorry if this came as a shock,' she went on. 'If I had known you would be there, I would never have agreed to the meeting. I've no wish to embarrass you, Gavin.'

His eyes narrowed. 'Aye, well ye could have fooled me, Mrs O'Byrne.'

'Och, come on – it's Frances, please.'

He shook his head in a hopeless gesture as if unable to find words to express his disillusion. 'Looks like ye got your feet tucked under somebody's fine table before he snuffed it.'

She wheeled round to meet his scornful gaze. 'That's not true – you know nothing about me.'

'I see ye sitting on the opposite side to me, is that no enough,' he shouted, blasting the words at her in a sudden assault. There was a pause then he lowered his voice to avoid attracting attention, asking exasperatedly, 'God woman, have ye no idea what position this puts me in – what the hell did ye come back for anyway?'

Frances felt wounded by his hostility. 'Merely to supervise the sale on the Thornton lease. I came by it unaware, through another transaction, and had no wish to hang on to it – I don't need to tell you why.'

'No indeed you don't! It wouldn't look too good for ye among all your posh friends if it was to get out who ye really are, eh?' He was shouting again so she raised her voice to match his.

'Or for you, Gavin!' He paused and she saw him digesting her words. 'Oh, don't worry, I'll no compromise your precious standing in the union – I owe you that much at least. As soon as this is settled, I'll be gone.'

'And you'll no care how it's settled, so long as ye get your

303

bloody price,' he hissed. 'It makes me sick to see ye holding the power to decide about men's lives – folk you lived among once, or did ye forget all that when ye came into your fortune?' He held up his hand to prevent her from interrupting. 'Aye, well, get one thing straight, fine lady, you'll no ride rough-shod over these men for you've me to contend with first!'

'Gavin, please, if you'd only listen to me. The last thing I want is to impose an unacceptable régime.'

'Och, spare me your platitudes and your fancy talk!'

'At least let me explain, tell you something about myself —'

'I've only got to look at ye – you're one o' them now, it's all I need to know.' He turned to face the window and gave a disdainful sigh as he gazed out over the grim colliery yard. 'Christ, to think that once . . .'

'Aye once,' she said quietly, moving across to where he stood. 'Does that no count for anything now?'

'After what you did to me?' Gavin swung round angrily and fixed her with a bitter stare. His words were level, measured in scorn and they made a knot in her stomach that threatened to choke her. 'I must be losing my touch. Am I no getting through to ye, Mrs O'Byrne, can ye no hear me? I feel only one thing in your presence – and that's mortal shame!'

Frances stood a few seconds in the corridor trying to compose herself before she went back to the boardroom. But it was hard to conceal her discomfiture from the anxious group who were patiently waiting. She looked pale as she spoke. 'Gentlemen, I see no cause for a further meeting at this stage, if at all.' They glanced from one to another, perturbed at the change in her tone. 'Mr Moffat, I have noted the points that have been made on behalf of the work-force and I want you to assure the men that I will give all consideration to their concerns while proceeding with the sale.'

'Er, am I to take it that ye intend to continue talks with the Fife Coal Company, Mrs O'Byrne?'

'You will be informed in due course. Thank you gentlemen, good day.'

6

Arranging a hurried meeting with the Fife Coal Company for that Thursday was easy. They were eager to do battle, confidently believing they now held the master cards. Frances too was in fighting mood. She had returned from the devastating encounter at Thornton Colliery hurt and humiliated, banging all the doors in the house and refusing supper, much to the chagrin of Mrs Heggarty. But, on the morning that she took the train bound for Dunfermline, her indignation was spent and had cooled to a plain determination. She was confirmed in her view that the trip to Scotland had been a mistake. All she wanted now was to conclude her business swiftly and without further rancour so that she could book her return passage and be home as soon as possible.

On arrival at Dunfermline station she was met by an imposing carriage and personally escorted to the company offices by the chairman of the board of directors. 'James Craig,' he said, introducing himself as he helped her into the waiting landau. 'Delighted to make your acquaintance at last, Mrs O'Byrne.' He was a tall, angular man with a very large nose, disfigured as though in some dreadful accident. Frances fought against the hypnotic need to stare at it and conversation was stilted as they made their way through the town. When they reached the imposing buildings of the Fife Coal Company, another official waited on the steps.

'This is Mr Harris, our company secretary.'

'So glad you could come to meet us, Mrs O'Byrne,' he said with an ingratiating stoop, his eyes moving over her as if peeling away the layers of clothing. He held her hand for an instant too long and Frances felt her skin crawl. But she had the measure of him. Already he was treating her as though this business was an amusing little hobby, something she could hardly be expected to take seriously.

'This way please.' Craig led her through a set of carved doors into a marble-lined entrance hall. A huge bell hung in the centre of the round area and she wandered over to inspect it.

'The shift bell from our first mine.' Harris was beside her, uncomfortably close again. 'All steam whistles now, of course. We've put a lot of new equipment into our mines. An expensive business.' Frances smiled to herself. The comment about expense

305

was not lost on her but, of course, that had been the intention.

The chairman waved towards the stairs. 'The boardroom is on the first floor. If you'll follow me?' He led the way and ushered her into a large oak-panelled room where the other members of the board waited. Frances found herself facing twenty-four men alone. A long round of introductions took place and she steeled herself for a weighty confrontation. There was a closeness, a hidden slyness about them she had rarely encountered in dealings with other businessmen. It felt as though she had stumbled into a nest of spies.

'Let me formally welcome Mrs O'Byrne to our somewhat hastily convened meeting,' Craig began, the implication being that they had inconvenienced themselves to accommodate her. 'As most of you will know, we have made some progress in our negotiations concerning the acquisition of the Thornton pit but there are still a few points on which agreement has yet to be reached – that is, before contracts can be exchanged.' He gestured to Frances. 'I believe, Mrs O'Byrne, that you wish to say a few words about this – please, the floor is yours.'

'Thank you.' Frances rose and looked round at the faces before her. They gave nothing away, their animal wariness and depth of cunning hidden beneath bland exteriors. 'I will come straight to the point, gentlemen. I am led to understand that you have certain reservations about the purchase of the Thornton Pit.' She smiled at them. 'It is always understandable to be cautious in any business transaction, but I think that here caution is being overplayed.' She pulled the summary sheets from her attaché case and passed them around. 'You have already seen the financial figures for the mine. These are historical and the forward evaluations I have made are based on conservative estimates of reserves, future markets and price variations. I take it there is no dispute on this matter?' She looked around and no one dissented. 'Good. Then we can progress to the matter of the work-force.' Several of the board members shifted in their seats. 'Now, Mr Craig, tell me when was the last time you were actually down a mine shaft?'

He was at first taken aback by the remark but quickly recovered his complacence. 'I am the chairman of the company board, not a labourer, Mrs O'Byrne.'

'Your tone implies contempt for your workers, sir. Yet should a paid officer not be aware of conditions at the coal face? You are in the business of mining but I rather think most of you have probably only ever observed it from the comfortable distance of the colliery office.'

306

Harris interrupted her rudely. 'Well, since the act of 1842 prohibited women down mines I think it highly unlikely that you can better this experience.'

'Actually you are wrong to make that assumption.'

The chairman's response barely concealed his irritation. 'Forgive me, dear lady, but a brief flirtation with gold mining in Canada hardly counts for much here.' He gave her a patronising smile and the others seemed amused at her discomfiture.

Frances tried to appear undeterred but decided against further disclosure of her past. 'Whatever you may think, gentlemen, I understand the life. It is a tough job and miners can be distrusting of change. A change of ownership is a daunting prospect for them – and their families.'

Harris spoke again. 'Mrs O'Byrne, that is all very well, but this company cannot afford to buy a Pit and also take on a long and possibly costly strike.' He glared at her. 'Which is what your men are threatening.'

'And do you know why, Mr Harris?'

She held his gaze until he answered her uncomfortably. 'Oh, it'll be something to do with new rotas, wage cuts, compensation I'll be bound.'

'You mean you have not even bothered to find out the cause of the unrest?' Blankly, they looked from one to the other and Frances let the silence speak for itself before she continued. 'Fortunately, gentlemen, despite the fact that I have only just acquired the lease, I have made it my business to show a little interest in more than just the selling price. For your information, the trouble seems to stem from the news that the Fife Coal Company is the intended purchaser of the mine.' She looked around again at the faces, none of them meeting her eyes. 'Now, that strikes me as very strange – can anybody here tell me why that might be?' She paused again to savour their unease. 'Well, no matter. I did some investigating myself and it seems your reputation in the region has preceded you. Forgive me, but that does not seem to me a good reason to drop my price.'

There was a little outburst of coughing and clearing of throats and Craig stood up. 'Mrs O'Byrne, we suggested a lower price because, as Mr Harris so rightly pointed out, a strike would cost us money. You say you have experience of mining, but I would wager it is some time since you yourself were nearer a coal face . . .' He smiled and broke off. 'I'm sorry, a gold seam, than the manager's office.' He held up a hand as she tried to speak. 'I think we are as aware as anyone else of the prevailing feelings amongst our miners and I respectfully suggest that you take care not to be wooed by excessive claims and demands. Many local men are fervent supporters of the new Independent Labour Party. They are nominating now for the general election in January.'

There were snorted mumbles of 'Disgraceful!' and 'Scandalous!' from the others.

Craig smiled wryly. 'Indeed, one of the union negotiators for Thornton has already been selected as a candidate. Frankly, madam, it matters little what the original cause of discontent might be. We cannot afford that kind of sedition to spread into our other mines. Perhaps if you were able to obtain guarantees from your work force about continued production, then we might be able to meet again on the basis of your initial price.' He shrugged and spread out his hands dramatically. 'But I doubt this will be feasible in the light of current unrest. All I can suggest is that you reconsider our revised offer and settle while you still have a proposal on the table. Do we not agree, gentlemen?' The board nodded as one.

Frances knew they were bluffing. She swallowed hard and tried to suppress her anger. 'In the course of my research I learned that although you may be the largest company in the area, you are by no means the only one.'

Harris eyed her sceptically. 'Really, Mrs O'Byrne, you cannot honestly expect to threaten us with that. If you have done your homework you will also know that among the handful of others that exist, there is not one company that could match your asking price.'

She looked at him and made no effort to disguise her contempt. 'Mr Harris, you are forgetting something – I may not have been prepared to accept a lower offer from the Fife Coal Company but I can drop the price for another buyer if I so choose.'

'If I may say so, that sounds ill-advised – er, in business terms.' His voice was agitated and his tone had grown conciliatory. 'Perhaps we should not rush into a decision at this juncture after all.'

Frances gathered the papers in front of her and pushed back the chair. 'Contrary to what you might think, gentlemen, this is not a rushed decision on my part. I had made up my mind before coming here but meeting you all merely confirmed I was right. I would not sell Thornton Pit to a parsimonious collection like you if my life depended on it!'

Craig was on his feet. 'Don't think you can make these outrageous, slanderous accusations and get away with it,' he barked.

Frances pulled on her gloves and swept to the door. 'Take me to court if you will. I can afford it and would welcome the opportunity to drag your odorous name through the mud.' Looking back at their startled faces, she nodded with satisfaction. 'Don't bother to get up, gentlemen, I'll see myself out.'

7

The days passed and though she was kept busy in locating a new buyer, Frances grew more and more detached from her surroundings. It was now mid-December and though she knew it would mean travelling home over the Christmas period, she was anxious to get away. The episode with Gavin had doused any vague thoughts she might once have had about being re-united with her family and she had successfully eluded drawing any attention from that quarter. Fortunately, too, the men from the Thornton bided their time, waiting for news and there was no immediate threat of unrest. By the twentieth of the month, she was able to confirm to Garston and the management that negotiations had been entered into with the Dundee and Angus Coal Company.

'The union will be well pleased with this, Mrs O'Byrne,' he said, equally delighted that he was to remain in post. 'I will announce it to them at once.'

'No, Mr Garston, it would be better to wait until everything is settled. With Christmas and New Year almost upon us, I would imagine that it will be early January before the contracts are exchanged. I will not be able to stay till then as it is time I went home. My return is long overdue.' They were speaking on the telephone and Frances looked through the window and saw the frozen outline of the laburnum shaken by the swelling wind.

'As you please.' He hesitated, wondering whether to say something complimentary. She had certainly opened his eyes to some remarkable skills, hitherto unacknowledged in a woman, and he had reluctantly developed a deepening respect. 'It has been a pleasure doing business with you —'

But the sentiment was not reciprocated. 'Thank you,' she said briefly, cutting him short. 'Mr Moskow will conclude the sale of the pit and once he has done so, you may make whatever announcements you wish to the work force.' With that, she replaced the earphone on its hook.

Frances had forgotten how quickly the weather could change in this part of the world. There was a threatening squall in the air and she changed her mind about walking into town. Instead, she asked Donald to get the motorcar ready to take her to the telegraph office where she was to cable Edmonton of her imminent travel plans. He appeared ten minutes later in a full chauffeur's outfit of dark-green brass-buttoned jacket, matching breeches, leather gaiters and gauntlet gloves. A peaked hat with fitted goggles sat snugly under his arm as he awaited her comment.

She smiled. 'Goodness, that's impressive. But is it really necessary?'

'Well, ye said it was your last trip in the automobile, madam, so I thought ye would like to do it in style.'

All heads turned as they chugged over the cobblestones and down into the body of the town. Donald delighted in broadcasting their arrival round every corner by pumping the hooter for all it was worth and, as they slowed to a halt, a little crowd quickly gathered. Frances was grateful however that their attention was drawn more to the vehicle than herself. When she re-emerged from the telegraph office, Donald was still engrossed in exhibitionist polishing of the mudguards and other superfluous chores.

Beneath an unseasonable striped awning to her left, a sign across a large plate-glass window proclaimed: REAL ITALIAN ICE CREAM. The exterior of the shop was painted in bright, gaudy colours and adorned by cunningly drawn pictures of heaped bowls of ice-cream, the mounds punctured by coronas of exotic wafers and slithering with sauces. Thus seduced, Frances decided to sample the wares. She glanced back at the preoccupied crowd around the car and slipped inside unnoticed. A bell tinkled in the back as she entered. The shop was busy, with a group of barefoot urchins clustered around the woman serving at the counter. The front part of the parlour was set out with small circular tables, each covered by a bright, red-and-white checked cloth, wooden chairs neatly tucked under the draped folds. A rich smell of vanilla and strawberries hung on the air.

'Can I have a cornet, Mrs Bagiotti?' A little girl's voice rose from the back of the clamouring children.

'Bide your time, lassie. I've only the one pair of hands.' It was the intonation that Frances recognised first and she stood rooted to the spot, gazing at the woman distributing cones and wafers to her eager customers. In sixteen years, Jeannie Adamson had grown from a plump young woman into the matronly figure they always knew she would become. Her reddish hair was pulled back and twisted into a bun at the nape of her neck, the pepper and salt effect of the grey somehow incongruous, framing the ruddy laughing face that still held a compelling freshness and innocence. Her eyes were lively, and she joked with the youngsters, all of them demanding to be served first.

Looking up momentarily, Jeannie saw the elegant woman standing uncertainly in the doorway. 'Oh, sorry to keep you waiting, madam. I'll no be a minute.'

Frances nodded, not trusting herself to speak. She felt nervous, wondering if she should just leave now and let the past lie undisturbed. The children had called her Mrs Bagiotti – of course, she thought, it had to be Carlo, and smiled inwardly recalling the brash young Italian who had vainly tried to woo Jeannie at the Links Market. He had obviously persevered and succeeded.

Jeannie called out to a door at the back of the shop. 'Marco! Maria! Get out here and give me a hand.' Two youngsters came through to the front shop, each unmistakably stamped with the Bagiotti image. The girl had the same dark hair and eyes as her brother, but as she approached Frances, her shy smile was Jeannie all over again. 'Can I get you something?' she asked.

Frances shook her head. 'I've not quite decided. Help your mother with the others and I'll have a think.' She watched Jeannie and her son and daughter serve the children and felt a sudden constriction in her throat. How tall Marco was, thin like his father, but with a hint of the man's strength to come. Rory would have been about the same age now.

The children, quietly concentrating on their ice-creams, scuttled from the shop and Jeannie's own two disappeared into the back again. The women were left alone. 'I'm sorry to have kept you, madam. What can I get you?' Jeannie looked respectfully at Frances. Not many of the local toffs came in by themselves for an ice-cream, usually they sent a maid with a big earthenware bowl to collect their indulgences.

Frances held her voice steady, unsure of quite how to play the situation. 'What flavours do you have?'

'Strawberry, vanilla, raspberry, chocolate . . .' Jeannie leaned forward as though confiding a great secret. 'But for the truly discerning sweet tooth, I would recommend the cassata. My Carlo makes the best cassata in Scotland, not to mention Italy.'

At the same time, a head appeared from the stairway that rose to a large steel trap-door at the end of the counter. 'What are you telling about me?' the man asked, wiping his hands on a cotton towel and pulling the trap-door shut. He bowed slightly, seeing Frances. 'Good morning, signora.'

She nodded back and smiled. He had hardly changed at all, still as thin as a whip, his hair black and gleaming. It was easy to tell who did all the tasting in this family. Carlo walked over to join his wife.

'I was just saying, how your cassata is the best there is.'

'Well, that is not for me to say – but it is all home-made. Downstairs I have the finest ice-cream factory in Scotland. All the equipment is imported from Italy, at great cost.' He broke off and looked hard at Frances. 'Excuse me, signora, but I know you?'

Jeannie nudged him in the ribs. 'Dinna be forward, Carlo,' she muttered.

Frances gave him a reluctant smile. 'Mamma mia,' he breathed and clutched Jeannie's arm, making her jump. 'Frances. It's Frances!'

Disbelieving, Jeannie's lips trembled as she stared across the counter. Frances's eyes misted with tears and she nodded her head. 'Och, Jeannie, do ye no ken me?' she whispered, hardly able to form the words. Suddenly her hands were grasped and she felt herself being pulled into a tight embrace. The next few moments were a confusion of tears and laughter, each of them trying to talk at once. Carlo ran to lock the door, putting up the CLOSED FOR LUNCH sign and Frances was led through into the back room, her old friend still sobbing incoherently and clinging to her hand.

'Come on, Jeannie,' she said, 'you'll make yourself ill.'

When the tears finally did stop, Jeannie sniffed into a large handkerchief and smiled up at her. 'I'd never have known ye. Never!' She looked at the enormous hat with its cornucopia of shivering black feathers, the embroidered beadwork on the collar, the kid gloves. 'My God, you two must have done well for yourselves out there!'

Carlo had joined them. 'Aye, and where is my friend William? Are you here on holidays – you did bring him with you?' he laughed.

Frances gripped Jeannie's hands. 'William died a year after we left. I — I'm sorry that I couldn't let you know,' she said, seeing the sadness on their faces.

'Oh, Frances, that's awful. Have ye been by yourself all that time?'

'No, not all the time.' She pulled out a lacy handkerchief and wiped her eyes. They wanted to know more but she attempted to steer the talk away from herself. 'Can we just leave that for now? Anyway, I want to know about you two. Look at how well you've

312

done. Come on, Jeannie Adamson, tell me how you let yourself get caught by this rogue.'

They took no notice. 'How long have ye been back, Frances?'

'About three weeks now.'

'What, three weeks and ye never came to see us? Shame on ye! But you'll have been to see the family though?'

'No,' she faltered. 'I've not been over there. It's difficult for me, you can understand that.'

Jeannie squeezed her hand. 'Aye, well, I'm right sorry about what's happened.'

'What? I don't know, tell me.'

'I dinna right ken where to start. Listen, I'll put the kettle on first and make us a cup of tea.' She rose and went through to the kitchen. 'Carlo, come and bring ben the tray.'

Frances felt her stomach churn, wondering what she was going to learn now. When they eventually returned with a large brown teapot, she asked urgently, 'Tell me now, please.'

Jeannie sat facing her and held her hand again. 'Your father. He died of a stroke about seven years ago.'

Frances was unmoved. 'I'm sorry but you know I'll shed no tears for him. What about my mother?'

'She's ... no well, Frances. Rob and his family take care of her now.'

'What's wrong with her?'

'Och, it's hard to explain – ye should go and see her. It wouldn't matter now your father's gone.'

'Rob's married, then?'

Jeannie nodded in reply. 'Aye, he got himself a right fine lassie from Methil. I think Maureen's her name.'

'And what about Chrissie and Jack, are they all right?'

'Would ye believe it, they're in New Zealand! Jack's chest got worse and the doctor said the climate out there would suit him better. They're doing right well, according to Rob. He gets a letter every Christmas.' She looked at Frances. 'But ye ken I dinna hear much of them now since I moved out of the Wemyss.'

'I know I should have gone to see them but I was scared, Jeannie. I didn't know what to expect.'

'You, scared? – ha!' Carlo gave an exaggerated laugh.

'Aye, me.' She smiled back at him. 'But come on, what happened with you two? Why did you not go back to Italy?'

In the midst of the story, once they had described the wedding and Carlo had reached the bit about having saved enough to buy

313

his own shop, the back door suddenly burst open and a crowd of children came rushing into the small room.

'Be quiet and behave! Can ye no see we have a visitor?' Jeannie's voice was formidable and Frances watched in astonishment as the children lined themselves up between their mother and father.

'Are they all yours?'

Jeannie nodded with pride. 'You've met the two oldest, Marco – he's fourteen.'

'I'm nearly fifteen,' the boy protested.

'Dinna interrupt. And Maria – she's twelve.' The girl smiled at Frances as her mother continued. 'Then there's Guglielmo, he's ten. Carlo named him for William.' She pushed forward a robust little boy whose hair was lighter than the rest. 'Say hallo to the lady.'

Frances held out her hand to him. 'Pleased to meet you, Guglielmo,' she said and he shook her hand shyly.

'And this little madam,' she affectionately pulled a gangly bright-eyed girl in front of her, 'is Francesca, your namesake. She is nine.' Tears clouded Frances's eyes as the girl bobbed a curtsey and shot back behind her mother's chair. 'Then we have Luigi, seven; the twins, Mario and Katerina at five; Angelo, four; and last but not least, Vincente – he's two.' She picked up the toddler, glancing at Carlo with finality. 'And he will be our last!'

'All fine Scottish names, Jeannie,' Frances laughed, bewildered by the row of faces before her. She turned to Carlo. 'You've been busy, Mr Bagiotti – and no just with the ice-cream!'

He grinned back at her. 'We need them all to grow up for to help us in the shop.' He waved his hands to indicate the small premises. 'Already we grow out of this place. Soon, I want to buy another shop at the end of the High Street.' He shrugged. 'Who knows? – one day, every town in Scotland will have la gelateria Bagiotti!' He shooed the children back into the kitchen and Jeannie got up to follow them.

'If one of us is no there to keep an eye on them at the dinner table, it's pandemonium,' she said to Frances.

'I should be going anyway.'

'Oh no, I'm not sending ye off yet, I've no heard all your news about Canada. But it'll be hopeless trying to talk with all that noise going on.' She jerked her head towards the kitchen. 'Tell ye what, why don't ye come back tonight and we'll have a special meal?'

'We insist,' Carlo added. 'And I will make a ragout!'

'How can I refuse?' Frances smiled.

314

Jeannie walked with her to the door. 'Will ye be going to the Wemyss then?'

'Aye, I'll take a trip out there now, while my courage holds.'

'That's right, I think ye should, Frances.'

'Well, after what you've told me I'm worried about my mother. And since I'm planning to leave tomorrow . . .'

'Och, I hate to think that you've been here all this time and we didna ken, and now you're talking of going back already.'

'To tell you the truth, Jeannie, I had some business here, the trip wasn't exactly planned. Once I arrived – well, it just seemed easier to be Mrs O'Byrne.'

Realisation dawned on Jeannie. 'Mrs O'Byrne! The papers are full of the Canadian woman in Fergus Place – and it's you!' For a moment she rummaged in a pile of old newspapers then abandoned the search. 'Where did you get the name? Ye must've married again after William died?'

Frances smiled and waved the questions aside. 'Yes, but I can't tell you everything at once – let's leave it till tonight, can we?'

'If you say so, I canna wait. Now, will ye be all right going to the Wemyss on your own? I could always come with ye if ye like?'

'Thanks Jeannie, but no. I should do it myself. Tell me, where will I find them?'

'Och, they're all in the same auld hoose, what do ye expect?'

Frances shivered. 'I'll be glad to come back here tonight – I might need a sympathetic ear.'

'Well, you're always welcome here.'

The two women embraced warmly and reluctantly let go. 'I'll see you later then.'

Jeannie tugged her arm. 'Oh, ye ken who you'll no see in the Wemyss?' she said, slyly. 'Gavin Douglas. He was awful quiet for a long time after – well, you know – but he's biding in the Coaltown o' Balgonie now. Done right well for himself with his union work, I hear. And, wait till I tell you – he's standing for election to Parliament with the Labour Party – would ye credit that?'

'Really?' Frances raised her brows in what she hoped was a gesture of detached surprise. 'Well anyway, like I said, I must be going.'

Jeannie could sense a discordant note in her voice and refrained from pursuing the matter. 'All right, we'll see ye later on,' she said. Then added hesitantly, 'Ye will come back now, won't ye?'

'Of course,' Frances laughed. 'Besides, I never got my ice-cream!'

8

The appearance of a motorcar in West Wemyss had heads poking out of every window as it made its bumpy progress along the main street towards the church. Frances stepped out and a blast of raw salt air stung her face. 'Turn round and wait for me along at the harbour end, Donald. I'll be a while.'

'Yes, madam.' He asked no questions, dutifully tipped his hat and returned to the driving seat. A crowd of curious children were beginning to gather. 'Keep your dirty paws off!' he snapped curtly.

Frances opened the creaking gate and made her way into the bleak, deserted graveyard. She had forgotten how small it all was. The cramped streets, the tiny houses backing onto each other – even the church that she had remembered as a large impressive edifice now seemed hardly bigger than a cottage. The graveyard too was crammed with stones, the dead as closely packed together as the living. As she moved slowly along the rows, suddenly an inscription caught her eye.

Elspeth Mary Douglas
Dearly beloved wife of
John.
Born August 12th 1810
Died April 14th 1893

What little space there was around the grave was trimmed and well tended and showed that someone came often, perhaps finding solace in the place. The thought left her sad as she remembered the gentle honesty of the old woman and she placed a kiss on her finger and touched Elspeth's stone as she passed.

Walking on, Frances came to the Rintoul family plot. Her grand-father lay here, apparently having died just a few months after she left. Poor old soul, she thought – coughing out his life in his surly son-in-law's cheerless hovel. But she was moved to see the headstone was carved in parrot coal, a fitting gesture to the old man. Next to this, her father's. 'Henry James Rintoul.' Defiantly she spoke the words out loud as if to challenge any residue of doubt about his passing. 'Rest in Peace.' She grimaced. 'Aye, ye deserve it – like

316

the peace ye gave to us.' But though provoked by bitterness, she knew he could not hurt her now and a vague relief remained.

The wind buffeted her clothes and she thrust her cold hands back into the snug sanctuary of her muff remembering all too well the frozen dampness in the air she once lived with. Then at last her eyes strayed from the church back down the main street towards the old Rintoul home. Frances sighed, unsure of what to expect. When they had driven past the family house on their arrival, she had looked away. Now, walking back towards it under the scrutiny of the faces at the windows, she felt more vulnerable and pulled her collar up to shield her identity. Pausing at the old familiar door she rapped twice, but cautiously. It was strange to await an answer and not to walk straight in.

A small, mousy woman opened the latch and peered out uncertainly. Her eyes widened in fear when she saw the grandly dressed stranger. 'What is it?' she asked nervously.

'Is Rob in?'

She shook her head. 'No, he's on day-shift. He's no back till four.'

'Can I come in?'

Again the suspicious look. 'What for? Are you from the Parish about his ma?'

'No.' Frances forced a reassuring smile. 'I'm Rob's sister. I've come from Canada to see him and my mother.'

'You're Frances? My God!' She looked her up and down. 'My God,' she repeated.

'Well, can I come in then and wait till Rob comes back from his work?'

The door was swung open. 'Aye, I'm sorry, come away ben.' The woman held out her hand awkwardly and Frances shook it. 'I'm Maureen, by the way. Rob's wife.'

The house had not changed at all and Frances doubted if it had been repainted since the day she left. A large fire burned in the grate and another wizened figure sat hunched in front of it, just as Grandpa had once done. But this was a woman.

'Ma?' Frances approached cautiously, hardly recognising the skeletal form in the chair. 'Ma? It's me, Frances.' Two vacant eyes stared up at her and the old woman made a vague, incoherent sound. 'Do ye no ken me, Ma?'

'She's no too well.' Maureen stood wringing her hands awkwardly. 'She's no been right since your Dad . . .'

'It's all right, I know he's dead.'

Maureen shook her head. 'No, it was before that.'

317

Something in her voice troubled Frances. 'What did he do to her?'

'I'm no sure I should be saying this —'

'Tell me, Maureen.' She snapped at the other woman, then tried to reassure her with a forced smile. 'I am family, remember?'

'Well, he'd been drinking right heavy, and laid off work ill. He come back one night and near killed her. Knocked her head about.' She looked away from the burning stare, her voice barely audible as she unfolded the dreadful truth. 'She got better, slowly. But she'd lost her wits – been like this ever since.'

'The black-hearted bastard!' Frances seethed with a rage that she knew had no outlet. She turned and looked at her mother, putting her hand tenderly on the frail shoulder, but the woman flinched and tried to pull away. 'It's all right, Ma. It's me.' Unaffected by the rebuff, Frances held onto her, stroking and soothing the pathetic, shaking wretch.

'She doesn't ken ye, I'm afraid – nor anybody else.'

'God, Maureen, this is awful. How do ye cope?'

'Och, we manage well enough. There's folks in the Wemyss worse off than us.' She smiled self-effacingly. 'But I'm forgetting my manners, would ye like a cup of tea?'

While Maureen busied herself with the kettle, Frances continued speaking softly to Jessie, but could elicit no coherent response. Time and again, her mother's eyes would stray to her face and move past, unrecognising. Reluctantly, Frances left her and was encouraged to sit at the table. The heat in the room was stifling and she removed her hat and gloves. 'How long have you and Rob been married?'

Maureen told her, adding, 'And we've just the three bairns. Henry, James and Robert. They're all at the school.' She eyed Frances curiously now, her initial fear gone. 'And you seem to be doing all right.'

'Aye, it looks that way, eh? Did Rob not tell you about me?'

Maureen looked uneasy. 'He never spoke about ye – none of them did.'

'What, not even Chrissie?'

'She was emigrated afore I knew Rob.'

Frances realised that Maureen had been told nothing and steered the conversation away from her past. 'It was New Zealand they went to, wasn't it?'

'Aye.' Maureen opened a drawer and pulled out a handful of letters. In one was a photograph taken in a studio in Nelson. Chrissie and Jack had been posed at a small table, surrounded by their children. Everyone was dressed in their best clothes with stiff expressions and it was hard to tell from their faces whether or not they were happy. Jack looked healthy enough though a hint of pain and tiredness still played around Chrissie's eyes. Frances jotted down the address. 'I'll need to write and tell her I've been back.'

The conversation between the two of them became easier, and they quickly lost track of time. Occasionally, Jessie would let out a soft moan and Frances would rise and go to her. 'Dinna bother,' Maureen said, 'she's fine. She just sounds bad.'

'What about doctors – the hospital, can't they do anything?'

'Oh aye? And where would we get the money for all that?' Maureen forgot her polite deference for a moment then quickly recovered herself. 'Anyway, the local doctor's seen her and he said there's nothing he can do.'

Before Frances could make any reply, the door opened and Rob strode into the room. 'There's a big fancy motorcar down at —' He stopped abruptly, seeing the elegant visitor. 'What the . . . ?'

Frances came over into the light. 'Hello Rob,' she smiled.

He looked at her closely. 'Frances?' She nodded and reached out to embrace him but he backed away and she stood uncertainly as he examined her. 'Is it yours then, that motor out there?'

'Aye.' She suddenly felt uncomfortable and embarrassed by the fact. 'But Rob, it's good to see ye.'

'Nice of ye to drop by and see how we're doing.' He gestured angrily around. 'Ye can tell we're doing fine.'

'Don't be like that, Rob. It's been ages since I've seen ye.'

'Aye, and no long enough if ye ask me.' He continued to glare at her in anger.

'Why are ye saying this? The past is done and over with.'

'It may be for you but it was us that had to live with it. Black affronted we were at the shame you brought on this hoose, whoring off with that brigger, and leaving your bridegroom standing at the altar. Aye, it was a fine juicy bit of gossip that kept the tongues in the Wemyss waggling for months.'

'Rob, for Christ's sake, that was nigh on sixteen years ago.'

'Ye thought we'd forget, eh? Is that why ye came back – so ye could shove your fancy clothes and shiny motorcar down our throats – make us look stupid again, eh?'

His face had flooded with high colour and Maureen grew anxious and gripped his arm. 'Rob, she's your sister, have a heart.'

'Shut up, woman! Ye dinna ken the half o' it,' he boomed. 'I suppose ye've just spent the whole afternoon bletherin' – where's my bath and my dinner?'

Frances was shocked by the outburst. 'I can't believe what I'm seeing, you're behaving just like him.'

Rob turned to her. 'Dinna tell me what I can and canna do in my own hoose,' he roared, threateningly.

Maureen intervened again. 'Rob, leave her be.'

He whirled round and thumped his fist on the table. 'I've told ye, woman, dinna interfere!'

Frances felt her breath coming in short gasps and fought to calm herself. 'What's happened to ye – why are ye like this?'

'Oh, ye expected me to be pleased to see ye then? We never heard a word from ye neither.'

'Is that what he told you? Did you not know I wrote to Dad seven years ago?'

'One letter, aye, and so ashamed he was, he couldn't even show it to the rest of us.'

'But I was trying to help.'

'Liar! I saw what it did to him. We dinna need your kind o' help. This family's always looked after itself.'

Her own anger burned now. 'Oh, aye? And what did you ever do all those times Dad raised his hand to me and Ma?' She spat the words contemptuously. 'I'll tell ye – ye crawled like a skelped dug into the back room and never looked near. Ye coward, ye were always the same and I see you've no changed.' He waved his fist in a furious gesture of frustration and she thrust her face towards him. 'Aye, go on, Rob, be a man. Hit me. Like father, like son.'

His whole body was shaking but he lowered his arm.

'Frances, you're wrong,' Maureen interjected, trying to take the heat out of the moment. 'He's no like his father,' she said quietly.

A loud moaning came from the corner as the old woman rocked back and forth in her chair. Rob went across to where she sat. 'These hands,' he said, holding them out to Frances and mouthing the words with his jaw taut, 'have ripped at a coal face down a bloody pit every day, year in and year out, to keep my wife and my bairns and your mother.' He shouted at her. 'Your mother, do ye hear! What did you ever do but make her greet?'

Jessie was screeching convulsively now, and trying to rise from her chair. Rob put his arms around her. 'It's all right, Ma, it's all right.' He glared back at Frances. 'See, you're upsetting her. So why do ye no just fuck off out o' here back to wherever ye came from.'

'Rob, that's enough of that talk!'

'It's all right, Maureen,' Frances said, grateful however for the support. 'I'm used to it and I see that's all I'll get here.' She looked sadly at her mother. 'But let me do something for her, Rob. Can we no at least talk?'

'You've nothing we need or want. Get to hell out of my hoose,' he bellowed, pointing to the door. Jessie clutched at the air and fell forwards, her lips flecked with foam and a low keening noise rattling in her throat. 'You did this to her,' he accused, jabbing his finger at his mother. 'You and your fancy notions.'

Frances shook her head. 'No Rob,' she denied coldly. 'It was him did this to her.'

He glared suspiciously at his wife. 'What have ye been telling her?'

Maureen was picking the old woman up from the floor. 'Nothing she couldn't work out for herself, Rob.' She looked at Frances. 'You'd best go.'

'Aye, but please think about it, I've got money now, I want to help.'

'What, so ye can buy yourself a clear conscience?' He came to stand in front of her and then barked with sudden violence into her face. 'We dinna want your filthy money. So just get out, and keep away from me and mine!'

'Please?' Frances begged in a weak voice. But Rob was unmoving and in the silence, she had no choice but to make blindly for the door.

As it slammed with finality behind her she felt the past repeat itself and dragged her feet slowly away. With a last despairing glance at the dismal row of cottages, the twitching curtains and the bell-tower between, she approached the harbour end. Even there she was faced with a humiliating prospect. She and Donald had reluctantly to elicit the support of several passers-by to help push the car back up the steep brae. It had been an easy free-wheel down into the village but leaving was another matter and the embarrassment for both of them was total. At the top, Frances gazed down again and, for a few seconds before she climbed back inside, the stiffening breeze from the Forth dried the tears that streamed down her face.

Frances had Donald drive her straight back to the ice-cream parlour and then dismissed him for the evening. It was a blessing to enter the warmth of a welcoming family atmosphere after the disastrous reunion in West Wemyss. She related the details in the kitchen while helping Jeannie to prepare the enormous dinner. Breaking down, she allowed herself to be comforted as she sobbed out the hurt and pain. Carlo listened sympathetically and waited until he judged the moment was right before coming to join them. Lightening the mood, he spouted snatches of Italian opera and Scottish street rhymes as he

321

cooked the richly seasoned ragout, not entirely trusting his wife, he reminded them, with so important a dish.

When it was ready, they were joined by the children and Frances quickly cheered up in their company. After enthusing at great length in praise of the ragout, they overcame their initial shyness and soon bombarded her with questions about life in Canada. 'Is it true ye bide with a real Red Indian squaw?' asked Marco, wide-eyed.

She nodded. 'That's right, her name is Pi'taki and she's very dear to me. As good a friend as your mother ever was – and is.' She held Jeannie's eyes and she blushed.

The meal was crowned by a Carlo's special ice-cream bombe, served on an enormous cut-glass dish and tasting better than any dessert Frances had ever eaten.

'I'm not surprised at the size of ye, Jeannie, when he feeds ye like this all the time,' Frances declared with a satisfied but discreet belch as they finished.

'Ye impudent madam! Just because there's no an ounce of fat on you, dinna get personal with me.' Jeannie grinned at her cheekily. 'Besides, think yourself lucky. He only ever cooks like this once in a blue moon. The rest of the time it's my mince and tatties and lentil soup.' The children all held their noses and made rude comments about their mother's cooking until she had had enough and sent them off to wash the dishes.

After the Bagiotti offspring had reluctantly gone to bed, the three happily retired to the over-stuffed armchairs in the living-room. Carlo opened a special bottle of wine for the occasion, though they all hesitated to call it a celebration. Still saddened by the news of William's death, he insisted they drank the first toast to his memory. Frances felt curiously detached however and although they plied her with questions about Canada, she was still pre-occupied with her mother.

'I'm sorry,' she apologised. 'I just can't get what happened this afternoon out of my mind, it pained me to see my mother in such a state.'

'We understand,' Jeannie said, patting her hand. 'But if you're away the morn, what can ye do?'

'What can I do if I stay?' She looked appealingly at the other two.

'Give it a bit of time?' Jeannie ventured. 'Maybe ye can talk some sense into Rob.'

'Do ye think so? He was like a demented thing, there's no way he will accept any help from me.'

'Well, you'll no change anything by getting on that boat and running away.'

'She's right, Frances,' Carlo joined in. 'What can you lose by staying a bit longer?'

Frances sighed. 'Oh, a few days wouldn't make any difference, it's not that, Carlo. I just don't want it all starting up again. All that bad feeling between me and the family. Rob and Maureen would be better off without me around to re-open the old wounds. I just seem to be trouble.'

Jeannie decided to intervene. 'Frances Rintoul, are ye telling me that a woman like you with all your money and connections and what have ye – that ye canna handle a wee nyaff like Rob? Surely to goodness if ye want to make provision for your own mother nobody can stop ye?'

Frances smiled. 'All right, you've made your point. I'm sorry but all this has just left me feeling like an outcast again. Now ye know why I didn't want to come back in the first place.'

'Aye well, you're no an outcast here.'

'I know, and I appreciate that, Jeannie.' Frances looked at her friends affectionately. 'Well, since it looks like I'll be here for Christmas, why don't you all come and spend it with me at the big house. Please, I'd really love that.'

They looked from one to another. 'That would be rare, Frances, we'd like that. And so would the bairns – they've fair taken a shine to ye!'

'Then it's agreed!' Frances glanced at the clock. 'Now I'd better go, it's been a long day and I'm near sleeping.' She rose and Carlo went to fetch her coat. He insisted that he escort her home, even though her house was but a few minutes' walk from their shop and, after many cheery goodbyes on the doorstep, they stepped out into the frosty air. A harsh wind was picking up, blowing leaves around their feet as they made their way uphill. But the wine and the friendship had warmed a glow within them. When at last they reached the drive and had trudged up to the front door, Carlo kissed her on each cheek.

'William was right about you, he said you were a brave woman. And after all you have told us tonight, I know it is true.'

Frances hugged him. 'Bless you, Carlo, for that. And for being here when I needed you.' She went indoors, promising to call in and see them the next day and make arrangements for Christmas.

9

By Christmas Day, the snow lay deeply in drifts against the wall of the house and the trees in the garden stood weighted by the heavy fall that sugared their naked branches. Everything was even and there was no end to the pavement or sign of where the road began. Periodically, a displaced heap would slide from the roof and smash into powder below but otherwise there was a smothered stillness in the air.

Inside was a different story. In the corner of the parlour a Christmas tree towered to the ceiling. Wreathed in ribbons and glittering trinkets, its resinous smell filled the room. The glass decorations shimmered in the gentle light of candles set around and the children's rosy faces glowed in front of a blazing fire. Oranges stuck with cloves, toasted marshmallows and chestnut cinders lay scattered in the grate before them. One or two were already feeling the weight of sleep on their eyelids. Vincente lay sprawled across the chaise longue with his head resting on Frances's lap. 'I don't think he's going to last out till tea-time,' she mused, stroking his hair.

Jeannie looked on. 'Ye should've had more bairns of your own, Frances. Think what a life ye could have given them.'

Carlo came and put his arm round his wife's shoulder. 'Jeannie is right, you know. Look how the children love to be with you. These holidays have been so happy for them, coming here to this house, riding in the automobile – it's like they have known you all their life.'

'Well, remember that when I go back, I'm holding you to your promise to come and visit. The bairns will love it. It's so beautiful there and has so much space for them to run around . . .'

Carlo saw the wistful look in her eyes. 'I can see you miss the place.'

She gave a sad smile. 'Aye.' She carefully laid the sleeping boy to one side and rose to her feet. 'Come on, I'll replenish our drinks.'

Jeannie followed her over to the glass cabinet. 'Why don't ye come with us next week to the Wemyss and see in the New Year at my ma's house? You shouldn't be on your own for Hogmanay.'

Frances shook her head emphatically. 'If I bumped into Rob, it would just ruin everybody's enjoyment. Thanks anyway,' she squeezed Jeannie's hand and smiled, 'but I would rather stay here and get my packing done.'

As the day progressed into early evening, the children, one by one, succumbed to sleep and Carlo carried their limp bodies upstairs to bed. Frances had let it be known that she would be holding open house for the night and a fiddler and accordion player had been brought in to provide the entertainment. The gathered visitors warmed to the cheery atmosphere, although many of the local dignitaries had called out of pure curiosity, under the guise of paying their respects. But they soon found themselves tapping their feet to the music as they were persuaded to relax formalities and enjoy the party.

Much of the talk was of the coming election and the demise of Conservative support. Frances was drawn into conversation with members of the local Liberal hierarchy who seemed confident of a landslide victory in the impending poll. She was not surprised at the dearth of enthusiasm for the new Labour Party and in different circumstances might have savoured the challenge of debating this new force in politics, flying in the face of social mores and relishing the opportunity to derogate the hypocrites in their midst. But the spectre of the pit dispute and her own position held her back.

She was biting her tongue as she listened to one particularly reactionary argument when Jeannie came over. 'Frances, look at who's just walked in,' she said, pointing discreetly to the door.

Frances had to look for some time before she remembered the faces. 'My God,' she breathed. 'Not the Doigs – what the hell are they doing here?'

'Arse licking, what else?' Jeannie glared at the couple who were beginning to circulate, looking for their hostess.

'Not in my house they don't. Come on.' Frances made her way towards them through the dense mass of people, Jeannie close behind.

'My dear Mrs O'Byrne,' Doig began as she reached them, 'allow me to introduce myself.' He offered his hand. 'Archibald Doig, works manager out at Nairn's Linoleum and Quality Flooring Manufacturers. You may have heard of them?' Frances was suddenly transported back in time by the fawning tenor of his voice and the shining, swollen face. She ignored his outstretched hand and he peered at her anxiously. There was an irritated cough from his left and he turned to acknowledge the abiding presence of his spouse, her tight mouth and narrow eyes screwed up in an ingratiating smile. 'May I introduce my good lady wife, Euphemia.'

325

'I know who you are,' said Frances, curtly, 'and I would be obliged if you would leave. Now.'

'I beg your pardon?' Doig stared at her in disbelief.

'You heard her,' Jeannie butted in.

'Adamson! What on earth are you doing here?' Euphemia Doig looked from one woman to the other and her mouth dropped open in comprehension. 'Archibald, it's the Rintoul girl.'

'Are ye mad, Effie?' he hissed. 'It canna ...' He stopped as he looked searchingly into Frances's outraged eyes. 'Good God Almighty!'

Frances thrust her face closer into his. 'Out! Before I have somebody throw you out.'

Doig looked like an over-ripe plum that was about to explode. He grabbed his wife's arm and tugged her away. 'Come, Euphemia. We're obviously in the wrong place.' Red-faced and mortified, they made their way to the door.

'Well, Frances did that make ye feel better?' Jeannie asked.

'You'd think it would, but no. There were times when I'd have given anything to get my own back. But it's not important any more.' She linked her arm in Jeannie's. 'Forget them. Finding you and Carlo happy means much more to me.' They started back into the heart of the gathering. 'Mind you, I never expected I'd find ye with all those bairns. Who'd've thought it!'

Jeannie laughed. 'That auld spaewife did. D'ye no mind the gypsy at the Links Market that told our fortunes? And you were that angered!'

'Oh, her.' Frances shrugged at the memory. 'She was a charlatan, said I'd marry a miner.'

'Ye did. Only it was gold and no coal he was digging.'

'I dinna think that's what she had in mind.'

'Well, she was right about me.' Jeannie hesitated. 'Nearly right anyway.'

Frances laughed. 'Did she have room in her crystal ball for nine bairns?'

'No, not exactly.' Jeannie looked uncomfortable and checked to make sure no one would hear. 'She said – well, she said I'd have thirteen —'

'Thirteen! My God!'

'Aye, but I've made up my mind – nine's the finish o' it.'

'And Carlo – have ye told him it's finished?'

'He does as he's told.' She saw the look on Frances's face and laughed. 'Aye, all right, I ken it takes two.'

'What takes two?' Carlo had come up behind them and Jeannie jumped.

'To throw out unwelcome guests,' Frances filled the sudden silence. 'We're just after putting out the rubbish.'

Reminded of the incident, Jeannie grew serious again. 'Still, I'm surprised you let them know who ye are. They'll no keep quiet about it.'

'Och, can you honestly see either of that pair telling anybody that they were thrown out of Mrs O'Byrne's because they once sacked her? Anyway, I'll be away in a week.' She waved away any further mention of the Doigs. 'Come on, we've a wheen o' partying to do, and I think it's time we got the dancing started.'

10

'Grandtully',
Fergus Place,
Kirkcaldy
Wednesday, 27th December, 1905

My dear Christian,

Learning of your recovered health brought me great joy and relieved some of the anxiety caused by my own culpability. Many thanks for the long letter relating all the news from Edmonton. I apologise if my delayed departure has caused you such worry but I trust you will heed Pi'taki – you commented somewhat sceptically that she seemed to sense all would be well with me here. Never discount her judgement for a moment – although things have developed in a way I would not have chosen, I still feel that I will have resolved matters to my own satisfaction before I leave.

I celebrated Christmas here with old friends, and the warmth and joy they occasioned made me very homesick for Canada. I trust that you, Pi'taki and the staff all enjoyed the festivities and promise to make up for my lack of presents (and presence!) upon my return.

I have enclosed with this letter some notes I made on the business matters we discussed. Please take care of these before I get back. As to when exactly that will be, I am happy to announce at last that I will be leaving Kirkcaldy on the second of January. The sale of the Thornton lease has not been as straightforward as either of us initially imagined, the main difficulty being to achieve a new owner who is acceptable in the eyes of the work force. As you know from previous dealings, this is an area about which

327

I feel most strongly. Fortunately, after exhaustive enquiries and negotiations, we located the Dundee and Angus Coal Company who seem to admirably fit the bill and I am delighted to say that contracts were exchanged today. I must inform you however that monies from the sale of the Thornton Pit will not be transacted through our Canadian bankers. The reason for this I will explain.

During my visit here, I have discovered that my mother is, and has been, seriously ill. It is therefore incumbent upon me to make adequate provision for her before I depart. This naturally was a contributory factor in delaying my return, which I am sure you will understand. My decision is to use the proceeds from the sale of the pit to set up a trust fund for the members of my family and the matter has been given over to Mr Moskow to make the arrangements – much as I dislike him, it seems simple enough even for his limited talents. In the meantime, will you please see to it that another letter of credit is sent post haste as I have incurred some unexpected expenses lately and have instructed the bank to wire money here for my other immediate requirements.

I will remain to oversee the transfer of monies on the morning of January second, after which I will be on my way. My ship sails on the fifth, and the journey should, weather permitting, see me home by the nineteenth. Please inform Pi'taki of this without delay! I was touched in your letter by your inclusion of messages from her. These were most welcome. Her familiar little grumps and groans make me think that there is not too much to worry about, but at her age we cannot be too careful. I do not need to emphasise that, should she take ill, no matter how seemingly insignificant the symptoms, she is to receive the best of every possible care. I reiterate that this is to be regardless of cost or how much she protests about 'quack doctors' and the like. You are of course free to read this out to her. I can hear her sniff loudly now, but we have no secrets. It goes without saying that along with my concern for her, I send all my love. My heart misses her more than even she could know and if it is within your power to do so, put your arms around her and tell her that from me.

I am not sure if I will be back in time for the local elections. If not, please retain any relevant newspaper clippings so that I can catch up with this on my return. As you are no doubt aware, there is to be a General Election here in two weeks and a most exhilarating campaign is being fought on all sides. However, in order to follow it through to polling day I would have to delay my departure and under no circumstances do I wish to tarry longer. My only desire now is to be back home as soon as possible.

Please accept my apologies again for having tried your patience over the past months. I am indeed sorry to have caused such distress

to you and those around me. Suffice it to say that I cannot wait
to be home and see you once more in good spirits. All my best
wishes go with you for the New Year.

Yours affectionately,
Frances

11

The house seemed shrouded in a mausolean silence. It was Hogmanay, and Frances sat alone in the drawing-room with her feet up.
A book lolled idly in her hands, slipped from her fingers and slowly
dropped to the floor. She yawned and did not bother to retrieve it.
The clock struck six but outside the late afternoon sky had already
turned to darkness. She had promised the staff New Year's day off
and could hear muffled sounds from below as they finished off the
last-minute chores before disappearing into the night to visit their
own folk. Though it was a far more widely observed holiday than
Christmas, Frances perversely felt the need to be alone on this great
family occasion. Lethargically she wandered to the window and
watched the lamps illuminate the deepening snowfall and veil the
garden in a bridal clarity. She sighed, feeling detached and restive
as her mind drifted aimlessly between desire to be out of the house
and a melancholy necessity to remain alone. Then, with a sudden
decision she pulled the bell cord.

The housekeeper entered, two spots of high colour glowing in
her cheeks. Obviously the bottle of whisky Frances had left for the
staff had been opened early to hasten the celebrations. 'Get me my
warmest coat, Mrs Heggarty and some stout boots that won't fall
apart in the snow.'

'You're surely not going out in this weather, madam?'

'Indeed I am, I need some air, please do as I ask. Oh, and
let me have a spare key in case you are all gone before I get
back.' Despite her misgivings, Mrs Heggarty did as she was bidden
and Frances left the house well muffled against the freezing chill of
evening.

In the darkness she made her way down into the town where
noisy revellers, some the worse for drink, were already filling the
streets. She had an impulsive need to walk one last time along the
shoreline before leaving and, breathing more easily now in the icy
freshness, she headed for the beach. Her route took her past the old

Corn Exchange and as she approached, she noticed the lights were lit inside and a sizeable crowd was thronged around the doorway. Curious, but unwilling to draw attention to herself by making enquiries, Frances glanced about for some explanation. A billboard caught her eye, revealing it to be the venue for a rally organised by the Independent Labour Party, with the local candidate, Gavin Douglas, as main speaker. The election was not far off now and, though triumph for the Liberals was being widely mooted in the press, for the first time it was considered that the new Labour Party might give them a run for their money. Intrigued, she edged her way discreetly into the packed hall. Looking about, she was surprised to see how much the place had changed – the layout so much more like a theatre than she remembered. The walls had been painted and covered in moulded plasterwork and great luminous chandeliers hung from the ornate ceiling. Banks of seating were arranged formally in front of a large, curtained platform at the end of the hall but the seats were already full and people were now standing in the aisles.

Finding a hidden corner, Frances concealed herself among the sandwiched bodies, their proximity at least bringing warmth to her frozen hands and feet. The air was thick with tobacco smoke. There seemed to be a commotion near the front and she craned her neck to get a clear view but it was impossible. Then the man before her moved a few inches and she found that if she stooped she could look through the crook of his arm. At last the speakers' platform was visible. One woman and three men sat at the table. A fourth man was on his feet attempting to introduce the main speaker but was currently engaged in deflecting abusive remarks from the floor.

'Please, now come to order,' he shouted above the noise. 'We canna expect to have a proper meeting if you'll no conduct yourselves in an orderly manner.'

The one woman on the platform sat motionless with her hands neatly folded before her. There was no acknowledgement of her presence and Frances was surprised that she should occupy such a favoured place. Gavin was next to her. Idly he perused his notes, seemingly unaffected by the heated exchanges that took place in front of him.

The speaker continued. 'Now, we've got here tonight the candidate for the Independent Labour Party in the Mid-Fife constituency. Some of ye will know him from his work with the union,' he said, his hands patting the air in an attempt to stifle the rumbling of discontent. 'It's my pleasure to introduce to ye Mr Gavin Douglas. So settle down all o' ye and for God's sake, give the man a chance.' Relieved that his official function had been accomplished, he regained his seat, wiping his forehead and glancing at Gavin as at one who is about to be thrown to the lions.

Gavin waited a brief instant before slowly rising to his feet. He put his hands in his pockets and confidently eyed the rabble before him. Frances noticed the alert expression on the woman's face, now turned towards him.

Somebody who obviously fancied himself as an orator shouted from the back. 'Ye must think we're all daft, Douglas – what difference can your puny Labour party make with only fifty candidates in the field?'

'No much, my friend,' came the reply. Gavin stroked his moustache with the flat of his hand. 'At least, not without your support. But those few could still change the tide of things . . .'

There were a few scattered laughs at this and another man shouted. 'Och, you'd just be hand in glove with the Liberals if ye got in.'

'Hand in glove? No comrades, I'd say more like a thorn in their side.' This time his retort was accompanied by a little rumble of approval. Gavin laid aside his papers and directed himself at the sea of faces. 'The Liberals have long claimed to carry the torch for the working man but it's a weak flame that puts profit and greed before the conditions of the workers.' The room was growing quiet now. 'It's a weaker flame that canna see the open mouths of hungry bairns.' There were a few grunts of agreement. 'And I put it to you, brothers, it's no flame at all that denies a man the right to strike and make his protest.' He paused and let the words take effect. 'Put us there, brothers and, whether all of us take our seats, or only one – I swear we'll never let them forget it!'

Frances was moved by the oratory and felt her heart thudding hard as she clutched her wrap tighter. Gavin continued to speak with all the old eloquence but now he was possessed of an authority that time had wonderfully matured. From all corners of the room they hurled denunciation and each verbal stone was caught, turned to his advantage and flung back in their faces. Slowly the crowd quietened to a respectful concentration and, gradually wooed by every word, they let him speak.

'Do ye no see? You've got to give us the power – not your landowners, shopkeepers and businessmen. What do they ken o' a working day, bent double clawing coal from the bowels of the earth? I ask you, what do they know of a life tied to the Company? Take your sitting member, the "honourable" Andrew Effington-Blane —'

331

'He's a good bloke, a proper gentleman,' somebody chirped from the sidelines but the others shouted him down.

'Oh aye, and what exactly does that mean, eh?' Gavin was indignant now. 'Are ye no a proper gentleman yourself? Ye work your fingers to the bone for twenty-five shillings a week to keep body, soul and family together and think yourself less of a man for it? Where's your pride, man?'

'Hear, hear!' There was a growing ripple of applause, only just drowned by the distracting sounds of further disorder. All heads turned as everyone's attention was drawn to the back of the hall. In the midst of the commotion a woman screamed and an usher ran down to the speakers' platform. Frustrated, the chairman rose and waved Gavin to sit down. 'There's too many people trying to get in,' he called out above the general noise. 'Can some of ye move down to the front here and let more folk in at the back.' He gestured vaguely at the crowd in front of him and slowly the people complied. To her dismay, Frances was propelled along with the surging mass, unable to hold back or reach any of the doors.

When some calm had been restored, Gavin stood again and stepped to the edge of the platform to resume speaking. Frances saw the woman's eyes follow him, shining with approval. 'Now dinna confuse us with the Liberals,' he continued in more irritated tone. 'I was one of a deputation from the Scottish Miners Federation that went yesterday to Dunfermline to see the Prime Minister. Believe me, brothers, we gave him our views in no small way. We let him know what we thought about the Miners Eight Hours Bill, the coal tax, the Miners Regulation Acts and the eviction of miners from their houses during strikes. And do ye ken what Mr Campbell-Bannerman had to say to us?' He looked around but no one answered him and his voice raised to a shout. 'He said he was sympathetic.' Gavin spat the words bitterly. 'He said that all his colleagues were sympathetic. But!' He stopped dramatically, lifted his hand and the silence in the hall was complete. 'But he said that he could not pledge the Government to introduce the measures we had outlined.' This provoked intermittent booing and cries of 'Shame!' from the audience. 'And do ye want to know why comrades? I'll tell ye why,' he boomed back at them, his voice resounding round the hall. 'Because, when ye come right down to it, they've a vested interest in pandering to the ruling classes. It's where most of them spring from anyway and in the end, make no mistake, they will protect them.' He gazed around the hall with almost tender affection at the faces to which he now appealed. 'Do

332

ye think we can ever hope to break the tyranny of the coal-owning élite in these parts?'

At this point his voice cracked and faltered and Frances realised with a mounting dread that he was staring straight at her. She wriggled in a futile attempt to move backwards, desperately trying to avoid his eyes. Gavin could see her discomfort as he continued his address, now directed personally at her. It did not matter that the crowd were unaware but Frances recoiled, feeling the pain of every word as his voice dripped contempt. 'I'm talking about those autocrats – the Wemyss, the Gourlays, the Raiths and the O'Byrnes – they that sit in wealthy ignorance of the working man but will cream off the profits of his sweated labour – your labour, brothers, and that of your wives and bairns! They feed on power and money and use them to their own degrading ends. They corrupt the system as they speak in its defence and, worst of all, they give their word as their bond then break it —' Grabbing a pencil from the table, he snapped it in two and threw the pieces on the floor. 'As easily as a child breaks a blade of grass.' Frances's eyes were blurred with tears as he went on. 'Sniff hard and ye can smell them. And brothers, they are closer than ye think, the stench of greed is here, like a decay that rots away the very fabric of society. You and me, we're chattels, goods to be bought and sold, profit margins on a set of accounts.' With one last disdainful look, he turned his eyes away from her and addressed the wider audience again. Frances fought to push back through the crowds. She put her hands to her ears but could still hear his powerful voice thundering after her in crescendo. 'Make no mistake, comrades, we'll have to wrest that power from them for they'll no give it up willingly. But, however they try to convince ye, they cannot speak for us. The Labour Party is the only true voice of the people in this country. I appeal to ye – dinna waste this opportunity, dinna settle for small change when ye can alter the course of your lives. Do ye hear me brothers? Do ye hear me at the back and outside in the street? Ye have one vote each but put them all together and ye have power at the ballot box to win victory for the Labour movement – victory for the people!'

There was a moment's utter silence then suddenly feet started stamping and the vast room went wild with cheers of approval and frenzied thumping applause. In the confusion, Frances was at last able to break free of the constricting mass around her as everyone surged forwards to the stage. Ignored by the enthusiastic crowd she made her escape, desperately pushing her way through to the doors, choking back the sobs.

333

Outside in the cold, clear air she grabbed a lamp-post to steady herself but could not control the sudden need to vomit, as though to cleanse her body of the vitriolic hate. Helplessly she crouched over the cobbles and retched, trying to free the twisted knot inside her chest. But there was little concern from the passers-by, too many folk were in the same condition that night. One passing couple noted her distress but she heard only disgust in their voices. 'Fancy seeing a woman in such a state with drink – it's criminal!'

Maisie answered the door and Frances thrust past her in her attempt to get safely inside. She was shaking, her face damp with sweat despite the bitter freeze and she pulled off her thick jacket and shawl as if they were somehow responsible for the feeling of degradation.

'Excuse me, madam, are ye all right?' the maid ventured, picking up the discarded garments.

'Of course I'm all right. What are ye staring at, girl – I thought I gave ye all time off for Hogmanay?'

'Well yes, Mrs O'Byrne, the others have already gone but I thought I would just stay on and keep the fires going – see if ye needed anything.' She paused. 'You're no going to bring in the New Year on your own?'

Frances ignored the question. 'Do you think I can't build a fire myself? It's your holiday, Maisie, away and get yourself off before I throw ye out!'

As she went into the parlour, the front door thudded behind her and the house fell into silence. Alone now she stood before the blazing grate and tried to bring life back to her numb fingers. She held her hands to the flames and saw that they trembled uncontrollably. The room was warm and yet she shivered almost convulsively and put her arms around her body to still the anguish that tormented her. In that half-way place between rage and despair she paced the floor, the only sure crumb of comfort being the knowledge of her imminent departure. Quickly she went upstairs. Flushed with emotion, she tore at her hat and her hair came down with it. Then hurriedly she peeled off her dress and blouse, her fingernails catching as she tugged at the lacing of her stiff corset. At last, unconstricted by the wadding and padding and boned undergarments, she put on her dressing-gown and walked over to the windows. Throwing them open to the night, she breathed deeply, as if it would dispel the tension that locked her body in its grip. A cold moon winked between the black interlace of the tree's branches casting a crystalline shimmer across the frozen garden. She felt the heat go out of her face and her anger slowly dissipated into sadness.

Midway down the stairs Frances stopped and sat with the forlorn look of a child, consumed by a desperate need for reassurance. At that moment she longed for Pi'taki's presence, more perhaps than in the darkest Dawson winter. She felt weak and vulnerable, aching for the support of a comforting word, a familiar face to renew the strength that had deserted her. Then the grandmother clock struck twelve, an awesome sound, giving birth to a new year and bringing only anguish and isolation. Two tears fell closely after one another onto her knees and she listened as each jarring chord drove through her, echoing without hope in the solitary silence.

Frances jumped. The eerie resonance had hardly faded when she was assaulted by the sudden brash jangle of the doorbell. Still crouched on the stairway she looked down into the hall and saw a dark shape through the glass of the porch. The tall figure loomed massively in the doorway and she saw the swirl of his frosty breath and heard the scrunch of snow as he stamped his feet to warm them. For a few seconds she remained rooted to the spot then rose slowly, her hand gripping the banister. The bell sounded again and jolted her to her senses. Trembling, she slowly descended and moved into the hall, all the time telling herself there was nothing to fear. Nothing more perhaps than the genial salutations of a thoughtful neighbour, a first-foot to welcome in the year. She opened the porch door and the cold blast of night greeted her as she tip-toed over the tiles and slid back the great iron bolts of the outer portal. Inching it ajar, she peered round the crack into the darkness.

'Frances?' The voice was unmistakable.

She gasped and tried to close the door but Gavin's hand thwarted the attempt.

'It's all right,' he tried to assure her but she cowered against the oak frame, barring his entrance.

'Go away, have ye no tormented me enough . . .'

His hand was caught, jammed next to her face where she pressed against the door but he ignored the pain. 'Please listen to what I have to say, I've no come to hurt ye.'

'For pity's sake leave me alone!'

'Frances, it's all right,' he said evenly, trying to calm her. 'I just want to talk to ye. I swear I'll no try to come in.'

Her heart thudded anxiously, torn between self-preservation and an overwhelming desire to believe him. She withdrew cautiously. 'Ye won't come in?'

'I promise.'

Slowly she prised back the cumbrous weight of the door. Gavin remained where he stood. In the pool of light cast by the carriage lamps, his face was raw and chilled, his expression weary. He pulled off his cap and looked up nervously as if unsure of how to begin. There was a veiled sadness in his eyes.

'I came because I wanted to apologise. What I did back there – what I said in the hall was wrong. I'm sorry, I just lost my head when I saw ye and didn't think about what I was saying. It wasn't until after the meeting they told me about Thornton – about you standing up to the Fife Coal Company and refusing to sell.' He hesitated. 'I ken I misjudged ye.' Then, taking a deep breath, he finished in an even humbler tone. 'What I'm trying to say is . . . will ye forgive me?'

She was inwardly astounded, aware of how hard it had been for him to form those simple words. Yet she shuddered from the knowledge that an even greater guilt should rest with her. Wanting to tell him so, she opened her mouth to speak but no sound came. She could only nod and they stood, uneasy in the smothered stillness. A little light snow fell, dusting his shoulders and sparkling against his eyelashes.

He looked down and noticed her bare feet beneath the robe. 'You'll catch cold,' he whispered.

Then she heard herself speak, as if from a distance. 'Aye, I suppose I better go in . . .' She waited a few seconds and slowly began to close the door.

'Wait.' He fumbled in his pocket and produced a lump of coal which he placed almost tenderly in her hand. 'A guid new year to ye, Frances.'

'And to you,' she returned softly, finally dropping the latch and shutting out the night.

Once inside, her heart resumed its fervid beating. She held the coal, feeling the cold hard facets of its gleaming surface as well as the rough edges and stared down at it as though it was a living thing. Then, placing it on the hallstand, she stood with her back to the wall, examining the black residue it had left on her palm. She swallowed hard to free the constricting dryness in her throat and noticed her hands were again shaking. Uncertainly, she glanced back at the porch and her breath caught short as she saw the dark figure still silhouetted against the glass. Then something involuntary moved her feet, her brain seemingly unconnected to the act, and she went towards the door. With a ponderous creaking it opened, light flooding the step. As she pressed herself into his arms she felt his chest heaving and the wet graze of his moustache over her open mouth.

The door thundered shut behind them as, still embracing, they found their way into the parlour. Frances reached up and pulled apart the collar of his jacket, hauling the sodden weight back off his shoulders. He was soaked through but he did not seem to care and kept drawing her back to him, as though fearful that she might disappear. She kissed his eyes and tasted the desperate tears that stung them, making her own breath falter.

'Oh Gavin, dinna do this to yourself. It's me that should be ashamed.'

He shook his head and sighed deeply into her ear as his mouth sought the once familiar crevices of her face, her neck, and he gave a little gasp of exquisite pain with every memory provoked. Her head lolled back as his tongue traced a line along her exposed throat and a groan rose from deep within her. She tugged at his waistcoat, tossing it over the arm of the sofa where it lay steaming before the fire's mighty blaze. Slowly he lowered her to the floor and she felt the irresistible weight of him press her to the rug. He eased her up, gently peeling back the silk gown where it lay in almost liquid pools at her side. She felt his strong fingers stroke her exposed skin. Tenderly he cupped her breasts in his hands and pushed them to his lips. His soft mouth circled each nipple in turn, swooping over her stomach and deep between the warm recesses of her legs. She gasped, at once shivering, then burning with the heightening tremors that surged through her body.

Frances leaned forwards, took hold of his shirt and heaved it urgently over his head. Reaching up as though in supplication, she ran her fingers from his taut neck down across his damp chest to his waist where the rigid muscles jumped at her touch. She urged him up and he stood looking down at her as she freed the buckle and with one motion drew the belt from his trousers. Slowly, without taking her eyes from his face, she slid her fingers behind the waistband and pulled them to the floor. He stepped out of the jumble of clothing and held her chin with his hand, urging her to rise. She resisted. There was an irrepressible need in each to give pleasure, to atone for all the pain they had caused each other. Gently, her tongue brushed his thighs. Resting her cheek against his belly, she slowly lowered her head and, with her hair falling all around, tantalising his skin, she echoed his own ecstatic sighs. Infinitely tender, she took him into her mouth, now guiding the responses of his body. She wrapped her arms around him, her fingernails digging into his legs, his back, as a fiercer passion now took hold of them. His breath started to come in rasping sobs and she released him, her own desire kindled to a fervent anticipation and intensity that drove out all conscious thought.

Spreadeagled, she stretched out for him and he sank to his knees, laying himself against her. His strong arms flanked her shoulders and her back arched as he entered her, his gaze holding her eyes for a second before their bodies, fused, began rhythmically to move as one. Her hands slid over the sweat of his back as they thrust at each other in momentum, driven harder by a mounting sensation. The height of pleasure, when it came, was almost intolerable.

She crushed his mouth with hers and stifled their shuddering cries. When he pulled away she groaned, still feeling the vibrant little spasms coming in the wake of ecstasy. Incoherent murmurs droned in her ears and Frances felt a langorous stillness sweep over her. She turned her head and stared into the virulent blaze of the fire that had scorched her body unawares. Clouds of deepest soot clung to the back of the chimney and in a tiny broken line, sparks climbed and glowed like soldiers in the night.

12

They lay like spoons in the dishevelled bed and Frances opened her eyes to the pale morning sun that seeped through the crack in the curtains. Sleep had come only with the approaching dawn when they had at last abandoned the hearth-rug for the bedroom. She felt the heat and measured breathing from the body that enveloped her and turned to touch his tousled hair.

'Well, here we are in the cold light of day,' she whispered, half-questioning.

Gavin stirred with a sensuous groaning sound and looked at her through heavy eyelids. 'Does it make a difference, Frances?'

'I don't know, I wondered if it might.' She tried to keep her voice neutral. 'People do strange things on impulse, things they afterwards regret.'

He propped his head on his hand and smiled at her. 'Och, come on, ye canna call this an impulse, no after sixteen years.' He kissed her. 'When I think of all that wasted time . . .'

She relaxed against him. 'Do you really mean that?'

'I could've married ye,' he said sadly, 'but for my own selfish stupidity. It was me that drove ye away . . .'

She smoothed her hand over his forehead. 'Aye, and me that left ye standing at the altar – don't take all the blame on yourself.'

He held her close and kissed her differently now.

Slowly his mouth moved down over her throat and breasts to her naked belly where he paused seeing the pearly streaks that feathered her skin. 'So ye did have children,' he whispered the thought aloud. Her muscles stiffened perceptibly and he glanced up.

'A wee boy. He was only six when he died.' Gavin was unprepared for the response. He made to interrupt but she silenced him with her fingers. 'It was an accident, nearly eight years ago. Don't ask me to tell you about it now.'

'Christ, Frances, I'm sorry.' He hesitated. 'Was he Munroe's or O'Byrne's? Och, I'm sorry – I should never have asked that.'

'Aye, what difference would it make? – I told you they're both gone now. But if ye must know, he was William's. It wasn't much more than a year after we left that William was killed and it all seems so far away now, sometimes it's almost like it never happened.' She sighed. 'Look, I know what I did to you was unforgivable but I canna pretend for your sake that I didn't care for him.'

'It's all right lass, I ken. And I understand the reasons better than ye know. One of these days I'll learn to hold my tongue – it's clear you've no had an easy time of it all these years.' He paused before continuing, fearful that his questioning might alienate her but so anxious to learn more. 'And what about O'Byrne, you've no said much about him?'

'He was a mistake,' she said coolly. 'If I lived my life over again I'd surely pull the trigger on that gun the day I met him.'

Gavin could not conceal his shocked amusement. 'That's a bit strong, isn't it? I mean you've no done that badly by him from the looks of things.'

'He got what he deserved, I'll no waste any grief on him. And I don't care how it looks; whatever ye think, I didn't court wealth.' Her tone softened. 'Honestly, you men are all the same, it wouldn't occur to ye that I worked for all this myself would it?'

Gavin laughed. 'Ye sound just like Margaret . . .' Then his face straightened and he checked himself.

'Oh aye, and who's Margaret then?' She was diverted for a moment by a frisson of pleasure as he began to arouse her again with generous nurturing strokes. Talk threatened to become insignificant but she was not to be so easily distracted. 'Come on dinna be shy,'

339

she goaded, drawing away. 'I've answered enough questions, now it's your turn.'

Gavin rolled onto his back. 'All right,' he conceded with a sigh. 'What do ye want to know?'

Frances leaned on his chest. 'Was she at the meeting last night – the woman next ye on the platform?'

'Aye. I've known her a long time, as a friend.' He looked uncomfortable. 'No, that is she was a friend. But we're closer than that now.'

'Close enough to marry her?'

'We've talked of it but things always got put aside, what with the campaign and everything. We decided to wait until after the election.'

'So soon,' Frances breathed, thrown a little off balance by the news.

Gavin shifted awkwardly. 'Och, let's not talk about her. Anyway I'll have to tell her it's over, I couldn't go on with that now . . .'

'Do ye mean that? What do you think she'll say?'

'I don't know. It won't be easy,' he sighed. 'She's a good lass. Been a tower of strength to me in the campaign.'

'Tell me more about her – what's she like?' Frances asked uncertainly.

'Well,' he began, 'she's an educated woman, well-read and very dedicated to the cause. There's no denying, I've learned a lot from her.' He paused then added, 'And she has a good heart.'

Her finger traced the broad line of his moustache. 'Aye, and I can see you're fond of her.'

'Well, I couldn't have done without her these past weeks. She goes over all my speeches and we discuss changes and issues that need to be addressed at the meetings.' He smiled unconsciously as he spoke and Frances sensed that the words hid more than they revealed. 'I rely on her to keep my campaign diary and she knows everything that's going on. You see she's so much more organised than me. If she was here now she'd have a list of commitments drawn up and she'd be reminding me about the next rally —'

'If she was here now,' Frances pulled him up sharp, 'I think she'd be more likely to throw ye out for what you've been up to!' Half-joking she blurted out the words but saw his face darken guiltily at the thought. The reality brought a change of mood. It was as if a keen wind had cut through the room, cooling their passion. Frances slipped out of bed, pulled on her dressing-gown and was through the door before Gavin could stop her.

Downstairs she busied herself building up the fires then went through to the kitchen and set the kettle on the stove. As she stood watching it she heard the sound of his bare feet on the tiled floor. She continued to make a show of being busy with little domestic tasks – hanging cloths over the drying rail, fetching milk from the cold cupboard, laying cups on the table. The kettle came to the boil and she looked round, asking briskly, 'Tea or coffee, maybe you'd like some breakfast? You must be hungry with all that political rallying and then hardly a wink of sleep —'

'What's the matter?' he cut in.

'Nothing.'

'Then why did you jump up like that and dash away downstairs?' He saw her knuckles tense and he walked across to where she stood, taking hold of her arm. 'Frances, it's you I want, can ye no see that?'

She looked at him steadily. 'My, Gavin how you've changed. I remember a time when your first thought would have been your responsibilities, the union, politics – and look at ye now. You're a Labour candidate, it's the middle of your campaign, you're as good as engaged to be married and does anyone even know where you are the day? Don't ye care about the scandal?'

'I'm willing to take the risk, if you are.'

She turned away. 'But what about Margaret, and the campaign? If this leaks out won't it ruin your chances in the election?'

He came up behind her and put his arms around her waist. 'I'll find the right moment to speak to Margaret and we can go on seeing each other if we're careful. No one needs to know until after the election.'

'But think about it, love, we'll have a job keeping this quiet.' She felt his hard nakedness against her back and gradually the doubts began to drain away as a glorious aching filled her body.

'Dinna worry, my darling,' he whispered, holding her tighter. 'We'll find a way.'

13

The coals glowed white-hot in the body of the fire, infusing the atmosphere with the smell of beeswax polish. In the faded elegance of 'Grandtully's' drawing-room, Frances lay across the plush velvet settee, restive and preoccupied with thoughts she could not share. Occasionally, she would pick up the slim book of verse Gavin had given her, but as often as not, she stopped half-way through a poem, the words of Robert Burns too accurately reflecting the feelings she fought to control. She alternated between fanciful imaginings of a future that allowed free rein to the indulgence of their love, and dreadful visions of scandal that would surely destroy them both. For three weeks now they had conducted a clandestine affair, meeting in the most bizarre of secret hideaways at whatever hours of the day or night could be snatched from Gavin's hectic electioneering schedule. When they were together, the times apart, like everything else, seemed not to matter – when she was alone, the separation was unendurable. Already, on more than one occasion, circumstances had forced him to cancel a rendezvous and Frances had returned home in frustrated anguish which put the household staff at a complete loss. The behaviour of their mistress had been unpredictable since she arrived, but it got so they hardly knew from one day to the next whether she would be in for meals, out for meals, receiving visitors or, as now, caged in uninterruptable seclusion.

There was a discreet knock at the door and Maisie crept in. 'Mrs Bagiotti is here to see you, madam. You did say you'd see her?' She waited anxiously for Frances's acknowledgement and showed in the familiar plump, well-wrapped figure.

'Jeannie, come and sit at the fire, you look perished.' Frances sat up and moved along the settee. She watched in amusement as her friend began the long task of unwinding the prodigious layers of clothes she wore against the bitter weather. 'Take these things and bring us some tea, Maisie.' The maid exited, loaded down with the coat and scarves.

Jeannie took off her hat and sat down at last. 'My, but it's snell oot there,' she shivered.

'So, what brings you here on such a day? Too cold for your customers to be buying ice-cream?'

'Well, business has no exactly been brisk since this cold snap started.' Jeannie laughed and held her chapped hands out to the blazing grate. 'Just thought I would come for a wee blether, since it will no be long now till ye go back to Canada.'

It was half a question and Frances smiled. She could always see through Jeannie when she was trying to elicit information casually. 'It's hard to say when I'll be going. There are still a few things to settle. I think I might be here a while yet.'

'Oh? I thought everything was sorted about your mother now – I mean the money and all that?'

'Yes, the trust fund has been set up but I need to make sure that

Rob uses it right.' She grimaced. 'Och, if he uses it at all. He's that proud and stubborn – just like my father.'

'Well, it's no been easy for him.' Jeannie held up her hand before Frances could say anything. 'I know, I know. You've told us about how hard things were for you, too. But Rob doesn't know that.'

'We've all had it hard at one time or another.' Frances's voice was agitated and she tried again to steer the talk away from herself. 'But take you and Carlo, another few years and you'll be living in a house like this.'

Jeannie looked admiringly round the large room. 'I hope so. We keep working and saving, and things are turning out right at last. Though I dinna ken if we'd ever be able to afford anything this grand.' Her eye caught sight of the newspaper lying beside the fireplace. 'Oh, have ye been reading about the election, then?' She picked it up and looked at the latest summary of results.

Frances nodded. 'It's hard to follow, but looks as if the Liberals have already got a majority – even with so many places still left to vote.'

'And what about the Labour? Have they won any more seats?'

'They seem to be doing not too bad.' Frances was relieved when at that moment the door opened and the tea-tray was brought in. 'Thank you, Maisie, I'll pour.' The girl bobbed a curtsey and left the room.

'They'll be voting here on Thursday.' Jeannie pursued the topic relentlessly. 'Do ye think Gavin stands a chance?'

Frances made a show of busying herself with the tea and took her time before replying. 'Oh, Jeannie, how would I know?' She passed across a cup and saucer. 'You've as much idea as me, more in fact – you live here.'

'Well, there's no need to bite my face off – I just asked.' She blew on the hot tea. 'Pass me one o' they cakes.'

Frances selected a choice cream puff with the silver tongs and smiled apologetically. 'I'm sorry, it's just that I have a few things on my mind.'

'Frances Rintoul, what have you to worry about?' Jeannie snorted and turned her attention to the luscious pastry. 'Anyway, the local talk is that Gavin will give the Liberal a run for his money. Funny that, him standing against a Liberal when they're talking about a coalition in government – makes it a harder campaign for him.' She chewed reflectively for a moment. Then, speaking with difficulty around the rich mouthful, she continued. 'But of course, Margaret's been a godsend to him.'

Frances hoped she had not flinched at the name. 'Oh you mean the lassie that helps with his work?' she asked nonchalantly.

Jeannie swallowed the last flaky morsel and nodded. 'Aye. She's a good match for the likes of Gavin. I mean, she's awful political herself. I dinna understand the half of what she talks about – women's rights and that. But she fairly organises Gavin and his meetings. A right canny woman, been well educated.' She sneaked a glance at Frances. 'I dinna ken where Gavin would be without her . . .'

'That's good.' Frances tried to appear uninterested though her hand trembled slightly as she passed the cake stand across again. 'Do you want another one?' Jeannie shook her head, licking the cream and icing-sugar from her fingers. She finished her tea and placed the cup back on the tray. Then she settled herself back in the deep cushions, as if waiting for something. The silence between them grew uncomfortable and Frances struggled in an effort to change the subject. 'Is Carlo looking after —'

'There's been talk.' Jeannie's voice was unnaturally loud in the blunt interruption, as though the words had been forced out. 'About you and Gavin.'

'What kind of talk?' Frances asked, looking away.

'That you're – you know, carrying on.' Jeannie lowered her voice, speaking the words with difficulty in a kind of reverent whisper. She paused. 'Well, is it true?'

Frances gave a little nervous laugh and stood up. 'What a load of nonsense,' she said, with a wave of the hand. 'Where did you hear that?'

Jeannie's eyes followed her. 'Och, dinna take me for an imbecile, it's written all over your face. I ken it's true just to look at ye.' She hesitated, almost as though she wanted to hear a further denial, but there was no response and she sighed. 'Why Frances? What's possessed ye?'

Frances walked across the room and stood at the dresser picking up things and putting them back again. 'It just – happened,' she said, embarrassed. Unable to explain what she herself did not understand, she shrugged and her voice faded. 'I dinna ken the why . . .'

Jeannie rose and came over to join her. 'You know,' she said quietly, taking her hand, 'all my life I wanted to be like you. I couldn't guess at the taste o' the plum for want o' nerve to shake the tree.' She took a deep breath. 'But I ken right from wrong, Frances. Dinna fool yourself with this. You're no sixteen any more and these are folk's lives you're playing with.' Frances's hand stiffened and she tried to pull away but Jeannie held on, pressing it hard into her own.

'Ye ken I'm telling ye this as a friend. What are ye going to do? Ye canna go on with it — for a start, there's Margaret to consider.'

'Don't you think we have been through all that? Over and over, time after time?' Frances broke free, hovering between frustration and tears. 'It's the last thing I wanted, but it's happened.' She looked steadily at her friend. 'Whatever you say, I'll no give him up now.'

'He's no yours to give up, he's promised to Margaret. She's a good woman and she's what he needs right now.'

'Oh aye, that's obvious every time he comes to my bed!'

'Dinna fool yourself, lassie — you'll ruin his life again if ye go on with this. Can ye no see that?'

Frances moved back to the fire, her cheeks flushed with anger. When she had composed herself she turned. 'Jeannie, you're a good friend, but don't overstep the mark. I'm old enough to know what I'm doing — and so is Gavin.'

'Is he?' Jeannie's tone was equally icy in its politeness. 'You'll be all right, you've nothing to lose. But if word of this gets out, he'll be finished in politics.'

'Not necessarily, and anyway, we've been careful —'

'Och, I canna believe you're so stupid. How the hell do ye think I knew?'

'Look, things will be difficult at first, till we can sort them out. But there's a good chance Gavin will get elected, and when he's in London it will be different. I'm sorry about Margaret, of course, but —'

'You're sorry?' Jeannie gestured in an angry flourish. 'I think your mind's turned!' She came across to where Frances stood and started to put on her hat again. 'Margaret's the best thing that's happened to Gavin — especially after what you did to him! Had you forgotten that? Has he?' Her rage was uncontrolled now. 'Mind you, I dinna suppose he'd be quite so interested if you'd come back as the poor widow Munroe instead o' rich Mrs O'Byrne?'

'Don't you dare talk like that!' Frances raised her hand and slapped her.

The blow in return was as hard and swift. They stared at each other in astonishment, the shock of the moment abruptly defusing their anger. Then Jeannie spoke again, but quietly now. 'Wake up, Frances. Look at what's happening.'

The maid entered without knocking. She stood, nervously crossing and uncrossing her legs, embarrassed by the scene. 'Excuse me, madam.'

Frances whirled round, annoyed by the interruption. 'What is it, Maisie? I told ye to say I'm no in.'

'This note came for ye, madam. The laddie said it was right urgent and I was to give it to ye straight away.' She handed over the grubby paper.

'All right, thank you. That will be all.' Frances unfolded it and as she read the scrawled message her face drained of colour. 'Oh, no,' she whispered, flopping down onto the settee. 'Oh, Jeannie, it's my ma. She's dead.'

The shocking news drove all talk and thoughts of Gavin away. Jeannie put her arms around her and held tightly. 'God that's awful, Frances, I'm that sorry.' She handed over a broad white handkerchief. 'Who sent ye the message?'

Frances passed it to her. 'It's from Maureen, bless her. She says they're burying her on Thursday. Oh, poor Ma, I canna believe it, what a life she's had. And that bastard prevented me from helping her, even in her last days.' She rose and paced the floor, clutching her hands in agitation. 'Well, he'll no stop me going to the funeral.'

'Now the last thing ye want is the family rowing at the grave – dinna go upsetting yourself the more.'

'She was my mother. I'll see her buried, whether Rob likes it or not.'

'Aye well, be careful, that's all I'm saying.' Jeannie made her sit again and patted her hand comfortingly. 'Do ye want me to come with ye?'

Frances looked into her eyes with remorse. 'Thanks, Jeannie, but I'll be all right.'

'Are ye sure now?'

'I'm sure.' She gazed into the smouldering fire, tormented by her last memory of Jessie staring mindlessly into her own cheerless hearth.

Jeannie seemed to sense her thoughts. 'Dinna think o' her like she was at the end. Mind all the good times.'

'Och, Jeannie, were there ever any?'

'Ye know there were.' She rocked Frances gently in her arms. 'D'ye no remember that time we dressed up in Chrissie's guid frocks? And your ma caught us in the midden, playing at being Lady Wemyss?'

Frances choked out a laugh. 'And we were fighting over who got to be the lady . . .'

'I mind it was you that won – as usual.'

'She wasn't angry with us – I thought she'd be that roosed but she let us play in the back room. And then washed all Chrissie's stuff before she found out.' Frances could see that day vividly, though it was over twenty years away, and with Jeannie's quiet coaxing, other memories were allowed to surface.

The rest of the afternoon was passed in a warm remembrance of her mother until Frances felt calm, ready to be alone. 'Come on, Mrs Bagiotti, it's time you were away to your own family.' She hugged Jeannie tightly. 'I can't say . . .'

'Ye dinna have to. Just ken I'll be thinking of ye.'

As Jeannie made her reluctant departure and the door closed behind her, Frances sat in solitary contemplation of the little note and weighed up its dreadful disclosure. Outside, broken shadows flashed against the window as a flock of pigeons rose on sudden impulse and flew home to roost across the rooftops.

14

On the Thursday morning, Donald drove Frances out to West Wemyss, this time wisely stopping the Daimler at the top of the hill. To re-enact the farce of having the car pushed back up would be unbearable, today of all days.

'Shall I walk ye down, madam?' he asked. The road was slippery with ice and a light snow had already fallen that morning.

'No.' Frances smiled. 'I've been up and down this brae more times than you could know. I doubt if I will be that long, but I know it's cold for you, hanging around.'

'Mrs O'Byrne, I'll wait as long as I have to.'

There was a fierce determination and pride in his young face and she was touched by his simple loyalty. 'Thank you, Donald,' she said softly, and meant it. Then, before any second thoughts could interfere with her resolve, she set off down the winding cobbled road, the bombazine mourning dress swinging and furling around her legs, the cape rising and falling gently with the rhythm of her stride. High trees on either side stood leafless and gaunt, their bare branches spearing the dim threatening sky. The light had that strange, washed-out quality that presages the coming of snow and sounds came muffled and indistinct across the empty winter fields.

At the foot of the hill she slowed, inhaling the salt-fresh crispness as she stared out beyond the line of houses. The waters of the Forth were glassy-calm, and seabirds glided low across the sands on the breathless air. As she turned into the little High Street, Frances could sense the inquisitive faces were there, at the windows. She lifted the black veil from her face and, holding her head defiantly high, walked slowly towards the graveyard. At each twitching curtain, she paused, deliberately meeting the eyes that peered back at her until nervous fingers let them fall and she continued on her way.

When she reached the wrought-iron gates of the churchyard, she could see the family group clustered around the gaping hole, a pyramid of freshly dug dirt heaped beside it. The minister, in his dark robes, stood at the head of the straggling circle and, between the legs of the mourners, she could just catch a poignant glimpse of the meagre wooden box. Frances remained at a distance, suddenly possessed by a sense of futility, a grief for which there could be no atonement.

The air was perfectly still and she could clearly hear the solemn words of the service. 'Man that is born of a woman hath but a short time to live, and is full of misery.' Thinking of her mother, Frances was struck by how tragically apt was the too-familiar phrase. A bitter taste rose in her throat as she recalled the image of the pathetic wretch sitting by the fire, the woman that had once been Jessie Rintoul. Her life had ebbed away in a dim twilight of madness and now she was being laid to rest eternally beside the very one who had dealt her the final blow – the monster whom she had once called husband and protector.

Frances watched as the six men holding the ropes slowly lowered the coffin into the ground. Rob held the first. Opposite him was a stocky young lad who she deduced from the dark Rintoul features must be her nephew, Henry. Beside the boy stood Gavin. Remembering how much her mother had thought of him, Frances was gladdened that the family had asked him to take a cord. For her own part, she had been unable to get in touch since learning of the death and was surprised and proud that he was there. It was polling day and she knew it must have been difficult for him to get away. As the coffin slid to its final resting place, he looked up, saw her, and their eyes lingered for a moment.

The minister spoke the timeless words over the grave. 'We therefore commit her body to the ground; earth to earth, ashes to ashes, dust to dust; in sure and certain hope of the Resurrection to eternal life through our Lord Jesus Christ.' As he led into the final prayer, Frances felt compelled to walk across the frozen grass and stand at Rob's side. Tentatively she reached out and touched his arm. He turned. His eyes widened when he saw her, a flush rose in his

348

pallid face, but he said nothing. Meanwhile the neighbours who were gathered at the grave peered curiously at the newcomer as they mouthed the last 'amens'.

The minister closed his prayer-book and Rob stooped to grasp a handful of the hard clay at his feet. He crumbled it roughly in his fingers, the grains spattering faintly as they dropped onto the lid of the coffin. 'Cheerio, Ma. Ye can rest now.' Since receiving the news, Frances felt her heart had hardened with the need for retribution but now, hearing these quiet words, barely audible and spoken in an echo of her brother's younger voice, she was moved to tears at last.

'Oh, Rob.' She clutched at his arm and strangely, he did not push her away. Bending again, he scooped another fistful of soil, pressed it into her gloved hand and, stepping back, he left her to move alone to the side of the grave. She let the earth fall, trickling through her trembling fingers like the sands of an hour-glass running out. Bowing her head, she stood still for a moment and said her own silent farewell to her mother. Then, uncertainly, she rejoined Rob. The other mourners filed by, murmuring their condolences, their eyes all the while curiously taking in the significance of her presence at his side.

Maureen came round and held both Frances's hands in hers. 'I'm glad ye came.' She spoke, heedless of Rob, and drew forward the three boys. 'This is your Auntie Frances.' They blushed uncomfortably and muttered their greetings before retreating behind their mother. Frances dabbed her eyes but could not speak.

'Will ye come to the house?' Maureen asked. 'We're having a cup of tea and that.'

'No, I don't think so,' she replied, looking at her brother. 'But thanks for asking me.'

'He's no as bad as ye think. Give him a bit of time, that's all.' She gave Frances a brief kiss. 'Ye ken you're welcome – and that means any time.' Rounding up the children, she ushered them towards the street. 'We'll wait for ye at the gate, Rob.'

Gavin too withdrew into the background till only brother and sister were left at the graveside with the minister. He was young and fair-haired, a contrast to her memory of the dour Reverend Black. 'Mr Rintoul,' he was saying, 'I know that this is a time of great sadness. But once the first grief has passed, be happy in the knowledge that your mother rests with the Lord.'

Rob nodded absently. The minister turned to Frances and smiled, unperturbed by her out-of-place elegance. 'You must be Rob's sister.'

He caught the look of surprise in her eyes. 'He's told me about you. In times like these, it's the family that counts most and I am sure it is a great comfort for him to have ye here now.' He warmly shook hands with them and walked back into the little church.

'Is it, Rob?' Frances asked. 'Is it any comfort at all?'

At last he spoke, though he could not look at her. 'For all that's happened, she was your mother too and you've a right to be here.' He turned to join his wife and children, but Frances caught his arm. Still he would not face her. He gazed out at the sea, his expression mirroring the flat calm of the waters as he waited to hear her out.

'I set money aside, Rob, for Ma. It was to help you look after her.' She clutched at the worn, shiny cloth of his best suit jacket. 'I know you didn't want it, but I had to do something. We canna change the past, and what's done is done.' She was crying again. 'But the money's still there, Rob, and I still want ye to have it. Even if you'll no touch it yourself, at least use it for your bairns. Get them an education, give them a chance to get away from here.' She tried to hand him the deeds of trust she had picked up from the lawyer that morning.

He shook his head, ignoring the papers, and finally turned and looked her in the face. 'Why is it,' he asked slowly, 'that all you ever saw was the road oot o' here?' At first, she could not understand his question and stared at him, bewildered. 'Frances, the world outside obviously gave you what ye wanted, and I suppose I should be glad for ye. But, some of us . . .' He shook his head, unwilling to say more. Then he took her hand and gently released it from his arm.

'Please.' Tasting the raw tears in her mouth, she tried again to press the roll of papers into his hand, to curl his fingers round it. He saw the pain in her eyes and this time he did not let go.

'All right,' he faltered, 'I'll no deny the bairns if that's what ye want. I'll see the money is used for them.'

Frances felt the breath of relief rush from her. She knew how hard it had been to speak those words and wanted to put her arms around him, hold him against her and make some recognition of their reunion. But already he was walking away.

'Rob,' she called after him.

He stopped without turning round.

Her voice was broken with tears. 'Maybe one day . . . ?' She could not finish the thought, and waited. He gave a barely perceptible nod then walked away.

Frances leaned on the stone gatepost, clinging to what vestige of hope he had aroused as she watched the little family group go down the length of the street. Hand in hand they walked until at last they disappeared behind the bell-tower and into the cottage that was their home.

There was a footfall on the path and Gavin was at her side. He pulled off a glove and gently traced the tears on her face with his finger. Then, raising her face to his, he kissed her forehead. 'Dinna be sad for her. She's better away than like she was.'

'I know that but I can't help thinking – with all I have, I couldn't even help my own mother.'

'Come on now, it's no good for ye that kind of talk. I doubt ye could have made much difference anyway. It was things far beyond your control that made her like she was, ye canna take on all the guilt yourself.'

'I suppose you're right but I just keep thinking, what if?'

'Oh I ken how ye feel, but I learned it'll no change what's done. When my Gran died, all I could think of was the things I never said to her.'

Frances blew her nose. 'Och, she knew how you loved her Gavin, everybody did.'

'Aye, maybe so, but did I ever tell her?' They were at Elspeth's grave and he brushed the brittle frozen snow from the headstone. 'You ken yourself how bad I was at saying things. And then, when ye want to, it's too late.' He stroked the cold granite of the memorial. 'But she was the one who always said ye must look forward, no back at something ye canna change. Remember that, Frances.'

She reached out and pressed his hand. 'It's good to have you here.'

He put his arms around her. 'It's where I wanted to be, lass. You should know that now.'

The minister came out of the church, locking the door and they quickly separated. He walked across to where they stood, and repeated his condolences to Frances before offering his hand to Gavin. 'It was good to meet you, Mr Douglas. I hadn't expected to see our candidate on polling day – at least, not without a speech and a soap box.'

Gavin smiled self-consciously. 'Aye, it's been a busy time. I'll have to get back to the committee rooms.'

Frances waited until the minister had left. 'I know you don't have much time but I wanted the chance to speak to ye, Gavin, could we walk for a bit?'

'Aye, I think we should.' He reached for her hand and led the way over to the side gate and out of the churchyard.

Once their feet touched the damp sand, some unspoken memory

drew them back towards the woods behind the beach. As they went through the old door in the wall, the trees swallowed them from view and they were alone again in the frozen stillness. The brittle undergrowth snapped beneath their feet while they walked and somewhere a collared dove crooned a throaty moan. It was a strange mood that prevailed, and both sensed it. Gavin stopped and leaned against an old gnarled tree, opened his coat and drew her inside it. She tucked her head under his chin and for a long time they held each other, listening only to the thudding of their heartbeats, feeling only the rise and fall of breath within their bodies. Not far from where they stood, a robin darted in a russet flash among the drab jumble of dead leaves. But the optimism broadcast in its cheerful song seemed singularly at odds with the loaded emotion of the day.

At long last Gavin spoke what was in their minds. 'Something's changed,' he said softly, 'hasn't it?'

'Yes.' Frances felt the word catch in her throat but by some instinct knew it was true.

They remained in mutual silence for a while, until the significance of their common decision was imbued with an acceptance. And in that understanding they both felt an odd, vaguely distant sense of relief that swept away apprehension.

'What about Margaret?'

Gavin responded, almost too quickly, as if he had anticipated the question. 'I never told her,' he said, without apology. 'I don't know why.'

'I didn't think you had.' Through her arms Frances felt him give a convulsive shiver. 'Come here and sit down,' she said, taking his hand and pulling him over to a fallen tree.

'Ye dinna look out of place in the Estate nowadays,' he commented as she sat and spread out the folds of her dress around her. 'It's hard to imagine you're the same lassie I courted in these woods.' He settled himself beside her with his arm around her shoulder and stared down at some tiny detail on the ground between his feet. 'Do ye remember it was here that I asked ye to marry me?'

'Gavin don't . . .'

'What a mess I made of it. I often wonder why ye didn't just turn me down then.'

'I wish I had now – it would have been the proper thing to do.' She looked into his face and saw the sadness spreading through his features. 'Ye couldn't see it then but even though I left, I loved ye.'

'Would we have been happy? I mean if . . .'

'Och, I think we both know the answer to that.'

The next question hung like a heavy drop of rain that weighs the petal of some brilliant flower. They looked at each other, both wise enough now to let it remain suspended.

'Frances.' Gavin took a deep breath and raised his eyes to the filigree of branches overhead. 'These past weeks, this time with you – it's been so perfect, so complete.'

She fumbled almost gratefully for his fingers, squeezing his hand tightly in hers. 'It's all right, you don't need to try to say it.'

'No, let me. I need to have ye know that the past is all forgotten. We've had more in a few brief days than we could have hoped for in a life of marriage and I wouldn't want to change any of it now.'

She released her grip on his knuckles and sagged sideways against him. Large snowflakes were starting to appear, drifting carelessly down through the skeletal coverlet above their heads. 'I don't deserve what you're saying,' she said, in a voice choked with emotion but the intensity in his eyes and the integrity in his voice told her that he meant it. She fought very hard against the pressing need to cry and could only muster a whispered scrap of words. 'Oh Gavin, how I love ye.'

'And I . . .' He could not finish the sentence and squeezed her to him, their heads pressed hard against each other in a last desperate embrace.

Frances felt her heart weaken as she had known it would when the moment came to part. Her eyes brimmed over and she raised her face and saw that he too was near to tears. 'Look at us,' she said softly, 'what a pair we are.'

He tried to smile but his taut expression collapsed. 'I hope we're doing the right thing. I was so sure about this when I came here, now I just don't know any more.'

'Yes you do,' she said, recovering slightly. 'We both know now.' She forced herself to stand. Even moving a few paces away from him her body ached, missing his touch already. 'But this brief time we've had was something very special – a gift.'

'Or a curse, Frances?'

She smiled at him tenderly. 'No, it was never that.' When she had brushed ineffectually at the gathering snow on her cape, she drew from the inside of it a little book. 'I read the poems ye gave me,' she said. 'But it was the lines ye wrote yourself that meant most.'

He shook his head and rose. 'When I wrote those words, I listened to my heart.'

Frances returned the precious book to her pocket. She could see the pain in Gavin's face but restrained herself from going

353

to him. Instead, she took a few more steps backwards, knowing that if she touched him now it would surely break their resolve. 'We canna heed our hearts now.' They stared at each other, fired with the need to reach out once more, equally desperate with the need to avoid it.

'Go then,' he said quietly, turning his head so he would not witness her leaving. 'And mind, a part of me will always be with ye.'

A light sprinkling of snow continued to fall, making brief gentle patting sounds as it touched the trees. 'Dinna stay too long out here in the cold, you've an election to win.' Frances choked her farewell, the tears warm on her cold cheeks as she walked away. 'Goodbye . . .' She raised a gloved hand but the wave became a fist which she pressed to her mouth, staving the cry within.

15

A swathe of sunlight slanted across the floor from the tall windows as Christian Ballantyne was shown into the dining-room. Frances and Pi'taki were just finishing breakfast.

'Good morning, ladies,' he smiled cheerfully. 'I think it would be fair to say that spring has definitely arrived out there.'

'I know,' Frances teased, mopping up the last of the maple syrup on her plate with a buckwheat pancake, 'I was out riding before you were even awake.' She grinned back at him.

'Hmm, is that so? Well, while some of us were amusing ourselves, I was collecting your post on my way here.'

'Anything interesting?' It was said with difficulty, while savouring the final mouthful.

He adjusted his pince-nez and rifled through the pile. 'Most of it looks like business . . .' He laughed as she screwed up her nose. 'Except for this, it's come from Scotland. I thought you'd want to see it first.' He placed a large wrapped newspaper on the table beside her and drew up a chair.

'That will be from Jeannie. I asked her to send me the paper with all the local election results and so forth.' She quickly wiped her hands on her napkin and tore off the wrapper. Flipping the pages, she scanned the headlines until she found what she was looking for.

'Surely you know the results already?' he asked. 'The Canadian papers may be provincial but they carried full coverage of the British elections.'

'That's not the same.' Frances waved him to be silent as she read the paper and Pi'taki raised her eyes to the ceiling in sympathy. She poured a cup of coffee for Ballantyne and then discreetly proceeded to feed some scraps to the eager dogs.

But Frances was unaware. She had found the page that Jeannie had marked with a pen: 'New Socialist Member Takes his Seat in the Commons' and read on in silence, oblivious of anything else.

> The King opened the new Session of Parliament today, giving little detail in His speech about the programme of legislation to be introduced by the Liberal administration. Mr Gavin Douglas, the recently elected Member of Parliament for Mid-Fife, joined the Labour Party contingent at the Palace of Westminster, sitting on the Government side. Mr Douglas, who was married only a few days previously, was accompanied to the State Opening by his wife. Mrs Margaret Douglas watched with obvious pride from the Strangers' Gallery as her husband took his seat on the benches. Mr Chamberlain, acting as Leader of the Opposition, made a speech . . .

Ballantyne eyed Frances over the rim of his cup. 'The news seems to have made you even happier than you've been since you returned.'

'Have I been? Happy, I mean?'

He nodded. 'Well yes, content I'd say. Maybe even serene.' He took another sip of his coffee. 'Whatever you call it, it's a definite improvement on your – shall we say prickly? – disposition before all this Scottish business.'

Frances laughed. 'You're surely not referring to me – such cheek!'

'I apologise unreservedly.' Smiling, he rose from his seat and gathered the remaining mail. 'Now then, there's a lot of work to catch up on. I shall go and make a start and wait for you in the study.'

Pi'taki patted his arm as he passed her and said, 'I am glad you are well now, Mr Ballantyne.' He paused, touched by the sincerity of the sentiment. Then he nodded respectfully to her before leaving the room.

The old woman eyed Frances as she drained her cup. 'He is right, Otanimm, you are changed since you came back. And it is good.'

'It's just because I am happy to see you all again,' she replied, kissing the wrinkled features. 'Give me a few weeks and I will be my cantankerous old self again.'

She stood to leave but Pi'taki held her hand. 'One day you will fool me, Otanimm. But not yet.' Lifting the battered little book from beside her, she smiled knowingly. 'You forget this – the one that never leaves your side.' Frances reached for it but the old woman held it a moment longer. 'You do not need it. It must all be in your head by now – or in your heart?'

As usual she was right. Frances turned and taking the precious book over to the window, she read the inscription penned on the inside cover: 'pick any page at random . . .' She closed her eyes letting the pages flutter in the draught from the window until the worn spine lay flat in her hand, as though in invitation. Her fingers traced the lines, running tenderly below them and her eyes opened to the words: 'The heart's ay the part ay, That makes us right or wrang.'

She looked up. Outside, a jaunty breeze had dissolved the last fragments of cloud from a promising blue sky. As the spring sunshine burst impatiently through the quivering trees, flocks of scattering blossoms caught the light and sent their careless shadows running free across the grass.